Salty,
Spiced,
and a Little
Bit Nice

Salty, Spiced,

AND A

Little Bit Nice

CYNTHIA TIMOTI

BRAMBLE

Tor Publishing Group

New York

This is a work of fiction. All of the characters, organizations, and events portrayed in this novel are either products of the author's imagination or are used fictitiously.

SALTY, SPICED, AND A LITTLE BIT NICE

Copyright © 2025 by Cynthia Timoti

All rights reserved.

A Bramble Book
Published by Tom Doherty Associates / Tor Publishing Group
120 Broadway
New York, NY 10271

www.torpublishinggroup.com

Bramble™ is a trademark of Macmillan Publishing Group, LLC.

The Library of Congress Cataloging-in-Publication Data is available upon request.

ISBN 978-1-250-34347-5 (trade paperback)
ISBN 978-1-250-34381-9 (ebook)

Our books may be purchased in bulk for promotional, educational, or business use. Please contact your local bookseller or the Macmillan Corporate and Premium Sales Department at 1-800-221-7945, extension 5442, or by email at MacmillanSpecialMarkets@macmillan.com.

First Edition: 2025

Printed in the United States of America

0 9 8 7 6 5 4 3 2 1

For Ludi, Maxwell, and Jasper

Salty,
Spiced,
and a Little
Bit Nice

CHAPTER 1

A Viral Beginning

Most people would agree that marriage proposals weren't supposed to make you nauseous. Yet here I was, a girl standing in front of a boy on his knees, with a stunning diamond ring in his hand, and all I wanted to do was hurl my dinner and hightail it out of the country.

The very prim and polished George Fitzgerald, aka the man of my family's dreams, smiled at me. "Elizabeth Rae Pang," he crooned my name, like it was a line in a Sinatra song, "will you marry me?"

The sparkly rock was winking at me, goading me to say yes. Our families were beaming at us, while all the guests had their phones up high, recording every glorious second. The Pangs' annual NYE bash had come to a grinding halt fifteen minutes before midnight, and I'd bet my entire savings the videos would be posted online before the clock struck twelve. Hell, we might even be live streaming right now. We'd only been going out for two months—two brunches, one (boring) date to the opera, and a handful of dinners—and he wanted to *get married*?

"Ellie?" George was still smiling. I never realized how disturbingly white and straight his teeth were. "What do you say?"

An involuntary shiver rippled through my body. Maybe the crystal chandelier above my head was too bright. Or maybe my glucose level was dipping low. Or because the band was playing a slow, romantic song that screeched like nails on a chalkboard to my ears. We were standing inside a heart-shaped spot, surrounded by dozens of long-stemmed roses and tealight candles floating in wineglasses. Apart from the obvious fire hazard, the proposal was textbook perfect, although all credits probably belonged to his PA.

How long had it been since George had finished his speech? I glanced at my family again, sighing when I saw Mom's face twisting with impatience and Dad's eyebrows knitting together. An eerie hush had enveloped the ballroom. The band was no longer screeching, and the only audible sound was my heart jackhammering behind my rib cage.

George shifted his knee, stoically hiding a wince. "I know this might seem sudden. But I think we have something special, and I want to spend the rest of my life with you."

Okay, let's pretend for a moment that I was delusional enough to consider his proposal. I'd do a pros and cons list on my listmaker app, and it would look something like this:

Pro:	Con:
1. He is kind, handsome, patient with children. He'd make the perfect husband, father, and son-in-law (100 points).	1. This was driven by a master plan to unite their family business with ours, which would mean I'd be pressured into working for them for the rest of my life (minus 2,000 points).

2. And the most important
pro of them all (not mine,
but according to both our
families): The lucrative
benefits and opportunities
that would result from
this (un)holy union.
Their score would soar past
10,000 points, and from
the looks on their faces,
everyone was champing at
the bit for me to accept.

This whole thing was never about love and marriage.

It was about profit and loss.

If I said no, my father would be furious, and my mother would say that I couldn't afford to be choosy, because apparently at twenty-eight, my childbearing ability was rapidly deteriorating. More importantly, our collective business ventures would go up in flames, because the rejection would be an enormous scandal. I could already picture the number-one trending YouTube video of the month: *Marriage Proposal Gone Wrong! Daughter of prominent businessman rejects the country's Most Eligible Bachelor!*

No. Pigs, turtles, and rabbits would fly, and hell would freeze a thousand times over before that happened. Maybe I should accept now, sparing our families the painful embarrassment, then quietly break the engagement after a few days. Just be kind, respectful, and honest, and everyone would understand.

Yes. Brilliant plan.

Then I opened my mouth, and my brain must have buckled under the pressure, because what came out was, "Nope, but thank you for asking."

George turned beet red, while gasps from shocked guests echoed around the ballroom, the loudest (and angriest) coming from my parents. I took a few steps back, ready to flee, when my heels knocked over the wineglasses.

Yep, the ones with the lit tealight candles merrily floating inside.

Horrified, I watched helplessly as the glasses tumbled over each other and crashed like dominoes and nightmares, setting the roses ablaze. The shocked gasps escalated to panicked shrieks, and right there and then, I knew one thing was certain.

My life, as I knew it, would never be the same.

Two days later, there was a knock on my apartment door. I ignored it, willing whoever it was to supernaturally receive my message and go away. My abysmal attempt at telepathy failed, because the knock got louder, followed by my brother's voice. "Ellie, I know you're home."

Sighing, I got up and peered through the security peephole before unlocking the door to let him in. "What do you want?"

Instead of my brother, another figure launched herself at me. My best friend, Naomi Park, squeezed me in a tight hug, doing her utmost to cut off the oxygen supply to my lungs. "Oh, thank God you're alive!"

Naomi and I had met on the first day of kindergarten, when we reached for the same wooden block at the same time, both refusing to let go. The wooden block was quickly forgotten when we saw we both had the same cute mermaid T-shirt on, and it wasn't long until we were laughing in the sandpit, building the greatest sandcastle ever known to five-year-olds. The sandcastle led to a playdate the weekend after, and we'd been inseparable ever since. We'd gone to the same schools, spent almost 24/7 together when we were teenagers, and had done the same finance degree in college. When she started dating my brother last year, both our families were thrilled.

Well, hers was—mine was slightly disappointed that the Parks "only" owned two very successful restaurants in Koreatown.

"Keep this up and I won't be." I pried open her suffocating embrace and nodded at my brother, who stood behind her. "Just the two of you? No cavalry?"

Although two years older than me, Eric was often mistaken for my younger sibling. We had the same chocolate-brown eyes and jet-black hair, only his was cut short, while mine was shoulder-length and slightly curly at the ends. He was the Golden Child: the chosen heir to the Pang Food Industries empire, the reliable one who put out fires and emergencies whenever and wherever needed.

Which was, apparently, right here, right now.

Eric closed the door behind him, a small frown on his face. "Just us. You've been ignoring our calls. We wanted to make sure you're okay."

"As you can see, I am." I collapsed on the sofa and picked up the remote. "Thanks for stopping by. Can you lock the door on your way out?"

"Ooh, you made brownies!" Naomi plopped down next to me and grabbed a piece from the plate on the coffee table. She bit into it, her eyes closed in bliss. "Mmmh. Seriously, El. Working in corporate finance is a waste of your true calling. Not to mention those pastry classes that you've been taking."

"Not working in corporate finance is a waste of my expensive college education."

"And we all know that's a cardinal sin." Eric's eyes swept my living room, his frown deepening when he saw the pizza box. "Pizza *and* brownies? Really?"

"Really." I flicked through my Netflix queue. "I'm starting a rom-com movie marathon, and pizza and brownies make it perfect. FYI, the brownies are carb-free, so they don't count."

Eric folded his arms, giving me a disapproving look. "You know what pizzas can do to your glucose levels, right? This is worse than I thought."

I snatched my phone from the table and waved it in his face. "*Nothing* could possibly be worse. Have you seen the video? Seven million views and counting. Tens of thousands of comments, ninety-nine percent of them laughing at me. Hundreds of texts from everyone and their grandmas wanting to know how I'm doing, while implying how ridiculous I was to have turned down the proposal. And don't ask me how many friend requests came in from random strangers." I shuddered. "It's creepy. The only silver lining was the firefighters got there in time, or I'd probably be in prison right now for burning down an entire ballroom."

"But you're not." Naomi reached for another brownie. "Can I take some of these home?"

Just then, my phone vibrated, and I groaned, tossing it to the sofa and covering it with a cushion. "On second thought, maybe prison is better. Mom has been calling to yell. At least twenty times. And Dad sent me a long email expressing his 'deep disappointment.'"

"You shouldn't be surprised," Eric said. "They had high hopes for you and George."

"We'd only been seeing each other for two months. Why would I say yes?"

"He's a great guy. Wonderful family. Why not?"

I scoffed. "You're just saying that because he's your business partner."

"No, I'm just stating the facts. You know the parents are only doing this because they want what's best for you."

"You need to get out of this apartment," Naomi smoothly interrupted, before I had a chance to retort. "Let's go somewhere fun, where you don't have to think about George, or the proposal, or creepy friend requests. How do you feel about some Japanese food?"

"I've got pizza and Netflix. I'm good."

But she was already ushering me toward my bedroom, and ten minutes later, I was being herded into Eric's car, my protests met with cheeky grins and wide, innocent eyes. Fifteen minutes after that, I finally accepted my fate as the three of us swung into a parking lot in front of a sushi train restaurant. Eric's phone buzzed as he turned off the engine, and he raised his eyebrows when he saw the caller ID.

"You two go ahead," Eric said. "I have to take this call."

Naomi linked her arm through mine as we got out of the car. "So here's the plan. We'll have lunch and some bubble tea as a treat. If you're still not cheered up, we might even go nuts and see a movie or two. Sounds good?"

"Sure. Maybe we should rewatch *The Proposal*."

She chuckled. "Seriously though, I've been so worried. How are you?"

I cringed as a couple of teenagers did a double take, staring at me as we walked into the restaurant. "Semi-famous. Thanks to YouTube."

Naomi waved her hands. "It's a video about *the* George Fitzgerald and his failed proposal. Plus, you nearly set the place on fire. It's bound to go viral, but it'll go away eventually." She lowered her voice as we were shown into an empty booth and sat down. "But why did you say no? You never told me much about him, but I thought you said he's not bad."

"Because I don't know him well enough. We'd only been going out for two months. And 'not bad' isn't exactly a ringing endorsement to accept a proposal, is it?"

"But when you know, you know, right?" Naomi argued. When I only made a noncommittal grunt, she raised her eyebrows.

"Well, why did you go on the second, third, fourth dates with him? There's got to be something that made you stick around."

I winced. I never told her this part because I was embarrassed. "Our mothers set us up. They encouraged us to meet for drinks, which turned into a few dinners, and now here we are."

Naomi groaned. "*Again?* Didn't we have a similar conversation already, when your mother tried to set you up with . . . oh, whatever the hell his name was. The heir of that Indonesian palm oil conglomerate?" She let out a dry laugh. "Ellie, we've talked about this so many times. Stop letting your family run your life."

I shrugged, pretending to be unconcerned. "If I said no, I'd hurt their feelings. They're just looking after me. That's what families do, right?"

Naomi's tone became gentler. "Sure, but mine doesn't set me up with rich heirs to expand our family business. Look, I know how difficult your parents can be, and how they handle you with kid gloves because of your diagnosis. But it's a super-thin, blurry line between looking after you and micromanaging your life."

"I'm used to it." She hit close to home, but I wasn't discussing my dysfunctional family relationship in the middle of a busy restaurant. Before I could change the topic, Eric slid into the seat next to Naomi.

"That was George. We haven't even launched the brewery, and the new CFO resigned this morning. Said she had an urgent family matter in her hometown." Eric's sharp gaze landed on me. "Could you handle the finance duties for us?"

My eyes nearly popped out of their sockets. "After I rejected his proposal? You're kidding, right? Also, news flash: I already have a job. In fact, I'm swamped right now, getting a client ready for their initial public offering."

"Is that a no?"

"You have two degrees and an MBA. I'm sure you can figure it out."

"Only until we find someone. You know how picky Dad is."

Eric had a point. Henry Pang had built his business empire from practically nothing, and earning his trust was tougher than teaching a donkey to play the piano. It took George's family a year of wooing and convincing Dad that they were the right business partner for Pang Food Industries, even though Fitzgerald Creek Wines was the biggest and oldest winery in the country. The partnership had resulted in Eric and George's new craft beer company. Eric had succeeded in expanding the family business into hotels, supermarkets, and catering companies, and this was the latest step in his bold conquest for world domination.

But after the NYE debacle, I wasn't going anywhere near the family business.

"Think of all the new experiences you'll be exposed to," Eric said. "You'll learn heaps."

Suuureeee, I'd always wanted to "learn heaps" while working with a guy I'd publicly rejected and humiliated. Almost as much as I wanted to do the macarena through Times Square buck naked during rush hour. In fact, they were items number one and two on my bucket list, ranked even higher than my dream of opening a bakery.

I sighed, stopping myself from thinking of more snarky comments. What was it that my mother always said?

"Sarcasm is the lowest form of wit, Ellie. It's inappropriate for a woman."

"We all know it won't be temporary. They'll guilt me into staying forever."

"I'll make sure they won't." When he saw my pained expression, Eric chuckled. "I promise. Once we find someone new, you can leave."

It sounded simple, but nothing was ever straightforward with my family, especially my mom. "I'll think about it." I ignored Naomi, who had paused from enthusiastically plucking plates of sushi rolls off the conveyor belt to give me a side-eye, as her words earlier came back to shame me. "Anyone want some genmaicha?"

"Sure. By the way," Eric turned to Naomi, his eyes softening as he watched her pour soy sauce into three small dipping bowls. "Alec texted. His sister's getting married in a few months. We're both invited."

Naomi squealed as my ears pricked up with interest. It had been a while since I heard that name. *Did Eric mean who I thought he meant?*

"Which sister? Is it Sienna?" Naomi's eyes lit up when Eric nodded. "Oh my God! Sienna's getting married?"

Okay, so it was exactly who I thought it was. Alec Mackenzie, who used to be Eric's Ride or Die, before he suddenly left the city without even saying goodbye ten years ago.

The guy who was my childhood crush.

But also, the absolute fucking bane of my existence.

A sudden wave of irritation surged through me because (1) Why wasn't I invited to the wedding? Followed by (2) Did that mean he was coming back home?

"I didn't know you two are still friendly," I said to Eric, my tone a little accusing.

"Are you still angry at him?" My brother shook his head. "It was a long time ago, Ellie. And it wasn't his fault. We talked about this."

Maybe we had, but that didn't mean I was ready to forget, forgive, and move on.

Because how do you forgive someone who not only broke your heart into tiny little pieces, but almost killed you, too?

CHAPTER 2

The Most Excellent Start to the New Year

It was a fact universally acknowledged that employee productivity dipped significantly post–end-of-year holidays, rendering the first few days pointless and ineffective. Case in point: Today was our first Monday back after the break, and nobody was even pretending to work. People stood around chatting, holding mugs of coffee while exchanging stories about their holidays, not caring whether they'd cleared the 1,828 unread emails in their inbox, let alone getting started on their first investment analysis for the year.

Not that I was any better. On the outside, it looked like I was hard at work, judging from the Excel spreadsheet I'd been frowning at for the past hour. In reality, I was focusing all my energy into ignoring my mother's face on my vibrating phone.

My father might have started the family business from zero, but my shrewd mother was the driving force behind every decision. Veronica Pang was ambitious, hardworking, and strong-willed, and the main reason my first-generation Chinese Indonesian migrant family had successfully built a multibillion–dollar business empire. The business was her whole life, her pride and joy, because it represented everything she'd worked so hard for. She always said that the one thing she feared the most was being poor and having no money. Which explained why she could be doggedly single-minded once she set her mind on something, especially when it was relevant to the business, exploiting all possible (often questionable) means to achieve her goals. And right now, her sole purpose in life was to rectify the crime I had committed by rejecting George's proposal.

Since ignoring her was an offense punishable by incessant nagging, she'd upped the ante and increased the frequency of her calls, harassing me six times a day like clockwork: twice in the morning, twice after lunch, twice at night. Sometimes she'd even throw in several text messages as a bonus. All her calls this morning had gone straight to voicemail, and her texts stayed unopened. I'd had enough of her harping on how I'd destroyed my life and future; how there wouldn't be anyone else interested in me after I'd rejected George; and why the hell did I turn him down, anyway? Finally, did I ever stop to think how selfish that was because it might damage our relationship with his family?

Nope, I didn't need to ruin my first day back at work by hearing any of that.

My phone stopped buzzing for five seconds, before going off again. Winnie, my coworker and usual lunch buddy, glanced at me. "Someone is dying to talk to you."

"I'm busy." I rejected the call, then clicked on a cell in my spreadsheet, pretending to check the formula. "It's just my mom. She'll call again tonight."

She gave me a funny look. "But it's your mom. What if it's urgent?"

I liked Winnie, but even though we hung out every day at lunch, I never told her—or anyone else at work—about my family. The less people knew about them, and how dysfunctional they were, the better. My mother never hesitated to use her money, or her network of powerful people, to make certain things go her way. But I was never comfortable with that, with people knowing how well-off my parents were. I'd learned (the hard way) that some people treated me differently once they knew, because of what they thought they could gain from my family by befriending me.

Before I could think of a believable answer, a door suddenly flung open from my right, and Stewart, one of the partners in the company, emerged from his office. "Ellie, can I see you for a minute?"

I closed my laptop, grabbed my pen and notebook, and followed him.

"Have a seat, please. Good Christmas?"

My stomach twisted. Stewart was known for getting to the point, so his making small talk *and* using the word "please" rang an alarm.

I cautiously lowered myself onto a chair. "Nothing eventful. Yours?"

"Oh, probably overindulged more than I should have." Stewart cleared his throat and clasped his hands together. "You must be wondering why I called you."

"Is this about the Axton Mining IPO?"

"No." He leaned across the desk. "The board had a meeting earlier. After the dreadful past two years, they want to restructure. Cut some costs. Merge some roles, streamline the operations."

The twist in my stomach tightened. *This sounds bad.*

"We have to let some people go," Stewart said, his hands still clasped. "You've been a great asset to the company. However, based on your last performance review, we feel you're probably better suited for a role elsewhere."

The twist in my stomach was now a Category 5 hurricane. "But why? I exceeded all my KPI targets last year. My last appraisal reflected that."

"Yes, but there are others who performed better. The decision wasn't easy, but it was based on the company's best interests. Nothing personal."

My head spun as Stewart continued talking about how much he valued my contributions to the team, his words going in one ear and out the other.

It didn't make sense. I was one of the top analysts for the company last year, and my clients consistently achieved higher than average returns on all their investments. Working in finance was never my first choice, but it was either this, or medicine, or law, because those were the only career paths acceptable to my parents. Arguing with them would be pointless, and I was good with numbers, so finance was the most sensible choice. Even then, there were many, many days when I hated my job and wished I were anywhere else but here.

Still, it was dreadful to have been told the company no longer required my services. On the first day back, no less.

I shifted and squirmed in my seat. *Way to make your family proud of you, Ellie.* All hell would break loose when they heard the news. My parents would hang their heads in shame, because to them, being fired from a job, no matter the reasons, was in the Top Three Things That Would Bring Lifelong Disgrace to Your Family. Another one was Rejecting a Lucrative Marriage Proposal from An Important Business Partner, so in less than a week, I'd succeeded in disappointing my family twice.

It's a sign, a small voice said, *that you should accept Eric's job offer. Not.*

"I can write you a recommendation letter, although you probably won't need it," Stewart said. "I'm sure your family can give you a job in one of your companies."

My head snapped up at that. "What?"

"Pang Food Industries. That's your family, right? One of the largest manufacturers and wholesale distributors of Asian food in North America. I saw the YouTube video."

That damned video would be the death of me. "Yeah, that's us."

"If I were you, I'd be living it up at the family business instead of slumming it here with the rest of us common folks. Two billion dollars turnover in the last financial year, multiple subsidiaries, and thousands of employees across the country. A brewery joint venture with Fitzgerald Creek Wines." Stewart let out a laugh. "You won't have any problems finding your next role."

I stilled. "How did you know about the brewery?"

He shrugged. "Everyone knows about it. It's public knowledge. There are social media accounts promoting it."

"But the joint ownership has never been publicly disclosed," I said slowly, my brain sifting through all the probable answers. "The only ones that knew about it were the people working for my family or the Fitzgeralds'."

For the briefest second, a look of guilt crossed Stewart's features. "No, I'm sure I read about it somewhere."

A siren wailed in my head as a disturbing possibility entered my mind. "My mother. Did my mother have anything to do with this? *Wait.* Did she pay you to fire me?"

The look of guilt returned to his face, giving me the answer I needed.

"Un-*fucking*-believable."

I stood up so quickly my chair toppled over backward. I'd been tolerating my family's interference all my life, but this was above and beyond. Was this their way of punishing me for rejecting George's proposal?

No, I realized. This was a ploy to force me into accepting Eric's offer. If I didn't have a job, then I'd have no choice but to say yes and join the family business.

And to think I had felt guilty for getting fired and giving them shame.

"You've just made the biggest mistake of your career." I pointed at Stewart. "I'll make sure HR and the Department of Labor hear about this. You won't be able to get a job anywhere in the financial services industry. I hope she paid you enough to last you the rest of your life, because you're going to need it."

With that last parting shot, I turned around and stormed out of his office.

An hour later, I arrived at the headquarters of Pang Food Industries. I *loathed* coming to this place, and in the twenty-five years since my parents started the business, I could count the number of times I'd been here on one hand. The first time was when I was seven, when I'd been too sick with a cold to go to school. Twenty-one years later, the memory was still fresh in my mind, as if it had only happened yesterday. They'd ushered me into an empty meeting room with my stuffed penguin, two Famous Five books, a bottle of water, and some rice crackers. The cleaners had found me wandering around after hours, because my parents had been too busy and had forgotten they'd stashed me there.

Then everything changed when I was nine.

My unexpected type 1 diabetes diagnosis completely redefined my life. My mom had been annoyed with me because I'd been waking up multiple times in the middle of the night feeling thirsty and running to the toilet almost every hour because I'd been drinking so much water. I started to lose a lot of weight and was constantly exhausted and irritable, which she'd blamed on my lack of sleep. That went on for a few weeks, until one afternoon after school, when I'd vomited violently while I was at Naomi's house.

Naomi's mother, unable to reach my parents, had rushed me to the ED, where the nurses and doctors took (what had felt like) gallons of blood samples. By the time my parents arrived two hours later, the doctors had returned, wearing very serious looks on their faces, and told me that I had type 1 diabetes. My mother had argued with them, disputing the results and demanding another round of blood tests, while Naomi's mother had given me a bone-crushing hug (everyone in their family was a tight hugger), whispering that everything would be okay. But I had no idea what it meant. Or how life would never be the same.

Because it had gone on undetected for a while, my blood sugar was off-the-charts high. The doctors told me that I was in diabetic ketoacidosis, which meant that my body didn't have enough insulin to process the blood sugar into energy, and started to break down fat instead, releasing acidic chemicals called ketones. If I hadn't been diagnosed and treated when I was, it could have been fatal. I had to spend a week in the hospital, hooked up with IV fluids and insulin to bring my glucose levels down, while learning new terms like "hypoglycemia," "basal insulin," and "bolusing."

The doctors had also said that the diagnosis shouldn't limit me from doing anything and everything I wanted, that I just had to learn to include my diabetes in my life. Still, it took me a few weeks to adjust, to come to terms with the fact that I couldn't just open the kitchen pantry and graze on whatever snacks I'd like throughout the day without giving it much thought; or that I'd have to count the amount of carbohydrates and give myself insulin for everything I ate. That I had to always remember to carry a small bag full of glucose tablets, jelly beans, and juice boxes, so I'd always have some sugar ready for whenever my glucose level was low.

My parents had blamed the foods I ate, ignoring the doctors' repeated explanations that type 1 diabetes was an autoimmune disease. After that, everything began to revolve around my glucose levels, and every single decision was made based on that. If my level was high, give myself more insulin. Lay off the carbs. Go for a run. If I was low, bring out the emergency apple juice stash from the back of the pantry. I once drank three juice boxes and ate two fun-size packs of Skittles in one sitting after a particularly grueling swimming session, just to bring my levels up. Everything was a balancing act, making sure that I was always within the acceptable range.

It had also transformed my busy, inattentive parents into their current state of workaholic, overprotective, and super-controlling parents. The first thing they'd ask about when they got home at night was my glucose levels. If my mom could somehow take time away from work, she'd stay and hover at the occasional birthday parties I was allowed to go to, to make sure I didn't eat more than my allotted tiny piece of cake. For the first few years, I relished the newfound attention, secretly thrilled that I was as precious as Eric the Golden Child. Then the overprotectiveness slowly mutated into oppressive and manipulative territory, and now, I'd give anything for them to regress to their old inattentive selves.

Soft instrumental music was playing as I pushed the heavy frosted-glass door and marched into the office, my face grim and my strides determined.

"Ellie! I haven't seen you in ages." Mimi, the longtime receptionist, beamed at me, then faltered when she saw me glowering. "What's wrong?"

"I need to speak to my mother. Where is she?"

"She's in a meeting," Mimi said, puzzled. "Would you like to wait?"

"No." I pushed the transparent glass door leading to the internal offices, ignoring her panicked shouts, and made a beeline toward my mother's office. The door was open, so I headed straight for her desk, convinced that I'd find evidence of her bribing Stewart there. Opening her laptop, I entered the password—Eric's birthday—and did a scan through her emails, files, and folders. Nothing came up, not even when I did a search for Stewart's name.

I released a frustrated groan. She was 100 percent behind this. Without a doubt. The question was, how could I prove it?

Footsteps echoed in the corridor outside, and my mother appeared at the door. "Ellie? Mimi called the boardroom and said—" She stopped mid-sentence, frowning at me. "Why are you on my computer?"

"Got fired today, Mom. I'm sure you've heard."

The frown turned deeper. "Don't be absurd. Of course I haven't."

"Let's not pretend you don't know what I mean," I said, saccharine ire dripping from my tone. "We both know you're smarter than that."

"You're not making any sense. Have you been getting enough sleep? Maybe you've been overworking yourself."

I wasn't even going to dignify that with a reply. If there was an Olympic sport for scheming and shaming, she'd be the all-time gold medal record holder.

Another set of footsteps approached, and Eric appeared behind her. "Ellie?" His eyes went back and forth between our mother and me. "Why are you here? What's going on?"

"I got fired this morning. The official line was 'company restructuring.'" I made air quotes with my fingers. "Imagine my surprise when my boss mentioned the brewery, something no one outside of this family knows about. Is this your way of making me accept your job offer, Eric? Because it's not very subtle."

He frowned. "What are you talking about?"

"Then it's her. She paid him to fire me."

Eric sighed, shaking his head at her. "Not again. Tell me you didn't."

I jerked my head up. "What do you mean, *not again?*"

She shrugged, her face the perfect picture of childlike innocence, while Eric tilted his head, clearly conveying, *come on.*

"Fine, I paid off your boss, who was more than happy to take the money." She narrowed her eyes at me. "I got you hired at that place, so I certainly can get you fired."

The loud thumping of my heart was deafening. "So the only reason I got my job in the first place was because you *bribed them?* Why would you do that?"

"Mom, she's an adult," Eric said. "You can't just go around payi—"

"I did, and I'll do it again if I have to." She glared at him. "It was for her own good. She was so adamant she didn't want to work in the family business. Now she can work at your brewery. With the family. With George. Because that's where she belongs."

"I'm standing *right here.*" I raised my voice. "Does it always have to be about the business? Is that all you care about?"

She raised her chin, looking indignant. "The business *must* come first. It's the only way we can give you and Eric a comfortable life. And," she said to Eric, "you know perfectly well why I did what I did. With her condition, I had to make sure she was employed at a place with a safe working environment. Nothing too stressful that can put her in danger."

"What danger? *What does that even mean?* I'm perfectly capable of looking after myself, so don't make this about me." I slammed the laptop shut.

Guilt roped around my heart as her eyes flared. Perhaps I was being ungrateful, and I was headed straight to the fiery inferno of hell the minute I walked out of this office.

"Ever since you were diagnosed," my mother advanced on me, her eyeballs almost leaping out of their sockets, as her face twisted in a furious scowl, "we've always kept you safe. Made sure you're well. And this is the thanks we get? Let's face it, Ellie. You have limitations. And you will never amount to anything without us."

"Mom," Eric said, his tone placating, "why don't we talk about this later?"

She ignored him and jabbed a finger at my chest. "Here's what you're going to do. You're going to call George to apologize. Get back together with him and accept his proposal. Then you'll start at the brewery, effective immediately."

I raised my chin at her. "What if I said no?"

Her brown eyes, so much like mine, narrowed with rage. "Then I will cut you off."

That's it. That was the last straw. As she glared at me, the past few days came flashing back, like a series of terrible movie clips you didn't really want to watch but had to because somebody threatened you with bodily harm: the public proposal from a man I wasn't even in love with; Stewart firing me; and the sad, nasty realization that I was, and always had been, a puppet to my controlling mother, who pulled the strings to suffocate my life.

Using my health as her excuse.

Naomi was wrong. The line between looking after me and micromanaging my life wasn't super thin and blurry.

It was nonexistent.

"Go ahead. Cut me off. Maybe it's time to test my so-called limitations." The words tumbled out of my mouth before I could stop myself. "See if I can survive without the family in my life."

"Ellie," Eric turned his world-class negotiation skills on me, "let's not overreact. I understand you're upset, but so is Mom. Why don't you go home, and we can talk once you've all calmed down?"

The thing about Eric is, he never subscribed to my manipulative-parent hypothesis. Sure, he conceded that they could be a bit much, but he always reminded me how they had sacrificed a lot for us over the years. How hard they'd worked for our family. Call me cynical, or him naïve, but he was a staunch believer that they always had our best interests at heart.

Whichever it was, I wasn't sticking around to find out.

"Not overreacting." I started toward the door. "Just doing what's right."

Mom placed her hands on her hips. "If you go through that door, you're dead to us."

I ignored her and walked out of the room.

"You hear me, Ellie?" She was yelling so loud, the staff outside her office were craning their necks to see what was going on. "I don't want to see your face ever again!"

Yeesh. She could now add "melodramatic" to her storied parenting career.

"Hey." Eric followed me out. "Where are you going? Don't rush into something you'll regret later. We can talk about this."

"There's nothing to talk about."

"Be reasonable, Ellie. What are you going to do?"

I had no idea, but I wasn't going to tell him that. "I'll keep you posted."

And with that, I pushed the front door open and left my family.

The minute I got home, I stalked to the kitchen and pulled out my mixer, some mixing bowls, and a cupcake pan. Then I dumped the bag of low-carb flour, cocoa, baking powder, and the carton of eggs on the counter, before flicking the oven switch to preheat. I needed to regroup and figure out my next move, and I did it best while beating some eggs and butter together. Baking had always helped me to relax and unwind, a safe space where I could just *be*.

I'd started experimenting in the kitchen a year post-diagnosis, because I was getting tired of my mother limiting what I could or couldn't eat. She had even gone as far as banning everything remotely sweet at our house; although she knew perfectly well that I could have anything I wanted, as long as I took the correct amount of insulin for it. My ten-year-old self had reasoned that maybe my mother wouldn't be so strict if I learned to make things with as little carbohydrates as possible. I'd borrowed recipe books from the library, spent endless hours watching the Food Network, then started with the easier stuff—brownies, chocolate chip cookies, blueberry muffins. Naomi was my number one ~~victim~~ taste tester, and although she never complained, I knew the first year was painful for her. I tried different types of natural sweeteners and sugar substitutes, while slowly improving (to Naomi's relief) and graduating from chocolate chip cookies to chocolate croissants, brownies to macarons, and muffins to kue lapis legit, a traditional—and very time-consuming—Indonesian type of layer cake.

Today I was trying a sugar-free salted caramel cupcake recipe that had been living rent-free in my mind for the past week. My hand worked rhythmically, whisking the flour and the baking powder together, while my mind began to plan.

Eric had made an excellent point about not rushing into something I might regret. For all my displays of bravado earlier, I didn't know what to do. I was jobless, the reluctant star of an embarrassing, viral YouTube video, and the black sheep of the family.

What a superb way to kick off the new year.

But things would never change as long as I lived in the same city as my family. I had to get away as far as humanly possible.

The ramifications of that might one day come back to bite me in the ass, but right now I was too fed up to care.

I turned the mixer on and slowly poured the eggs and melted butter in. *It's time*, a small voice piped up at the back of my brain. *Dust off that plan. There's nothing, and no one, to stop you from going ahead now.*

Turning off the mixer, I poured the batter into the cupcake pan and shoved it into the oven. I glanced at the messy countertop as the sweet scent of caramel infused my apartment, and just like that, I knew what I had to do. Naomi was right—it was time to finally put those baking classes to good use. It might be an enormous gamble, but I had no job, and anything was better than living under my mother's manipulative thumb. I was finally going to take the plunge; expensive education be damned.

For as long as I could remember, my dream had always been to open a bakery. Not just *any* bakery, but one that could cater to clientele like myself. A place that offered a wide variety of options for people who wanted healthier, guilt-free alternatives to traditional desserts. I'd been saving up since my first-ever paycheck years ago, done extensive research and put together an equally extensive business plan for it, and created at least fifteen Pinterest boards full of ideas and inspirations for my dream décor. I'd never had the guts to do anything about it, because it had always been too scary, too uncertain, and not worth the hassle of upsetting my parents.

But it was a whole different ball game now.

Grabbing my laptop, I opened the plan I'd prepared a long time ago. I scrolled through it, pausing to read the list of pros and cons I'd put together:

Pro:

1. I'd be doing something I really loved. Something I was passionate about. And if my business concept worked, then I'd also be helping people live a healthier life (1,000 points).

2. I'd have full control over everything. It would mean independence, flexible hours, and no more pressure from my parents to join Pang Food Industries (1,000 points).

Con:

1. It'd be risky as hell, and the possibility of failure is high. Statistics show that only half of new businesses survive five years or longer, and only one-third are around a decade after launching (minus 1,000 points).

2. No steady paycheck— I'd have to rely on my savings for a while, because it could be weeks, months, even years, before the business became profitable (minus 500 points).

The place that I'd had my eye on was on the other side of the country—a beautiful coastal city called Port Benedict, population 29,171, around an hour and a half from Seattle. A recent report in the World Fitness Index listed the place as one of the most health-conscious cities in the United States, stating that over 85 percent of its residents engaged in regular physical activities and were mindful of what they consumed. The healthier lifestyle proved to be attractive to a lot of people, because it was also ranked number seven in the top ten most livable cities in America, while being one of the fastest-growing cities in the country, increasing by a rate that would double the population in eight years.

Which was excellent. More potential customers for my bakery.

I'd also narrowed down my research to a neighborhood that would suit the type of bakery I had in mind. The city was home to a shopping center called Port Benedict Plaza that housed two department stores, seventy-five specialty stores, a food court, two supermarkets, a boutique hotel, and a rooftop entertainment precinct that was home to a multicultural mix of cafés, bars, and restaurants. The location was perfect: the Plaza was within walking distance of downtown Port Benedict and the Waterfront, a bustling tourist strip lined with trendy eateries facing the shores of picturesque Port Benedict Bay. There was only one French pâtisserie in the shopping center, which meant I'd have very little competition.

The specific area that I'd set my sights on was a strip of shops adjacent to the shopping complex. The rent was much more affordable than what it would cost in the main Plaza building, and the vibe was utterly warm and charming. Google Maps showed that it was flanked by rows of tall trees, with cobblestone pavements and renovated brick buildings, housing some of the most chic shops I'd ever seen. There was an art gallery, an antique shop, and a florist. I could just picture a bakery—*my bakery*—joining those businesses.

I took a long, deep breath.

It was time to take the plunge.

Jumping on a real estate site, I searched for shops for lease at that row of stores. There were only a few available, and after crossing off the ones that were out of my budget, I was left with two final options.

The first one was a spacious corner shop, currently occupied by a secondhand bookstore. It was newly renovated, and sat next to an organic juice and smoothie bar, so what I had planned should fit right in. But the detailed descriptions said the owner strongly preferred businesses wanting to lease the store for a minimum of five years, which wasn't ideal. What if my brilliant bakery idea turned out to be a flop?

The second, slightly smaller option, looked much more promising. Not only was the rent lower than the first one, but the shopfront also had a gorgeous glass-panel door and wide bay windows. The store was sandwiched in between an adorable yarn store and an old-timey ice-cream parlor, and the best part was, it would be available in two weeks, which was perfect timing-wise, because it would give me plenty of time to organize the move.

A hopeful flutter went through my stomach. *This might actually work.*

Before I could change my mind or second-guess anything, I sent off an email to the Realtor to enquire about the property. Feeling optimistic, I opened my list-maker app, my brain racing as I put together a list of things to tackle if I was really doing this: pack up my stuff, find a place to live in Port Benedict, and start short-listing suppliers for the bakery.

The oven dinged, just as I finished typing the last item on the list.

I might be jobless, but things were already looking up.

After all, what better way to kick off the new year than starting over thousands of miles away from your controlling family?

CHAPTER 3

You Have Arrived at Your Disaster Zone

Three thousand miles, forty hours, three cheap motel rooms, and hundreds of dollars of gas later, I finally arrived in Port Benedict, hungry and exhausted, and for the one-hundred-millionth time, wondering if I'd committed the biggest mistake of my life.

Well, too late to do anything about it now.

The exhaustion that seemed to have taken over my body had evaporated the moment I drove past the WELCOME TO PORT BENEDICT sign. There was a quaint small-town vibe and laid-back charm to the city, contrasted by several high-rise buildings towering in its center. My insides practically vibrated with anticipation at the thought of seeing my new shop; the place where I was supposed to start over, as evidenced by the five suitcases, three duffel bags, the cooler bag for my insulin vials, and seven cardboard boxes crammed inside my car.

My CR-V sputtered, probably feeling the long journey it had just gone through. Eric had warned me it was unwise to drive the twelve-year-old car across the country. But I was on a tight budget, so upgrading to a newer car was fresh out of the question. And besides, the car was a gift from my father's parents, my Engkong and Emak, when I first got my license, and now that they were both gone, it was the only thing that reminded me of them.

I took a long sip from my water bottle while eyeing the road for signs to Port Benedict Plaza. I'd been driving since the crack of dawn, only making a quick stop at the Realtor's office to pick up the keys.

Everything had worked out perfectly. Within forty-eight hours of making my inquiry, I had signed the lease for the shop, then spent the next two weeks packing up my belongings. I'd only told Eric and Naomi where I was going and no one else, not even my parents. And by doing that, I had successfully checked the last item on the Top Three Things That Would Bring Lifelong Disgrace to Your Family: moving across the country to escape my meddling parents.

When I finally reached the Plaza, I circled the busy parking lot twice before finally finding an empty space. Switching the engine off, I took a deep breath, quietly reflecting on what I'd done: left the safety of my family and the city I'd grown up in, relocated to the other side of the country with no familiar faces, and sunk almost all my money into starting a business. It was daunting, but it was a fresh, exciting start to my new life.

I got out of the car and pulled up the directions to the shop on my phone. Walking past the main building, I headed toward the row of shops on the fringes of the shopping complex. The area became quieter, with fewer customers milling around. I kept walking, until my phone quietly announced, "You have arrived at your destination."

I looked up and my face spontaneously broke into a grin.

The pictures I'd seen online didn't do the place justice. It was as if the store had been lifted out of an idyllic countryside and plunked in the middle of this shopping strip. The walls were made of beautiful recycled red bricks, giving off a timeless, warm, and rustic charm. The door and the windows had charcoal-colored trims, with a black metal hanging sign dangling above the door. The cute yarn store next to my shop had painted white bricks, a blue door, and blue window frames, while the ice-cream shop on my other side had striped, red-and-white awnings with vintage wrought iron chairs and tables outside on the sidewalk.

It was *awesome*.

I was vibrating with excitement. *This is the start of the greatest year of my life.* Fishing out the keys from my pocket, I unlocked the front door and walked in.

Only for my jaw to practically clatter to the ground.

Instead of an empty space full of hopes and dreams, I saw a mess of catastrophic proportions and my life flashing before my very eyes. A long, thick piece of tree limb had impaled the roof at the back of the store, which was why it wasn't visible from outside. There was a massive hole where a significant part of the roof used to be, and a pile of debris littered the floor: a bunch of broken roof tiles, some plasterboard sheeting, chunks of drywall, shattered floor tiles, and bits and pieces of twigs and leaves. The tree had also knocked out part of the back wall where the pipes were, causing water to slowly trickle onto the floor.

It took me a few minutes to fully comprehend the scene in front of me, because I was too busy flexing my multitasking muscle: gawking at the unholy mess that was supposed to be the start of my new life, whilst excavating my jaw from the ground and simultaneously brainstorming multiple doomsday scenarios in which I had to declare bankruptcy and beg strangers for mercy at the side of the road to survive, or worse, go home and *beg my parents for their forgiveness.*

No. That was not an option. I was *not* going back home, no matter how bad things were. I gingerly stepped around the debris, jumping when something hairy—a squirrel? No, *two squirrels*—

climbed down the fallen tree from the hole in the roof, before scurrying out through the open front door. As I stared at the disaster that was nowhere near my worst nightmare, it became harder to stay calm. I wondered if this so-called fresh start was actually the first step toward permanently screwing over my life and whatever hope I had of a future away from my family. The quiet reflection from earlier had vaporized, replaced by fear, mercilessly seeping into my pores, and I began to hyperventilate, as panic threatened to overtake me.

Inhale, exhale.

Maybe I should count to ten and think of my happiest child-hood memories. There weren't many, but I should be able to conjure one up if I really put my mind to it.

Inhale, exhale.

Nope, epic fail. Maybe I should close my eyes to avoid looking at this atrocious sight in front of me.

That didn't work either because the vision was already permanently imprinted on my brain. This entire thing was my own fault. I had brought this on myself. None of this would have happened if I hadn't had the brilliant idea to start my own bakery, would it?

Get a grip on yourself, Ellie. Swallowing the scream that was threatening to spill out of me, I took a few deep breaths, counted to twenty, then opened my eyes, feeling my heartbeat slowing down.

Okay, shit happens, right? Problems and challenges are part of life. It was how I reacted to them that mattered. Having type 1 diabetes taught me how to be flexible, to adapt to things quickly, and to always be prepared for all kinds of possibilities. Underestimated my carb count? No worries, I had my trusty insulin pump for that. Gave myself too much insulin? Nothing a juice box or some glucose tablets couldn't fix. Unsure how much carb was in that plate of fettuccine carbonara? Just make my best educated guess and adjust for the difference later.

Finding a ruined store on the first day of the rest of my life? It was nothing I couldn't handle.

All I had to do was call the Realtor that had handled the lease, explain the situation, and they would organize for the landlord to fix the damages, just like what the owner at my old apartment used to do.

I pulled out my phone, and in my calmest, most professional voice, informed the Realtor that I had found substantial damage to the property, only for them to remind me that I had signed a "triple net lease," which meant the tenant—*me*—was responsible for all expenses of the property, including any repairs and maintenance. It had been storming and raining heavily for the past two weeks, which had probably caused the tree to fall and part of the roof to collapse.

Internally screaming, I thanked the Realtor and hung up. Fine, surely the insurance company could help, right? But after being put on hold for over an hour, the cheerful voice at the other end told me that because they had been inundated with calls, they wouldn't have an available claim adjuster to assess the damage until *next month*.

If my mom were here to witness this, she'd probably shake her head patronizingly and murmur choruses of, "See, Ellie? You couldn't survive out in the world on your own."

Yes, I can. She was wrong, and I'd prove it to her. I had everything riding on this, and I'd rather forge a friendship with all the squirrels in the world than crawl back home, admitting defeat. I had to turn this around, come hell or high water.

So I looked up building contractors in the area and called them one by one. But they were all tied up in various projects, and one hour and thirteen unsuccessful phone calls later, I was ready to pull my hair out. The earliest someone could start working was in nine weeks.

Nine. Fucking. Weeks.

Not knowing what else to do, I called Eric.

"Ellie! I was just about to give you a call. How's the new place?"

"A disaster." I told him about the property as I fought to keep my voice steady. "Nobody is available to fix the place for another nine weeks. I don't know what to do."

There was a long pause, before my brother's voice came back on the line. "Let me make some calls. But you've got to promise me that you won't be upset."

I frowned. "What do you mean?"

"I know someone who can help. But you can't be mad."

"You're helping me. Why would I be mad?"

"Give me an hour. I'll see what I can do."

He hung up, leaving me alone with my thoughts and my disaster of a place. I glanced around, and uncertainty rained down on me again, hard. When I'd conducted my research and business plan, I'd been confident with my niche, even thinking that I could make a difference by helping people to live healthier. That had to count for something, right? But after this morning's setback, I was scoring very low on the confidence graph, and very high on the freaking out chart.

Time to assert some control over this problem. I didn't know what Eric was going to do, but I couldn't just wait around for him.

After moving my car to a closer spot in front of the shop, I hauled my backpack inside the store, then sat on a debris-free spot on the floor. Pulling out my laptop, I began to rework my finances, figuring out where to cut costs so I could reallocate the funds for the repair expenses. Accommodation took up a significant chunk of my budget, so I had to do something about that. Find somewhere cheaper to live, or maybe, if push came to shove, and things got really bad, I could *probably* temporarily camp out in the shop. I wondered if sleeping in a commercial space was illegal and made a mental note to check on that.

Reaching for my phone, I opened my list-maker app, then started a new To-Do List and a To-Buy List. On the top of the list: disposing of all the rubble, then buying some cleaning supplies and running a mop soaked in hospital-grade disinfectant through the floor. Some duct tape to put over the leaky pipe. A ladder, and tarp to cover the hole in the roof.

An hour later, I had a good plan going, and my confidence was slightly restored. Going back to my car, I decided to find my sleeping bag. The chances that I would sleep there tonight with the squirrels treating it as their stomping ground was less than 5 percent, but just in case.

As I turned around to go back inside the shop, I missed the five dogs happily stampeding in my direction, followed by their teenage dog walker, who was staring at her phone as if her life depended on it. In the split second it took me to notice the canine entourage, my feet snagged on the crisscrossing leashes, and like a bad slapstick routine, I tumbled, ass over teakettle. My sleeping bag went flying as my hands shot out to cushion the fall, and my left forearm heroically scraped the cobblestone pavement, saving the day.

I groaned as the dogs continued their journey unfazed, and my fresh wound began to sting. A car door slammed somewhere in the distance, and there was the faint sound of footsteps pounding the pavement. But the sidewalk was quiet, and nobody had witnessed my fall, so perhaps I could stay down for a while. After the busy past two weeks and the stress of this morning, the brief respite felt wonderful. I could probably close my eyes and doze off for a few minutes . . .

A firm hand clamped around my arm, interrupting my precious nap. *How rude.*

"Are you okay? Shit. Wait here, don't move."

Glad whoever that was had left me in peace, I turned my body sideways, hoping to find a more comfortable position. Only to be interrupted by the same person.

"Your hand is bleeding." Those firm hands gently touched my face, then felt around my head. "Your head seems fine, though."

Who is this guy? Why is he back?

I was faintly aware that the owner of said hands was squatting down and dabbing at my bloodied arm with something soft and wet.

"Ellie? Can you hear me?" There was a tinge of worry now in the voice. "Are you feeling dizzy or shaky?"

How does he know my name?

And why does the voice sound oddly familiar?

I opened my eyes to find a pair of eyes the color of matcha infused with lightly roasted cocoa beans, and framed by incredibly long lashes, peering down at me. From memory, I knew that the frown on his face hid a lone dimple on the left cheek. A faint scar cut through his right eyebrow, making him look like he'd been in a knife fight. Some people had argued that the overall combination could be called hot, but I wouldn't go that far. Maybe he could be classified as cute, at best, but I certainly wouldn't be caught dead saying that—at least not within hearing distance. He smelled as nice as I remembered, too, like citrus, spice, and sunshine.

Him.

The last person on Earth I had expected to see.

CHAPTER 4

An Annoying Blast from the Past

My first instinct was to snatch my hands away and make a run for it. But he was too close, so I'd have to push him off or elbow him in the ribs if I wanted to escape, and my injured left arm didn't really feel like it was up for the task. And if I wanted to be reeealllyy honest, his warm hand on mine felt kind of . . . nice.

I blinked once, then twice, trying to make sure that he wasn't a figment of my imagination. Then to be extra, doubly sure, I lifted my good hand and poked twice at his right cheek, then his left cheek, and pinched his nose for good measure. Extra hard.

"Ouch." He frowned at me, still dabbing at my left arm. "What was that for?"

Okay, so he *was* real. Alec Mackenzie, aka Sir Annoying Mc-Grumpyface, formerly known as Eric's BFF, was actually here. In the flesh.

Right in front of me.

"You." I narrowed my eyes and glared at him. "Why are you here?"

He stopped cleaning my arm and stared at me, before returning my glare. "Eric called me."

Him? He was THE HELP Eric had promised me?

This officially catapulted the day from bad to super-extra-extremely-the-worst.

This time, I really did snatch my hand away. "What? Why would Eric call *you*?"

"You should ask him that." Abandoning the first-aid attempt, he tossed the wet tissue into a nearby trash can, then stood up, giving me my first real good look at him. He was wearing a scowl on his face and a well-fitted charcoal suit, looking like ~~a snack he'd just finished a GQ photoshoot~~ he'd come straight from work. He seemed different from the young man I remembered, because this version of Alec had sharper features and crinkle lines around his eyes.

He must have noticed that I wasn't making any attempts to get up, because he offered his hand. "I saw what happened. Then I thought maybe you were having a hypo. A thank-you would've been appreciated."

My jaw unhinged, and I stared at him, unblinking. *He remembered . . . about hypos?*

Alec McGrumpyface had been an all but permanent fixture in our house when we were younger. He was Eric's best friend, and the two of them used to always turn heads wherever they went—my friendly, charismatic brother with his dazzling smile; and dark-haired, green-eyed, smoldering Alec, who charmed his way into girls' pants with his devastatingly attractive grin and an arrogant crook of his finger. He unleashed said charm and grin on everyone, excluding me. No matter how hard I tried to win him over, his life's mission had been to annoy, irritate, and exasperate the hell out of me.

Then that fateful night ten years ago clinched the tone of our relationship, affirming that I should stay as far away from him as possible. I could probably have forgiven him had he only broken my heart, but I drew the line when he nearly caused me to cross to the other side, then disappeared without so much as an apology.

Living at opposite ends of the country had been an excellent start.

Until now.

Ignoring his outstretched hands, I pushed myself up, wincing when my wounded forearm protested. "I don't know what Eric told you, but I'm fine. I don't need your help."

Alec snorted. "That's not what your brother said. He asked me to keep an eye on you and gave me the address of this place. I believe his exact words were, 'Ellie needs help, and you're the only one I can trust.'"

If I somehow survived this ordeal, the first thing I'd do when I saw my brother again would be to kill him. Slowly and excruciatingly.

"Do you live here? In Port Benedict?"

"Been here for ten years."

"And Eric knows about it? How often do you two talk?"

"Once a week, maybe." He looked almost bored with my questions. "What, you think our friendship was over just because I moved to a different city?"

What were the odds?

Alec's mother and mine used to be semi-friendly with each other, as they had a similar background—both came from Indonesia to the States as students, before becoming American citizens. But that was where the similarities ended. The two of them had lost touch, as my mother had married my father, a fellow Chinese Indonesian migrant, and then gone on to build a successful business empire, while Alec's mother had married a Scottish American.

The two families had reconnected during an Indonesian community gathering, where Eric and Alec hit it off like a house on fire, much to the displeasure of my mother, who thought the Mackenzies were not affluent enough for the likes of our family. She'd never warmed up to Alec, even though he'd been thick as thieves with Eric when we were growing up. The only reason she tolerated Alec hanging around our house so much was because she wanted to save face, and not be seen as a heartless grouch who banned her son from making friends with those less wealthy. She had always treated his family with curt indifference, never going out of her way to be nice to them. Not even after Alec's parents separated, leaving his single mother struggling to raise three children on her own.

"Why here, of all places?" Although I knew the answer. Fastest-growing city and all that.

Alec raised his eyebrows. "I'm sorry, I didn't know I needed your permission to live here. Are we done with the interrogation? Because I have somewhere else to be," he glanced at his watch, "in forty-five minutes."

"You're free to go. Tell Eric everything's under control."

But instead of leaving, he cast a disinterested look at the shop. "Is that yours? What do we have here?"

"Nothing," I said, a little too quickly. I wasn't going to admit to the most irritating man I'd ever met that I was desperate for help. "We have nothing. Thanks for coming, and I'm sorry you had to drag yourself away from whatever important things you were doing. Goodbye now."

I picked up my bundle of sleeping bag, then started toward the shop, hoping that he wouldn't follow. But because the universe seemed to be intent on giving me nothing but trouble today, of course he *did* follow.

"Is that a sleeping bag?" He fell into step beside me, his eyes laser-focused on the bundle in my hand. "Are you planning on sleeping in the store? Because I'm pretty sure living in a commercial space violates a law or two."

That meant I definitely had to figure out a cheaper housing situation, fast. "No offense, Mackenzie, but it's none of your business."

"It *is* my business, because I've had to cancel a meeting to come here." Alec gave me an annoyed once-over. "If it weren't for Eric, I wouldn't be wasting my time babysitting you."

I came to an abrupt stop to face him and drew myself up to my full height. "Eric might have called you, but I didn't. I never asked you to cancel any meetings, and I don't need anyone to babysit me. This has been an enchanting conversation, but I'm sure you have somewhere else more important to be, and so do I. So, again, you're free to go."

He was standing a bit too close for comfort, assaulting my nose with a whiff of citrus and spice. His voice turned low, sending all kinds of shivers down my spine. "I would have already left if it hadn't been for the sleeping bag, Ellie. Now show me the store."

I wondered if the hospital-grade disinfectant I was planning to buy would be strong enough to also repel him from showing up unannounced. Knowing he wouldn't budge until he got what he wanted, I stalked past him and pushed the front door open, then dumped the sleeping bag on the floor as he walked in. A cloud of dust from the debris flew up, making him cough.

Mwahahahaha. My inner supervillain twirled an imaginary mustache and cackled with unhinged mirth. *Serves him right.*

The cough stopped—unfortunately—replaced by him swearing under his breath when he saw the collapsed roof.

"It's not as bad as it looks," I said, even as my brain roared in laughter and called me all sorts of liars. "I've already made calls to a few local contractors."

"Really? How did that go? Eric said the earliest someone can start is in nine weeks."

Seriously, I was going to have some very stern words with my favorite sibling about the importance of *not* oversharing. Right before I strangled him with my bare hands.

"I can help." Alec turned to me. "I don't know if Eric mentioned—"

"He told me nothing. I didn't even know you're still alive."

"—but I work in the property industry. I know people who can do the repairs."

His phone buzzed, interrupting him, while my brain perked up with interest. *He does?*

That was how desperate I was: I was actually willing to consider an offer of help from the only man that I couldn't stand. Without anyone holding a gun to my head.

I must be out of my fucking mind.

Maybe the enormous shock from seeing this place had fried the neurons in my brain, because the correct answer was, I'd rather burn in hell than ask *him* for help. There are eight billion other humans in the world, so there had to be another option.

But this handsome man is the most logical choice, my insubordinate brain argued. *Do you know anyone else who's a local and works in the property industry? Go ahead, name someone else better than him. I'll wait.*

I mentally scrolled through my phone contacts, trying to think of someone else who might be able to help, but came up with nothing.

Maybe I could do the repairs myself. That was what Siri and the internet were for, right? I'd save some money, and my budget could have some breathing space. I'd never replaced roof tiles or fixed leaky pipes before, but I'd cross that bridge when I came to it.

But that line of thought was instantly nixed when an errant piece of roofing decided to no longer fight gravity and crumbled on top of my head. I let out a yell and jumped to save my life.

See how bad things are? Insubordinate brain was triumphant. *He's obviously the best man for the job.*

No, no, not so fast.

The man in question was frowning at and typing on his phone, so I quickly made a mental pros and cons list:

Pro:

1. He's the only person I know in Port Benedict. And he works in the property industry, so he must have connections that could help turn this place into a functional, tasteful, state-of-the-art bakery (200 points).

2. He is probably the only person Eric would trust with his life, which was why my brother had called him for help. Ergo, I should be able to trust him with mine (501 points). *Theoretically.*

3. I'd rather deal with him than going back home to my parents (10,000 points).

Con:

1. We have history. Bad, unpleasant history. He shattered my heart into pieces, then nearly committed homicide, and he is the world's most annoying man (minus 500 points).

It was crystal-clear. Asking my sworn enemy for help *and* sharing the same city with him wasn't in my bingo card for the year—or ever—but I had no other choice. The more I thought about it, the more convinced I was. Living in the same city as Alec Mackenzie? No problem, because after almost three decades of parental oppression, I'd take that as a win any day.

"I accept."

Alec looked up from his phone. "Accept what?"

Was he making me beg? I swallowed my pride and ignored the way his ~~deep, smooth~~ voice sent waves rippling through my stomach, and employed my most professional, businesslike tone. "I accept your offer of help." Then I forced a polite smile on my face. "Thank you."

"Okay." He shrugged. "I'll make some phone calls and let you know."

"How long do you think it'll take to get everything fixed?"

Alec pocketed his phone and stood next to me. "A few weeks, depending on how busy the tradesmen are. But from the looks of things, you won't need any other major repairs." He gestured to the massive hole in the ceiling, his arm brushing mine. It sent a tiny electric zing jolting through me, traveling from my fingertips to my toes. "Apart from the collapsed roof, the structural foundation is solid. There's no rotting, no cracks any-where, no significant damage to the beams and the walls. All you need to do is replace the roof tiles, the floor tiles, and fix the plumbing. Then a thorough clean and a fresh coat of paint, and it'll be good as new." At my doubtful look, he added, "Trust me. I've been doing this for a long time. It might look bad now, but you're pretty lucky to have snagged this gem, because the location is golden."

He might be right, but my entire existence had been reduced to this sorry excuse of a shop, an old car, and the suitcases and boxes inside said car. Asking me to be positive right now was akin to buying a one-way ticket to Byron Bay and hoping to score a date with one of the Hemsworths.

"By the way, who was the Realtor that handled the lease?"

"A guy called Phil Anderson," I said. "From Anderson Real Estate."

"I know of him," Alec said, nodding. "Solid reputation. He's a business associate of my soon-to-be business partner."

"Soon-to-be?"

A proud grin lit up his face. "Yeah. Goodwin Property Group. One of the biggest commercial property developers in the country. They own multiple developments and shopping complexes, including this one. They approached us last month and expressed an interest to acquire almost half of my company."

"Impressive." I popped my eyes open and gave him a mock innocent look. "Did you have to pay someone to make that happen?"

"Funny, very funny. Anyway, it's been real, but I must run. Congratulations, good luck with everything, et cetera. I'll be in touch."

"I think 'congratulations' isn't the right word." I marched toward the door and opened it for him. The sooner he left the place, the better. "Thanks for stopping by."

But instead of walking out like he was supposed to, he didn't move, his eyes narrowing at the sight of my sleeping bag. "You're not really going to camp here, are you?"

I wasn't, but he didn't need to know that. "Really? You're still hung up on that?"

"Yep. Because it's a certified health hazard."

I crossed my arms in front of my chest. "What if I don't have a choice? I'll need a lot of money to fix up this place, so I can't afford to rent a flat, or a hotel room, or an Airbnb. What am I supposed to do, Alec?"

He grew quiet, the silence stretching long and painful between us. "I'll probably regret this tomorrow," he mumbled to himself, and took a deep breath, as if mentally preparing for his next sentence. "My place is only ten minutes away, and you can have the spare room until you get back on your feet. I'm rarely home, so you won't see much of me around."

My stomach turned. Staying in the same house with my sworn enemy? That held as much appeal as crawling back home to my family. "No thanks. I'll be fine."

"I wouldn't have offered if I didn't mean it. You don't have to pay rent. If the situation was reversed, Eric would've done the same thing for my sisters in a heartbeat." He looked pained, as if saying the words was making him die a slow and agonizing death. "We're adults, and I know you don't like me, but I'm sure we can be civil for a short time."

"*We* don't like each other," I pointed out.

"Same difference."

The offer was very tempting, because it might be a while before I could afford my own place, and I wasn't going to risk breaking the law and getting fined for sleeping in the store. And really, if I wanted to be honest, the prospect of setting up camp in a place with no toilet, no shower, with squirrels and maybe even rats to keep me company, wasn't at all appealing. He might be a ~~much~~ slightly better alternative than the rodents, but sharing the same house with him might spark the next Civil War.

Time for another quick list:

Pro:	Con:
1. A proper bed to sleep in, and a decent toilet and shower (100 points).	1. I'd have to live under the same roof with him (minus 200 points).

2. I could kiss the squirrels, the rats, and whatever
animals currently mak-
ing plans to nest in the
fallen tree limb goodbye
(no, eww, not literally, of
course) (200 points).

An uncomfortable twinge of guilt tugged at my heart, admonishing me for being so ungrateful. *Be nicer, Ellie.* After all, he was being generous, helping me with the repairs *and* offering me a place to stay. Sworn enemies or not, the least I could do was be civil and respectful to him. And really, let's face it: I was desperate. What other choices did I have?

"Thank you. I'll take it," I said, forcing myself to sound polite. "But I'm paying you rent, even if it's not much. I don't want to be indebted to you for the rest of my life."

"Whatever. Good thing I showed up, huh?"

"Absolutely. You should make a full-time job out of it. 'Knight in shining armor for hire' has a nice ring to it, don't you think?"

He gave me a dirty look, before pulling out his phone. "What's your number?"

"I don't give out my numbers on the first date. You need to buy me dinner first."

He blew out an exasperated sigh, looking as if his patience was on its last legs. "Your number, Ellie. I'm texting you my address and the security code to disarm the front door."

"Why didn't you say so?" I gave him an innocent look as I took his phone and typed in my number. "Should have opened with that."

Alec scoffed as he took the phone back. "Why else would I be asking?"

"Actually," I said, as my phone pinged with his text, "I might need another favor."

"For someone who doesn't like me, you seem to be needing my help a lot." This time, he did walk out the door. "Keep it up and I might start charging you."

"Can you not say anything about this to anyone back home?" I ignored his jibe and followed him to his car. "That I'll be living at your place?"

"Why? Are you on the run from your family? Eric knows you're here."

"Yeah, but he doesn't need to know where I'll be staying. I don't want him and Naomi to, uh, get any ideas."

Alec stopped next to his car and raised his eyebrows at me. "What kind of ideas?"

"Just . . . the wrong kind of ideas." I made a vague gesture with my hands. I trusted Eric and Naomi, and I knew they would never say anything to my parents, but the fewer people from home that knew I'd be living with him, the better. "If Eric asks, tell him that you don't know where I live."

He let out a mock exaggerated sigh. "Asking me to lie will cost you extra. And you forgot to say please."

"*Please?* My family doesn't need to know about our living arrangements."

Something flickered in his eyes. "Fine. I won't tell anyone. Not that your parents would ever get in touch with me, anyway. Your mother hates my guts, too. Seems all the women in your family are immune to my charm."

I smiled a little. "At least there's one thing she and I agree on."

As he drove away, I blew out a breath, while crossing my toes and fingers, hoping I hadn't just made the second biggest mistake of my life in less than a month.

Because—zings or not—I was about to share a house with the devil incarnate himself.

CHAPTER 5

Pancakes and Glasses Are Essentially Lethal Weapons

A tall, dark-haired woman was standing in front of the neighboring yarn store, looking curious as I walked back toward the shop after Alec had left.

"Hey there," she called out. "I saw you going in earlier. Are you the new tenant?"

"I am." I smiled and introduced myself.

"Oh, awesome." She offered her hand. "I'm Kimiko Halim. You look so much friendlier than the grouchy old man who was here last. All the tenants in the neighborhood didn't like him, and we were all so glad when he finally decided to retire."

I grinned at the woman, instantly liking her. "Lovely to meet you, Kimiko." I tilted my head at her. "Halim? Is that an Indonesian surname?"

Her eyes lit up. "Yeah. How do you know? It's from my father's side of the family. And please, call me Kim."

"My parents are Chinese Indonesian," I said. "They were born in Jakarta but moved to the States."

My new friend clapped her hands in delight. "My grandpa is going to be so happy to hear about this." She gestured to the yarn shop next door, its window display full of colorfully knitted sweaters, bright scarves and beanies, and cute crocheted animals. "That's mine. Well, technically it still belongs to my grandparents, but I'm running it now. Are you a knitter?"

"Afraid not."

She shrugged. "That's okay, I won't hold it against you." She shot a curious look toward my store. "What are you planning to do here?"

"A bakery. Specializing in low-carb, sugar-free desserts. The usual things like brownies, donuts, cupcakes, and cookies, but we'll be using natural plant-based sweeteners." My confidence took a sharp nosedive when a slight crease appeared on her forehead. I struck a pose, like a 1980s game show model showcasing a product, trying to cover my awkwardness. "We offer healthier choices, but with the same great taste!"

When I said it out loud like that, the idea seemed silly, not worth the huge gamble of uprooting my life and investing all my savings into it.

"That sounds great." Kim gave me an approving nod. "I promise I'll be one of your most loyal customers. We small business owners must stick together."

"Thanks. I don't know when we'll be able to open, though." I pointed at the store, gesturing for her to peek inside. Her eyes went wide at the sight.

"That's an enormous piece of tree."

"And the best part is, it comes with its own squirrels."

"Gosh." She let out a low whistle. "You really have your work cut out for you."

"Yeah. But a supposed expert in the building industry said I should consider myself lucky, because the location is excellent, and he thought I won't need any other major repairs."

"Better get that so-called expert to help you with the work, then. But he's right, the location *is* excellent. Anyway, good luck, and let me know if you need any help." She tilted her head, her brows drawing closer. "You look familiar. Have we met before?"

Damn YouTube video. "Don't think so. I'm from out of town. It's my first day in Port Benedict."

Kim beamed at me. "Right. Must've mistaken you for someone else. Well, good to meet you, Ellie. I should get back to my store, but we should get together for dinner sometime."

I returned her smile. "That would be lovely." It was nice to meet a friendly new face in the middle of this debacle of a day.

Hopefully that was a sign that things were looking up.

Back home, my usual morning routine was to wake up at six, go for a forty-five-minute run, then take a quick shower before breakfast. The exercise helped me start the day energized and focused, while keeping my glucose levels under control.

But of course, I wasn't home right now. I was in a new place, in a different time zone, three hours behind my hometown. And without my approval, my body clock had decided to forge ahead and take charge, stirring me at three in the morning because, hey, *who needs an alarm clock?* It insisted I open my eyelids, although the pitch-black darkness outside wisely recommended that I snuggle back under my comfortable blanket.

Heeding its advice, I tried to go back to sleep. Until images of gigantic tree limbs, hailstorms of chipped roof tiles, and squirrels as big as my arms innocently waltzed into my brain, finally catapulting my eyes wide open.

It wasn't a nightmare. I really *was* thousands of miles away from home, the proud new tenant of a severely damaged store, and sleeping under the same roof as Alec McGrumpyface.

Cue loud groan.

Fully awake now, I padded out to the guest bathroom and jumped in the shower, relishing the wonderful feel of hot water drumming on my back. I shuddered a little, because less than twenty-four hours ago, I was actually desperate enough to even consider a very different, way more ridiculous scenario, where I'd wake up freezing my ass off, with a scurry of squirrels masquerading as my blanket.

Sir McGrumpyface might be the most infuriating person in the universe, but I'd be forever grateful for his offer. His home was a renovated, two-story townhouse nestled at the top of a hilly street, with a clear, gorgeous view of Port Benedict Bay in the distance. The spare guest room that I was staying in was on the second floor, with a view of the neatly kept backyard, and tastefully furnished with a beige queen-size wrought iron bed, teak bedside tables, and a beautiful mahogany chest of drawers. The room was across the hall from the guest bath and his bedroom, separated by a cozy rumpus area.

A million things ran through my mind as I got dressed. I needed to check off as many things as possible from my To-Buy List, starting with some cleaning items and basic handyman tools. Rolls of duct tape, a ladder, a large piece of heavy-duty tarp. A chainsaw to cut up the broken tree limb into smaller pieces, because that would be faster than a regular handsaw. If I could start the cleanup so the place was ready for the contractor to start the repairs, it would save me some time and money.

The soft clanking of pots and pans echoed throughout the house, interrupting my thoughts. I trotted downstairs, where a shirtless Alec puttered around the kitchen, displaying a prize-winning torso. My traitorous brain whistled in appreciation, because the Alec I remembered from our younger years definitely hadn't been *this* buff. He wore a pair of gray shorts, with his hair messy and sticking out every which way.

Holy abs, Batman. This wasn't such a terrible view to start the day.

Then I realized he had a pair of tortoiseshell glasses on.

My heart pounded quicker. This was not good. *At all.* I didn't know what it was about men wearing glasses, but I'd always had a bizarre infatuation with them. Seeing Alec with a pair right now sent a battalion of butterflies crashing through my stomach. And for the love of all that is holy, who knew that shoulder blades could be so . . . interesting?

Stop staring. He's annoying, and you don't like him.

"Heard your shower running. Coffee?" He didn't look up from the stove. "Mugs are in the top right corner."

"Put a shirt on. My eyes are hurting me." I opened the cupboard and took out a mug, careful to maneuver my way around him. The last thing I needed at five in the morning was to have that smooth, solid skin touching mine. *Ugh.* "Got any teas?"

He glanced at me over his shoulder, blinking twice. "You don't drink coffee? What's wrong with you?"

I was about to retort with a snarky response, but a voice at the back of my brain reminded me: he was helping me with the repairs. He gave me a place to stay. The least I could do was be friendly and polite, no matter how challenging it would be.

"Coffee and I don't get along. One cup, and my heart thumps like it's about to run a marathon."

"You sure you're related to Eric? The man has coffee flowing in his veins."

"Eric, my mother, and my father. I'm the black sheep of the family." I pulled out a box of Lipton green tea from his pantry, placed a tea bag in my mug, then poured hot water and left it to brew for a few minutes. "When did you start wearing glasses?"

Instead of answering, he turned around and slid a plate in front of me. "Whole grain buttermilk pancake, with my mother's homemade strawberry compote."

Okay, glasses + pancakes = a dangerous combination. *Must tread carefully.*

"Thank you." Raising my eyebrows, I sat on a kitchen stool. "Are they edible?"

"Totally not bragging, but I've received multiple five-star reviews for those." He leaned against the kitchen counter, presenting me with a close-up view of his chest. "Some girls have been known to profess their undying love for me after tasting them. Just saying."

"Count me out." I gestured in the general direction of his body. "Ew. I said, shirt on."

He smirked and put the spatula down, disappeared into the laundry room, and returned wearing an old T-shirt. Plating a second pile for himself, he sat across from me and lifted his mug in a toast. "Here's to a few weeks of coexisting under the same roof in peace."

"Without maiming each other. Temporary truce." I took out my insulin pump to bolus for the pancake. "Did you say this was whole grain?"

At his nod, I did some quick mental math to estimate the amount of carbs in the meal, then entered the number into my pump, which gave me the amount of insulin I should be taking based on my current glucose level. I pressed the blue tick mark to confirm the bolus, then slipped the pump back in my pocket. When I glanced at him, he was watching me, an unreadable expression on his face.

I lifted my chin at him. "What? Have I got strawberry jam on my face or something?"

I'd had countless curious, pitying, and sometimes even disbelieving looks from friends and strangers when they learned I had type 1 diabetes. Some even made the obnoxiously ignorant comments that I'd been "eating too much sweet stuff" (I hadn't), and "you'll grow out of it when you're older" (I wouldn't), or "don't worry, it's not life-threatening" (it could be). At first, I used to get really worked up when people said those things, but after a lifetime of hearing them, I'd grown accustomed to it. A tiny part of me still got fired up sometimes, but I'd learned to not let it bother me.

But *him*—I didn't want him to look at me that way. Nor did I need his sympathy or pity, or worse, treating me like I was fragile. I was poised for battle, ready to defend myself, if he even so much as grazed anything along those lines.

"Nothing on your face. I started wearing glasses last year. Getting old, I guess."

Huh. Not what I had expected.

Alec dug into his food, so I bit down my reply and started on mine. When the heavenly combination of sweet strawberries and gooey, fluffy pancakes exploded in my mouth, I let out a low, throaty moan that wasn't suitable for the breakfast table.

Those girls he was talking about? Yeah, they knew what was up, because honestly, who wouldn't want to be eating these for the rest of their lives? ~~Just for the pancakes alone, I'd marry him in a heartbeat. Men who can cook are hot AF.~~ He was an excellent cook.

Perhaps that first bite was a fluke. I was starving, so my tastebuds were probably warped. But when the second and third bites were followed by the second and third moans, it became obvious that his pancakes were making me experience something orgasmic.

In fact, the closest thing I'd had to a non-battery-operated orgasm in a while.

"Who *are* you?" I looked up to see him staring at me, his eyes darkening, and his fork suspended midair. "Eric never mentioned his friend being a culinary genius."

He slowly lowered the fork, his eyes still on mine. "Told you so."

"Relax. I won't leap over this countertop and profess my undying love to you, or, God forbid, jump your bones." I speared the last piece, then wiped the remaining strawberry jam with it, making sure not to miss a single morsel. "Not even your pancake can make me like you."

"Maybe my homemade waffles could change your mind."

Glasses + pancakes + *waffles*? I could be in huge trouble.

"Anyway, I spoke to a few of our regular contractors," Alec said, his attention already back on his food. "Most of them are in the middle of other projects, so the earliest someone could start on your shop is in four weeks."

Relief whooshed through me. I would have liked someone to start as soon as possible, but that was still much better than the nine weeks I was told yesterday.

"But he's got a reputation for overcommitting to too many projects. I'm waiting to hear back from one more guy, who's away on holiday. He's not due back until next week."

"Great. In the meantime, I was planning on cleaning up the debris in the shop, so it'll be ready for when the contractors start working. Can you recommend a good brand of chainsaw?"

He looked up, his eyebrows disappearing into his forehead. "A what?"

"A chainsaw. To cut up the fallen tree into smaller pieces, so it's easier to dispose of."

He placed his fork on his plate. "Ellie."

"Alec." I echoed his tone.

"Have you ever used a chainsaw before? Or any other power tools?"

"What kind of question is that?" I pretended to be offended. "You think I've never used a power tool just because I'm a girl? That's very condescending."

"Both my sisters know their way around power tools. Being

condescending is the last thing on my mind. Just answer the question."

"I'm an expert with a drill." I held back a grin, because it was kind of fun to wind him up. "I assembled my IKEA wardrobe back home all on my own. With a sliding door. Have you done one before? Those things are hard to put together."

Alec let out a loud sigh. "Let me try again. Do you have any *real* renovation or building experiences outside of IKEA wardrobes?"

My grin finally broke. "If you have to be that specific, then no."

"Do you know that a chainsaw in an untrained hand is practically a lethal weapon?"

"Now you're just being dramatic."

"No, I'm being realistic." His tone was growing impatient. "Eric will never forgive me if I told him that you've lost a hand—or both, or your feet—because you used a dangerous power tool without training. You should wait for the tradesmen, because they'll have the proper tools, and they can get it done in no time."

"I'm not going to lose a hand, or a foot, or any parts of my body." My grin vanished. "Because you know what? I don't have much of a choice. The repairs are going to drain almost all my savings, so the more things I can do by myself, the more money I can save."

Alec was quiet, looking thoughtful, giving me the impression that he was regretting his careless remarks. But a minute later, he shrugged. "Suit yourself. Don't say I didn't warn you. FYI, the nearest hospital is fifteen minutes away. Please don't list me as an emergency contact."

And just like that, our temporary truce flew out the window and was shattered into a billion tiny pieces. "Don't worry. Not even if you're the last man in the whole universe."

"Good." Polishing off his last piece of pancake, he stood up to rinse his plate and stack it in the dishwasher. "Great chat, but I have an on-site meeting at seven." Without another glance, he bounded up the stairs.

Alone at last, I redirected my brainpower onto the day ahead and went through my plan again. Despite my show of confidence earlier, I had (less than) zero faith in my power-tooling abilities. Give me a balance sheet and a cash flow statement any day, but this was foreign territory to me. Not that I would ever admit it to him—I'd rather bite my own tongue and disappear into the ether. But I had to give it my best shot.

Because what other choice did I have?

"I'm leaving." Alec jogged down the stairs a few minutes later, dressed in a dark suit and a crisp white shirt, sans glasses. Grabbing his keys, he shoved his phone into his back pocket. "I'll be back late tonight. Give my regards to the squirrels."

"So I don't have to wait up?" I yelled as he slammed the door behind him.

CHAPTER 6

A Deal with the Grumpy Devil

Fifteen minutes later, I repeatedly kicked the tires of my formerly dependable CR-V, venting out my frustration. My sweet old car had decided to die on me. I didn't have time to service the car before I left home, and this was my payback.

Walking it was, then. Google Maps estimated it should take no longer than fifty minutes to Port Benedict Plaza, plus another ten for a quick stop at a nearby Home Depot.

Two hours later, I was huffing and puffing as I unlocked the door to the shop and flicked on the lights, thankful the electricity was at least working. I dumped the box of cleaning supplies and tools on the floor, then took several minutes to catch my breath, before straightening up and glancing around the place. And despite the dreadful, dystopia-lookalike scene in front of me, a spark of hope bloomed inside my chest. I still had a long road ahead, but this—no matter how atrocious things might seem right now—was still one step closer toward my dream.

I rolled up my sleeves and donned my new protective gear. My goal was to chop up and remove the fallen tree by the end of the day, cover the hole in the roof and clear the rest of the debris by tomorrow, and figure out how to fix the leaky pipes on the third day. It might be a tad ambitious, but I was confident I could finish everything before the contractor came in.

Taking out my brand-new chainsaw from its box, I sat on the floor and read the user manual from cover to cover, then looked up a YouTube video on how to safely operate one. The woman on the instruction video sounded positive and encouraging, so my confidence was at an all-time high. With my phone propped up and the YouTube tutorial playing, I picked up the chainsaw and turned it on.

It took me a few—okay, *a lot* of—tries before I could finally get the hang of it. But still, it wasn't as easy as I thought it was, and by the time I stopped for a lunch break, I'd only managed to cut up a very small section. Either the tree was larger than I'd expected, or my power-tooling skills just weren't up to scratch. At the rate this was going, I'd be lucky if I could remove the tree by the end of the month.

As I slumped into a defeated heap on the floor, I blew out a long breath, wondering if my mother was right, that I couldn't survive unless my family supported me. Maybe she knew me better than I knew myself, because she had never trusted me with bigger responsibilities. Because she'd already foreseen what was going to happen: that I'd probably fail and come crawling back home, with my tail tucked between my legs.

After all, mothers always know best, right?

Enough with the sarcasm, Ellie. Lowest form of wit, remember?

As if on cue, my phone vibrated with an incoming text. My mother was still sending me messages and emails, demanding to know where I was, and livid that I'd been ignoring her. This latest one was short but not sweet, with a not-so-subtle threat saying that if she didn't hear from me by the end of the week, I'd be hearing from her lawyers.

I had to read the message three times before finally registering her words. Was she threatening to *sue me*? On what grounds? What was she expecting to achieve by doing that? Did she really not know when to back off?

Anger—and a healthy dose of fear—gnawed at my brain. I couldn't afford to wait four weeks for Alec's contractor, because who knew what other kinds of nasty, horrible damage she might be able to pull off in that time?

Fueled by new resolve, I deleted the message, then went back to my chainsaw and the tree. I yanked the starter several times, but no matter how hard I tried, it still refused to start.

It was a brand-new chainsaw. Why wasn't it working?

Groaning with exasperation, I Googled the symptoms, and found that it was most likely flooded. The solution, according to an arborist chat forum, was to "remove the air cleaner, the spark plug, the bar and chain," and that was when I stopped reading, because they could be speaking in an alien language for all I knew.

With my frustration bubbling over, I reached for my phone and called Naomi. She picked up on the second ring, her familiar voice instantly cheering me up.

"Ellie! How are things going out there?"

"Could be better, but I shouldn't complain." I told her about the store and felt myself begin to relax. "How have you been? How's my favorite brother doing?"

"We're good. I've been busy with work, and Eric has been running around getting the new brewery ready for opening."

"Tell him not to work too hard. Even the Golden Child needs a break sometimes."

Naomi snickered. "I'll tell him that. You know how much he hates that nickname."

"Make sure you do. Hey, um, have you heard from George?"

"Saw him last week," she said. "He's fine, if that's what you're wondering about. You did the right thing, and it's better for both of you in the long run."

This was why Naomi and I had been best friends for so long. We always supported each other, no matter what. She was with me when I was diagnosed, when I went through my first heartbreak, and I had consoled her when she broke up with her first girlfriend. She had always stood behind every decision I made, good or bad, not even flinching when I told her I was moving to Port Benedict, because she knew how long I'd been wanting to chase my dream.

"Eric said Alec's helping you with the repairs. How's that going?"

"It's going fine, although I'm not happy about it. We're tolerating each other. Barely."

She only chuckled. "Well, make sure you stay away from him then, because I don't want my best friend killing my boyfriend's best friend. And if you *are* going to murder him, I'll need twelve hours' notice to fly over and help you get rid of the body." Her voice softened. "How does it feel to see him again, though? Are you doing okay?"

Because of course Naomi knew about my crush on him. She knew how devastated I was when he had left without even saying goodbye.

"I'm fine. It was an old childhood crush. Don't worry, I've grown out of it."

We spoke for a few more minutes, and she told me about the short getaway Eric had planned for them the next weekend. When I hung up, my mood was considerably lifted, giving me a fresh dose of confidence.

Come on, get your act together, Ellie.

I'd gone this far from my old life, and I wasn't going back. The only way out of this mess was to push forward and get this place up and running.

Because the alternative wasn't even worth thinking about.

My top was drenched in sweat as I turned onto Alec's leafy street, just as his car swung into the driveway. Slamming the door closed, he rushed toward the front door, stopping short when he saw me walking up.

"Holy shit." His eyebrows went up as he eyed me from head to toe. "Did you stop for a swim at the pool or something?"

"Sure, after my daily one-hour jog by the beach." I gave him an exaggerated eye roll. "I walked back from the shop. Why are you in such a hurry?"

"Who says I'm in a hurry?" He frowned, his eyes darting to the curb to my CR-V. "What's wrong with your car?"

"It decided to take a well-deserved holiday."

"Good thing you got into town before it conked out. Probably just the battery. I can jump-start it tomorrow morning before work." He considered me for a second, then said, "Call me next time, and I can give you a ride. Saves you from having to walk back."

I was about to thank him for the offer, but then I remembered his rudeness this morning, and that the temporary truce had been indefinitely suspended. "I appreciate the offer."

"I can smell a 'but' coming."

"But I prefer walking barefoot across flaming hot coals, surrounded by flesh-eating piranhas, to riding in a car alone with you."

He ignored my dig. "The offer still stands. I thought exercise and temperature can affect your blood sugar levels. They can make you low, right? I remember that night. All that walking, and that's when you . . . you know." His face turned the slightest shade of pink, and he actually had the grace to look uncomfortable. "And the alcohol you had didn't help. You had, what, two Bud Lights? And a margarita?"

My jaw dropped and practically crashed on the gravel driveway.

Because he didn't say "beers" and "cocktails."

He said, very specifically, "two Bud Lights and a margarita."

How did he still remember the exact drinks I had?

Somewhere deep in the bowels of my brain, a group of minisized counselors and psychologists hastily convened to hold an emergency meeting, dissecting and analyzing the shocking revelation that *Alec remembered what happened ten years ago in great detail!*

It might seem like a trivial detail to obsess over, but it was hugely significant to me. I'd always been under the impression that he never cared about what happened that night. But now . . . the fact that he still remembered the simplest, tiniest little details . . .

I filed away that interesting piece of information so I could overanalyze it later. Shrugging, I tried to appear nonchalant. "Chalk it up to teenage rebellion. After years of being told to watch what I ate, being able to taste a drop of alcohol was pretty damn liberating."

Our eyes met, knowing that it was more than just teenage rebellion. It had also been heartbreak, anger, spite, and foolishness.

All of it mine.

"It wasn't just 'a drop.' Otherwise you wouldn't have ended up in the ER."

For several beats, his eyes held mine, and my brain failed to instruct my eyes to look away. Right now, the fact that I couldn't stand him had faded into the background, replaced by a shared memory that he'd once witnessed one of the most terrifying moments of my life.

A series of angry car horns blared in the distance, and he blinked twice. The next second, whatever moment we'd just shared vanished along with the fading car horns.

"I have to run." He cast a furtive look at the street and unlocked the front door.

I narrowed one eye at him, before following him inside. "What's going on? You're looking very suspicious."

He let out an indignant huff. "Nothing, and no, I don't."

"You sure? Because you look like you're hiding something. Are you in some kind of trouble that I should know about? Follow-up question, are you running away from the authorities?"

"No. I just need to change before my next meeting." He gestured at his attire from this morning. "Stop asking so many questions. Don't you have better things to do? Weren't you supposed to be busy at your store? Chopping off trees for firewood or something?"

"Yep. Day one of my To-Do List successfully completed," I lied through my teeth. "Tree's almost gone."

"And all your limbs are still intact? Congratulations."

"What meeting is it? Since you're my landlord for the next few weeks, I need to know if you're planning a criminal activity."

"You caught me. I'm plotting my next move to topple the free world." He placed his keys and phone on the kitchen counter. "Want to join the cause? I could always use another henchman."

"Again, I appreciate the offer. But honestly, I'd rather be sucked into a supermassive black hole instead."

"First piranhas, now black holes." He shrugged his suit jacket off. "I'm starting to think you don't like me."

"Well done, you finally figured it out. Is it a cult?"

A corner of his mouth lifted at the tiniest, most miniscule angle. "I asked you to stop with the questions. Terrible at following instructions, are we?"

"Not a criminal, not a cult. Secret girlfriend, then?"

"Wow. The things that go through your mind." Disappearing into the laundry room, he came back wearing a dark pair of jeans and a fresh light-blue shirt. "Must be fascinating to live inside your brain."

"It's the happiest place on Earth. You know I won't stop until you tell me what it is."

"Fine." He released a long-suffering sigh and cast a cautious look at the front windows, as if someone were standing outside with a recording device, ready to catch him saying something illegal. "I'm meeting a woman named Audrey."

"Oooh, a secret girlfriend," I sing-songed. "I was right."

"Not my girlfriend. I'm paying her to be one."

My eyes widened. "You're hiring an escort?"

"I said a girlfriend, not an—" He stopped, his lips pursed into a thin line. "Why am I explaining myself to you? Forget I even said anything. It's none of your business."

"Seriously? You can't just drop a juicy bombshell about hiring a girlfriend and expect me not to question you about it."

Alec smirked. "Watch me."

"But why? Are you really that desperate for some human touch?"

He choked a laugh as he pocketed his keys. "I'm not desperate."

"If you're hiring a girlfriend, you are. I can even smell the stench of desperation," I said. "Here's an idea. You've had girl-friends in the past, right? Why don't you just get back together with one of your exes? Send them flowers. Grovel and beg until they take you back. Wouldn't that be easier than paying an esco—I mean, hiring someone to be your partner?"

Alec stared at me, looking like he wanted to strangle me and feed me to the wolves.

"You can be a bit annoying, sure. But maybe one of those exes is gullible enough to be willing to sacrifice their prime years and spend their precious free time with you?"

"You don't know when to stop, do you?" He arched his eyebrows. "Still as stubborn as ever. Some things never change."

"Not stubborn. I persevere. There's a difference."

"Fine, if you really must know, I have an important work event this weekend, and long story short, it'll look bad if I came alone. Audrey is a freelance actor for hire, so I'm meeting her to go over our cover story, how we first met, all the backstories."

A few minutes passed as I gaped at him, trying to process his answer. "That," I finally said, struggling to contain my laugh, "is *the most* ridiculous thing I've ever heard in my life."

"I didn't ask for your opinion." Alec lifted his shoulders, not looking the least bit concerned that I'd just insulted him. "She costs a fortune, but this function is important, so I'll pay her whatever she wants. Now, if you're finished judging me, I have to go."

"Wait." A lightbulb flickered in my head, as my mother's latest threatening text came back to taunt me. "How important is the event?"

He pocketed his phone. "Very. Everything hinges on this."

I put two and two together. "Is this related to that acquisition you were telling me about? Goodwin Property Group?"

"Maybe."

"Come on, Mackenzie. Stop being so secretive. How is hiring a pretend girlfriend going to make or break the future of your business?"

He hesitated for a few seconds, before answering, "The woman who owns Goodwin Property Group is interested in both my company and me."

"Saucy." I whistled. "She's got terrible taste, though."

He ignored my comment. "She's a wonderful person, and she's been upfront about the whole thing, which I appreciate. But I didn't want to jeopardize the deal by repeatedly rejecting her dinner invites. I felt really bad, so on the spur of the moment, I lied and told her I already have a girlfriend."

"Did they teach that in business school? Start your business partnership with a lie?"

"That's why all I need to do now is find a convincing girlfriend for the next few weeks. Once the acquisition is completed, we'll stage a respectable breakup. I'll get my deal, and Audrey will have enough money for her next holiday or a deposit on her first home."

The bulb grew brighter. It was an outrageous idea, but it might be my best bet to get things up and running as quickly as possible, before my mother had a chance to follow through on her ridiculous threat. She would stop at nothing to make sure I failed, and I wouldn't put it past her to do something vile, like suing me or reporting me to the authorities with false accusations. I ran a quick pros and cons list, but it was really a no-brainer, because this was a win-win situation.

"You don't need Audrey," I said slowly.

Alec raised an eyebrow. "I don't?"

"You don't. I can help you."

"*You?* Want to help me? Why?"

"Because we're old friends, and that's what friends do."

"*Friends?*" He snorted loudly. "We're not friends. You don't even like me."

"Well, we've known each other for a long time. Maybe longer than I would have liked." I forced out a smile. "The point is, I'm offering my help. I'll even do it for free."

"For free," he repeated, his expression incredulous.

"With one condition."

"Obviously you don't know the meaning of the word 'free,' but I'm willing to let that slide." He folded his arms, leaning against the kitchen countertop. "Let's hear it."

My words came tumbling out before I could stop myself. "I can be your pretend girlfriend for the next few weeks, or however long you need me to be, if you help me with the repairs at the shop."

His forehead creased. "I thought you said you had it under control."

"I don't. I'm way in over my head. The tree is still there, because I spent the entire day cutting off a tiny section before flooding the chainsaw. You know the contractor that could start in four weeks? If you can get him or someone else to start tomorrow, I'll be your Audrey."

Alec stared at me. "Let me get this straight. You want me to help you, in exchange for you being my girlfriend. Have I got that right?"

"*Pretend* girlfriend," I emphasized. "One word can make a huge difference."

"Why? If I remember correctly, someone told me a few minutes ago that it was the most ridiculous thing they'd ever heard in their life."

"I changed my mind."

"But there's no way I can pretend to be madly in love with you." He repressed a shudder.

"Think about it. You're a savvy businessman. You'll save some money, and since we're old friends—"

"Do I have to keep reminding you that you don't like me? You've been nothing but unfriendly from the moment I saw you yesterday."

I pretended not to hear him. "—we won't need to make up any backstories, or cover stories, or any other fibs. Less risk of accidentally saying the wrong thing and having her discover your elaborate lie."

He studied me, the cogs clearly spinning inside his brain. "You do have a point."

"You know I do. It's the offer of a lifetime, Alec."

"I wouldn't go that far."

"Still, it's too good to pass up," I said, using my sweetest, most coaxing tone. "Didn't you say Audrey costs a lot?"

"She does. I could utilize the funds better elsewhere, especially with the expansion we're planning after the Goodwin investment." He rubbed his chin, looking thoughtful. "And all I have to do is find someone to help you with your shop repairs?"

"Find me someone who could start *tomorrow*. I don't care if you do it yourself, or someone else, just as long as they're reliable, affordable, and they can get the job done ASAP."

After a long pause, he nodded. "Okay." He offered his hand, and my stomach fluttered as his palms gripped mine. "But we'll need to sit down, work out a detailed plan, then go over it repeatedly until you can recite it in your sleep."

I grinned at him. "Consider it done. Trust me, we're going to do great."

"We better." He pulled out his phone and scrolled through his contacts. "Looks like I have to tell my pretend girlfriend we're no longer dating."

CHAPTER 7

Nobody Checks Their Emails at Midnight

Loud, insistent knocks jolted me awake the next morning, followed by Alec bellowing from the other side of my door. "Wake up, Ellie! We're leaving in thirty."

Groaning, I groped for my phone, my eyes popping wide when I saw the time. "Somebody better be dead," I muttered.

Another loud, impatient rap. "Come on. Burning daylight here."

Jumping off the bed, I flung the door open and glared at him. "*What daylight?* It's five in the morning!"

His eyebrows, already furrowed, climbed upward. "Yikes." His gaze traveled down my length. "And you complained about *me* not wearing a shirt?"

My cheeks heated when I belatedly realized that I was in my old, ratty Hello Kitty pajamas. It was my oldest, most comfortable sleepwear, with fading pictures on the thinning white top and pink pants, and ~~probably~~ *most definitely* inappropriate for public view. It wasn't the same as him being shirtless, but from where he was standing, he could probably see what was underneath. And as if on cue, my uncooperative yet friendly nipples had apparently decided that it was time to join the party and introduce themselves.

I crossed my arms in front of my chest and glared at him. "This had better be a life-and-death situation."

"We're meeting my contractor in an hour." He leaned against the doorframe, his eyes lazily wandering back up to my face. "Sent you an email about it last night."

"Didn't get it."

"Did you check your email?"

"I did, before I went to bed. Nothing from you."

"Check again."

I marched over to the bedside table and snatched my phone. Sure enough, the last item in my inbox came from him, sent just five hours ago.

"Who, in their right mind, sends an email about an appointment, at two minutes past midnight, to someone living in the same house?" I waved my phone, repressing the urge to hit him on the head with it. "Why didn't you just knock? Slip a note under the door? Or use this nifty little platform called WhatsApp? *Who the hell checks their freaking emails at midnight?*"

"Any budding entrepreneur who wants to succeed. Breakfast is ready downstairs."

"You can't boss me around. If this is how it's going to be, I'm canceling our deal."

"Your loss, Hello Kitty. It's not me who has their future riding on a badly damaged building." He pushed himself off the doorframe and headed toward the stairs. "Best of luck, Godspeed, and all the rest of it."

Damn him, because he was right. Whether I liked it or not, I needed his help.

I slammed the door, ignoring his evil chuckle from the other side.

As if being abruptly woken up at the crack of dawn wasn't bad enough, the car ride to the shop was even more excruciating. Alec had put on a podcast about the construction industry that droned on and on about the importance of workforce management. No amount of tea, energy drink, or even coffee would ever be enough to help me endure this kind of mind-numbingly dull talk so early in the day.

"Do you seriously listen to this on your way to work? Every day?"

His reply was a grunt, his eyes focused on the busy morning traffic.

"This is awful. No wonder you're so grumpy and annoying."

There was a *tsk* before he replied. "I'm not grumpy, and this is how I start my day. It pays to keep myself up-to-date with the latest changes in the industry."

"I mean, I'd probably be grumpy, too, if I had to listen to this every morning. What about some upbeat songs to boost your mood and start the day right?"

"My mood and my days are just fine."

Was it wrong that I felt a perverse satisfaction in riling him up? "Have you ever heard of BTS? That super popular K-pop boy band? They've got some catchy songs to cure your crankiness. You don't even have to understand Korean."

"Anyone ever told you your taste in music is appalling?"

"Beyoncé? John Legend? Old Dominion?" I went on, knowing full well that he was getting annoyed. "Michael Bublé? You can't go wrong with easy, jazzy Bublé."

"Look, Hello Kitty." He let out an extra-long sigh. "When

we're in your car, you're free to play any songs you want. K-pop, rock, country, operatic arias, I don't care. When we're in mine, *this* is what we listen to."

"You're being very close-minded." He was so easy to tease, and I might have found my new favorite pastime. "There's a whole world outside of construction podcasts, you know. You should open yourself up to new possibilities."

"Goddamn it, Ellie. If you keep this up, one of us isn't going to survive the next few weeks. And yes, by that I meant me."

He turned into the shopping complex and found an empty spot not far from the shop, then leaned around to grab his jacket from the back seat, his arm brushing mine. His now-familiar smell of citrus and spice made its way into my nose, and I closed my eyes, discreetly taking a deep, greedy inhale. The construction podcast might be torture, but this more than made up for it.

"Everything okay?"

My eyes snapped open. He was watching me, with a smirk on his face.

So much for being discreet.

Without warning, the next few weeks flashed before my eyes. I was practically snorting him into my nostrils after a short ten-minute car ride. How on Earth could I pretend to be his loving, devoted girlfriend without driving myself up the wall? If I kept this up, *I'd* be the one who wouldn't survive.

Well, should've thought about that before offering to be his fake girl-friend.

I suppressed a shudder, regretting my reckless suggestion.

But as I unlocked the door to the shop, the awful sight slapped me back to reality: however hard it would be, I had to suck it up because my entire future hinged on this deal.

"I tried to jump-start your car this morning," Alec said as we walked in. "It's not the battery, so I'll give you the contact details of my mechanic. He can get the car fixed in no time. And I'll pick you up at six for dinner."

"Dinner?" I flicked on the lights. "What makes you think I'm going to have dinner with you, Sir Grouchiness?"

He bristled. "It's business, not a date. We need to hash out the details of our deal. And I'm only picking you up so you don't have to walk, and possibly die on my watch, because Eric would never forgive me."

This time, it was my turn to stiffen. "I'm perfectly capable of getting to wherever I need to without your help. Besides, if I had to listen to another second of your boring podcast, my brain cells would probably shrivel up and die."

"Hey, Alec." A deep voice interrupted his reply, and I turned to see a hazel-eyed, brown-haired man dressed in a fluorescent orange vest striding into the shop. The two of them performed one of those bro-handshake-slash-hugs that guys do to make them seem cooler than they really are.

"Rob, this is Ellie Pang," Alec said. "Ellie, meet Rob Carmichael, the builder I told you was away on holiday. He was the contractor I worked with on my first development. Best in the business, but likes to think of himself as a comedian."

"Nice to finally meet you." Rob smiled at me. "You must be a very important person. This one sent me an urgent email last night, asking me to scramble a team and be here first thing in the morning. Anyone else, I'd tell them to go f—"

Alec cleared his throat.

"—find someone else." Rob raised his eyebrows at Alec. "Honestly, Mackenzie. What did you think I was going to say?"

Finally meet me? I returned his smile. "Thanks, Rob. Appreciate you coming at such short notice. But I thought Alec said you're not back until next week?"

"And he would be right. Except I was more than happy to cut

my holiday short when he contacted me." Rob gave me a lopsided grin. "It's my extended family's annual get-together, and there were more relatives than I could tolerate. I'd rather be knee-deep in debris on a job site than endure another day of nosy questioning about my love life."

"I can relate. They sound like mine during Lunar New Year. It's the worst."

"Oh, exactly. They don't know when to stop."

Alec glanced at his watch. "Okay, you two need to wrap up the bonding session. We haven't got all day."

Rob gave me a knowing look. "He thinks he's the boss."

"Tell me, Rob. How do you put up working with someone this curt and rude?"

"He can be charming if he wants to. But you want to know my theory?" Rob leaned over and mock-whispered, "I think he does it to keep his distance from people, especially the ones he cares about. It's his defense mechanism. A way to protect himself so he doesn't get hurt."

Alec sighed. "Are you done psychoanalyzing me? You two want to get started now?"

He ignored our snickers. Rob and I started walking around the place, discussing what needed to be done. He said he'd be able to fix the roof, the floor tiles, and the leaky pipes in one week, before remodeling and refitting the shop with ovens, commercial refrigerators, sinks, and the prep areas. I explained my idea of having an open-plan style kitchen with glass windows, so customers could see the behind-the-scenes process. Rob took notes and offered suggestions, including installing energy-efficient appliances to reduce the shop's carbon footprint.

"We can finish in two, three weeks at the most," Rob said when we were done. "I've got a crew ready to start today. You won't recognize the place when we're done."

I released a breath of relief. "That's perfect. We haven't discussed the budget, though. Can you email me your quote for the project?"

"We'll do it at cost, plus the labor expenses to pay my guys." Rob chuckled at my widening eyes. "You should thank him." He pointed at Alec, who looked up from his phone. "I owe him big time, so I'm just paying it forward."

Baffled, I turned to Alec, but he only shrugged.

"I have to run. I'll leave you two to it." He gave Rob a friendly slap in the back, then glanced at me. "If you don't want me to pick you up, we'll meet somewhere nearby."

"I said no dinners." I followed him as he stepped outside. "Also, what's the deal with Rob? I can't let him work for free."

"You *are* paying him. For the materials and the labor costs."

"But that's not fair to him. He needs to make a profit, right?"

Alec sighed, because I was clearly stretching his patience. "Rob is a shareholder in Mackenzie Constructions. He heard about the Goodwin offer and asked if he could buy a stake in my business. We worked out a deal where I gave him ten percent ownership in return for him doing some jobs at cost."

"Oh," I said, surprised. "He must be a really good friend."

"He is. Rob was the first person who gave me a chance when I moved out here, when nobody else did. I'm just returning the favor."

I didn't want to admit it, but I was secretly impressed. "That's very kind of you. And thanks. That would really help my cash flow."

He made a noncommittal grunt. "See you at six."

"Absolutely not. We can work out whatever details we need via email."

"Says the woman who doesn't even check her emails."

"Send them before ten P.M., and I'll guarantee you a reply the next morning."

"There's an Indonesian restaurant nearby." Alec suddenly spun around and sent me crashing into his chest. "I'll text you the address. Six o'clock. If you're not there, deal's off."

I couldn't answer, because my brain must have gone on a tropical holiday somewhere. Or maybe the cells *did* shrivel up and die from listening to the podcast earlier. Perhaps, more accurately, it was because my face was firmly planted on his solid chest, which had the audacity to smell so nice *and* feel so good. Both my hands shot up to anchor myself against him, and I took one tiny, reluctant step back, not wanting to extract my face and deprive myself of such a heady, glorious feeling. My traitorous nose decided to go ahead and inhale his scent again, slowly and thoroughly like it was a lifeline, before I flicked my eyes upward and met his.

My breath caught in my throat as I met his gaze, because he was staring down at me. Was it my imagination, or had his eyes turned darker?

"If someone insisted on wining and dining me, I'd jump at the offer."

Both our heads turned at the voice. My next-door neighbor was grinning at us, her keys poised over her shop door. A dark blue, beat-up Hyundai was parked in front, next to Alec's car, and a curly-haired woman sat behind the wheel, resting her chin in her left hand, watching us with a curious smile on her face.

I beat a hasty retreat from that solid (and annoyingly warm) chest. "Hey, Kim."

"Hey." She tilted her head, giving Alec a curious once-over. "Is this the building industry expert you told me about?"

"She said that?" Alec gave Kim a bright smile, cranking up to full wattage, giving me a brief flash of his dimple. I swore Kim's eyelashes fluttered a little as he offered his hand to her. "Alec Mackenzie. Nice to meet you."

"Kimiko Halim. That's my housemate, Jenna Ng." She pointed at the woman in the Hyundai, who lifted her right hand in greeting.

"Great setup you've got there." Alec gestured at her shop. "Very charming."

"That's very nice of you to say." Kim beamed at him. "Are you helping Ellie get her place up and running?" She gave me a not-so-discreet thumbs-up. "Does that mean we'll be seeing a lot more of you?"

"You'll see more of my partner, Rob. But I promise we'll stay out of your way, so you won't get sick of us."

Kim chuckled, obviously thoroughly charmed. "Oh, I'm sure we won't."

I let out a quiet scoff. "I'm sure *I* will."

"Well, it's been such a pleasure meeting you, Kimiko. And your housemate, too." Alec gave the other woman—still watching from the car—a little wave. He turned back to me, his smile dimming. "I'll see you at six."

Without a second glance, he walked away, as Kim, her housemate, and I all watched.

After Alec had driven off, Kim finally opened her door and grinned at me. "He's a cutie. If I were you, I'd keep him around."

CHAPTER 8

No, We Are Not Adorable

Java Spice was a hole-in-the-wall, blink-and-you'll-miss-it Indonesian restaurant, wedged between a takeaway burger place and a travel agency. Google told me it was two blocks away from Port Benedict Plaza, and a short stroll from the Waterfront. When I walked in at six fifteen just to make a point, Alec was already sitting at a small table for two at the back, chatting with an older, kind-looking Asian gentleman.

He flashed me an annoyed glance as I pulled out my chair. "You're late."

"I'm here, aren't I?" My knees knocked against his under the tiny table as I sat down. There was nowhere to escape, so I braced myself for the long haul.

Alec gestured at the older man. "This is Mr. Tanujaya, the owner. He makes the best beef rendang and nasi goreng in the whole country." He pushed the menu in my direction. "But honestly, everything's good."

I scanned the pages, my mouth watering at the colorful photos and list of familiar food: sate ayam, nasi gudeg, soto Betawi, sop buntut, and gado-gado drenched in peanut sauce. They also had Indonesian sweet tea and avocado juice, which I hadn't had in forever.

When I was little and my parents still had time to spend with us on weekends, we sometimes went out for Indonesian food. I might have been born in the States, but both my mom and dad were born overseas, so they would introduce Eric and me to the different cuisines they'd grown up with. But that tradition stopped as their business expanded and they became busier. The last time I had proper Indonesian food was two years ago, when my dad's brother and his family came from Jakarta to visit, and my young cousins were so homesick that we took them to an Indonesian restaurant to cheer them up.

"I can't decide." I looked up at the owner. "Can I just order everything?"

"I recommend our rendang. We make the spice paste from scratch, and the beef is slow cooked for eight hours. Very tender and melts in your mouth."

"Sold." I smiled at him and returned the menu. "Just a warning, I may never want to leave your restaurant, ever again."

The older man beamed at me. "Any friend of Alec's is always welcome here." He half bowed at us and disappeared into the kitchen. A minute later, there was the unmistakable sound and smell of garlic being tossed into smoking hot oil, and the metal spatula scraping the wok.

"Are you a regular here? It's cozy." I took in the restaurant's décor. The wall closest to our table had framed black-and-white photos of old Chinatown storehouses in Jakarta, while front-to-back mirrors covered the opposite side, lending a larger feel to the tiny restaurant. Two white lucky cats perched by the cash register, their mechanical left paws slowly swaying back and forth, often believed to bring the shop owners wealth and prosperity. Next to them was a miniature figurine of becak, the Indonesian version of a rickshaw.

"Found this place when I first moved out here. I was missing my mom's cooking, so I went hunting for authentic Indonesian cuisine. The food's delicious, and Mr. Tanujaya is always happy to chat whenever he's not busy. Plus, it's not part of the Waterfront, so I can always get a table, but close enough for a walk on the beach after." He clasped his hands together. "Anyway, enough small talk. We're here for business. Let's get started."

Following his cue, I said, "Give me some background on your acquisition. I looked up Goodwin Property Group. Didn't realize they're everywhere."

"They're huge." Alec leaned back in his chair. "They control around two-thirds of the commercial property market, and they want to acquire forty percent of my business, which means I'll continue to hold control."

Our drinks came, and I smiled to thank the waitress as she poured the steaming tea into our cups. I took a small sip, and the rich taste of the sweet black jasmine tea instantly transported me back to my childhood.

"Having GPG as a shareholder will open more opportunities. We'll have enough capital to build residential projects in other states and diversify into commercial developments. It's something I've been working on for the past few years."

"Gotcha." In other words, this was massively important for him. *No pressure.* "Tell me about the owner."

Alec blew on his tea. "Her name is Jacqui Goodwin. Very smart, very business-savvy. One of the few female CEOs in the industry. She told me she came from practically nothing and started working part-time jobs at fast food restaurants when she was only fourteen, determined to make something of herself. She saved enough for a deposit and bought her first investment property when she was eighteen, then aggressively grew her portfolio, and started branching out into commercial real estate six years later."

"That's incredible." My biggest achievement at eighteen was landing myself in the ER in a valiant—and misguided—effort to impress this guy. If I had only gotten the memo that one could start amassing properties at that age, life probably would've looked very different now.

"The company is based in Seattle, and they've been selectively buying smaller companies around the country these past few years. All the businesses they've acquired have been doing exceptionally well so far."

"What happens if *this*," I gestured back and forth between us, "doesn't convince her, and she finds out you're starting your business partnership with a lie?"

"There's no *if.* It has to work."

I pulled out my phone and tapped open my list-maker app. "Okay. So our deal goes on until (a) your acquisition is formally signed, and (b) my shop repairs are completed."

"Correct. I'm estimating no longer than four, maybe five weeks."

I could tolerate him for five weeks, no problem. "Sounds reasonable."

"We'll also need to follow each other on social media. Post an occasional picture."

I stopped typing on my list, as a prick of uneasiness went through me. "Our families will see, though."

"Ah, but the thing is, Jacqui's a bit old-school, so she's not on any other platforms except Facebook. Since she's our only target audience, that's where we'll be uploading the photos. She's never overly active anyway, but we'll still need a few posts, just in case. And Facebook lets us choose who can see our posts, so we can exclude our families from seeing them."

"Okay. That might work."

"We'll need to post a few selfies together," he said. "Stage a picture where we stare adoringly into each other's eyes."

"Is that necessary? Why can't we post artsy pictures of our meals instead?"

A loud snort answered me, just as our food arrived. "I need to convince Jacqui I'm in love with a real human being, not with this plate of nasi goreng, no matter how good it looks."

"Fair point." I cringed as the waitress set down my plate, her eyebrows shooting to her hairline when she noticed me. "Speaking of social media, someone posted a video of me several weeks ago, and it went viral. You probably wouldn't want Jacqui to see it."

"I heard. Eric told me about it when we last chatted. It'll be okay. Jacqui runs a multimillion-dollar company. Her days are full of back-to-back meetings, business lunches and dinners, and then more meetings. She has better things to do than watch videos online."

"Fine." I was quiet as I opened the CGM app on my phone to check my levels, took out my insulin pump, and bolused for the food.

"I've never told you this, but I think you're one of the toughest, strongest people I've ever met." Alec broke the silence. He looked up from his food and met my gaze. "I can't imagine what you had to go through from such a young age."

A blanket of warmth enveloped me as I raised my eyebrows, attempting to hide the heat shooting to my cheeks. "Did you just compliment me?" Picking up my phone, I tapped the video button and aimed it at him. "This is rarer than a super blood moon eclipse. Can you repeat that?"

An unexpected, full-blown laugh escaped him, and for a few brief seconds, his entire face lit up; it presented me with a rare appearance of his dimple, and never-before-seen footage of Alec Mackenzie laughing and being friendly *with me*.

It was possibly the most glorious view on Earth, bar none.

"I mean it," Alec said. "Don't let it go to your head."

Our eyes held for a few more seconds, before I did a mental kick and pretended to find my rendang immensely fascinating. My brain was running a hundred miles a second, my nonchalant demeanor hiding the raging thoughts running amok in my head: Alec Mackenzie had given me a rare compliment—and ugh, why did he have to look so good when he's laughing? Also: *I made him laugh like that.* It was addictive, and now I wanted nothing more than to do it again. Repeatedly.

But as the thought went through my head, another burst in, asking a grim question: *What the hell are you getting yourself into, Ellie?*

Nothing. I wasn't getting myself into anything, because I needed to remember this was purely a business transaction.

"The CGM and the pump makes life so much easier, though," I said. "I can't even remember what my life was like before these devices."

"CGM? That's the coin-sized device on your upper arm, isn't it? To monitor your glucose levels continuously?" He shrugged when he saw my jaw dropping. "I've been doing some reading. Just a little. You know, just the basics."

I stared at him, flabbergasted.

He's been . . . reading up on diabetes?

Because of me?

Maybe I heard him wrong. Because that didn't sound like the same Alec who used to ignore me when we were younger. Who never saw me as anyone other than Eric's little sister.

What was happening here?

"I felt it was my responsibility to be prepared, since you're a guest in my house," he quickly added. "If something happened to you, I'd have to answer to Eric, and he can be damn scary when he's angry. I'd prefer to avoid that."

"Yeah." I finally found my voice. "The CGM sends the information to my pump and the app on my phone. I don't have to keep pricking my fingers to check my levels, unless the CGM stops working, or when I'm feeling extremely low."

"Gotcha." He nodded. "Anyway, back to Jacqui. Is your favorite food still pizza?"

I blinked at him. "Yes, but what does it have to do with her?"

"I thought we could go through what we remember about each other. See if anything's changed. Things like favorite color, favorite movie, favorite sport."

This should be interesting. "Why don't you start?"

"Sure. Your favorite color is mint green. You like dramas and comedies. Can't stand gory movies. Hate carrot cakes but will never say no to brownies. You love all animals, except spiders. Your favorite candy is Reese's Peanut Butter Cups. You can't stand bullies and attention seekers. You'll try everything in life once, because you want to prove that you can live as normal a life as everyone else." He stopped at the dazed look on my face. "What? Have I got it all wrong?"

That was the problem. He didn't.

He got all of them right.

"Impressive," I managed, not knowing what to do with the fact that he knew—and remembered—those things about me. "Dramas and rom-coms now. And sushi, to add to the pizza. But yes, the rest are correct."

"Your turn."

How was I supposed to compete with that? "Your favorite movie genre is sci-fi. You hate reality TV shows. Favorite sport, basketball. You don't have a favorite food, because you'll eat just about anything, except licorice." I gave him a questioning look. When he nodded, I continued, "You hate self-centered people. And you look up to your mother the most, because she sacrificed so many things in life to provide for you and your sisters. How did I do?"

A look of surprise briefly crossed his face. "Passed with flying colors."

I grinned. "What about pet peeves? And maybe childhood crushes?"

"Why are those important?"

"Just in case."

"My biggest pet peeve is people asking me about pet peeves. No childhood crushes." He pulled out his phone and leaned his head toward me, before snapping a selfie of us.

"Let's do another one." I grabbed his phone and smiled at the waitress. "Hi, would you mind taking a photo for us?"

She took the phone as Alec stood up and came over to my side of the table. My eyes widened as he gently tugged me up, then sat down in my chair and pulled me down onto his lap. "What are you doing?" I hissed, as his hands went around my waist.

"Posing for a picture." He propped his chin on my shoulder, assaulting my senses with his citrusy scent, and he was so warm and so close I wondered if he could hear the taiko drums putting on a performance from under my rib cage.

Maybe not, because he was flashing the waitress a charming smile, totally oblivious.

"Can you take a few? My girlfriend has this terrible habit of closing her eyes or looking somewhere else." He gave me a nudge while I glared at him. "The camera's over there, *sweetheart*."

Gritting my teeth, I hammed it up for the picture as the heels of my boots found his toes and firmly dug in. A corner of his mouth curved up, hiding a wince.

"Aww, you two are adorable." The waitress handed his phone back with a smile. "I hope there's a good one in there."

Thanking her, I pushed his arms away and stood up, then sat in his vacant chair. Alec scrolled through the pictures, leaning across the small table to show me. There were four or five photos, and although the first two were of me scowling at him, the last few were decent.

"This." He double tapped on the last picture to enlarge it. "This is the one."

The photo was perfect. It looked natural, even. The waitress had said something funny, and I was laughing at her joke. But Alec—the taiko drums did an encore here—wasn't looking at the camera. He was watching me instead, with a small smile playing on his lips. Goosebumps erupted on my arms, because to strangers who didn't know any better, his look could easily be mistaken as infatuation. No wonder the waitress had called us adorable.

Gah. What infatuation? I was losing the plot. Just business, remember? Maybe I should get a reminder tattooed on the inside of my eyelids so I wouldn't forget.

He was oblivious to my exhausting mental gymnastics, his fingers still dancing across his screen. "It's uploaded on Facebook, and you're tagged. Both our families are excluded, so they can't see anything. Should we change our relationship status? Is that still a thing?"

I poured more tea to avoid looking at him. "No one does that anymore." I sure as hell wasn't going to announce to the world that I was in a relationship, albeit fake, with *this* man. Reopening my list-maker app, I asked, "Have we covered everything?"

"One more thing." He put his phone down and looked at me, his gaze serious. "We shouldn't be seeing other people until after we fake break up."

"That's easy. I don't know anyone else here anyway, apart from you and Kim, and whatever free time I have, I'll be at the shop."

"You've met Rob."

I feigned a dreamy sigh. "True, and I already like him better than you. Handsome, funny, and polite. What's not to like?"

"I'm sure he'll be thrilled to hear that."

"Don't roll your eyes at me. You can learn a thing or ten from your charming friend."

"I'm good. Let's talk about this weekend's function. It's a charity fundraising event for Jacqui's foundation, supporting underprivileged women who want to start their own businesses. She's inviting the who's who of business owners in Port Benedict."

"She'll ask how we first met," I said. "How long we've known each other."

"Eighteen years." His reply was quick. "You were ten, and I was twelve."

My eyebrows shot up, impressed by how quickly he answered, without hesitating or struggling to remember. "Have we really survived that long without injuring each other?"

He chuckled. "Not that hard. We didn't see each other for ten out of those eighteen."

"Why did you leave?"

His eyes narrowed at my abrupt question. "What?"

"You left without saying goodbye. All Eric said was that you'd moved away. Why?"

"Job opportunity. With Rob. Too good to turn down." He cleared his throat, looking uncomfortable. "We were never that close, anyway."

That hurt, because even though he'd always been more of Eric's friend than mine, I'd spent most of my teenage years mooning over him, and that deserved at least a courtesy goodbye, right?

It doesn't. Stop being delusional. Stop thinking about the past.

"We've always kept in touch, but we've only been together for two years. Long distance," Alec continued, and I realized that he'd gone back to the cover story for Jacqui. "You finally decided to move out here this year, because you couldn't bear to be apart from me."

"I couldn't, huh?" I pushed my delusional, irrational thoughts aside. "I shouldn't have suggested this. How can I convince people I've been madly in love with you for the past two years? That's going to be a hard sell. Why don't you have an actual girlfriend, anyway? Someone to take photos with, bring to these functions, and protect you from flirtatious property magnates?"

"What's with all the questions? If I'd known you were going to be so nosy, I would've stuck with Audrey."

Folding my arms, I assessed him. "Seriously, though. On paper, women should be lining up-to-date you. You're successful, mildly attractive, and can be charming if you want to." My fingers made a circling gesture at his face. "You've got that tall, mysterious, and brooding appeal that most women seem to go for. Is something wrong with you?"

"Did you just call me mildly attractive?" His face broke into a *very* attractive grin. "I believe the word you're looking for is 'handsome.'"

"That wasn't it. And it wasn't 'humble,' either."

"Humble? I'm not familiar with that term." He smirked at me. "Obviously."

"But to answer your question, I've just been too busy. I had to help my mom, because she relied on me sending money home to help with the finances to send my sisters to college. Relationships take a back seat because I don't have the time or energy for someone else."

"How old are your sisters?" I racked my brain, trying to remember the bits of information I'd heard from Eric over the years. "As your fake girlfriend, I need to know these things."

A genuine smile lit his face up. "Sienna is twenty-four, and she's getting married in a few months. Gemma is twenty. They're both working now, but things were tough for a while."

"I heard about Sienna's wedding. Are you going home for that? Eric and Naomi are coming, aren't they?" I wasn't being petty, but the subtext was clear here: that *I* wasn't invited.

He must have caught on, because he gave me a sheepish, apologetic look. "She wanted a small, no-frills celebration with close friends and families. And I'm going home, yes."

I didn't think his sister had been *that* close to my brother and Naomi, but I let it go. "And when did you last see your dad?" There were a lot of framed pictures of his mom and sisters at the house, but none of his dad.

Alec's face turned tense. "Don't remember, don't care. We're better off without him."

We were quiet as he poured us both more tea. Eric never told me what exactly had happened, only that Alec's dad had walked out on them years ago. My heart swelled a little, imagining him as a young man, taking on the enormous responsibility of helping his mother look after the family. Something suspiciously resembling awe and admiration started to brew in my chest, and for a moment, it was as if eighteen-year-old me was the one sitting here, back again in a foggy haze of lifelong, die-hard crush on him.

Snap out of it. You're not that teenager anymore.

"At least that's something we have in common." I gave him a smile, trying to brighten the mood. "Challenging parents, am I right?"

"I've only got one difficult parent, and he's no longer in my life, but both yours are challenging," he said. "Honestly, you're really brave to move away from your family. On your own, thousands of miles across the country. Not everyone has the backbone to do it."

I raised two fingers, hoping he wouldn't notice the flush creeping on my face. "You've complimented me twice in less than an hour."

"I'm not keeping track, but sure, if you say so."

"But it's unheard of." I frowned at his cup. "Maybe the tea is laced with alcohol."

"Seriously?" He rolled his eyes. "You don't know how to accept a compliment?"

"I don't know what that is. I'm too profoundly damaged, thanks to twenty-eight years of rigorous parental manipulation."

He choked out a laugh. "I was being serious."

"So was I."

His gaze softened a little. "But you know that moving away from your family doesn't solve the problem, Ellie. Whatever issues you have with them, you'll have to face them again eventually."

"They're on the other side of the country. They don't even know where I am. What can they possibly do?"

Alec scoffed. "I'm familiar with your parents. They make my dad look like the pope, okay? My point is, they're still around, and you can't avoid them forever."

He might be right, but I wasn't going to worry about it now. "Fifty bucks says I can."

"You can't," he said. "They're coming for you. And when they do, you better brace yourself, because it sure as hell won't be pretty."

CHAPTER 9

PSA: Don't Forget to Regularly Service Your Car

"R ob Carmichael," I stared at the wonderful sight before my eyes, "you're a miracle worker. A fairy godfather. A heavenly angel sent from above."

After only three days of work, Rob and his crew had removed the fallen tree, patched up the gaping hole in the roof, and replaced all the rotting roof tiles. The leaky pipes were gone, and in their place were brand-new heavy-duty brass pipes instead. His team was now replacing the damaged floor tiles, and the speed and competence with which they worked on everything had obliterated any lingering doubts I'd had about faking a relationship with Alec. If he hadn't introduced me to Rob, I'd probably still be hacking away at the fallen tree right now, because no matter how many video tutorials I watched, I could never do what they did.

"And you, Ellie Pang, are good for my ego." Rob grinned. "You might sing a different tune once you've started painting the walls though. Sure you're up for it, E?"

"Absolutely. Anything I can do to help."

"Knock yourself out, then. Sing out if you need anything."

I donned my protective gear and spread the drop cloths on the floor, then got to work. Two hours later, I had just finished applying the first coat of paint to the last section of the wall, when an unknown number flashed on my phone.

"Is this Ellie?" A friendly voice rumbled from the other end. "I'm Mike Chang, the mechanic who picked up your Honda the other day."

"Hey, Mike. Did you find out what was wrong with it?"

"We did. When was the last time you serviced the car?"

My stomach sank. "A while ago. Close to a year, maybe."

"No wonder your engine failed." There was a low chuckle. "The level of oil in your car is practically nonexistent. Alec told me you've just driven it across the country?"

Oh fuck. "Yes."

"When the oil is low, it damages the engine. You could have avoided this if you had serviced it regularly. Sorry to tell you this, but you'll need to replace the engine."

Another point to add to my parents' list on how I couldn't survive on my own. How many disasters had I notched under my belt in less than a week?

"Sure." I pressed my thumb to the bridge of my nose, mentally preparing myself. "How much would that be?"

"Around eight to ten thousand. I could also rebuild the old one for half the cost, so about four to five. You'll get better gas mileage out of a rebuilt engine, and it can usually last as long as a new one." The low chuckle returned. "Just don't forget to service the car."

A headache began to pound at the back of my head. *Eight to ten thousand.* That would throw my budget way off and stretch my already thin account balance to its very last legs.

"Or you could look at buying a secondhand car and sell your old one for scrap metal."

I didn't know whether to cry or laugh, because even though he meant well, it was the most absurd suggestion I'd ever heard. The only way I could afford a secondhand car was to sell one of my kidneys, or other non-vital body organs. Plus, the CR-V was my first-ever car, and I'd learned how to drive in it. It had scratches and dents, and it wasn't perfect, but getting rid of it would be like saying goodbye to my own beating heart and letting go of the last tangible reminder I had of my Engkong and Emak.

It was clear: I wasn't parting with the car, or my heart, or any of my kidneys. I had to save money somewhere else.

"Did you say rebuilding the engine would be cheaper? Let's go with that."

After agreeing on the cost and timeline, I hung up and looked around the shop with exasperation. In a few days, I'd be at least four thousand dollars poorer. A few minutes ago, I'd been pleased with the progress, but right now, the self-doubt came back in full force.

Am I biting off more than I can chew?

No. I steeled myself. This was only a minor setback. All I had to do was readjust the budget, and things should be back on track. The clock was ticking, so I had to dust myself off, stop the moping and the pity party. The only option was to keep pushing forward.

Abandoning the paint, I picked up my phone again and scrolled through my emails. Rob had sent me a list of materials and estimated costs for the work, so I made a mental note to chat with him to see if we could substitute some things around.

Just then, my phone pinged with a reminder that I needed a dress for this weekend's function. I'd donated all my fancy party dresses before I left home, so unless I wanted to turn up wearing these dusty, paint-splattered overalls, I had to find a presentable (and affordable) outfit in less than forty-eight hours. The thought of spending what little amount I had in my bank account on something so frivolous plunged me back into the deep, dark well of gloom and dread.

"Hey, neighbor." There was a rap on the front door, and Kim strolled in with a grin. "You want to grab dinner together later?"

"Sure. What do you have in mind?"

"There's this awesome Japanese fusion place over at the Plaza's rooftop area called Ocha Izakaya. They have the best sushi tacos and sake in the city. I've been flat-out busy at the shop, so I need to unwind and chill out tonight. My housemate Jenna is coming, too."

"I'm in." An idea popped into my mind. "Before that though, can I steal you for an hour? To help me find a dress for an event?"

Her face lit up. "Hell yes. Absolutely."

"Great. I'm broke, so something not too expensive. If you could also recommend a good hairdresser, that'd be awesome."

"Consider it done." Kim rubbed her hands, looking excited. "I know the city like the back of my hand. You, my friend, won't even recognize yourself when we're done."

That afternoon, Kim took me to a vintage boutique inside the Plaza. Jenna met us there, and they led me to the back of the store, where there were racks upon racks of secondhand dresses and gowns. We found a few that still had tags, which they glee-fully thrust at me. Both of them grabbed a few dresses for them-selves before ushering me into the changing room.

"Where's the party?" Jenna's voice carried across the partition from the stall on my left, as I removed the first dress off the hanger.

"Not sure." I slipped into a cute, patterned navy dress. "I'm just going as a favor for a friend. He needed a plus-one."

"Is this 'friend' the building industry expert we met the other day?" Kim asked, her voice coming from the stall on my right. There was a soft curse, followed by the sound of a zip being pulled up. "*Ouch*. The tall, cute one?"

Next, I tried on a mint-green plaid shirtdress and instantly decided to add it to my collection. "Alec? I guess he *is* cute, if you like the guarded, brooding type."

"Who doesn't?" Kim chuckled. "I'd sign up, too, but he's obviously taken with you."

"Me?" I paused halfway through zipping up the last dress. "No, he's not."

Jenna said, "Ha!" as Kim's chuckle turned into a scoff, her voice announcing, "You need to get some prescription glasses."

We all stepped out of our changing rooms, and they both nodded in approval at the black wrap dress I'd just put on. The material hugged my body, and the V-neck plunged deeper than I was used to, exposing a hint of cleavage.

Kim gave me a wolf whistle. "You look stunning."

"I second that," Jenna said.

"It's not too much?" A splinter of nervousness poked at me. "I don't really need to look good, just presentable. This isn't a date or anything."

"Still, it doesn't hurt," came Kim's cheerful reply. "Sexy dress, flirty heels, new hairdo. It'll make you feel good, and you can't go wrong with that, right?"

At their prodding, I bought all three dresses, a pair of black stiletto heels, plus a pair of jeans that still looked brand-new, and managed to leave my bank account with minimal damage.

"Let's do something about your hair." Kim scrunched up her nose as she gave it a thorough appraisal. "When was the last time you colored it?"

"Never?" I raised my eyebrows at Kim's disapproving look. "What's wrong with that? I've always had dark hair."

"Then it's high time for a change."

They led me out of the vintage boutique and into a nearby Korean hair salon, where I spent the next hour having my head massaged and my hair trimmed, curled, and highlighted. When the hairdresser finally whipped off the barber cape with a flourish, I gaped at the mirror, not believing it was my reflection that was staring back. Shimmering ribbons of ash-brown strands now swirled through my locks, and the ends of my hair had the prettiest waves I'd ever seen. I looked different and refreshed, nothing like my old self. I even *felt* different. Like my new hairdo made me powerful enough to take on anything in the world.

Like I was finally taking control of my own life.

"You look amazing," Kim announced, as we headed to dinner. "Trust me, Mister Building Expert won't know what hit him."

"He won't notice. It's a business function. He'll be busy networking."

Kim snorted. "If he doesn't notice anything, then you *both* need glasses."

Jenna gave me a wide smile when she caught my eye. She was an Asian Australian who had migrated to the States for work a year ago. "A magnifying glass, maybe?"

"My eyesight is fine," I said, as we arrived at the restaurant. "Trust me, getting involved with him is a horrible idea. There's too much baggage between us."

"Why?" Kim's eyes were curious. "What happened between you two?"

"It's a long, boring story."

A waiter ushered us to our table. Ocha Izakaya was a delightful mix of traditional and contemporary, with simple, modern wooden tables and chairs, soft lighting from the Japanese-style lanterns hanging above, and prints of mountains and cherry blossoms decorating the walls.

"We've got all night." Kim picked up the menu, gave it a cursory once-over, then slid it toward me. "Try the spicy salmon sushi tacos. Highly recommended."

"I'm having the tempura udon," Jenna said. "Also highly recommended."

I chose the sushi tacos and the dragon avocado roll, then looked up at both women, who were watching me with expectant looks on their faces. Maybe I should try changing the topic . . .

"So, Jenna. Which part of Australia are you from, and how do you like living in the US?"

She grinned. "I'm from Melbourne, and love the States, but we're not talking about me."

Kim lifted a warning finger. "Don't you dare change the subject. You're free to ask Jenna about her country and the kangaroos and the spiders later, but first we want to hear all about your sordid past with Monsieur Building Expert."

I hesitated, but the glint in her eyes told me she meant business. "There was an incident. Ten years ago."

"What kind of incident?" Kim wriggled her eyebrows. "The sexy kind?"

"No. I used to have a crush on him when we were teenagers."

"Who wouldn't?" Kim smirked, as Jenna murmured her agreement.

"He was my older brother's best friend. I foolishly thought I was in love with him, so convinced we belonged together. But he's always been so cold and unfriendly with me, even though he's charming with everyone else. God knows how many hours

I wasted trying to make him notice me, hoping he'd return my feelings."

The bottle of sake came, and Kim motioned for me to continue as she poured some of the clear liquid into three cups.

"The week I turned eighteen, we went out to celebrate my birthday. Me, my brother, Eric, Alec, and my best friend, Naomi. We went skating, played a few games of mini golf, then had dinner. It was one of the best nights of my life."

"Ahh, young love." Kim sighed.

"After that, Alec and my brother went to see some of their friends, and Naomi and I tagged along." I cringed as memories of that night came flooding back. "I remembered thinking, 'maybe he'll notice me now because I'm finally a grown-up.' So I waited for the right time, then cornered him alone and professed my undying love."

"That's very gutsy." Jenna gave me a supportive nod. "What did he say?"

"Nothing. He just stared at me. I thought maybe he couldn't hear me because the restaurant was too loud, so I repeated what I said."

Kim's eyes widened. "And?"

"He was quiet for the longest time. Then he said, very bluntly, that he wasn't interested in me. He didn't feel the same way, and he never would, because I meant nothing to him but as Eric's little sister." Ten years later, and it still stung. "Then he walked away."

Jenna gasped, while Kim hissed under her breath, "Jerk."

Our food came, and I bolused for the sushi before continuing the story, but my appetite had disappeared. "A few of their friends were egging me and Naomi that night, daring us to drink, making bets on who was the more sensitive lightweight between the two of us."

Kim frowned. "Is this where things get ugly?"

Nodding, I inhaled a long breath. "Eric was on a call outside, so it was just me, Naomi, Alec, and those other guys. Alec just sat there, looking bored, uninterested in everything. Didn't say a word, didn't tell those guys to leave us alone. And you know what I thought?" My laugh sounded hollow, as my captive audience shook their heads. "I thought, maybe it's my chance to impress him. Maybe he'll finally see me as an adult, not as Eric's uncool little sister."

Jenna winced. "Oh, Ellie."

"Naomi tried to stop me, saying we're not supposed to, and how we could get in trouble, but I was so determined to impress him. So I took a sip. Then another sip, until I ended up finishing an entire bottle of beer. And the next bottle, then a cocktail. That's when the shit hit the fan. I had a severe hypo and passed out."

Jenna interrupted, "Wait, what's a hypo?"

"It's short for hypoglycemia. That's when my glucose level drops too low, below what is healthy for me." I shuddered as I thought of what could have happened. "In severe cases, it can cause the person to become unconscious, and if left untreated, it can be fatal."

There was an "Oh my God!" from Jenna, and a quiet "Fucking hell," from Kim.

"They rushed me to the ED. I knew I brought it on myself for having those drinks without thinking of the consequences. But for a long time, I blamed him for what had happened, because he could've stopped those jerks from taunting us, but he didn't."

"But you're drinking alcohol now." Kim gave me a puzzled look and pointed at my sake cup. "Why couldn't you then?"

"It's different for everyone, but for me, it was a combination of too much physical activity and too much alcohol that night. It was also my first time drinking, and I didn't know how to properly estimate the insulin for the drinks," I said. "It decreased my blood sugar down to a dangerous level. Not long after, Alec left home, and I never saw him again until last week."

"Was he the reason you moved here?" Jenna asked.

"No. I didn't even know he lived here. I needed to get away from my family and that disastrous marriage proposal, and the right opportunity just happened to be in Port Benedict."

Kim raised an eyebrow. "What marriage proposal?"

I told them about George and the viral video, and both their eyes bulged.

"I *knew* you looked familiar when we first met." Kim whistled. "Wow. You were almost engaged to *the* George Fitzgerald?"

"You made the right choice," Jenna said. "He's rich and good-looking and all that, but he seems too uptight. Good on you for listening to your heart and saying no."

"Hottie Building Expert is way sexier than George Fitzgerald anyway." Kim frowned. "Although after hearing your story, maybe you should've said yes to George after all."

I shook my head. "No, it was the right decision."

"Having said that," Kim continued, "A lot of things can change in ten years, and I could tell that Alec likes you now, because the man couldn't take his eyes off you when I saw you two that morning. I'd probably be wary of him, too, if I were you, but there's nothing wrong with keeping your options open and exploring new possibilities. He might be a completely different person today compared to ten years ago."

I made a noncommittal grunt, not willing to admit that she *might be* right.

"And, by the way, you were making moony eyes at him, too," Jenna added. "Your chemistry could light up this whole city. Cliché, but true."

"He's just a friend now." I wasn't ready to tell anyone about our fake relationship agreement. "What happened between us is in the past. And I've got too many things on my plate to worry about unnecessary distractions."

Both my friends gave me dubious looks, as if they weren't convinced with my statement.

I couldn't blame them, because neither was I.

CHAPTER 10

Time to Put Your Fake Relationship to the Test

At five to six on Saturday night, I paced back and forth in my room, slowly losing my confidence to proceed with the farce. For the umpteenth time in the past fifteen minutes, I smoothed the hem of my black wrap dress, wondering if I could still cancel everything. Plotting a fake relationship inside a tiny Indonesian restaurant was one thing; actually having to act it out at a massively important event was an entirely different matter.

He lived up to his end of the bargain, a small voice reminded me. *It's your turn now.*

Alec had his back facing me when I went downstairs. He must have heard my footsteps, because he turned around, blinking twice when he saw me.

"Hey," I said, hoping to disguise my nerves by sounding casual. "Ready to go?"

"Yeah." His eyes slowly traveled my length from head to toe, then back up again. "You look great."

My cheeks turned warm from his gaze. "You clean up pretty

well, too." He was wearing a dark gray suit paired with a light-blue shirt, with just the right amount of scruff on his jaw, looking like he'd probably skipped shaving this morning.

A corner of his mouth quirked up. "Glad you approve."

Jacqui Goodwin's home was in one of the most expensive areas of Port Benedict. Tall palm trees lined the street, and huge gated properties flanked it on both sides. The house was bathed in bright lights when we arrived, with the sounds of classical music filtering out of the windows, and rows of expensive European cars lining up at the front.

I whistled with appreciation. "Wow. Her house is incredible."

"She doesn't even live here." Alec turned into an empty car spot. "This is her holiday house. One out of her many properties all over the country."

Before I could unbuckle my seatbelt, he'd already gone around to my side of the car and opened my door. It was a silly thing, but coming from an Asian family, I'd never had men opening car doors for me. Of course I didn't need anyone to—I was perfectly capable of opening my own door—but I found his gesture oddly endearing. He offered a hand to help me up, and I felt a tingle running down my spine as his warm hand gripped mine.

"It's showtime, Ellie."

I ignored the goosebumps erupting all over my body, chalking it up to nerves, because I was walking into a party hand-in-hand with a man I hadn't even been friends with a week ago. Because a lot was riding on this for him, and I didn't want to screw anything up.

Or was it because he was pressed so close to me, feeling and smelling incredible?

Taking a deep breath, I tried to refocus while pushing the thought of him out of my mind. And no, I wouldn't screw anything up, because we'd gone through every plausible scenario in minute detail. We could recite each other's quirks, likes and dislikes, even our SAT scores. I could even do it half asleep; that's how perfect of a fake girlfriend I was. If there was a test on fake-girlfriendship, I'd score an A+, and probably even win multiple awards.

"Let's find our host. I'll introduce you, make some small talk, then we'll leave."

I nodded. "Good plan."

He led me inside, and my eyes widened at the opulence. Marble floors stretched as far as the eyes could see, and the dining room walls were draped with strings of curtain lights, giving it an ethereal, otherworldly feel. Two long tables stood in the middle of the room, full of plates upon plates of food, all made brighter by the chandelier above. The place practically shimmered with glitz and glamor.

Plucking two champagne flutes from a passing waiter, Alec handed one to me, then downed his in one swift guzzle. He tapped his fingers on the empty flute, eyes darting around the room as he slowly exhaled, and I realized he was nervous.

"Hey, we got this." I rubbed his arms, soothing him. "I got your back, okay?"

"Alec!" A melodic voice called from behind us. He tensed and tightened his hold on me, as if I were a buoy keeping him afloat. Fixing a bright smile on his face, he turned around and briefly disentangled his hands from mine to hug a beautiful brunette, who was probably in her late thirties. She was impeccably dressed in an elegant, lacy white dress, had legs for days, generously dimpled cheeks, and exquisite ocean-blue eyes with lashes I would kill for.

Alec must be out of his mind, because Jacqui Goodwin was drop-dead gorgeous.

"Glad you could make it." The woman beamed at Alec. "Where's Rob?"

"He couldn't be here tonight. He sends his apologies."

"Too bad. Maybe next time." She switched her attention to me, those blue eyes curiously assessing. "You must be Ellie. I've been hearing so much about you."

Hearing so much about me? I shook her hand, keeping a smile plastered on my face.

"Thank you for having us, Ms. Goodwin. Your home is lovely."

"Call me Jacqui. It's so nice to finally meet you. This one," she gestured at Alec, "wouldn't shut up about you. Now I know why he's been turning down my dinner invites."

I didn't know how to reply, so I only smiled wider, probably looking like a madwoman. Nobody had warned me that being a fake girlfriend would be complicated. What was I supposed to do next? Pretend to be offended because she'd been hitting on my boyfriend? Act as if it wasn't a big deal and laugh it off?

When this whole thing was over, I should write a handbook about it. Or start a business: a fake-relationship-planner-slash-coach, to guide newbie pretend couples, so they could avoid the pitfalls and awkwardness of being a fake partner.

"Have you met Phil?" Jacqui gestured to the tall, bearded man next to her. "Phil is the founder of Anderson Real Estate. You've probably seen some of their offices around."

"We spoke on the phone," I said. "I'm the one who leased the shop at the back of the Plaza, next to the yarn store."

"I remember," Phil said. "It's one of the best locations in the entire city. Close to the Plaza, to downtown, to the Waterfront. You were lucky to snap it up when it became vacant."

"That's what I told her." Alec grinned at me.

"I've known Phil for a long time. We've worked with Anderson Real Estate for nearly ten years. One of the best in the business." At this, Jacqui sent Phil a pointed look. "I'm a firm believer that we should work in an area that focuses on our strengths.

I wouldn't know where to start marketing a property for sale. That's *your* area of expertise. Right, Phil?"

That's weird. I wasn't an expert in real estate, but her harsh tone, followed by the way Phil's posture turned stiff, gave off a strange vibe that had nothing to do with properties or marketing.

"Sure." Phil gave her a tense smile before turning his attention to Alec. "Anyway, heard you'll be joining forces with GPG."

"Hopefully, yes."

"You struck gold, son. Couldn't find a better partner anywhere else. And I've heard so many wonderful things about Mackenzie Constructions. Three years in a row!" He directed his next sentence at me. "You must be so proud."

"Oh, yes." I pasted a bright smile on my face, although I had *zero* idea what he was talking about, realizing I'd made a newbie fake girlfriend blunder: I knew everything there was to know about Alec, except his company. How could I recite his SAT scores but know next to nothing about his business?

I mentally added a line on my To-Do List: *Look up Mackenzie Constructions.*

"So," Jacqui grabbed a champagne flute and took a sip, her eyes full of speculation, "how did you two meet?"

Okay, so she was a straight shooter. Maybe that was one of the qualities that helped her be so successful from such a young age. I should probably take notes so I could follow in her formidable footsteps.

Alec was the first to transform into his role of The Adoring Boyfriend Character. "Ellie is my best friend's younger sister. She's been following me around like a lovesick puppy since I was twelve, always trying to impress me and get my attention. Remember, babe?"

"Lovesick puppy?" I smiled at him through gritted teeth. "Aww, that's cute, but that's not how I remember it, darling."

"Pretty sure it was, sweetheart." He gave me a (fake) loving smile, as if the two of us were sharing a secret joke. "You even followed me into my college lecture once, didn't you?"

"I was there to see Eric, honeybunch, not you."

"Your brother wasn't even enrolled in that subject, pumpkin. It's okay. You can admit you've been smitten with me from the first day we met."

Had I been that obvious? From the very first time I laid eyes on him, I'd put him on a ten-foot-high pedestal—this cool, aloof, handsome older boy, who was way out of my league. I'd watched him from afar whenever he came around to our house, hoping he would notice me. He never did, until one day, when I was having one of my low episodes. I was slumping on the sofa, quietly munching on some gummy bears, watching him defeat Eric in one of their racing games. He'd glanced at me, then came over and handed me a fun-size Snickers bar.

"You look like you could use one of these."

Without another word, he walked away and resumed his game. And just like that, I was gone. One Snickers bar, and I was head over heels, madly and hopelessly in love with him. I was *that* pathetic. None of the guys I'd dated were ever memorable enough, and maybe that was the main reason things didn't work out with George, too. Because I was always comparing them to Alec.

He had always been, and probably would always be, my unicorn.

"Oh, I adore childhood sweetheart stories," Jacqui said, snapping me back to the present. "Was it love at first sight for you, too, Alec?"

"It was, but I was too stubborn to admit it." His hand circled around my shoulder and started stroking my arm, as if showing affection. What it was doing, though, was short-circuiting my nerve endings. "She has this endearing habit of making a list for everything. If it was an important decision, she'd make a pros and cons list. If she had things she needed to tackle, it would be a to-do list. I swear, she couldn't survive a day without making one. It used to annoy me at first, but that was one of the things that made me fall in love with her."

I turned to stare at him, speechless. *He noticed that?*

The only people who knew about my list-making habit were my family and Naomi. It was something I'd started not long after I was diagnosed, because I used to feel like diabetes was dominating my life, telling me what I could or could not do. The lists were my way of establishing some sort of control over my otherwise overwhelming life.

"But even at the age of twelve, I knew I was going to marry her one day."

Ooh, he was *good*, lying so effortlessly through his teeth. What I didn't expect though, was how those lies were making my insides a tiny bit gooey. How my inadequately prepared heart was eating up every single word, along with his (fake) adoring look.

"That's sweet," Phil said. "How long have you been together?"

"Not long," I replied, at the same time Alec said, "Two years."

Three pairs of eyebrows went up—including my fake boyfriend's.

Yikes. First test, and I'd already failed. This was why professional athletes put in countless hours of practice before competing in a match. Or why surgeons had to study for a million years before they were even allowed to come near a patient with a scalpel. The more often you do—or say—something, the quicker it gets ingrained in your muscle memory.

But I was nothing if not a quick study. And a decent improviser.

"I meant two years isn't long *enough*," I smoothly corrected my blunder. "Let me tell you, two years of a long-distance relationship was hard. Thank God for video calls."

"Do you fly back and forth to visit? Your frequent flyer miles must be piling up."

Man. The Spanish Inquisition had nothing on Jacqui Goodwin.

"We take turns," Alec replied smoothly, quoting our well-rehearsed answer. "Our rule is, never go more than two months without seeing each other. And this year, we finally decided it was the right time for her to move out here."

I sipped my champagne, hoping for liquid courage to get me through the night, and only wriggled my eyebrows in agreement.

"Being so far from me was taking a toll on her. She couldn't sleep, couldn't eat, couldn't work, too lovesick to function. Cried herself to sleep at night. Didn't you, lovebug?"

I nearly spat out my drink. "I *what*?"

His teasing grin was infuriating. "That was a joke, baby." Pulling me closer, he planted a quick kiss on my cheek, sending tingles down my spine.

Phil chuckled, but Jacqui was relentless with her questions. "Alec tells me you're starting a bakery?"

I nodded wordlessly, my brain still unwilling to move on from that kiss.

"Ellie bakes the most amazing things. All sugar-free, but you wouldn't know it because they're so delicious. When we were younger, it was one of the things I'd most look forward to whenever I went to her house."

Huh. Was that true, or just another lie? I glanced at him, and my heart did a backflip when I saw him watching me with a smile, looking every inch like The Adoring Boyfriend Character he was so brilliantly portraying. He still had his hand wrapped around my shoulder, and I was acutely aware of his warmth on my bare arm.

And was it so wrong that I loved the way my name rolled off his tongue?

Jacqui gave me her first smile for the evening. "Let me know once you're open. I might have some orders I could send your way."

"That would be wonderful." I gave her a grateful nod. "I appreciate that."

As she turned to say something to Phil, Alec planted another kiss on my temple, while whispering into my ear, "You're doing so well. Such a natural-born liar."

I shivered a little, because even though I knew he did that for our audience's benefit, the not-fake kiss felt *so* good. And maybe it was me being delusional, but I could have sworn he lingered longer than he should have.

Jacqui waved at someone from across the room. "I should go mingle. But I'm staying in town for the weekend. Maybe we could all catch up for brunch tomorrow."

Recoiling, I glanced at Alec. Things had gone well so far, but if I had to do an encore performance within twenty-four hours with fewer people and far more scrutiny, I didn't know how convincing I'd be.

"Don't we have that appointment?" I said pointedly to him, hoping he'd play along. "That, uh, lunch thing with your friends?"

"They canceled." Alec smiled, ignoring my low growl. "See you both tomorrow."

As soon as they walked away, I hissed at him, "I can't do two days in a row. She's so nice, and I feel guilty lying to her face. She's already convinced, right? So we can wrap this up. Tell her we're not going."

"We had a deal," Alec hissed back. "Remember your store?"

We had a glare-off, although I knew he was right.

"Please, Ellie. You know how important this is for me." He switched tactics, his eyes now pleading. "We've gone this far, and she'll be expecting us both tomorrow."

My biggest mistake before we started this charade was failing to give a heads-up to my naïve heart, followed by a stern warning that we shouldn't, under any circumstances, fall for Sir Grouchiness and his charms. Because right now it was begging me to say yes, since (a) what kind of heartless monster would reject his desperate, heartfelt pleas? And (b) a lot *was* at stake for him, so how could I live with myself if my refusal to see Jacqui tomorrow ruined his business deal?

"No more than one hour."

"Two hours, and I'll knock five percent off your rent."

"Ninety minutes, and ten percent."

He grinned at me. "Eight percent, and you have yourself another deal."

"Done." I offered my hand to shake on it.

Ignoring my outstretched hand, he pulled me in for a hug, wrapping his arms around me. My overexcited heart let out a thrilled whoop, while my nerve endings went on high alert and hummed with pleasure, because I could feel the sharp outline of his hard body molded against mine. My nose was nestled into his neck, and this time I inhaled his scent without shame.

"It'll look suspicious," he murmured into my ear, making me shiver even though the air inside the room was warm, "if they saw us shaking hands."

He pulled away and gazed down at me. My heart was thumping loudly, because he was so close—all I had to do was tilt my head a little to the left, and I could be kissing him.

Whoa, wait. What the actual WHAT?

Okay, time for a hard mental slap, plus maybe ten roundhouse kicks for good measure. That reminder tattoo inside my eyelids was starting to look like a brilliant idea.

Nobody was going to kiss anyone, definitely not while I was alive and breathing, because none of this was real. It was all make-believe, and the quicker I could drill those cold, hard facts into my thick skull, the better it would be for all parties involved.

Especially for my gullible, unsuspecting heart.

CHAPTER II

We Were Both (Not) Moving in Sync

*A*lec's initial plan of leaving the party early was flushed down the toilet almost instantly. He spent the evening talking to too many people, and we ended up staying for over three hours. By the time we walked out into the cool night air, he was more than a little tipsy.

"You're not driving. In you go." Opening the passenger door for him, I pried the keys out of his hands. I bent down and reached across the passenger seat to buckle him up, ignoring the delicious feel of his solid body beneath mine. "How much food have you had tonight?"

He peered at me from under his eyelashes, looking indignant. "A lot, if you must know. I ate three of those mini shrimp thingies." He held up two fingers to emphasize. "Three."

"That's it? No wonder the alcohol is partying in your body. Next time eat first, then go forth and network. Got that?"

"Yes, ma'am. The shrimp thingies were soooo yummy." He yawned, then audibly sniffed. "Ooh, *you* smell yummy. Like a bouquet of flowers."

My breath caught when he leaned forward, his nose nuzzling the sides of my neck.

"Is it roses? Lavender? Tulips?" He wriggled underneath me a little, and I stopped breathing when his lips made the lightest contact with the dip in between my collarbones.

I ignored him and pulled away before one of us—my bets were on me—lost our mind. Slamming his door, I took a deep breath before getting into the driver's side.

"Roses, lavender, and tulips are now my favorite flowers," he announced, his words slurring. "Hey, where are we going?"

"Home, Alec. Party's over. We're going home."

He shifted in his seat to peer at me. "You're cute. Have I ever told you that? C-U-T-E. Cuuuuuuteeeeeee."

My heart jumped a mile high, because he had *never* said anything like that to me before. But my rational brain took over, telling me to squash any absurd thoughts immediately, since he wasn't himself, and the alcohol was obviously flirting on his behalf.

So I only chuckled, hoping it sounded cool and casual, while I eased his car into the queue of vehicles leaving the Goodwin mansion. Sober Alec might be grouchy and annoying, but drunk Alec was downright adorable. "Well, Kim thinks *you're* cute."

Another yawn answered me. "Kimwho?"

"My next-door neighbor at the shop. You've met her, remember?"

My reply was a deafening silence. Alec was already asleep, his mouth slightly open, snoring softly, and his head slouching to the side. His suit jacket was draped over his lap, and the sleeves of his shirt were rolled up, showing off some impressive forearms. I drove back to his house; the only audible sounds were of his steady breathing, Taylor Swift on the radio, and the gears of my brain turning.

The past three hours only confirmed that I was completely unequipped to be in a pretend relationship with this man. At least, if I wanted to emerge from this with my heart unscathed. Right now, at the rate I was going, I'd come out the other side bruised and battered; an even worse repeat of ten years ago.

What I needed was a solid plan. A detailed list to keep me on track, resist his charms, and focus on the bigger picture: getting the bakery up and running ASAP. *Yes, that's it.* The first thing I had to do once we got home was to work on that lifesaving plan.

Alec was still out cold when I pulled up at the house. Opening his door, I gave him a gentle poke. He groaned, then turned his face to the other side to dodge my nudging. I briefly considered leaving him in the car the whole night, but unfortunately my parents had raised me better than that.

"You owe me big time, Sir Grouchiness."

I took a deep breath to prepare myself for the challenging task ahead, then dragged him out of the car, nearly buckling under his solid weight. Good thing I was stronger than I look—all those early morning runs had prepped me for this. It took me ten minutes to finally get him inside the house, up the stairs, and into his room.

"Okay, sleeping beauty. Let's get you ready for bed."

I pushed his door open and flicked on the lights. My guest bedroom was bathed in light colors, but his room was the complete opposite. The walls were painted gray, and artsy black-and-white pictures decorated the room. Two bedside drawers flanked the dark-framed king-size bed, covered with a gray blanket and white pillows. It was neat, fuss-free, and it fit him to a T.

I guided him toward the bed and dumped him unceremoniously onto it. Alec continued to snore, with his hands spread wide at his sides. Staring at his unmoving figure, I once again contemplated leaving him be, but he looked uncomfortable lying on his back with his legs hanging off the edge of the bed, and he obviously needed help to get out of his formal attire.

Somewhere at the back of my brain, a wise voice warned me

this might not be a good idea. Still, my feet propelled me toward his drawer, where I pulled out a white T-shirt and an old pair of gray sweatpants.

"Here we go," I mumbled.

First his shoes came off, followed by his socks. Then I undid his shirt, my eyes concentrating hard on each button, because the temptation to stray and stare at his chest was too enormous. I worked as fast as humanly possible, pulling and tugging at his sleeves, until I finally slipped the shirt off him.

I took a long, steadying breath before tackling the next piece of clothing.

Unbuckling his belt was the easy bit. Unzipping the pants, then pulling them off his long legs, while doing my best to ignore the intriguing bulge under his black trunks, was the tricky part. Then, although I'd never live it down if he found out, I paused to admire the glorious view that was almost-naked Alec.

Kim was wrong, because he was anything but cute. He was *gorgeous*. A beautiful male specimen who was even more attractive now than the young Alec I had crushed on ages ago, because underneath his grouchy exterior, there was gentleness and kindness, and a hidden vulnerability that I'd never seen before.

Which was why, as soon as I was done covering him with some clothes, I had to get started on that Stay on Track Plan.

Alec stirred, reminding me to get on with the job. Picking up the T-shirt, I lifted his upper body and slipped it over his head. It was no easy feat juggling his weight with one hand and putting his T-shirt on with the other, while simultaneously trying not to ogle his chest.

"Ellie?"

He groaned, his eyes drifting open.

I froze.

"What are you doing?" His sleepy gaze swept over me.

Fuckity fuck fuck fuckkkk. I was bent over him, with one hand underneath his head and the other tangled in the T-shirt around his neck. His eyes were still bleary, but they were fixed on me, unblinking. His gaze dropped to my mouth, and I sucked in a breath.

I didn't know if I was the one lowering my face down to his, or if he was the one lifting his face up toward mine, but it seemed like we were both moving in sync, with the exact same goal in mind, and nothing else in the world mattered but that.

Except it was all, apparently, only a wild imagination in my head.

At the very last second, before our lips touched, sense must have kicked into him, because his eyes suddenly turned wide at the sight of me looming over him. There was a low "Oh, fuck" and then I was flipped on the bed, followed by Alec rushing to stand upright. Those green eyes were now staring at me, clear and unmistakably horrified, as his hands worked furiously to cover himself with the T-shirt and sweatpants.

"I'm so, so sorry." He took a step back and ran a hand through his hair. "That should never have happened. I don't know what I was thinking."

Well, maybe he didn't, because he was drunk. But I was 100 percent sober, and I was *mortified*. Beyond belief. What was wrong with me? I was all but begging him to kiss me, for fuck's sake.

Clearly, nothing had changed: my crush had returned with a vengeance; but he was the same Alec who wanted nothing to do with me. The only reason he was being nice was because Eric had asked him to keep an eye on me. After all, that was his lifelong MO: looking after his family after his dad left, and now, looking out for his best friend's little sister. Kissing him, or worse, falling for him—*again*—would be beyond foolish, because I'd be serving my heart on a silver platter, practically begging him to stomp all over it. It was clear as day, and I didn't even need a pros and cons list to know that it was the worst idea in the world: falling for him twice in my lifetime was a big, fat, capital HELL NO.

"You don't have to apologize." I got up, not meeting his eyes. "Nothing happened, right? I should go. See you in the morning."

He opened his mouth, then closed it again.

I went around him and opened the door. And without another glance, I disappeared behind it, ready for the floor to swallow me whole.

CHAPTER 12

I Felt A . . . Thing?

The minute I opened my eyes the next morning, memories of last night immediately came rushing back. Groaning, I pulled my blanket over my face, embarrassment washing over me. How could I face him today, pretending that less than twelve hours ago, I hadn't been practically frothing at the mouth at the possibility of him kissing me? And worse, how would I fake a loving relationship with him for the next few weeks?

But nothing actually happened. Which meant I could classify it as a nonexistent event, right? Yes. Yes, I could. We had an agreement, and my future was riding on it. I had to do this, come hell or high water. Pretending to be in love with Alec Mackenzie, and *not* falling for him? I could do it with my eyes closed. Piece of cake, easy as pie, as simple as ABC.

As soon as I finished that way overdue Stay on Track Plan.

Alec was already busy in the kitchen when I returned from my run. I cleared my throat to announce my presence. "Morning."

He didn't turn around from the stove. "Breakfast is on the table."

My brows shot up at the spread on the dining table. There was a stack of whole-grain toast, a jar of no-sugar-added strawberry jam, a bowl of oats porridge, some apple slices on a small plate, and a tub of blueberry yogurt next to it.

"No pancakes or waffles today?"

"I've read that low-GI foods are better for someone with diabetes. It raises your blood sugar gradually, right? I looked up some breakfast ideas last night and thought I'd give it a try."

Last night? I gaped at him. Was that before or after the humiliating event that shall now and forevermore be dubbed as The Kiss That Never Happened?

This was, hands down, one of the nicest things anyone had ever done for me.

"That's very thoughtful," I managed. "You really didn't have to."

"It's not just for you." He finally turned around, revealing the crimson tinting his cheeks. "I'm always looking for healthier options, too."

"But I thought . . . aren't we meeting Jacqui for brunch?"

Alec brought a pan over, slipping a silicone trivet underneath before placing it on the table. He'd made skillet-baked eggs with mushrooms, spinach, and tomatoes. "It's not for another two hours. Figured you might need something to eat before then."

My heart stumbled over and swelled a hundred times. "Thanks. I appreciate that."

He pulled out the chair across from me, a muscle in his jaw twitching. "I need to apologize for last night. We had a business agreement, and what I did was unprofessional and unacceptable. I shouldn't have gotten drunk at the party, especially to the point where I passed out . . . and even tried to kiss you."

My cheeks felt like they had been lit on fire. *No, it was me who tried to kiss you.*

"I promise it will never happen again. But if you want to reconsider our agreement, I'll understand. I'll still honor my end of the bargain, but you don't have to."

He looked uneasy as he said that, but it was clear: he was giving me an out. My brain raced, frantically creating a list of whether I should accept or reject the offer, and all the points were firmly in the pro column. It was perfect, and I'd be a fool to say no.

But *his* deal was equally important to him. It was a huge opportunity that probably wouldn't knock twice, and it would crush him if he lost it. And for reasons I'd rather not delve too much into, ending our agreement this way wasn't something I felt comfortable doing.

"You sure it's an apology?" I raised my chin at him. "Smells like a bribe to me."

"It's not. I don't do bribes. Just say the word, and I'll cancel brunch, and you don't have to continue with the rest of our arrangement."

It's your chance, my brain whispered. *Go ahead, nod and say yes . . .*

"No. We agreed to do this until your acquisition is completed," I said, as my brain cells threw their hands up in exasperation and screamed *FOOL!* while my heart cheered and tossed colorful confetti to celebrate. "So that's what we'll do."

His gaze never wavered from my face. "Are you sure?"

I nodded, trying to portray a confidence I didn't feel. "Positive. As long as we move on from last night. Nothing happened, so let's not talk about it anymore. We will both be professionals from now on. Is that a deal?"

"Yes." A smile lifted the corners of his lips. "So we're good?"

"Totally awesome." I hoped my enthusiastic tone convinced him.

Now all I had to do was to convince myself.

By the time we were on our way to meet Jacqui, last night's embarrassing Kiss That Never Happened was a distant memory, securely tucked away in a dusty compartment at the back of my brain, never to be revisited. As an addendum to his apology, Alec agreed to swap his podcast for my Spotify playlist and was now humming off-key to a Coldplay tune.

I smirked with satisfaction. *Boring podcasts: 0, Ellie Pang: 1.*

"Told you I'd convert you."

Alec only grunted a response, but his mouth twisted into a smile. He was wearing a navy button-up shirt and dark-gray pants, dressed like he was going to a magazine photoshoot instead of a casual weekend brunch at a seaside restaurant. We stopped at a red light, and while waiting for it to turn green, he took one hand off the steering wheel to roll up one of his sleeves.

I pretended to look straight ahead, but I was really watching him from the corner of my eyes. I'd never thought that the simple act of someone rolling up their sleeves could be that appealing, but here we were.

Eyes away from the arm porn, Ellie.

"Hey. It's Sunday."

"Whoa." He snorted. "Your wisdom knows no bounds."

"It's Sunday, smart-ass, and you're wearing a shirt and dress pants."

"Because I'm meeting a potential business partner. Let me share a free tip with you: it pays to present yourself well and make a good impression."

"Doesn't mean you have to be stiff and uptight about what you wear." I gestured at my mint-green shirtdress. "Exhibit A. My casual look is still presentable and acceptable for a semiformal business meeting on the weekend."

He spared me a brief glance. "You look nice."

"This is how I rolled out of bed." I ignored the warm fuzzy feels from his compliment. "You're dressed like you're going to a job interview. Jacqui wouldn't judge you or your business based on what you wear on a Sunday."

"Well . . . old habits die hard."

"You mean you've always been this uptight? Were you born that way?"

He ignored my quip and drummed his fingers on the steering wheel. "Only since my dad left, I guess. A few guys I used to hang out with made fun of my family because my parents separated." He let out a bitter laugh. "I was ashamed at first. For some people, apparently it meant that my family was somehow inferior to theirs. Like I wasn't good enough to hang out with them, just because I didn't have a father figure in my life, or because we weren't rolling in cash since we had a single mother supporting our family."

Something tugged at my heartstrings, instantly wiping the smirk off my face. I'd never heard him mention anything this personal about his father before.

"But your brother," he smiled a little, "reminded me that those guys aren't my true friends. That I wouldn't want people like them hanging around me anyway. How it was better not to have a father, rather than having one who never wanted to be in my life, and that having my mother and my sisters was more than enough. That I had nothing to be ashamed of. And he was absolutely right. So to me, dressing up nicely is a way of showing people that even though my dad left us, we're still doing okay." He looked embarrassed. "It's silly, I know."

My heart broke for him. "Not silly at all. Do you miss him?"

His jaw hardened. "No. He hasn't reached out to us, so I'm not going to try to find him."

"How old were you when he left?"

"Just before I started college. The first few years were hard. My mother had to work a few jobs to support the family. Being a first-generation immigrant, the opportunities afforded to her were limited, even though she went to college here, and her English is excellent. So I decided to quit college and help her."

"Did Eric and my parents know about this? It would have been easy to find your mother a job at one of the companies within Pang Food Industries."

The minute I said those words, regret came over me. It sounded so obnoxious, like something a spoiled, privileged person would say to someone less fortunate. Like something *my mother* would say, and it was a stark reminder of how his family and mine were so different. I knew how lucky I was, because I'd never had to work to put myself through college or worry about student loans. But on the other hand, I envied Alec for the relationship he had with his mother, because it was something I'd never had, and probably could never have, with mine.

"No." At my question, something resembling disgust briefly flashed across his features, but it was gone the next second. "The thought never crossed our minds. We survived just fine, without anyone's help." He paused, seemingly debating what to say next. "And I knew your mother never thought much of me. She'd always made it clear that I wasn't good enough to hang around your family. That I didn't deserve to be friends with Eric and you because of my dad."

"Well, she's wrong. And you more than survived, because you're doing very well now, and you should be proud of yourself." I paused. "Thanks for sharing that with me."

He glanced at me, and our eyes held for a few seconds.

My brain sighed and mumbled *Here we go again*, while my heart urged me to reach across and give that young man who had to put up with so much shit because of his father a comforting hug.

Strictly business, Ellie. No hugs or actual feelings allowed here.

Time for a topic change.

"By the way, you never told me that Jacqui is drop-dead gorgeous."

He was already concentrating on the road again. "Didn't see why that would matter."

"You've got to be kidding me. She's stunning, smart, *and* rich. Most men would probably give up a kidney for one night with her. She had her eyes on you, and you're not tempted?"

"If I were, you wouldn't be here, and we wouldn't be having this conversation."

"Why not give it a shot? Just go on one date with her."

"She's not my type."

"That's not possible. Someone like Jacqui is *everybody's* type."

"Not mine. I kinda have my eyes on someone else already." He sounded sheepish. "And before you say anything, let me clarify that it's nothing serious yet. I'm aware that we're not supposed to see other people, so I won't make any move until this is over."

Jealous Ellie reared her head, and it wasn't pleasant. She was snarling, demanding to know who that someone else was, and if that was the case, then why the hell did The Kiss That Never Happened . . . uh, happened?

There was only one plausible explanation: he had been very, truly, incredibly drunk, and hadn't realized who was in front of him. He'd probably been imagining that other someone, which explained why he'd been so horrified to find me instead. After all, to him, I was only Eric's little sister, wasn't I? He had nothing but substitute-big-brotherly feelings for me. Wasn't that what he had told me all those years ago?

But there had been nothing brotherly about the way he was looking at me last night. I was 100 percent sure of that, because I'd replayed that moment a thousand times in my head, over and over again.

Well, duh. Of course, because he was thinking of someone else, wasn't he?

Goddamn it. I needed to get out of my head, because even I was going mad listening to my neurotic thoughts.

"Good for you!" My voice came out squeaky and high-pitched, so instead of seeming like I was genuinely thrilled for him, I sounded like a frog was stuck in my throat. "She must be a saint, if she's willing to put up with you."

Alec let out a strangled laugh. "She must be."

"Why don't you ask her to be your date to all these Goodwin functions, then? Saves you from having to put up with me." I pointed at myself and made a self-deprecating face to emphasize what I meant.

"I don't mind spending time with you. You're not so bad. Somewhat tolerable."

"Aww, look at you, being so generous with your compliments."

"And besides, she and I are very new. I don't think we're at that stage yet."

"Which stage?" *Mine is currently at the lusting-over-your-fake-boyfriend stage.*

"Introducing her to my colleagues and business partners. It seems too . . . serious. We're still getting to know each other. I don't want her to get the wrong idea."

"Tell me about her." *Why am I torturing myself?* "What's her name? What does she do? Does she know you're pretending to be someone else's boyfriend?"

"Too many questions." He indicated left, his eyes scanning for a free parking spot. "I can't choose which one to answer first, so I'm ignoring them all."

"But I'm intrigued about this woman who voluntarily agreed to date you. Was she under duress? Is her experience with men so limited that she didn't realize there are plenty of other fish in the sea? Oh, wait. Are you her *first boyfriend*?"

"She's not my girlfriend yet. Are you always this chatty?" He slid the gear into park and turned off the engine. "I don't remember you talking this much when we were younger."

Probably because I had always been too nervous to speak when he was around. And right now, because my chattiness perfectly disguised my disappointment at knowing he was interested in someone else. "Compared to you, Sir Grouchiness, a rock would be considered chatty. And you have answered none of my questions."

"Maybe one day. When I have ten free hours."

I rolled my eyes as we got out of his car and started walking toward the row of restaurants along the Waterfront. "If you expected me to spare ten precious hours of my life for you, you've got another thing coming."

"Three at the party, and ninety minutes today. They all add up."

"Speaking of the party," I said, suddenly remembering a moment from last night, "what's the deal with Jacqui and Phil? I thought I picked up some tense vibe between them."

His eyebrows quirked up. "Did you? Very observant."

"One of my many talents." I twirled my hands with a flourish. "It was something Jacqui had said about how marketing a property isn't her expertise. Phil didn't look very impressed."

"Word on the street is, Anderson Real Estate is in some serious financial trouble. They've had to close three offices alone in the last year. Rumor is, he's approaching Jacqui to invest in his company so he can save the business."

"And she wasn't interested, judging from what she said last night?"

He shrugged. "Your guess is as good as mine."

We walked in comfortable silence for a while. It was a cool but beautiful sunny day, and the Waterfront was packed with tourists and locals wanting to enjoy a slice of sea and sunshine. Families with kids frolicked on the sand, while couples young and old strolled hand in hand along the gorgeous white-sand beach.

"Can I ask you a question?" I broke the silence.

"If I say no, you're still going to ask, aren't you?"

"Why is the Goodwin deal so important to you, anyway?"

"Didn't you write all this down? Check your notes."

"I mean, I know it's a great opportunity," I said. "But from what Phil mentioned yesterday, you seem to be doing well for yourself. I understand that GPG could open new opportunities for you, but you're giving up half of the business you've worked so hard for."

"Because they're the Holy Grail of the construction industry. Imagine if Martha Stewart knocked on your door tomorrow and offered you five million dollars for half the stake in your bakery. I bet you'd jump at the chance."

"I wouldn't take anything less than fifty." I grinned.

But he wasn't listening. "Jacqui is a savvy businesswoman. People like her do their research, their due diligence, and they don't just offer to invest in any business unless they're certain it'll be profitable. This is a once-in-a-lifetime opportunity, and it will give me a chance to branch out of Port Benedict and expand the business all over the country."

"You could open an office back home. Be closer to your family."

His face clouded. "No. Not back home."

Before I could ask why, he lowered his head. "We're almost there, and Jacqui and Phil are sitting outside, looking in our direction. I think they're talking about us."

I snuck a glance at the restaurant we were heading to. He was right: the two of them were at the outside dining area, chatting as they watched us approach.

"They definitely are." We were walking too far apart for two people who were supposedly in a loving, committed relationship. "Should we hold hands or something?"

"Sure." Without hesitation, he laced his fingers through mine. "Maybe you could also gaze adoringly into my eyes."

I turned my scoff into a cough, then forced out a bright smile to avoid looking suspicious to our audience. "Why should I be the one to gaze adoringly at you? It's an equal opportunity world, so *you* can gaze into my eyes."

Alec suddenly came to a complete stop and turned me around

to face him. He cupped my face with both hands and stared deeply into my eyes.

"Is that better? Is my gaze adoring enough?"

I struggled to contain my giggle. *Giggle? I don't do giggles. Be professional, Ellie.*

So I returned his stare, gazing back into his eyes, only that was a mistake, because standing this close, I could see every single brown fleck in them, and could count each and every strand of those long eyelashes.

"Your hands are hanging by the sides of your body." His voice was low, husky.

"Of course they are. Where else are they supposed to be?"

"We look awkward. Not like two human beings who are passionately in love." Alec took a step forward, closing the small distance between our bodies, his hands still holding my face, his eyes fixed on mine. "Put your arms around me."

I wanted to protest, but his thumbs began to stroke my cheeks, and my hands moved on their own volition, circling around his waist. We were now standing toe-to-toe, staring into each other's eyes, with squawking seagulls soaring above and the glistening ocean as the backdrop, as if we were the main characters in a romantic movie scene.

"There. Happy? Now what?"

Instead of answering, his eyes dropped to my mouth, lingering there for a while, then back up to my eyes. The longing in them was so intense, I might have forgotten to take a breath.

Okay, this was clearly getting out of hand, but luckily, what little was left of my brain cells decided to take over. *Let's not embarrass ourselves again here. Remember yesterday? And what he said in the car, about being interested in someone else? Well, news flash, girl: he's intensely longing for* her, *not you.*

"Are they still watching?" Alec asked.

I stole a stealthy glance at Jacqui and Phil, and the two of them were craning their necks, practically trampling over each other trying to get a better view of us. "Yes."

He sighed. "What should we do now? Will it look suspicious if we break apart?"

"How should I know? You're the one who got us into this position."

There was a flash of hesitation in his eyes, but it solidified into steely resolve the next second. "Then we better give them something to talk about."

"Are you . . . wait, what are you going to do?"

"I think I might have to kiss you. But I promise, it will be quick and painless. Just a one-second peck on your lips. You won't even feel a thing. We're both professionals, and this is strictly business. Is that okay?"

I nodded. Strictly business. One-second peck. Got it.

The next thing I knew, he brushed his lips over mine, and not that I was counting, but it was certainly more than one second, and I *definitely* felt something. A lot of things, in fact, and none of them were even remotely close to the words "business" and "professional." My knees buckled, and my heart thumped so loudly I wondered why it hadn't burst out already, then it whooped and cheered, because someone sighed (me), and someone else deepened the kiss with a soft groan (him). Nothing else in the world mattered but those perfectly warm lips devouring mine. I didn't know how anyone could taste this intoxicating, and I wanted to stop time, right here, right now. Obviously I had no dignity and self-respect, and I should rethink all my life choices, because my immediate thought was, *I want more.*

No. This wasn't real, and nothing positive could come out of this.

But there was nothing wrong with enjoying the moment while it lasted, right?

Someone passed us and let out a wolf whistle. "Get a room, guys."

That snapped me out of . . . whatever the hell this was. It took all my willpower to pull away, and when we finally broke apart, I was dazed and breathless, and my remaining brain cells had packed up for early retirement.

Alec was staring down at me with glazed eyes, as if the kiss had affected him as well. A flash of guilt crossed his face, but it was gone the next second.

"Thanks for playing along." He was the first one to speak.

I only nodded, not trusting myself to say anything.

Alec let go of my face and took a step back, and I curbed the irrational urge to grab his hands again. Placing one hand instead at the small of my back, he gently prodded me to start walking, because my feet were cemented to the ground. "You ready?"

Another quiet nod, because my brain cells had decided that retirement was so much more fun than dealing with this blasted nonsense, so coherent words had escaped me.

He stared at me for a few beats, then linked his hand through mine again. "Time to convince them we're madly in love."

Of course it was only to convince Jacqui. What else would it be?

I had the sinking feeling that it had also convinced my poor, unsuspecting heart.

CHAPTER 13

I Had Dinner with Him and Everyone Survived

We were only a few days into our fake courtship, and we'd already gotten a routine going, just like any normal fake couple: I'd start the day with my morning run, and by the time I returned, Alec would have breakfast ready in the kitchen. He'd drop me off at the shop on his way to work, sometimes picking me up in the afternoon, and for the last few days, it felt like our pretend relationship was blossoming into a tolerable friendship.

But yesterday's Strictly Professional Kiss seemed to have changed everything.

Alec was his charming self during brunch with Jacqui and Phil, but as soon as we left the restaurant, it was as if the past few days and our newfound camaraderie had never even existed. He'd relapsed to his grumpy, clammed-up self, quiet on the car ride home, only speaking whenever necessary, then spent the rest of the day avoiding me. I'd racked my brain trying to figure out what could possibly have caused it, but came up empty.

This morning, gone was the thoughtful breakfast, and on the

way to work, his boring podcast was blaring at full volume. Today's topic was legal tips for astute property developers, and I thanked the Good Lord that the drive only lasted ten minutes, because any longer, I'd probably have flung myself out of the moving vehicle. The air inside the car was sub-zero, and he hadn't said a single word since we'd left.

After five minutes of uncomfortable silence, I attempted to break the ice.

"Busy day planned at the office today?"

"Mm-hmm."

"Lots of meetings? Site visits?"

"Yep."

I tried again. "Did you see the weather forecast? It's going to be a cold day."

"No."

Perhaps I should have left it at that, but persistence was my middle name. I gave it one last shot. "How's your family? Your mom and sisters well?"

"Great."

We made a new friend: the infamous curt, one-word answer. Effective, but annoying.

"By the way, Rob asked me out to dinner tonight. Don't wait up for me because I'll be staying at his house having hot, wild sex all night."

Didn't know why I said that, but it got his attention. He screeched to a halt at the next red light and turned to frown at me—the first time he really looked at me today.

"What?"

"I thought that would encourage you to use your words."

"That's not funny." He bestowed an icy glance on me, then turned his eyes back to the road. "Rob has a girlfriend. For a minute I thought he was cheating on her."

"I didn't know he has a girlfriend. That's too bad, because he'd be perfect." For Kim, because I'd been meaning to introduce them, but I stopped myself from saying that.

No answer.

I jabbed at the infotainment screen to turn off his painfully uninspiring podcast. "Okay, I'm clueless here, Alec. Things were fine yesterday. What's going on?"

He switched the podcast back on from a button on the steering wheel. "Nothing. Busy day ahead. Got a lot on my mind."

I turned it off again. "Liar. I'm practically freezing here from your frostiness."

The podcast came back on. "Don't know what you're talking about."

He made a right turn and stopped in front of my store. The second I got out of his car, he peeled away as if he were exiting a Formula One pit stop.

It was official: Sir Annoying McGrumpyface had made a triumphant comeback.

Gritting my teeth, I pushed the shop door open. Was I disappointed that he was being a hostile pain in the butt again? Yes, because I thought we were finally becoming friends, but obviously he didn't share the sentiment. I shouldn't let it bother me, nor the fact that any trace of The Strictly Professional Kiss seemed to have vanished the moment we said goodbye to Jacqui and Phil yesterday. Should I try to analyze what was going on? No, because he wasn't my actual boyfriend. Should I move on and focus on the rest of my day as if nothing had happened? Hell yes, if I knew what was good for me. In fact, I should follow the steps of my freshly completed Stay on Track Plan:

1. First and foremost, focus on getting the bakery up and running.
2. Distraction is king: I need to spend more time doing things I love—getting back to the kitchen to test new rec-

ipes, and working through my Netflix queue and Kindle to-read list.

3. Minimize contact and establish clear boundaries with him. DO NOT, under any circumstances, not even in the name of fake courtship, KISS HIM AGAIN. Not even if the universe was coming to an imminent end and kissing him is the only thing that could save humanity from destruction and/or extinction.

4. List his negative qualities and reasons we're incompatible: he's arrogant, annoying, listens to awful podcasts, and sees me only as Eric's little sister. Possibly has a (soon-to-be) girlfriend.

5. If all the above fails, remember: he nearly killed me ten years ago. Fine, it wasn't technically his fault, whatever, but he was the one who had triggered the whole thing.

When I walked in, Rob and his team were already knee-deep in wires and electrical switches. The work was progressing nicely, and things were taking shape. I pushed aside my frustration and disappointment with Alec to admire the view: the previously drab walls were now freshly painted in beige, and the floor tiles had been cleaned and polished to gleaming perfection. My shiny, beautiful, new commercial oven was delivered yesterday, and Rob had scheduled the installation this week. I couldn't stop grinning as I ran my hand across its sleek surface. Things were moving forward, and on budget, bringing me closer to achieving my dreams.

I spent the day checking things off my To-Do List: planning several menu options for the bakery, ordering kitchen tools and equipment, and chasing city officials to make sure the permits and licenses would be ready in time.

That afternoon, as I switched off the lights and locked the door, Alec's SUV swung into the empty spot just vacated by Rob's truck. He got out, his face as surly as it had been this morning. I schooled my features to match his unpleasant scowl.

Alec nodded at me. "You ready to go?"

Shoving my keys into my bag, I lifted my chin. "No. I don't accept rides from rude, unfriendly faces. I can get home on my own, thank you." Shouldering my backpack, I started walking toward the main Plaza building, where the bus terminal was.

He growled from behind me. "Stop. You're being stubborn again."

"Stop calling me that."

"Where are you going?" He marched after me, catching my arm to anchor me in place. "You don't have a car, and I'm trying to help. The least you could do is say thanks."

I snatched my arm away. "I have been *nothing* but grateful for everything you've done for me. But I don't appreciate you shoving that in my face as an excuse for your grouchiness. So thanks, but no thanks, because I don't need your help."

"I know you don't, but I promised Eric. He would've done the same thing for my sisters."

The hairs on the back of my neck prickled. Eric, Eric, Eric. I loved my brother, but I was so sick of hearing Alec wonder, *What Would Eric Do?* The only reason he was being thoughtful was because he promised my brother to look out for me. The wisest thing to do was to pour cold water on whatever feelings I was redeveloping for him, because they were only setting me up for a much harder fall.

I swung around and hissed at him, "You know what, Mackenzie? You're *the most* frustrating man alive. I thought we had a good weekend. We were an awesome team, we charmed Jacqui, and I was even under the delusion that we were finally becoming friends. Yet for some unknown reason, you've gone back to your old irritating self this morning."

He pursed his lips but said nothing.

"Sure, if that's what you want, I'll play along," I said. "We don't have to be friendly and civil to each other outside of our agreement."

He closed his eyes and rubbed a hand over his face.

"We're done here." I gave him one last stink eye and walked away.

"Wait," he called out, his footsteps echoing behind me. "You're right. We do make an amazing team. You completely charmed Jacqui yesterday. I couldn't have done any of this without you."

I kept walking. He kept following.

"I owe you an apology. For being rude this morning, and for the kiss."

My steps faltered.

"I know I said we should be professionals, but I swear, I didn't mean for it to happen for that long. It was just something I thought of on the spot to convince Jacqui."

I stopped and turned around to face him.

"I've been thinking about it the whole day. I was angry at myself, and I felt so guilty about it," he continued. "You made an excellent point about limiting our interaction outside of our agreement. That should minimize any . . . unnecessary physical contact."

Unnecessary physical contact? A chaotic smorgasbord of emotions rumbled inside my heart. That hurt, because obviously for him, the concept of touching and kissing me thoroughly revolted him. Then jealousy, because understandably, he felt guilty because he was kissing me when he liked another woman. But most of all, I was furious with myself, because I felt jealous *and* disappointed, and I had no right feeling any of those things.

Whatever it was, he was right. It was the appropriate thing to do. And if in doubt, refer to the Stay on Track Plan.

"Fine. Apology accepted, and we're limiting our interactions. I'll see you around."

He jabbed a thumb toward his car. "Can I give you a ride? It'll save you a forty-five-minute bus trip home."

"That totally defeats the purpose of what we just discussed ten seconds ago."

"We can start tomorrow. I'm already here, going in the same direction as you are."

My stomach seized that very moment to rumble, loudly demanding that it needed to be fed. A corner of his mouth quirked up at the sound.

"It's almost seven, so maybe we can go to that sushi and sake place at the rooftop area for dinner. Don't you need to eat something so your blood sugar doesn't go low?"

It was comments like these that made it supremely difficult to stay annoyed at him. My heart aahed and awwwed with adoration, while my brain sighed in resignation and created a brand-new list to add my collection: Alec's Supremely Thoughtful Gestures.

"*Sushi and sake?* I can't keep up with you. Doesn't this count as social interaction?"

He shrugged. "Yeah, but I'm only offering because—"

"Let me guess." My tone was flat. "Because that's what Eric would do?"

His face split into a grin. "No. Because I'm also starving."

Ocha Izakaya was packed, so we were ushered to two empty seats at the sushi bar. We placed our food orders and some hojicha, then quietly watched the sushi chef in front of us fill a wooden sushi boat with salmon and tuna sashimi slices.

"Mike called today," I broke the silence. "My car should be done in a couple of days."

"That's good. I forgot to ask, what was wrong with it?"

"Engine failure. He's rebuilding the old one, because that costs less and I'd have better mileage out of it."

Alec set his cup of tea down. "How much is that going to cost you?"

"A few thousand." I winced a little. "It's a bit tight, but I'll make it work. It's cheaper than a new engine or a new car."

Just then, his phone trilled. He excused himself, then walked away, while muttering a low "hey" into his phone.

Nope, not going to feel jealous that *that* was probably a call from the girl he had his eyes on. Absolutely none of my business.

Just then, my phone vibrated, too. I tapped the green icon to answer the video call, grinning when Naomi's smile filled my screen.

"Ellie! So good to see your pretty face." She peered at the screen, trying to work out where I was. Waiters with black T-shirts and red aprons bustled behind me, carrying trays of sake cups and sushi platters. "Are you at dinner? I can call back."

"No, that's okay. What's up?"

"I've got big news." Naomi's voice crackled on the phone, the smile on her face enormous. "Remember I told you about the weekend trip Eric organized?" When I nodded, she went on, "Guess what happened."

My eyes widened as she brandished her hand in front of the camera, showing me a big, blindingly beautiful ring on her finger.

"We're going to be sisters, El!"

I let out a squeal, attracting Alec's attention, who'd just returned to our seats. "Oh my God, that's awesome! Congrats, you two!"

"Hey, Naomi." Alec leaned to peek into the call frame, whistling when he saw the sparkly ring. "Is that what I think it is? Finally! Congratulations, so thrilled for you and Eric."

Naomi's face froze mid-smile, her eyebrows hiking up so high they practically disappeared into her hairline.

"She's not moving," Alec observed. "Bad phone connection, maybe."

"Or extreme shock. Naomi? Blink once if you can hear me. Blink twice if you can't."

My friend blinked rapidly, finally showing signs of life. She squinted closer at the camera, her eyeballs filling the frame, as if that would help her see him better. When that obviously didn't work, her dilated pupils swiveled toward me. "You. Are having dinner with Alec? *Alec Mackenzie?*"

"That's me."

I shrugged, keeping my face blank. "Well, he's the only Alec I know in town."

"That's true. I've never met another Alec here. Plenty of Alexanders, though."

"But . . . but . . . ," Naomi spluttered, giving me a quizzical look, "you said you're not happy about having to ask for his help. That you're barely tolerating each other. When did that turn into buddies having dinner together? Why wasn't I briefed about this significant development in your relationship?"

"Because there's no relationship," I replied. "It's just dinner. Very casual. Lots of other people here, too, see behind me?"

"Lots of other people." Alec nodded, looking serious. "When's the big day, Naomi?"

"We haven't decided," a familiar voice murmured behind her.

Naomi beamed, all her shock and bafflement forgotten, as my brother's face popped into view. "Hey, kiddos."

"Eric, congratulations!" I shrieked, while Alec said, "Well done, man."

My brother was smiling from ear to ear. "Thanks. How are things? Good to see you two hanging out together and playing nice."

"I'm always nice," Alec said. "Took me a while to convince Ellie, but she's finally coming around." He grinned at me. "I'm starting to grow on you, aren't I?"

Both my brother and my best friend turned their curious faces on me. Naomi's eyes were narrowed, full of speculation, while Eric just looked amused.

"I'll get back to you on that," I said, before directing my next sentence at Eric and Naomi. "Anyway, what's been happening back home? Eric, how's the brewery going?"

Naomi gave me one last raised eyebrow before answering, the unspoken threat loud and clear: *I demand a full explanation later.* "Things have been busy and chaotic, as usual. Babe, tell them about the drama with your parents."

"Oh, man." Eric rolled his eyes. "El, you remember old man McKay, don't you? Their eccentric neighbor? You're gonna laugh when you hear this."

As he told the story, my mind drifted away, and I was suddenly overcome with sadness. I spoke with Naomi and Eric often in our group chat, but I hadn't spoken to my parents since the day I stormed out of their office. My mother hadn't followed through on her threat to sue me, thankfully, and apart from the occasional angry text messages, she hadn't made any real attempts to contact me. Knowing my mom, a world champion at holding grudges, it could be a long while.

There was an old saying in Indonesian that my mother used to tell us when we were little, that "heaven lies under the feet of mothers." It meant that a child must respect their parents, specifically their mother, to "gain passage into heaven." She'd grown up listening to that, so she was never one to disrespect her parents and her in-laws. That was how I'd been raised, too: by being told to *always* honor your elders. They were always right. Even if they were wrong and you didn't like what you were being told to do, well, tough luck, because you need to suck it up and do it anyway. Apparently, it was the Chinese Indonesian way, or at least, it was *my* Chinese Indonesian family's way.

But for me and Eric, being raised in a Western society, we were also taught from an early age to express our opinions and question things that didn't make sense to us. Which was what we did, whenever we could, just as long as it was within the acceptable confines of my mother's expectations. This was the longest I'd gone without speaking to my parents, because in the past, I had always given in and apologized, then done what was asked of me.

Until, of course, a few weeks ago.

I wondered how they'd taken the news of Eric's engagement. They liked Naomi and respected her family enough to approve of her dating Eric, but it was never a secret that my mother had always wished for a more dynastic marriage for him. Someone richer, with more powerful connections, who could be a mutually beneficial partner for my family.

Someone just like George Fitzgerald.

Without warning, George's public proposal flashed into mind. The YouTube video was now sitting at eleven million views, and random people I passed on the street still gave me double-takes sometimes. Hearing about Eric and Naomi's happy news triggered a tiny seed of doubt, clawing and nagging at me: What if I'd said yes to George? I wouldn't be here right now, working my ass off trying to get a business up and running, while involved in a confusing non-relationship with this frustrating man next to me. Instead, I'd be marrying a perfectly decent guy, from a highly respectable family, and we'd probably have an idyllic marriage with beautiful kids and a beautiful house, and my familial ties with my parents wouldn't be this fractured.

But as Eric finished his story, both Naomi and Alec laughing at the absurdity of it, I thought, *I'm good here.* Even with the uncertainty of my future, and the impending doom that I was undoubtedly heading into with *him*, I'd rather be here— anywhere—than home.

"Hey, Eric. How's George doing?"

My brother chuckled. "He's fine. You know who he brought into the office the other day? Emma Ryan. Remember her? Her family used to supply fresh produce for Dad's restaurants. Looks like he's gotten ov—*ouch*." He glared at Naomi, who was out of frame, then turned back to me, looking sheepish. "Anyway, he's well. He sends his regards."

"That's great. I'm happy for him." I really was, and relieved as well, because George was a great guy, and he deserved to be with someone who truly loved him for who he was, not for the continued success of our family's business relationships.

"By the way, Mom asked if I'd heard from you."

"She did?" The sadness multiplied, and a sharp jab of guilt hit me. She and I might've not seen eye to eye, but no matter how challenging she could be, she was still my mother. "How is she? How's Dad? Are they well?"

"They're both fine. But they haven't forgiven you for turning down George. They're *still* talking about that."

Of course. I forced out a smile. "So . . . nothing's changed."

"Anyway, she asked if I've heard from you. Don't worry, I didn't say a word." He paused. "I never asked, actually. Where *are* you staying now, anyway?"

I opened my mouth, then closed it again, glancing at Alec for help.

"She doesn't live far from me," he answered, without missing a beat. "Within walking distance from my place."

I snorted, turning it into a cough when Naomi shot me a suspicious gaze.

"Thanks for looking out for her, man. I owe you one," Eric said. "How's work going?"

"You'd have done the same for my sisters," Alec replied. "And work's been busy. Had a big work function on the weekend."

Heat flooded my cheeks as a full-length movie of The Strictly

Professional Kiss began playing. I stole a glance at Alec, but he seemed unfazed, so obviously he'd forgotten all about it, and I was the only one still affected.

Our food came, and we said our goodbyes, with Alec promising to catch up with Eric and Naomi at his sister's wedding in a few months. I bolused for my food while Alec poured some soy sauce into two small dipping bowls, then mixed a generous blob of wasabi into his.

"Did you know? That he was going to propose?"

I shook my head. "No. Great news, though. Couldn't be happier for them."

"Not Eric." Alec picked up a piece of salmon sashimi and dipped it in his mixture. "George's proposal. I watched the video."

I groaned. "Yeah. You and eleven million other people."

Alec grinned. "It *is* entertaining. I might have contributed quite a bit to those eleven million views. Why'd you say no?" He turned to watch me. "He seems like a nice guy."

"He is." I swiveled in my own stool and returned his stare, our gazes holding for a few beats, and I couldn't tear my eyes away. "Just not the right guy for me."

I knew I was setting myself up for a long, hard fall, but right now, in this crowded Japanese restaurant, I couldn't see anyone else but him. I realized he would never be mine, so I might as well make the most out of whatever time I had with him in the next few weeks.

Even at the risk of having my heart bruised and battered for the second time.

Alec was the first to break the moment. "By the way, just in case the topic ever comes up with Jacqui," he said, turning his attention back to his food, a teasing smile playing on his lips, "my favorite movie of all time might be that YouTube video."

CHAPTER 14

How to Un-Fake a Fake Relationship

wo days later, I was alone in the shop, setting up the bakery's new accounting software I'd just installed on my laptop, when a loud knock broke my concentration.

"Ellie Pang?" A lanky, dark-haired man was standing at the door, his cap in hand.

"Hi, yes." I recognized his voice from our calls. "You must be Mike."

He nodded and handed me my car keys. "Your car's outside, ready to get back on the road. We've rebuilt the engine and performed a tune-up. Checked and rotated the tires, too. If something doesn't sound or feel right, bring her back."

"Great. Thanks so much for dropping the car, I appreciate it."

"No problem. I don't normally do it, but Alec asked me to, and you're on the way to my other appointment anyway."

I mentally added another item on the list of Alec's Supremely Thoughtful Gestures. "How much do I owe you?"

Mike handed me a folded piece of paper. "Here's your invoice."

I opened it up, reciting a silent prayer. His initial estimate had been four to five thousand, so if I was lucky, it would be at the lower end of that quote.

"*Three* thousand? That can't be right. Didn't you say four to five?"

"I did." Mike smiled, showing off perfect rows of white teeth. "But once we started the work, it turned out the damage wasn't as extensive as we first thought."

I gaped at him, then at the invoice, and back to him again. "Are you sure?"

"Absolutely positive."

Both my budget and I let out a relieved sigh. "I'll organize payment this afternoon."

"Sure." He shoved his hands in his pocket and looked around the shop. "Nice space you got here. What are you opening?"

"A bakery."

"Sweet." He grinned at me, clearly proud of his pun. "Alec said you just moved here?"

"Brand-new transplant from the East Coast."

His face turned curious. "You settled in so far? Explored our lovely city yet?"

"Not really. I've been focusing on getting this place up and running."

"I'd be happy to show you around." The curious look turned into a charming smile. "If you're a coffee aficionado, there's this awesome coffee shop that roasts their own gourmet beans. And they make these exquisite red velvet muffins." He made a kissing gesture on his fingers. "It's the best in the entire city."

"Thanks, but I'm busy for the next few weeks. And coffee isn't really my thing."

His smile became flirtier. "That's okay. We've also got tearooms, excellent locally brewed beers, and award-winning wineries."

I chuckled. He was cute, but the last thing I needed right now was more distraction. "Look, Mike. You seem nice, but we just met five minutes ago. What if you're a dangerous axe murderer, or an organ trafficker planning to drug me and harvest my kidneys?" I tempered my words with a small chuckle.

A grin spread over his face. "Alec can vouch for me."

Alec. We weren't supposed to see other people during this deal, right? Even he himself had put a pause on pursuing his new relationship until after this was over.

"But sure, I totally understand if you're not comfortable. You've got my number if you change your mind."

This isn't a date, though. My brain swiftly ran an internal pros and cons list. It was a smart business move, an opportunity for me to network and meet more people. Mike was obviously a local, and he might be useful in helping to spread the word about the bakery.

Plus, he might take my mind off Alec. Which was exactly what I needed.

Mike was walking toward the door. "You enjoy the rest of your day."

"Saturday morning, one hour, in a public café," I said, stopping him in his tracks. "Just in case you *are* an axe murderer, there'll be witnesses who can testify that I was with you."

"Cool. I'll pick you up at, say, nine?"

"Text me the address. I'll meet you there."

"Awesome." Grinning, he put his cap back on and pushed the door open. "I promise I'll leave my axe at home."

That night, I was back at Ocha Izakaya with Kim and Jenna, all three of us nursing cold drinks after a very long day. Rob and his crew had finished the kitchen today, and some of the tables and chairs I'd ordered were delivered this morning. We were ahead of schedule, and I was breathing a little easier because things were finally taking shape.

"We should make this a weekly gig." Kim clinked her Sapporo with my Coke Zero, looking like she was well on her way to tipsiness. "The alcohol's probably not good for my health, but I get to hang out with two wonderful friends and flirt with the cute chef. Win-win."

"He's been checking you out, too," Jenna said. "Go talk to him."

Kim considered this, then shook her head. "Maybe not. He looks a bit like Leo, my ex-fiancé. Don't need another Leo in my life."

Jenna did a spit-take while my eyeballs nearly spilled out of their sockets, then we both started talking over each other.

"Shut the front door! You were *engaged*?"

"You kept *that* tiny bit of information a secret from your housemate? *How dare you?*"

"Who's Leo? How did you two meet? How long were you two together?"

"Why did the engagement end? Are you still in love with him?"

Kim raised a finger, silencing us. "We were engaged for a few years. Classic case of him being a dickhead and screwing around. But I don't want to waste my breath talking about him, because he's ancient history. Prehistoric. I prefer to live in the moment, okay? Let's talk about something else."

"Fine. But you're not off the hook," Jenna warned. "I have the means to pry secrets out of someone, and I'm not afraid to use them."

"Bring it." Kim stuck out her tongue at Jenna, then turned to me. "Have you thought of a name for your bakery?"

"Of course I have." I beamed at her. "I'm calling it Sugarless Goodness."

Kim grimaced. "Do you want me to be polite, or should I be brutally honest?"

It was my turn to wince. "I thought it perfectly conveys the concept of the bakery—desserts that are sugar-free and good for you."

"It does, but I think you can do better. Any other alternatives?"

"There's Sugarless Pleasures, Sugarless Bakeshop, or Sugarless Cravings."

"Those are the best you could come up with? Anything without 'sugarless' in them?"

"I also thought of Twisted Sweets, Guilt-free Pleasures, and Heavenly Cravings."

Kim snorted, apparently having given up all pretenses of being diplomatic and sparing my feelings. "Why don't you just call it Ellie's Den of Heavenly Pleasures?"

"It's a bakery," I protested. "Not a harem."

She grinned. "Well, with those names, it might as well be."

"I vote for Twisted Sweets," Jenna helpfully said. "I like that one the best."

"I disagree." Kim shook her head. "You need to find something catchier. Bolder. Something that will make people look up and pay attention."

"Like what?" I raised my eyebrows. "The Whisk Warrior? The Naked Baker?"

"There you go. *Now* you're talking."

Jenna frowned. "I'm not going into a bakery called The Naked Baker."

Kim scrunched up her nose. "Eh, true. People might go in expecting some kind of Magic Mike situation. You're not licensed for that." She sighed. "Well, keep brainstorming. Anyway, how did it go at the function with Cutie Building Expert? Did he swallow his own tongue when he saw you in that black dress?"

"I told you, he's just a friend."

Kim scoffed. "Keep telling yourself that, and maybe one day you'll believe it. Remember what I told you about that morning when we first met him? There was *nothing* friendly about the way he looked at you. Jenna, back me up here."

"I concur." Jenna wriggled her eyebrows suggestively at me.

"In case you didn't catch the meaning, allow us to translate. It announced that he wanted to kiss you and undress you and do filthy things to make you scream. I personally think, woman to woman, the least you could do is let him try, so I can live vicariously through you."

"We," Jenna added. "So *we* can live vicariously through you."

I choked out a laugh. "I'll pass."

"Why not? It's okay to admit that you're attracted to him," Kim said. "And you both live in the same house, which means you've cut down on commuting time, so you've got even *more time* to do all those things. Maybe you could make *him* scream. Or growl your name. Groan in ecstasy. I'm not a romance novelist, but you get the idea."

Uninvited images of a naked Alec on top, moaning and moving against me, sneakily slid into my brain, making me hot all over. I shook my head to chase them away. "No. No one's getting any ideas."

"All I'm saying is," Kim said, "you've been working too hard, and you deserve a break. Just start by asking him on a date, and the screaming and the moaning can happen after."

"I already have a date. Well, technically a non-date."

"Yes!" Kim brightened. "With Sexy Building Expert?"

"With the mechanic who fixed my car."

"NO!" She looked scandalized. "Lord Building Expert isn't going to like it."

"I'm just meeting the guy for coffee. No big deal."

"Alec still won't like it," Jenna agreed. "Kim's right. I can tell when a man looks at you like he wants to strip you naked and do dirty, delicious things to you all night long."

Kim nodded, lifting a finger to stop me when I started protesting. "And please don't insult our intelligence by reciting that spiel about 'just friends' again."

I wondered if I should tell them about the fake dating arrangement. Naomi was very suspicious and had asked lots of questions when I'd called her after the dinner, but I didn't tell her anything. I trusted her, but the fewer people that knew about it back home, the better. And since I couldn't tell Naomi, these two women were the closest friends I had in this town.

"Can you two keep a secret?"

Jenna nodded, her face solemn. "I don't have any other friends, so I can't tell anyone."

"That's not true. She has more friends than you and I combined." Kim sipped her drink. "And of course I can. My lips are sealed tighter than Fort Knox."

"Okay." I took a deep breath. "Alec and I are in a pretend relationship. He was going to hire a fake girlfriend, so I offered, in return for his help finding a contractor to repair the shop."

My friends' eyes grew larger, followed by a few moments of silence.

"Back up a little," Kim said. "Start from the very beginning, pretend we're a couple of one-year-olds, and go reeeaalllyy slow. What on God's green Earth are you talking about?"

They both listened, unblinking, as I told them about our agreement. Our food and drinks sat untouched until I'd finished recounting the story.

"Interesting," Kim said. "One question. Is there anything in your agreement that says you're not allowed to consummate the fake relationship?"

"Kim!" I groaned, as Jenna roared with laughter. "*That's* your takeaway from the story?"

"I'm just saying, he looks like he'd be interested in taking your fake relationship further and un-fake the hell out of it." Kim grinned, before her face turned serious. "Joking aside, though.

How do you feel about it? You kept saying he's just a friend, and you don't have any feelings for him. But has anything changed?"

I considered her question. "I don't know. I know that things are different between us now," I said. "He's definitely not the same person he was ten years ago. He's much friendlier now, and he keeps doing these sweet little things that surprise me. Thoughtful things I wouldn't have expected from the Alec I used to know."

Jenna smiled. "And you're starting to have feelings for him again."

"Maybe a little, yeah," I admitted. "But I'm not going to do anything about it. Because he said he's interested in someone else, so I'm convinced he's only being nice to me because he promised my brother to look out for me."

Kim frowned. "If he's interested in someone else, why is he asking you to be his pretend girlfriend?"

"He said it's still very new. They're still getting to know each other."

"I think he's lying." Jenna piped up. "I think he told you he likes someone else as an act of self-preservation. Because he's afraid he'll fall madly in love with you, but he thinks you still blame him for what happened ten years ago. So he's pretending not to be interested in you, to protect himself from getting hurt."

My mind flitted back to Rob's theory about Alec being curt as a defense mechanism, and for a brief, hopeful minute, I wondered if Jenna was right.

But what if she's not?

I curbed that tiny flicker of hope. Whatever it was, it didn't matter. My priority right now should be to get the bakery up and running, and I had no time for anything else.

Especially to un-fake a fake relationship.

CHAPTER 15

A Birthday Revelation

Ever since I was young, my parents were never big on birthdays. I didn't know if it was because they were always so busy working and building their empire, or because their deep-seated Asian frugality prevented them from cutting loose and celebrating.

Before I was diagnosed, birthdays were always "just another day," as my mother liked to call it. They meant quick, subdued dinners at home, always featuring noodles of some kind, because it was supposed to signify a long, healthy life.

But after the diagnosis, it felt like birthdays—especially mine—ceased to exist. And slowly but surely, other children's birthdays, too, because parties meant cakes, cookies, junk foods, and tons of sweet, sugary treats, which sometimes translated to persistent glucose level highs and sleepless nights trying to bring it down to an acceptable range. Every year, without fail, I'd get a nod and a curt "happy birthday" from my father, followed by a bulging angpao from my mother. No cakes, no birthday songs, no hugs or kisses.

Which was probably why I woke up this morning not even

recalling that I turned twenty-nine today, only realizing it when I opened Naomi's text, full of celebration emojis, and Eric's not long after. Nothing from my parents—not that I was expecting one. It was a good thing nobody here knew about my birthday. Less fuss, and I could enjoy it quietly on my own tonight.

In lieu of my usual morning run, I decided to celebrate by testing a recipe I'd seen for chunky Oreo and white chocolate chip cookies, but with my own twists on it. The house was still dark when I went downstairs. Early morning when everything was calm and still were always my favorite time to bake. It gave me a chance to think and reflect, and the process of measuring things and methodically following instructions to create something always soothed me, setting me up in the right mood for the day.

Switching on the lights above the kitchen island, I turned on the stove and started melting some butter. I poured it into a mixing bowl, then added some monkfruit sweetener, an egg, a splash of vanilla extract, then whisked it until it became light and fluffy. And here was the twist I was planning: instead of Oreo and white chocolate, I was using matcha and dark chocolate as substitutes. The carbohydrate content in matcha was super low, so I wanted to experiment with different recipes using matcha powder, hoping to offer several items in that flavor at the bakery.

After adding some plain flour, baking powder, a pinch of salt, and some matcha powder, I mixed them all to form a dough, then added some dark chocolate chips and several crushed matcha cookies into the mixture. Scooping up large chunks of the dough, I rolled them into plump balls, then arranged them on a cookie tray. I set the oven timer then went back upstairs for a quick shower.

When I bounded down the stairs fifteen minutes later, the sweet scents of the cookies filled the kitchen. Alec was already up, holding a steaming mug of coffee, and he was—*damn it*—wearing those tortoiseshell glasses again. Without warning, Kim and Jenna's theory came to mind. *Could they be right? That he's only pretending to be interested in someone else?*

I mumbled a "good morning" as I walked past him and took the cookies out to cool.

"You've had a busy morning." Alec took a sip of his coffee. "That smells fantastic."

"I'm testing a new recipe." I went to find a mug, then busied myself with the tea bag ~~while trying not to stare at him and those distracting glasses~~ and concentrated on brewing my tea. "How would you like to be my unofficial, unpaid taste tester?"

"I thought you'd never ask."

"Matcha and dark chocolate chip cookies. Tell me what you think."

Alec set his mug on the kitchen counter and took one, before tearing it into halves. The cookies turned out better than I'd expected. Perfect dark green color, with gooey dark chocolate oozing out of the center. I sipped my tea and watched nervously as he bit into one half.

"Wow." His eyes widened. "Ellie. These are delicious."

"Yeah?" Relieved, my face broke into a grin. "Not too much matcha? Or maybe more dark chocolate?"

"No. It's perfect. I think you've ruined me for other cookies. Are you going to sell these in the bakery?"

"That's the plan, yeah."

"It'll be a huge hit." He swallowed the last piece in his hand, then reached for another one. "Hey, you got any plans for today?"

"I'm meeting Mike this morning, then I'll be at the shop."

"Mike?" Alec's eyebrows hiked upward. "As in, Mike Chang, my mechanic?"

"Pretty sure he's the only Mike we mutually know." I drained my tea, then started plucking the rest of the cookies off the tray to store them in an airtight container.

His eyebrows plunged, forming a frown. "I should've warned you about him. Great with cars, but not with women."

A tiny jab of thrill shot through me. Could he possibly be . . . *jealous*?

"Plus, I thought we agreed. Neither one of us could date other people for now."

"I'm aware. But it's not a real date. We're just meeting for coffee."

He scoffed. "Your definition of a date is clearly different from mine."

"It's only an hour of getting to know a new friend. Or networking, whatever you want to call it." I placed the dirty cookie tray in the dishwasher. "That's not violating our agreement. And anyway, aren't you the one who told me you're interested in someone else?"

"Yeah, but I also told you I'm putting a pause on it. I'm not setting up coffee or dinner dates with her, am I?"

The thrill disappeared, and my heart dropped at his answer. Because it confirmed that Kim and Jenna were wrong, and that he really *did* have someone he was interested in.

Someone who wasn't me.

"This could potentially jeopardize my deal with Jacqui. If anyone sees you with him and Jacqui hears about it, she might get suspicious and call off the acquisition."

And that was my reminder that he couldn't possibly be jealous, because this entire thing was nothing more than a business transaction to him.

"You're being a bit reckless, and I don't think you've thought this through."

"It's just coffee, Alec," I repeated, suddenly feeling exhausted. "I'll be super careful. I promise I won't do anything to risk your deal with Jacqui."

Without saying another word, I grabbed my bag and keys, then walked out the door.

Mike was already at the café, waving from a table at the back when I arrived. Casting furtive glances around, I made my way to him. Alec did raise a valid point, so I was just making sure that Jacqui, Phil, or anyone else from Jacqui's party wasn't anywhere nearby.

We ordered drinks and started chatting, and after a few minutes I relaxed, glad I'd said yes to this non-date. Mike was flirty and funny, listening to my every word and chuckling at all my terrible jokes. The complete, total opposite of Alec. Maybe once the fake dating arrangement with Alec was over, I should consider an actual date with Mike. He seemed to be kind, hard-working, and honest. Plus, he genuinely wanted to get to know me because of who I was, not because of who my brother was. And more importantly, he was someone who had never hurt me in the past.

In short, someone who was *not* Alec Mackenzie.

Stop thinking about him.

"How long have you been working as a mechanic?"

"Since I was sixteen. Never liked school. Decided early on that I wanted to do something with my hands. I started working at my uncle's garage, then saved enough money to start my own business two years ago."

"So it's your own garage." I was impressed. "How's it going so far?"

"Been quiet since the end of the year. But things are picking up now."

"I feel like I should apologize. My car repair fees probably didn't help much with your cash flow."

"Don't worry about it." Mike waved a dismissive hand. "It's not a big deal."

"It's a *huge* deal. Thanks for not charging me an arm and a leg. A lot of other people would probably have taken advantage of it and invoiced me for the full quote. You're honest, and I appreciate that."

Discomfort flickered over his face. "Yeah, but seriously, you don't have to thank me."

"Of course I do."

"Really, you don't." He gave me an awkward grin. "You're right, I would have charged you the full quote if it weren't . . ." He trailed off, as if realizing that he'd said something he shouldn't have.

I raised my eyebrows. "If it weren't . . . ?"

He was shaking his head, seemingly regretting having said anything in the first place. "Never mind. You sure you don't want to try their red velvet muffins? It's del—"

"Mike." Something fishy was going on. "You need to finish what you were talking about. Or I might be inclined to do something to embarrass you in public, and it'll be *so* humiliating, you'll be the talk of Port Benedict for the next ten years. Trust me, you don't want that."

I was bluffing, but my tone and the steely glint in my eyes must have tricked him into believing me, because his eyes widened in fear.

"Fine. Alec subsidized your repair fees," he blurted out.

I frowned. "Subsidized?" My brain was slow to register his words. "What do you mean?"

He looked at me like I'd just spoken in tongues. "You know, when someone else pa—"

"I know what the word meant." I was getting impatient. "Are you telling me he *paid* a portion of the repairs? For my car?"

"Uh, yeah, he did." Mike's worried eyes darted back and forth to the door, as if Alec might appear any minute and slug him on the head for spilling the secret. "The original invoice was for five thousand. He paid two, so we only charged you three. Look, I wasn't supposed to tell you, so you didn't hear this from me, okay?"

Alec did WHAT?

"You need to say something." Mike peered at me, looking wary. "Are you okay?"

I was most definitely *not* okay. Eyes popping, jaw agape, I held my cup suspended in midair, as if I'd just witnessed Mike magically levitating and evaporating into nothingness. Meanwhile, my brain was cheerfully reminding me to add this to the list of Alec's Supremely Thoughtful Gestures.

Which, at the rate he was going, would probably fill up an entire notebook in no time.

"You're kidding, right? Why would he pay for almost half of *my* car repair fees?"

"You'll have to ask him. He called the garage the day before I delivered your car and asked how much it would be." Mike's eyes turned curious. "That's very generous of him. I've known Alec for a while, and he's never done anything like that before. You two must be close."

"He's my brother's best friend." I swallowed the lump in my throat. "He's just looking out for me because my brother asked him to."

Are you sure, Ellie?

A confusing concoction of emotions churned around in my head. Was that really why Alec did it? To keep a promise he'd made Eric to keep an eye on me?

Because no matter how good of a friend he was with Eric, everything that he'd done so far was above and beyond "keeping an eye on me."

Hope bloomed in my chest. Maybe because he was . . . starting to care for me?

But a small part of my brain nagged at me, reminding me that this was all too similar to what my mother had done: paying someone behind my back. Sure, their motivations for doing so might be completely different, but it still hit just a little bit too close to home.

Shame, guilt, and a tiny bit of disappointment clouded my brain. My family had been overprotecting me since I was young, and whatever Alec's reasons for doing this were, I didn't want—or need—him to treat me the same way. I wanted him to see me as someone who was perfectly capable of looking after herself. Someone independent, and capable of making her own decisions.

As someone else other than his best friend's younger sister.

I took a deep breath. *You're being ungrateful, Ellie.* He knew that I was on a tight budget and had obviously just been trying to help. My throat started to clog up. I should be thanking him and paying him back. Every single cent.

Because otherwise, I'll know that I have truly failed to come into my own.

CHAPTER 16

Childhood Crushes Do Matter, Damn It

When I got home that afternoon, Alec was lounging on the sofa, staring at the TV. He was wearing the same pair of shorts from this morning, although the glasses were gone, and the T-shirt was different. His hair was damp, as if he'd just stepped out of the shower.

"Judging from your clothes, I'm guessing you haven't left the house the whole day."

He made a noncommittal sound, not taking his eyes off the TV.

"What are you watching?" I adopted a cheerful tone, then glanced at the screen and made a mock gasping sound. "*The Bachelorette*? I thought you hated reality TV shows. See how good of a fake girlfriend I am? I remembered that useless trivia about you."

Alec sighed, my quips clearly testing his patience. "Well done."

I sat down next to him, pointedly ignoring his sulkiness. "Having a lazy day off today? Thought you'd be at the gym, or hiking, or canoeing, or whatever it is you do on the weekends. Your girlfriend's busy again?"

"She's not my girlfriend."

"Sorry. Your *potential* girlfriend."

His jaw ticked. "She was working. Not that it's any of your business."

I ignored the small thrill I felt at realizing that he wasn't spending time with the woman he was interested in. "Are we back to being frenemies? I thought we'd gone past that."

He finally glanced up at me. "How was your coffee date?"

I gave him a teasing grin. "Jealous, are we?"

He gave a low scoff. "In your dreams."

"Relax, sweetheart. My heart belongs to you, at least until our fake courtship is over."

"I'm not jealous. I'm upset, because you don't seem to care that your date with Mike could jeopardize the deal with Jacqui. Did you ever stop to think about that?"

"Nobody saw us," I said. "Even if they did, we didn't do anything. He's just a friend. We went to a café, I drank some tea, we had a chat. I didn't make out with him in public."

Annoyance flashed in his eyes, and the jaw tics became more pronounced. "I'm respectfully asking you to refrain from making out with him in public until our agreement is over. After that, you're free to see and do anything with anyone."

An unexpected flurry of frustration swirled inside my head. He didn't care who I'd be seeing once this fake relationship was over? That annoyed me more than I thought it would.

"Actually, I'm seeing him again next week. I could use more friendly faces in this city, since the company I'm presently in is so insufferable."

This time, a vein popped in his neck. "Is that so?"

Mike's words from earlier came back, shaming me and reminding me again that after everything Alec had done for me, I shouldn't be behaving this way.

"Listen, I don't want to fight. I got you something." I placed the brown paper box I'd been holding on the sofa. "I've been wanting to check out the place, and their pastries are highly recommended by Kim and Jenna. I was going to bake you some brookies, but I got sidetracked and didn't have enough time." I pointed at the box. "Open it."

His gaze was suspicious. "Are they poisonous?"

"I won't lie, the thought did cross my mind."

"You do realize that if you tried to poison me, Rob knows you live here, so you'll end up becoming the first and prime suspect."

"Naomi's going to help me get rid of your body. No one's going to suspect anything."

He rolled his eyes. "Pretty sure that's not how it works."

"Just open the damn box already, will you? Fine, I'll do it." I lifted the lid with a flourish, revealing a dozen mini éclairs inside. "It's from the French pâtisserie inside the Plaza. Wasn't too sure what your preferences are, so half is chocolate, because you can't go wrong with chocolate, and the other half is mocha, seeing how you inhale coffee every morning. I don't know how to make these myself, so I thought these would be a nice treat for you."

His eyes narrowed. "What's this for?"

I took a deep breath. "If I tell you, promise you won't be angry at Mike."

"Really? We're *still* talking about Mike?"

"He told me you paid for some of my car repair fees."

Alec pursed his lips. "Did he, now? First date, and you're already sharing your innermost secrets with each other?"

Deciding to ignore the snarky comment, I reached into my bag and took out the check I'd written for two thousand dollars. "This is yours. I appreciate your help, but I'm paying you back. Did I tell you, by the way, how I got hired at my last job?"

Confusion crossed his face at my abrupt change of subject. "No."

"My mother secretly paid them. To hire me." I chewed on my lower lip, trying to keep my bubbling anger in check. "And then to fire me, too."

The confused look slowly cleared, replaced by understanding. "I didn't know."

"Neither did I, until a few weeks ago. I know you were just trying to help, and I really, truly, appreciate you so much. That," I pointed at the box of éclairs, "is me saying thank you. But in the future, please don't go around paying people behind my back without letting me know about it."

"I won't. I promise." His face turned sheepish. "I'm sorry. I was only trying to help because you've been having a rough time with your finances. Eric—"

"Would have done the same for your sisters, I know."

Alec nodded, his expression slowly softening. "Why don't you hold on to this for now? Pay me back once you've made some money." He handed me the check. "I'll keep the éclairs."

"Please take the check. And the éclairs. You've done more than enough."

"Actually, you know what?" A wide grin split his face, showcasing his dimple, and he let out an evil chuckle. "I should probably charge the repair costs to Eric, plus interest. God knows he owes me from all those times I lied to your parents, covering for him."

I couldn't respond, because the grin had transformed his surliness into sunshine, inviting me to come closer and bask in his warmth. Maybe he'd done me the favor because of Eric, but right now, I didn't really care. I just wanted to stay in this spot and be on the receiving end of his smile and kindness.

Before it was time to say goodbye.

I forced myself to snap back into the present and pushed the check back at him. "I'm sure he'll appreciate that. But it's my car, so I'll pay for it."

Alec sighed, then nodded. "Okay. Thanks again for the éclairs." He suddenly perked up. "Which reminds me. I've got something for you, too. Wait here." He leapt up the stairs to his room and came back a few minutes later with a blue paper bag.

It was my turn to be suspicious. "What's that?"

"Your present. Happy birthday." He handed it to me.

My eyes widened. "You . . . remembered?"

"Yeah." Red tinted his cheeks as he gestured for me to open the bag. "I didn't know what to get you. I hope you like it."

My jaw went slack when I pulled out a plaid pajama set.

In mint green.

My favorite color.

Here's the thing: most—90 percent, maybe—of my wardrobe consisted of striped and plaid designs. On any given day, I'd be wearing either a striped tee, or a plaid shirt, or a dress in any of those motifs. I'd been known to own other types of clothing, but if one took a sweeping look at my closet, the emerging pattern would be clear as day.

Which meant Alec had been paying attention to what I'd been wearing.

I swallowed to get past the thick lump of emotions lodged in my throat. "You shouldn't have," I whispered.

"Too late, I already did. You can retire those holey Hello Kitty pajamas." His cheeks now resembled a ripe tomato. "Anyway, when I asked about your plans this morning, I thought we could go for lunch to celebrate your birthday. There's an awesome Italian restaurant that makes the best wood-fired smoked salmon pizza in the entire city. The entire country, even. You haven't lived until you've had one of those."

Oh.

"Then fucking Mike Chang had to go and ruin my plans."

OHHHHH.

That's why he was upset this morning.

He quickly clarified, "I was *really* looking forward to that pizza."

I reached out and gave him a hug. "I love this, Alec. Thank you."

His fresh soap smell surrounded me, and I greedily inhaled it, not even stopping myself from burying my nose in his neck, or caring if he could hear the brass band booming behind my rib cage. My heart was full, overflowing with awe and gratitude. This man not only remembered my birthday, but gave me an extremely thoughtful gift (in my favorite color), and had even planned a birthday lunch (of my favorite food, too) for me. I could feel my self-control slowly slipping, falling more and more under his spell, as his hand gently, absentmindedly, rubbed my shoulders.

Brain to Ellie, a small voice addressed me. *Remember the Stay on Track Plan?*

Yes. Yes, I do. I reluctantly pulled away, not meeting his eyes. He got up and padded toward the kitchen, beckoning me to follow him.

"I hope you have no plans tonight. Because what you'll be doing," he announced with a wink, "is celebrating your birthday with me."

"Whatever happened to limiting our social interaction?"

"It's your birthday. We'll make an exception." He uncovered a dish on the kitchen counter, revealing mouthwatering fried noodles, with sliced chicken, eggs, prawns, and veggies. "I made some mie goreng earlier, because we have to have noodles on our birthdays, right?"

I was the human equivalent of a goldfish. Eyes bigger than five-cent coins, mouth hanging open, at a loss for words.

"I also ordered some food from Java Spice." He pulled out a few takeaway containers from a brown delivery bag. "We've got some sate ayam, oxtail soup, and gado-gado with extra peanut sauce. When Mr. Tanujaya heard that it was your birthday, he even threw in some pandan cakes for free."

I closed my mouth and opened it again to say something.

Only my brain wasn't capable enough of forming a lucid, thoughtful sentence. Instead, what came out was, "What about that pizza you really wanted?"

He shrugged. "That can wait. I've also got some wine. Plus, I remembered how your mom used to freak out whenever there was a birthday. So," he opened the freezer with a flourish, "I present to you, a low-carb ice-cream cake. You can probably make your own, but birthday girls shouldn't be making their own cakes."

I croaked out, "You did all this for me?"

"Well, it's not my birthday."

Peering at him, I touched his forehead with the back of my hand. "You don't feel feverish. Are you okay? You're not dying or anything, right?"

"I'm perfectly fine. This is *my* thank-you for being such a good sport and for charming Jacqui last weekend." A satisfied grin lit up his face as he closed the freezer. "How did I do? Your mother would be proud of me for choosing the low-carb cake."

"She'd be so proud, she'd probably adopt you into the family in a heartbeat."

Alec snorted. "She wouldn't."

"You're right, she wouldn't." We both laughed at that, although a twinge of sadness filled me at the realization: that it would take a divine miracle for my mother to like and accept Alec and his family in this lifetime. "By the way, just so you know, I don't have to totally cut off cakes and cookies and other sugary stuff."

"You don't?"

"Yep. I'm not limited in what I can or can't have, as long as I take the correct amount of insulin to balance the carb intake. Although of course, healthier options are always better."

Alec gave me a puzzled look. "Then how come your mother used to go berserk whenever you got invited to a birthday party?"

"Because she was being a control freak, even though she knew that if my level was high, I can give myself a correction dose to bring it down to an acceptable range."

"Right. Looks like I still have a lot to learn."

Ignoring the way that made me warm all over, I gave him another hug. "This is so thoughtful of you. You're not so bad, Sir Grouchiness."

His arms wrapped tightly around me. "I know. I'm the best."

"Your potential girlfriend doesn't mind that you're hanging out with me tonight?"

"No." This time, he was the first to pull away.

Immediately missing his closeness, I cleared my throat. "So, she knows about us? About our agreement, I mean."

"She does." He started opening the takeaway containers.

"And she's okay with her boyfriend pretending to date another woman?"

"I'm not her boyfriend yet. And yeah, she's totally fine with it."

"Sounds like a keeper." I squashed the jealousy nibbling at the edges of my heart and helped him plate the food. "When are you going to introduce us?"

"One day. You two have a lot of things in common. I think you're going to like her."

Don't be so sure about that. "I'm sure I will."

Right then, my pump beeped urgently, needing my attention. "The insulin in my pump is running low. Give me a few minutes while I change my pump site."

Alec stopped plating the gado-gado. "Is it okay if I . . . observe how to?"

I gaped at him. "Why?"

"So I can learn." He looked dead serious. "Just in case you needed help."

My brain wasn't fast enough to come up with an answer, so I

just stood there, staring at him. Nobody else, not even my brother and Naomi, had ever said that to me, even though they'd seen me do it a lot of times. If something were to happen and I needed someone in my family to change my pump site, I'd probably be dead before they figured it out, because none of them had done it before.

And this man . . . wanted to *learn how*?

"Let me go grab my stuff."

When I got back to the kitchen, he'd already finished plating the food and was wiping the counter with disinfectant wipes, preparing the space for me and all my supplies, then went around to stand next to me.

"Okay. First, I need to suspend the insulin delivery on the pump." I leaned toward him so he could have a look. "Then I need to remove the old line. It's currently at my back." I felt around my lower back and unplugged the pump, then tried to pull out the steel needle that was inside my body.

"Here, let me."

He moved closer, his breath warm on my neck. One of his hands pressed at my spine, spreading heat as he held me steady, while his other hand gently peeled off the adhesive around the thin metal needle, then pulled it out. He did the same with the connecting piece, then wordlessly used alcohol wipes to clean my skin.

Damn. This felt intimate on a whole 'nother level. My back felt like it was on fire from his touch, and my cheeks were burning, and I had to concentrate on what to do next, even though I'd done this so often I could probably complete the process with my eyes closed.

"Now we're going to fill a new cartridge with insulin." I reached for a sterile syringe and showed him how to use it to draw insulin from the vial. "Make sure you get rid of any air bubbles in the syringe, because that could affect the insulin that gets delivered into my body. Then we fill the cartridge, and once that's done, we load it onto the pump."

Alec didn't say anything, just intently watched what I was doing. He looked so serious, I was half expecting him to whip out a notebook to jot everything down or record the entire thing on his phone.

"Now I'm inserting the new site." I lifted my top a little, pinched a bit of skin on my stomach, then stuck the new steel needle in, ignoring his wince. "Finally, I'm resuming the insulin delivery. And we're done. Did you remember all that?"

"Most of it. I might have to see it a few more times before I can remember everything. How often do you have to do that?"

"Every two to three days. My CGM, every ten days."

He nodded, looking like he was processing all the information as I cleaned up and safely disposed of the used needle and syringe.

"By the way," he tilted his head at me, "what on Earth is a brookie?"

"You don't know what a brookie is?" We each pulled out a kitchen stool and sat down. "You've never had one?"

He shrugged. "Can't say that I have."

"It's a mash-up of brownies and cookies. And you're in luck, because there's a recipe for peanut butter cheesecake brookies that I've been wanting to try. I could use another taste tester."

"Sign me up."

"Anyway, how are things with GPG?"

"Jacqui is looking over the final numbers. We should be signing the deal soon."

"That's great. I guess she's convinced we're a real couple, then."

He grinned. "Yeah. Those lovey-dovey eyes you've been giving me paid off."

But as he said that, his eyes sparkled, and for the first time I realized what Kim and Jenna had been talking about: that *he* was also making lovey-dovey eyes at me.

That night, after slipping under my comfortable blanket, I finally did what I should've done weeks ago: I Googled the hell out of him.

His entire career history was on LinkedIn. He'd started Mackenzie Constructions seven years ago, and more cyberstalking unearthed articles about how his company had won awards three years in a row for building environmentally sustainable homes. They were also a major supporter during a fundraising drive for a local children's hospital. I found pictures of him dressed as the Easter Bunny, smiling with his arm around a bunch of cute little kids, and my heart melted into a puddle on the floor.

I saved the articles—for research, obviously, so if someone quizzed me on my fake boyfriend's company, I could recite the answer like it was implanted on a chip in my brain—when my phone pinged several times in a row, notifying me of a social media tag.

Alec had posted pictures from Jacqui's party and the morning brunch with Phil on Facebook. There were also photos from a few hours ago, of me blowing the candles on the ice-cream cake, and a selfie of us making funny faces at the camera. Ninety-two people had liked the selfie, including one Jacqueline Goodwin and one Robbie Carmichael (who'd left heart-eyes and fire emojis in the comment). Neither Eric, Naomi, nor his sisters had liked it or left any comments, so Alec must have remembered to exclude our families in the post.

A tiny part of me was slightly disappointed because he'd turned my birthday dinner into a social media opportunity, no doubt in the name of further convincing Jacqui. But at least it reminded me that I should curb my growing feelings.

Because this. Was. Not. Real.

Still, that didn't stop me from liking all his pictures and downloading a few good ones. If anyone asked, I'd be able to show a picture of me and my fake boyfriend.

Oh, who am I kidding? He was signing his deal soon, and the work on the store was nearly completed. In a few weeks, these photos would be my only memories of him.

Even though it was late, I started scrolling through his older posts. One photo became two, then five, and then I moved on to his other social media accounts, and went down the dark, deep rabbit hole of scrolling through all his pictures. There were lots of him with his mother and younger sisters, from when they visited him in Port Benedict. Shots of him and Rob with their group of friends. There were even a few funny throwback photos with Eric in them, and I chuckled at how young and innocent they looked. An hour later, I'd gone back and liked his very first post from many, many years ago. My excuse was that it would show Jacqui—or anyone else who bothered to check—that we really did have a genuine relationship from way back when.

Yep, I took everything in life seriously, including my fake girlfriend role.

Speaking of girlfriends . . . I scrolled back up to his latest posts. Maybe I could find this so-called potential girlfriend that he'd been so secretive about. There were several recent pictures of him at a group lunch with Rob and a few other people. Alec sat next to a cute, petite brunette, and could be seen chatting and laughing with her in the background in a few other photos, looking very cozy together. She was tagged in one of the pictures, so I clicked on her profile and saw that Alec had liked every single one of her posts from two months ago.

This had to be her. The potential girlfriend he was taking things slow with.

Or she could be anyone, my brain argued. *She could just be a very good friend.*

I huffed out a frustrated breath, pushing thoughts of him *and her* out of my mind. Whatever, not my business, because I shouldn't be thinking about and obsessing over Alec.

Finally turning off the lights, I snuggled deeper under my blanket and tossed my phone on the bedside table when it pinged, alerting me to a WhatsApp message. It was past one in the morning, so I ignored it, only for it to ping again.

> Did you just do a deep dive into my Insta and Facebook accounts? 😵
> You did. All the way to the first photo I've ever posted.

Sighing, I typed back a reply.

> It's one in the morning, Alec.
> I'm sleeping.

The two blue check marks immediately appeared, followed by his response.

> You just spent the last hour liking all my photos.
> Are you okay?

> Stop exaggerating. I only liked a few.

> A FEW? 😂 😂 😂
> Sending cold hard evidence now.

I snorted when his photos popped up—screenshots of rows and rows of notifications that I'd liked photos after photos, all within seconds of each other.

Busted.

> Okay fine, more than a few. Happy?! 😫
>
> But it was an hour well spent.

I'd forgotten about your rockstar wannabe period. That pic of u and Eric with the matching bandannas was sooooo cute! 😈

Not me. Must've mistaken me with someone else 😑

My cheeks were hurting because I was grinning from ear to ear.

> Thanks again for today though.
>
> One of the best bday dinners I've ever had.

Not THE best?
Okay, challenge accepted.

> What challenge?
>
> I never challenged you to anything.
>
> Are you hallucinating?

Making your next birthday THE best you'll ever have, what else?

My heart stumbled. Was he implying that he'd be around for my next birthday?
As friends, Ellie. As friends. Remember the Stay on Track Plan?

> Yours is in October, right?

Very impressed you remembered. 👍

Of course I did. I remembered everything about him.

> I memorized everything.
>
> All the mostly useless facts about my fake boyfriend.

Although there are still things I don't know about you.

Like what?

Your favorite book,
favorite movie,
What your last meal would be,
And I still don't know who your childhood crush was..

There was a long pause before his reply popped up.

Maybe I'll tell you that last one, if you tell me yours too.

I hesitated, then typed my reply.

You know who mine was.

The blue check marks appeared, followed by the longest, the most excruciating silence.

But that's ages ago and doesn't matter anymore!
So we can forget about that, right? 😊
Also, Zac Efron.
Not ashamed to say I can recite every line from
high school musical 1 2 and 3 . . .

I released a relieved breath when he started typing back.

Good choice 💯
Even I think he's gorgeous.

Your turn now

Childhood crushes don't matter anymore.

Didn't you say that?

That only applies to MY answer.

Wait let me guess. Angelina Jolie?

You seem like the type that would go for Jolie.

Wrong.

J-Lo? Jen Aniston?

Sandra Bullock! Cameron Diaz?

Nope.

okay, now I REALLY HAVE TO KNOW!! ••

Why are we still talking about this? 🐌

Because u said you'd tell me if I told u mine!

I'm going to sleep now

Your messages will remain unread and unanswered.

💀 💀 💀

No! You're not playing fair 😾 😾

Don't make me come and kick down your door.

You've got 2 mins!

Alec I'm warning u!!

The two blue check marks appeared, but there was a long silence until, finally, his reply popped on my screen.

And nearly sent me into cardiac arrest.

You.

My childhood crush was you.

CHAPTER 17

Bubble Tea Makes Everything Better

If birthdays were deemed an unworthy celebration in my family, Lunar New Years were the complete opposite. Traditionally, it was the perfect time to catch up with relatives, to eat an obscene amount of food, and for kids to collect piles of angpaos. Everyone would be encouraged to wear new clothes, preferably in red, famously believed to scare away bad spirits and represent success and good fortune. It was one of my favorite celebrations of the year, because I got to see out-of-town or overseas cousins that I wouldn't normally see otherwise.

When my Engkong and Emak were still alive, and whenever they came for a visit to the States, they used to tell me stories about how their families couldn't celebrate their heritage back home in Jakarta. The early Indonesian government had prohibited their citizens of Chinese descent from observing traditional Chinese customs and strongly encouraged them to shed much of their Chinese identity. As a result, people like my parents and Alec's mother had grown up with Indonesian as their mother tongue and had adopted Indonesian-sounding names. My father's surname, originally Pang in Cantonese, was altered to the more acceptable Pangestu. The owner of Java Spice, Mr. Tanujaya, would formerly be a Tan. Kim's family name, Halim, would be an Indonesianized version of Lim.

But even though the discriminatory laws had been revoked after Indonesia's fourth president, my grandparents said it was still felt in many areas, causing many Chinese Indonesians to flee overseas. For some people, the minute they settled in a new country, they reverted to their Chinese surnames and began to observe the traditional customs again, keen to rediscover their ethnic traditions. Like my parents. Not only that, but all our celebrations were also tinged with touches of Indonesia, so to me, Lunar New Year represented a delightful fusion of the two cultures that were the essence of my family.

And, of course, my parents, being my parents, had taken it a step further: using the occasion as the perfect time for them to network and show off.

Every year, without fail, they would invite their wealthy friends and business partners over. The preparation for the day would take at least a week, with my mother meticulously planning and executing everything with military precision. She'd have long, strategically planned lists of gifts and hampers to be sent to said friends and business partners. Our house would be cleaned from top to bottom; every corner wiped and dusted, every nook and cranny swept and scrubbed, any unnecessary clutter ruthlessly discarded. Eric and I had had to show her that our rooms were spotless, and it had probably been one of the more stressful times of my life, waiting for her to finish her thorough inspection.

Then there was the food. She always made sure we served an elaborate, lavish banquet that could put even the poshest Michelin star restaurant to shame. Eight different whole fish dishes; platters of oysters, crabs, and lobsters; gourmet spring rolls; all kinds of noodles and dumplings; egg tarts and sesame balls; and plates of yee sang—the good luck salad. We'd also have some Indonesian-style desserts: kue keranjang, lapis legit, and bakpia, along with piles of oranges, pears, longans, and lychees. Everything was supposed to represent wealth and prosperity, but more importantly, it was designed to impress their important guests.

Once everyone was fed, it was time to trot out the lion dance troupe. I didn't know how our neighbors tolerated the noise, year after year. Because for the next twenty minutes, the house would be filled with loud, thunderous beats of drums, cymbals, and erupting firecrackers.

It was basically similar to our annual New Year's Eve bash, only on steroids.

But even though my parents had placed a slightly twisted importance on the tradition, I'd always associated Lunar New Year with joy, and a fun day of celebration with family and friends. So when Jenna sent digital flyers about the annual parade and festival happening in Chinatown to our WhatsApp group chat, we immediately made plans to check it out.

It was a gloomy Sunday, but not even the imposing gray clouds looming above could stop the hundreds of people crowding Port Benedict Chinatown. It stretched between three streets in the middle of the city center, about fifteen minutes' walk from the Plaza, marked at the entrance with a magnificent red gateway and two stone lions on each side. Rows of Asian restaurants, grocery stores, hairdressers, and cute boutiques lined the streets, with colorful signs in Mandarin, Japanese, or Vietnamese.

Right then, the street fair was in full swing. Bright red-and-yellow lanterns hung above, strings of firecrackers were draped across shop entrances, and the various stalls selling food, drinks, and decorations were all packed with customers. All the wonderful festivities should have brought back some fond memories of home, but somehow, this year, I couldn't get into the right frame of mind to enjoy the celebration.

Kim and Jenna were walking ahead of me, and I could hear Jenna telling Kim about the various Lunar New Year festivals they had in Australia, in her hometown of Melbourne.

"There'd be one every weekend in different suburbs," she was saying. "But the biggest one is in Melbourne Chinatown, where they'd have the dragon dance parade. The whole of February would be chock-full of these festivals and eating a shitload of food." She sighed. "I miss it. My mother wanted me to come home this year, because we had relatives visiting from Singapore and Malaysia, but work has been super busy."

"That sounds awesome," Kim said. "I wish I'd grown up with those traditions. My grandparents don't really celebrate them anymore. We didn't even do red packets when I was growing up. Hey, maybe we should make this our new annual tradition!"

They continued chatting, and I heard Kim telling Jenna about an artisan brand of hand-dyed alpaca yarn she'd found online. I zoned out after a while, as my mind drifted back to Alec's last message. The revelation was too much for my brain to comprehend. And I had *so* many questions. Why hadn't he said those words when I confessed my crush to him all those years ago? Why was he so cold and aloof when we were younger? I'd been obsessing, analyzing, and re-analyzing his five short, devastating words, alternating between disbelief, thrill, anger, and finally defeat, because after all these years, he'd obviously gotten over his crush, since he was now interested in someone else, wasn't he?

"Whoa." Jenna gasped loudly, stopping in her tracks, causing me to bump into her. "Ellie, is that Chris Pratt?"

I blinked. "Huh?"

She pointed to a man standing at one of the stalls on my right. "There. Wait, it's Chris Pine." She squinted her eyes, presumably to get a better look at whoever she was looking at. "No, hang on, it's the first Captain America himself."

"What?" I craned my neck, as Kim let out a snicker. Realizing that I'd fallen for their joke, I rolled my eyes. "Ha-ha, hilarious, you guys."

"You've been off in la-la land for the past ten minutes." Jenna grinned, as we continued walking. "I had to get your attention somehow."

We stopped at a bubble tea stall, and I waited to answer as we ordered our drinks. "Sorry. I had a late night," I said. "Anyway, what were you saying about the artisan yarn, Kim?"

"I'm stocking them, they're coming next week. But never mind that, how are things with Signor Building Expert?"

"Nowhere. Confusing. He's interested in someone else, remember?"

The bubble tea lady called out our number, then handed us Kim's brown sugar milk tea, Jenna's lychee oolong tea, and my oat milk tea.

"He's not," Kim insisted. "I'm even willing to bet my entire shop inventory, including my brand-new expensive artisan yarn. That's how confident I am."

"You're wrong. I saw pictures of them looking very friendly together."

"Show me."

I pulled out my phone, thumbed open his account, and showed them photos of Alec and the cute brunette.

"That's not her," Kim immediately said.

"How do you know? He liked all her most recent posts."

"I liked all your posts," Kim pointed out. "Doesn't mean I'm interested in you. He could just be a very supportive friend, like me."

Jenna was scrolling through the photos. "They're mostly group pictures, and she's not overly touchy-feely with him. I don't think there's anything between them."

"Then why did he tell me he liked someone else? I don't understand."

"I told you already," Jenna replied. "Self-preservation."

I decided I needed to tell them both because I had spent way too much time overanalyzing my own thoughts. "Something happened."

Kim's eyes widened. "Between you and Signor Hottie?"

Jenna looked excited. "Something of the sexy, moaning, groaning kind?"

Sipping my tea absentmindedly, I told them everything, including his last text messages. Jenna was smiling from ear to ear when I finished, while Kim was watching me with a shrewd look on her face.

"You know what that means, don't you?" She waved her cup of milk tea at me. "Jenna and I were right. He likes you."

Jenna nodded. "Otherwise he wouldn't be going out of his way to do all those things for you. He got you cute pajamas in your favorite color, for goodness' sake! It might seem simple, but trust me, it speaks volumes. It shows that he's paying attention. I've never had anyone I've dated in the past buy me cute pajamas or made me birthday noodles."

"You need to find better exes," Kim commented. "But I agree."

"My point is," Jenna continued, "I understand that you might be reluctant to trust him and admit to yourself that you like him, because it's scary. You're scared that he might hurt you again. But he's doing all the right things now. So maybe he's not the same person that had hurt you in the past. Maybe he's changed."

Her next words were drowned by the booming, rhythmic drumbeats, and the cymbals and gongs that filled the air, signaling the start of the dragon dance performance. Ten costumed dancers, each holding poles attached to the long body of a giant, fierce-looking red-and-gold dragon puppet, began to move in time with the beats; swaying and swishing the poles in a wavelike motion, bringing the puppet to life. The crowd took videos as the dancers holding the heads began jumping over the dragon's middle section, followed by the rest of the performers, before turning around in a spiraled formation, creating a mesmerizing visual spectacle.

But I wasn't paying attention to the dragon dance, or the lion dancers that appeared after.

I was thinking about what Jenna had said.

Because she was right.

The younger Alec from a decade ago probably wouldn't even remember when my birthday was, or what my favorite color was. He wouldn't even know what low-GI foods or insulin pumps were, let alone want to learn about how they work. That Alec had run for the hills at the first sign of trouble.

But the older version of him had more than proven he had changed. That he wasn't the same person who had hurt and abandoned me all those years ago. He did thoughtful things to look after me, wonderful things that made me realize that he accepted and appreciated me for who I was, diabetes and all. He made a conscious effort to get to know the real me, to be involved in my world, even though a lot of other people didn't care to, or even want to. And if I ever needed proof that he was now a different, a better person, all I needed to do was look at the ever-expanding list of Alec's Supremely Thoughtful Gestures.

Maybe Jenna was right. That it was okay for me to finally admit that I like him.

That I *more than* like him.

My stomach sank as realization hit me: I was falling for him again, in a major way. It was inevitable, hurtling toward me at a breakneck speed.

And no matter how many lists or plans I made, there was nothing I could do to stop it.

CHAPTER 18

Always Heed Your Internal Alarms

GPG get-together tonight with Jacqui, 7pm. U free?

I'll pick u up at 6.

My stomach did a somersault when I read the message.

"Everything okay?"

I looked up at Mike. We were at Java Spice for lunch, and I'd been scrolling through my emails as he chatted with Mr. Tanujaya when Alec's message popped up.

"All good." I tossed my phone back in my bag without replying to the message. I needed time to think it through, maybe do a pros and cons list before replying. The right thing to do was to say yes, but I wasn't ready for the awkwardness that would inevitably set in. I hadn't seen him for a few days, because he'd been leaving the house earlier and coming back later than usual, presumably to avoid me after the weekend's WhatsApp conversation.

"Hey, I wanted to ask you last week, but where are you from?"

"Didn't I tell you? I moved out here from the East Coast."

"No, what I meant was, where's your family from?" Mike pointed at himself. "Me, for example, my father was born in the States, but his grandparents migrated from Taiwan back in the 1800s. Is your family Chinese? Korean? Japanese?"

"I was also born here in the States, but my parents are Chinese Indonesian. They migrated from Indonesia when they were younger."

"Ah. That's why you wanted to meet here for lunch." He nodded. "You ever visited your families overseas?"

"Several times. Would love to go back someday."

Our food came—grilled chicken and rice for him, and mie goreng for me. I ~~might have~~ definitely did not order that dish because it reminded me of what Alec had made for my birthday.

"I haven't been to Indonesia, but I heard it's beautiful. Bali's on my bucket list. Maybe we can do a trip together, see the country, visit your extended family."

I raised my eyebrows as an alarm quietly rang at the back of my brain. One coffee meet-up and one lunch, and he was already inviting himself to go on an overseas trip to visit my family? "Uh, maybe we can talk about it later."

"Of course." He gave me a warm smile. "I think you're really cool. I'm so glad we met."

"Thanks." I stopped myself from singing him the same praise.

Mike dumped a spoonful of chili sauce on his chicken, his smile growing bigger. "You know, I'm a strong believer that we don't meet people by accident. Our paths crossed for a higher reason. Both my brothers got married in their midtwenties, and they were already expecting their second child at my age. Clearly I have to make up for lost time, don't I?"

I blinked at him once, then twice. The alarm became louder, and suddenly it seemed like spending two hours in the car with

Alec and faking the role of his girlfriend in front of Jacqui wasn't such a terrible idea.

Did I hear him right? Was he implying that our paths crossed because we were meant to be together? After two (non) dates?

First George, now him. What the hell was wrong with these men?

I should at least give him the benefit of the doubt. Maybe I was getting ahead of myself and unnecessarily jumping to incorrect conclusions.

I reached for my pump to bolus for my food, only to remember that my insulin reservoir was running low. I was rushing this morning and didn't have time to change my pump site before leaving, so I'd have to revert to using an insulin pen for now.

"Sounds like you're close with your siblings." I took out the small pouch that always lived in my bag, filled with my insulin pen, my glucose meter, and a bunch of test strips. I chose a new sterile needle, attached it to the insulin pen and primed it, then checked my levels on my CGM app. "Does your family live in Port Benedict too?"

"*Whoa.*" Mike recoiled, his eyes going wide. "What are you doing? What's that?"

I'd forgotten he'd never seen me do this. The last time we went for coffee, he didn't even notice me bolusing with the pump. "I should've explained." I gave him an apologetic smile. "It's an insulin pen. I have type 1 diabetes. I need to take insulin before any meals, so my blood sugar doesn't skyrocket. The insulin in my pump is running low, so the pen is my backup."

"*Diabetes?* You're what, twenty-three, twenty-four? How can you have diabetes already?" Mike stared at me, his mouth gaping open. "What, have you been eating too much sweet stuff your whole life?"

The alarm was now blaring louder than a police siren. I recapped the pen, preparing myself for a lengthy explanation. "It has nothing to do with eating sweet stuff. More to do with the fact that my pancreas isn't producing any insulin."

Mike raised one skeptical eyebrow. "That doesn't sound right. Are you sure about that?"

"One hundred percent positive." I gave him a sweet, syrupy smile. "Would you like a full medical explanation on how my pancreas stopped working?"

"No, thanks." He scrunched up his nose with distaste. "My grandpa is also diabetic, but he said it's probably because he practically lived on Coke and junk food when he was young. He's never had to do any injections though, so yours must be really bad."

If I had a dollar for every time I had to explain this to people. "That's because your grandpa is a type 2, and they don't always require insulin injections. Whereas someone with type 1, like me, is insulin-dependent for life. This," I pointed at my pen, "is a lifesaving device."

He rolled his eyes. "You're exaggerating."

This guy was stretching my patience. "I wish I was, but I'm not. Insulin is an essential hormone. Since my body can't produce any, if I don't have these injections, I couldn't survive."

Mike let out a disbelieving scoff. "Come on, that sounds so dramatic. So you can't eat sweet stuff, right? No big deal. You won't die from it or anything."

"Actually, if my blood sugar drops very low, I could lose consciousness and die. Or the opposite, if it stays too high for too long, I could die as well."

"Shit." He blew out a long breath. "Glad it isn't me. I think that's enough medical lecture for today. I'm gonna start eating before it gets cold."

I'd lost my appetite, along with my interest in this so-called lunch date. The only reason I still tolerated him was because I needed to have something to eat, otherwise my glucose level might dip. I uncapped the insulin pen again. "Go ahead. I'll just do this first."

Mike shuddered. "Can you do that somewhere else? I hate needles."

"I'm doing it under the table." I was gritting my teeth. "You won't see anything."

"But I still know you are." He was cringing, waving his hands as if shooing me away. "Seriously, I can't stand them. Go do it in the toilet or something."

What an asshole.

I strongly considered throwing the contents of the teapot in his face, but I didn't want to make a scene. Although his reaction didn't surprise me, because this wasn't the first time someone had had a strong reaction to my using an insulin pen. An older man once saw me doing it in a restaurant and told me that it was disgusting and inappropriate to do in public, and that I should go to the bathroom instead. Then he called the restaurant manager on me.

But I knew it wasn't worth my time and energy to pay attention to people like that elderly man or Mike. I could be frothing at the mouth trying to explain to them about my condition, but if they refused to open their mind and listen to my explanation, then there was nothing else I could do to change their minds.

And at the end of the day, their opinion didn't really matter to me.

Without saying another word, I did my injection on the spot, ignoring Mike's repulsed looks, then finished my lunch in record time.

Alec had been wrong: Mike Chang wasn't only after a good time.

But he was, most definitely, one of the most unpleasant men I'd ever met.

The minute lunch was over, I deleted Mike's number, turned my phone off, and buried myself with work.

After I changed my pump site, I called a friend of Jenna's who was looking for work. I only had the budget to hire one person right now, and she was so bubbly and nice, I decided to hire her at the end of our call. Then I ordered boxes, paper bags, and stickers with the new bakery name. I'd finally settled on Twisted Sweets, because it perfectly described the concept I was going for. I also signed up for every social media account in existence and posted teasers across all the platforms: photos of some freshly baked croissants and cinnamon scrolls; a buy one, get one free offer for the first opening week; and a short video on how to frost cupcakes.

I spent the afternoon testing low-carb donut recipes with my new oven, experimenting with different fillings. By the time the donuts were cooling on the rack, I'd added three flavors to my menu rotation: cinnamon sugar donut, blueberry cheesecake donut, and my personal favorite, the chocolate hazelnut donut. Before I knew it, it was almost six, and I was turning off the lights when a knock at the door startled me.

"Good. You're still here." Alec pushed the door open and strolled in. "I've been trying to reach you. You haven't replied to any of my messages."

"Oh, hey. I turned my phone off." I reached into my pocket and switched it back on. There were three new messages from him, the last one an hour ago, saying he was coming to pick me up. "I've been swamped with work. And obviously not dressed for a corporate shindig." I pointed at my T-shirt and old jeans, covered in flour and blueberry stains. "Just tell Jacqui I'm unwell. Give her my regards, will you?"

"We'll swing by the house so you can change. We just need to show up, chat with her, and shake some hands. It won't take too long. One hour, tops."

"The last time you said something similar, we ended up staying there for three hours, and you were intoxicated." I locked the door as The Kiss That Never Happened suddenly flashed back in clear, vivid images, and I mentally stomped on the memory with a fierceness that could have eradicated whole civilizations.

"That won't happen again. We're so close to signing the deal. This will be one of the last things you'll have to do. I promise."

After the horrible lunch with Mike, I wasn't in the mood to socialize and play fake loving couples for Jacqui. But he was right—we were almost at the finish line, and I couldn't jeopardize this for him.

"Fine. No more than one hour."

"Awesome." A big grin split his face, the dimple winking at me, and suddenly the thought of having to endure polite fake chats with Jacqui was worth it. He unlocked his car with a beep and opened the passenger door for me. "Might be easier if we leave your car. I can drop you off here tomorrow morning."

I paused. "Will I have to listen to your God-awful podcasts again?"

"I only play construction podcasts in the mornings. I listen to history podcasts at night. Halfway through the history of Byzantium right now."

My eyes widened.

"Did you know the Byzantines loved sweets and desserts more than anything, and they were the first to use saffron in their cooking? So fascinating."

"Hell no." I slammed the door shut, nearly dismembering his fingers. "I'm not getting in your car if I have to listen to history podcasts. No offense to history enthusiasts, but that was one of my worst subjects in school, so I'm steering clear of it for the rest of my life. Not even if you threatened to tor—" I stopped at his amused look. "Listen, I'm nothing if not generous, so I'm willing to compromise. No history podcast, but we can listen to one of your construction ones on the way there. And we're putting on my playlist on the way back."

"I was kidding." Alec chuckled. "You should see the horrified look on your face. I wish I had taken a picture."

I could still hear his amused chuckles even after he'd closed my door, sending warm fuzzy butterflies swarming through my stomach.

Leaving me to wonder how I'd survive the next few hours.

CHAPTER 19

Descending into Madness and Hell in 3 . . . 2 . . . 1

Halfway through the drive to Seattle, and my mind was blown.

"You know, these construction podcasts aren't so bad after all. Who would've thought?"

Alec was concentrating on the road, but he had a small smile on his lips. "Told you."

"What this guy is talking about can be applied across any industry." I paused to catch the end of the episode we'd been listening to. "I mean, of course I knew the importance of innovation, but what really resonated with me was when he said that business owners need to have a specific innovation plan and strategy in place. I'd never thought of that."

"We have one. Rob and I worked on it not too long ago."

"I'll have to prepare one for the bakery. I'm going to share this with Kim, too, for her yarn store. Is Rob coming tonight?"

Alec nodded. "He left before us, so he should be there by now."

"What's this get-together for, anyway?"

"Jacqui said it's an informal gathering after their quarterly board meeting today. She wanted to introduce us to her board of directors and the senior management team."

"Sounds like the acquisition is a done deal, then."

"It is. We're signing the agreement on Friday."

I tilted my head at him, curious. "Then you don't really need me to come tonight."

"She asked about you, and I thought it'd be good for her to see us together again."

Something inside me deflated a bit hearing that. Maybe I was expecting too much, but after everything that had happened, I was—foolishly—hoping that a part of him might be asking me to go to these things for Jacqui because he wanted to spend time with me. Clearly I couldn't be more wrong, and if I'd hoped he was asking me for anything else other than a show for Jacqui, then I was kidding myself.

"You've done it. You got what you've worked really hard for. Congratulations."

"Thanks. I couldn't have done it without you." He gave me ~~an adoring an affectionate~~ a warm smile.

"Just give me ten percent of your profit for the year."

His smile turned into a chuckle. "I'll see what I can do."

"By the way, I had lunch with Mike today."

"Did you?" The smile dimmed.

"It wasn't good." I told him what happened, and although his eyes were fixed on the road, his face twisted into an annoyed scowl.

"That's unacceptable. He was being extremely disrespectful to you." His tone was calm, but there was an undercurrent of anger underneath. "I'll have a word with him."

"Don't waste your time. He's not worth the effort." A sliver of irritation poked at me. "He acted like I disgusted him. I couldn't care less about what he thinks, but it's still annoying."

Alec was quiet for a while, until we came to a stop at a red light. He turned to me, and one warm hand shot out to squeeze mine. "Listen, Ellie. Don't let the Mike Changs of the world get you down. Trust me. You're the bravest, strongest woman I've ever met."

Warmth suffused me as I glanced down at his hand covering mine. *How did I ever think I needed someone like Mike to take my mind off Alec?* That WhatsApp message nudged me, saying, *He used to have a crush on you. Aren't you going to ask him about it?*

We hadn't addressed *that,* and I wasn't sure how to react if he broached the subject. Maybe I could feign amnesia. Or pretend I didn't know what he was talking about.

It was past seven when we arrived, but the twenty-story building that housed the GPG office in downtown Seattle was still buzzing with activity. Weary-looking employees filtered out of the foyer, some seeming like they could fall asleep standing on the curb.

According to Alec, GPG owned the building (naturally), but they only occupied the top three floors. The building directory told me that an investment bank, an insurance company, a law firm, and a recruitment agency were among the companies leasing the other floors. A security guard checked us in, then sent us to the twentieth floor, along with several other guests. The ten-second elevator ride felt like two hours, because I was pressed close to Alec inside the small space, his front to my back, making me hyper-aware of his presence, his warmth, and his scent. By the time I heard the *ding* signaling our arrival, my brain had successfully memorized every ridge and contour of his body.

The elevator opened to reveal a floor filled with guests chatting and laughing, everyone holding either a champagne flute or a wine glass. Caterers weaved around the crowd, carrying trays of drinks and hors d'oeuvres. Some people were helping themselves to the food on the linen-covered table—there were trays of sandwiches and mini beef sliders, fruit platters, and gorgeous charcuterie boards. Floor-to-ceiling windows surrounded us, proudly displaying a spectacular, unobstructed view of the bright city lights.

Holy shit. *This* was her idea of an informal gathering?

"Alec! About time you got here." Rob waved as he made his way toward us. He cocked his head at me, looking puzzled. "Everything okay, E? Why are you looking at me like that?"

"Making sure you're the same Rob I saw a few hours ago." I was assessing him from head to toe. "Never seen you in anything but orange vests and work boots. You clean up pretty well."

"I do, don't I?" Rob proudly tugged on the lapels of his charcoal suit, a grin splitting his face. "I'm like an unpolished diamond, just waiting for my turn to shine."

Alec sighed. "Can we not make his head bigger than it already is?"

"What's wrong, Mackenzie? Jealous?"

"Of course not." Alec avoided my eyes, and nodded toward the end of the room, where Jacqui stood chatting to a man with his back to us. "There she is. We should go say hi."

Alec took my hand in his, smiling at people as the three of us made our way to Jacqui.

"She's talking to Phil." I tugged at his hand, motioning to where the pair was standing. "Don't think they're comparing notes about the weather."

They were both raising their voices, although I couldn't hear what they were arguing about. Phil shook his head in exasperation, before rolling his shoulder in a "whatever" shrug. He turned around to leave, giving us a curt nod as he passed, not bothering to stop and say hi.

Jacqui, on the other hand, looked positively unperturbed. Spotting us, she waved her hand, beckoning us to come over. "Glad you all could make it." She shook Alec and Rob's hands, then gave me a hug. "How's the bakery going?"

The tiniest shred of remorse tore at me, because I was deceiving this kind, wonderful woman. *It's just a business transaction.* I squashed my guilt into a pulp and offered Jacqui a smile. "We're opening very soon. You should come by sometime."

"Actually, I'm celebrating my fortieth next month. I'll get my PA to place an order for the party. You're all invited, of course."

The guilt returned, larger and meaner than before, coupled with shame instilled from a lifetime of strict and manipulative parental upbringing, berating me for deceiving her: *She's helping you with your business, and you're lying to her face in return?*

I was *so* going to hell for this.

"Come with me," Jacqui said. "I'll introduce you to our board."

For the next half hour, I smiled and shook hands with God knows how many suited men and women Jacqui had foisted on us. Everyone expressed their excitement to Alec and Rob, raving about how delighted they were that they'd be working together. Then Jacqui's PA ushered us into a group picture, and I fixed a bright grin on my face, wishing that I was snug and comfortable under my blanket instead of being here.

Well, once Alec signed his agreement, I wouldn't have to do this anymore, and we could start planning our fake breakup. Then I could stop lying and deceiving everyone, especially Jacqui, giving my overworked guilt a much-needed break.

It was an excellent plan, so why did it still feel like the world was about to be plunged into an eternity of gloom and despair?

Because once this is over, it's time to say goodbye.

"By the way," Jacqui said once the board members had dispersed and mingled with the other guests, "we're having our annual company outing this weekend. You should all come along, celebrate our new partnership. Three days, two nights at one of our beautiful resorts. We leave Friday afternoon."

"This Friday?" Alec asked. "As in, the day after tomorrow?"

"Yes. We'll sign our agreement in the morning and celebrate

on the weekend. It'll be great!" She nodded at her PA. "Carmel will be in touch with the details."

Three days, two nights?

With Alec? Faking being his girlfriend in view of everyone?

My brain went into panic overdrive, and I blurted out the first excuse I could think of. "I can't. We're opening soon, and I can't leave, there's still so many things to do . . ."

"We're pretty much done," Rob unhelpfully announced. *The traitor*. "We're ahead of schedule, and everything's under control. You don't have to worry, E."

"It's only a few days." Jacqui gave my arm a friendly pat. "You look pale. Maybe you've been working too hard. This is the perfect chance to take a break." She directed her next sentence at Alec. "Oh, and I'll have Carmel send a draft of the press release about the acquisition to you first thing tomorrow morning. Let me know if you want any changes with the wording."

As soon as she was out of earshot and Rob went to look for food, I pulled Alec aside.

"*Company trip*." I let out a growl. "Do you know what that means?"

He raised an eyebrow at me. "That we're going for a short getaway?"

My eyes bulged at him. "She'll be expecting us to sleep in the same room. We can't—I can't—*no*. No way in hell."

I didn't even need to do my usual pros and cons list to know that saying yes would be the worst idea of the decade. *Of the freaking century*. Sharing the same house with him was hard enough as it was, especially after that WhatsApp revelation. I wasn't foolish enough to torture myself, but if I were, I'd rather have papercuts all over my fingers than spend two nights in the same room with him. There was no way I could survive without slowly descending into madness and hell.

"Madness and hell, huh?" He made a "pfft" sound, as I realized

I'd voiced it out loud. "Come on, Ellie. I promise this is the very last thing you'll have to do. I'm signing the agreement on Friday. Work at your shop is almost done. After next week, we can go our separate ways."

Think of it as a goodbye trip, my heart gently coaxed me.

I silenced the small thud of gloom that went through me. This would probably be my last ever chance to spend some time with him. Because he was right. In less than two weeks, he wouldn't be in my life anymore, and we'd be living completely separate lives.

Three days will be over before you know it.

And so, to the boisterous victory cheers from my heart, I said, "I'll go, but you get the pull-out sofa, and if there's even the tiniest hint of a snore coming out of you, I swear I'll smother you with a pillow."

"How come you've never told me about this spot?"

"My deepest apologies." Alec placed a palm over his heart, his expression contrite. "Shall I make a list of all the places I frequent for your approval?"

Rolling my eyes, I took out my pump and bolused for the food. "Your mother ever told you that sarcasm is unbecoming?"

"Sarcasm? Who, *me*? I'm offended."

We were at a lookout area, on one of the highest points of Port Benedict. A few other cars were nearby, their passengers sitting on the hoods, chatting and enjoying the view. Glittering stars liberally dotted the night sky, and beneath us, Port Benedict and the bay lit up, showing off its beautiful, sparkly lights.

Alec opened the tailgate of his SUV, and we both sat there cross-legged, opening a brown paper bag filled with burgers and fries. He'd kept his promise—we left GPG after an hour, apologizing profusely to Jacqui. We only had finger food at the party, and we were both still hungry, so Alec had suggested grabbing some burgers and stopping here before going home.

"The view is gorgeous." I tore open the packet of ketchup, squirting it into a puddle.

"It is, isn't it? I come here when I need some peace and quiet." He pulled his burger from the bag, unwrapped the greasy paper, then bit into it.

I unwrapped mine, while following and tracking his movements from the corners of my eyes. Never had I thought that the simple act of eating a burger could look so sexy, but I couldn't stop watching him. A dash of sauce smeared his lips, and he used his thumb to wipe it, then sucked it clean, sending a jolt of lust reverberating throughout my body.

Taking a deep breath, I silently recited the Stay on Track Plan. For a few minutes, it worked, because I successfully convinced myself he was off-limits and this was not real and it was ending in a matter of weeks and *I should just concentrate on my damn food.*

But then he had to open his mouth.

"We need to talk. About my last message."

I picked up some fries and dunked them into my puddle of ketchup, which had suddenly become very interesting. "Which one?"

A pause, then, "About how you were my childhood crush."

Points to him for being upfront about it. My heart started to round up the brass band players. "What about it?"

Points *to me* for being so blasé about it.

"I feel like I should clarify. Clear the air."

Nope, screw being blasé.

"Okay, then clarify." I shifted to face him. "Was that a joke? Because if it was, then you have a seriously warped sense of humor."

His gaze never left mine. "Not a joke. I really did."

The brass band began pounding loudly. *Did*. That was the operative word. He had been interested once, but not anymore.

"You had a funny way of showing it. You were so unfriendly, I thought you hated me."

Alec barked out a dry laugh. "I never hated you. It's my method of self-preservation."

Jenna Ng, you're a fucking genius.

"But that night, when I told you how I felt . . ." I trailed off, a thick lump suddenly forming in my throat, as the humiliation came searing back. *Pull yourself together, Ellie.* "You said you'll never feel the same way, because I was nothing to you but Eric's younger sister."

"I didn't handle that very well, did I?" He grimaced.

"Oh, you think?"

"I was wrong. I shouldn't have said that."

"I didn't catch that." Grinning, I placed a hand behind my ear. "Was that an apology?"

"It is." He looked serious. "Eric knew I liked you. He knew that your mother never really warmed up to me, so he warned me that your parents would never approve of you being with someone like me. Someone whose family isn't as affluent as yours, and because of my dad, too. So I promised him I'd stay away."

"Eric said that?" I squished my eyebrows together. "And you believed him? That was enough to convince you?"

Alec tilted his head. "You remember that guy who used to follow you around in high school? Scott something or other?" When I nodded, he went on, "Do you remember that he suddenly left school? Have you ever wondered what happened to him?"

I could feel my eyebrows drawing together. "Did my family get rid of him?"

He gave a solemn nod. "Eric thinks your parents used their influence to bankrupt Scott's family and sent them packing to another state."

"I never knew that." I groaned.

"So that night, when you said you liked me, I panicked. I didn't want the same thing to happen to my family that happened to Scott's. I figured if I said enough hurtful things, you'd be upset and stay away from me."

Well, it worked, because I not only stayed away from him, but had also spent the past ten years hating him with every fiber of my being.

"But what did you mean, because of your dad? Because he left your family?"

"More than that." He stared at his burger. "He left us for another woman. It had been going on for a while, and when my mom found out, she kicked him out of the house."

My heart broke for his mother, for Alec, and his siblings. "That must have been horrible for you. I'm so sorry. But that shouldn't make your family . . . unsuitable."

"No, but it wasn't good enough for the well-respected Pang family, right?" His laugh was bitter. "That's not all. Dad even had another family with that other woman. While he was still married to my mother."

I gaped at him. "What?"

"He had two sons, who'd probably be in their teens now." Alec rubbed the back of his neck, not meeting my gaze. "Anyway, don't know if you remember, but I used to date this girl, Anna, first year of college."

Of course I remembered. I'd envied Anna with every fiber of my being.

"From the first minute of our first date, I knew it would never work out. Because I kept comparing her to you. And all the girls, too. I'd be thinking of what you'd say, or do, imagining you were with me instead of them."

My breath left me in a whoosh, and that brass band had morphed into the Royal Edinburgh Military Tattoo.

"But a part of me kept thinking that your parents were right. I was convinced that I wasn't good enough for you, that you deserve someone better than me." He finally glanced at me. "Especially after I found out about my dad's affair. His second family. What if one of these days, I turn out just like him? Someone who turned his back on his family, on the people that he was supposed to love and care for?"

"Don't listen to them." My heart broke for him, while raging at my family. "You're not your dad. The fact that you put your family first and worked to help your mother raise your sisters, that's enough proof that you're nothing like him."

"I know, but I'm still his son." His laugh was dry. "And I've done it once, Ellie. That night when you had your extreme hypo. I could've stopped those douchebags from making you drink that much, but I didn't. I turned my back on you, and I've always felt guilty about it. You could've died, and to think that I did nothing to protect you . . ."

I didn't know what to say, knowing that he'd been living with his guilt all this time. Then another thought nagged at me. Was that why he'd been doing all those thoughtful things for me? Not because he was starting to care for me, but because he was trying to atone for his guilt?

"I did blame you," I said. "For the longest time. But I knew that it wasn't your fault. I was trying to impress you, so I was the one to blame."

Alec shook his head. "But if I hadn't said those hurtful words to you first, you wouldn't have tried to impress me."

"It was my decision to have those beers, so it was on me."

"And I should've stopped you, but I didn't."

I threw my hands up in the air. "Okay, let's split the blame. What happened that night was half your fault, and half mine. Sounds good?"

"But what about those jerks that taunted you and Naomi? Are

we letting them off scot-free?" He was shaking his head. "That doesn't seem fair."

"Oh, *now* you want to blame them?" I rolled my eyes with a laugh. "Fine, it's entirely *their* fault. We are both free of any future guilt and responsibilities. Are we happy now? Can we move on?"

He returned my grin. "Yes. I can finally sleep well at night."

Just then, his phone rang. Glancing at the caller ID, he smiled a little before excusing himself, and walked away while muttering a low "hey" into his phone.

A call this late at night, and him answering with a goofy smile on his face? It had to be the girl he was interested in. No, I most definitely was *not* jealous. Our fake relationship was ending, and no matter how I felt about him, we would be going our separate ways soon.

I crumpled my greasy burger wrapping paper and threw it back into the bag.

So why did I have this sinking feeling that I had missed out on the very best thing that could've happened in my life?

CHAPTER 20

Front-Row Seat of a
Damn Hot Show

Since we were going away for the weekend, I worked overtime on Thursday to check items off my To-Do List. I still had two weeks to make sure that everything was in place before the grand opening, but I didn't want to worry about anything while I was gone.

My phone trilled, bursting my concentration. A crisp, business-like voice greeted me from the other end. "Ellie Pang? This is Carmel, Jacqueline Goodwin's assistant."

"Hi, Carmel. How can I help?"

"Ms. Goodwin would like to place some orders for a party. I had a look at your social media pages, and I understand you make custom-decorated cookies. Do we have to come up with a design, or can you supply us with one?"

A sliver of guilt briefly cut through me, because Jacqui was being so kind, but here I was, deceiving her and letting her think I was Alec's girlfriend. She had been nothing but supportive, and I should be ashamed for taking advantage of that.

No. This was business. Nothing personal.

"I can design one for her." I went back into professional mode. This was our first big order, and there would be lots of important, well-connected people at her party. This was my chance to impress. I shifted the phone to my right hand as I grabbed a pad and a pen, poised to take notes. "Is there a theme that Jac—Ms. Goodwin would prefer?"

"Yes. I'll email you a list of things we'd like to order, including specific requests to incorporate in the designs. The party is on the first weekend of April. Does that work for you?"

I nearly crapped my pants. That wasn't too far away. "Absolutely," I said, portraying a confidence I didn't feel. "We have plenty of time."

"Excellent. I'll go ahead and send the email. Let me know if you've got any questions."

The minute she hung up, I tapped my inbox open and refreshed it every few seconds, until her email whooshed in a few minutes later. They wanted five dozen each of the dark chocolate cronuts, peanut butter cupcakes, mini baked cheesecakes, and red velvet brownies. On top of that, they'd also ordered five hundred cookies in the shape of birthday cakes, champagne flutes, and wine bottles. It took me a few minutes to read and reread Carmel's email, making sure I wasn't imagining things. If the rough calculation I ran in my head was correct, the order would add up to almost six thousand dollars. It could cover my expenses for the first few weeks.

My face breaking into an excited grin, I let out a loud whoop and jumped up to do a happy dance. Someone believed in me, and trusted me with their important event, and my heart felt like it was going to burst out of my chest, because *I was finally living my dream.*

With a thousand things running through my head, I tapped

open my list-maker app and started a new to-do list for Jacqui's party. I had so many things to do in such a tight timeframe, and I couldn't afford to mess up. But the longer the list grew, the more neurotic my thoughts became. Self-doubt crept in, sending those thoughts snowballing further and catapulting me into a tizz of panic. What if I couldn't pull it off? What if I screwed up my first big order, and business became so bad that we'd have to shut down within the first few weeks?

Then my mother would have the last laugh.

And I couldn't let that happen.

Taking a deep breath, I closed the list, and decided to do some baking to calm my overthinking brain. I went to the kitchen and preheated the oven, planning to make the peanut butter cheesecake brookies I'd promised Alec. I took out a mixing bowl and some low-carb cookie dough from the cabinet, then broke the dough rounds apart in a bowl. I added a couple of eggs and mixed it, then poured the batter into a pan.

Things had been going well so far, and I had my plans and my lists to guide me. Come hell or high water, I had to prove to my parents that I could survive without their constant interference. This had always been my dream, and now that I'd come this far, there was no turning back.

Failure was not an option.

In another bowl, I beat some cream cheese until it became fluffy, then added some no-added-sugar peanut butter into the mix. Once it was smooth, I spooned the cheesecake mixture over the cookie batter and spread it evenly, then set the timer on the oven.

I kept working, melting some organic dark chocolate chips and chopping up some peanuts for the top layer, while slowly feeling myself calm down, and all the doubts melting away. I counted to ten, pep-talked myself, and finally kicked the crippling self-doubt to the curb as I cut the brookies into rows of six by six.

I can do this.

Everything would be just fine.

The house was dark and quiet when I got home. I stored the box of brookies in the fridge, left a note for Alec on the kitchen counter, then headed up to my room. Tossing my phone and bag on top of the dresser, I decided that a relaxing bubble bath was just what I needed to end the long day. Taking off my pump and grubby clothes, I wrapped myself in a towel, then padded out to the guest bathroom.

The spare bathroom was spacious and bright, with large windows and modern white furnishings. On the left side was a glass-walled shower, while the bathtub was hidden in a corner nook at the right side, which I headed straight for when I walked in. I ran the bath, dropping jasmine bath salts in it, then turned off the lights, letting the moonlight shine through the windows. I slipped in and let out a long, relieved breath, relishing the soothing feel of the warm, fragrant water quietly lapping around my body.

A few minutes later, there was the faintest sound of the front door opening and closing downstairs. I could hear Alec's footsteps on the staircase, followed by the firm click of his bedroom door. Taking a deep breath, I closed my eyes, letting the tension of the day slowly ebb away.

My eyes snapped open as the handle of the bathroom door suddenly rattled, and I belatedly realized it wasn't locked. I'd never needed a reason to lock it—Alec had his own bathroom, so this one was practically mine.

But the next second, the man himself strolled in.

While unbuttoning and stripping off his white shirt.

My breath caught in my throat, and I silently sank lower into the bubbly water, with only my eyes peeking out. He flicked on the lights, then hung his shirt on the towel ladder, not noticing me. I was holding my breath, trying to stay very, very still, and very, very quiet. My eyes nearly popped out of their sockets, horrified yet fascinated, as he unbuckled his belt and unfastened his pants, letting them drop to the floor. He had his back to me, presenting me with the amazing sight of his perfect ass, his black boxers snugly hugging it.

Instead of a relaxing bubble bath, I had a front-row seat to an impromptu striptease. By my ~~ridiculously gorgeous~~ *fucking hot* fake boyfriend.

The polite thing to do would be to close my eyes. Or yell out to announce my presence. Probably both. But I wasn't feeling very polite right now, so instead, I resurfaced and craned my neck to get a better look. And anyway, it was undoubtedly way, way too late. Should have said something the minute he walked into the bathroom. I'd just wait this out—it would be over in a few minutes.

Then he slipped out of those snug boxers, and my heart nearly stopped.

With his back facing me, he stepped into the shower, still oblivious that I was hidden in the corner bathtub, unable to take my eyes off him. Turning the faucet on, he drenched himself under the stream of hot water, before picking up my shampoo bottle, sniffing it, then squeezing out a generous amount. His hands worked methodically, kneading and massaging the shampoo all over his hair. Next, he pumped out blobs of my soap onto his hands, rubbing them together before lathering it all over his body. First on his neck, then on his arms, then on his back, followed by his chest.

This wasn't just your normal, everyday, run-of-the-mill striptease. It was a real-life porn movie, and I was enjoying it too much to tear my gaze away. He stretched his neck, trying to get water onto his left side, and turned around, giving me a full-length, uncensored, breathtaking view of a gloriously naked Alec. *So. Very. Naked.*

His hands kept working, rubbing the soap on his stomach, then down his thighs, all around his legs and backside, making showering look so sexy like it was nobody's business.

That was when my mouth decided to betray my brain, producing a low, breathy sigh I'd *never, ever* heard before in my whole life, alerting him to my presence. Startled, he looked up and locked eyes with mine.

Wet, naked Alec Mackenzie caught me watching him rub soap all over his body.

My breath hitched, before stopping for a few seconds. Maybe even a few hours, for all I knew. If I died right now, it would entirely be his fault, no two ways about it. The coroner should rule out foul play, but they'd probably announce that my cause of death was a rare but deadly combination of prolonged breathing difficulty and striptease-induced extreme arousal.

What a way to go, though.

My only regret was that I wouldn't have the chance to say my goodbyes to Eric, Naomi, Kim, and Jenna. Make amends with my parents. Or update my will. Run a marathon, float in the Dead Sea, build white picket fences and live happily ever after, the list goes on.

But back to the more pressing matters at hand.

Alec had stilled, his eyes slowly widening, his hands paused between his legs. Swallowing, I forced myself to blink, debating my next move. But before I could decide, his eyes turned darker, and his hands started moving again. My eyes followed them as he deliberately and slowly lathered more soap all over himself: his chest, his abs, then back between his legs, where a part of him stood up to attention.

Wet, naked Alec Mackenzie *got hard* watching me watching him rub soap all over his body.

I had never, ever been so turned on in my whole life. If I could fan myself, I would.

He took his sweet time rinsing the soap off, a seductive smile teasing the corners of his mouth. Reaching behind him to turn off the water, he stepped out of the shower, grabbed a towel, and wrapped it around his waist, never once breaking eye contact with me. Then he strolled over and kneeled at the side of the bath, casually propping his dripping wet arm on the edge of the bathtub, his face only inches away from mine.

"I hope you enjoyed that." His voice, rough as gravel, rumbled in my ear. I shivered, as if he'd touched and caressed every single inch of my bare skin. Dropping his eyes to my mouth, he gave me one last sizzling look before standing up. "I sure as hell did."

Fuuuuucccckkkk.

He walked out without another word, and I let out a long, ragged breath. My heart had made a huge, nonstop ruckus throughout Alec's performance, and it was a miracle I had survived the earth-shattering act.

The bath water had turned cold, but I wasn't going to risk getting out of the bathroom now. I'd wait until he was safely tucked in his room, maybe even stay here until next week, if the situation called for it. I could Uber some takeaway food so I wouldn't starve.

But while waiting, there was nothing wrong with replaying those red-hot moments on repeat, right? I wasn't even going to overanalyze his words, because I was already teetering on a precariously slippery slope, in danger of plummeting headfirst into a dark, bottomless abyss, crushing my head—and my heart—with no way up.

A long time later, when I'd been sufficiently pruned, finally confident it was safe to go out, I rinsed the bath and reached for my towel.

Only to find that it was missing.

Alec had taken *the only freaking towel in this bathroom.*

Panic threatened to overtake me. There was nothing else I could use to dry off and cover myself. The only items that would even be remotely useful were a mediocre-sized facecloth, a soggy bath mat, and his old shirt and pants. The facecloth barely covered my face, the bath mat was out of the question, so that left me with two lousy options: (a) slipping on his old shirt; or (b) sprinting stark naked to my room while praying nobody (*him*) caught me.

All the points in the pros column were overwhelmingly in favor of the shirt, so I gingerly slipped it on. It smelled of citrus and spice and him, and against my better judgment, I lifted the collar to my nose, inhaling his scent. After doing the top two buttons, just enough to cover the run to my room, I opened the door and peeked outside.

Silence. The coast was clear. *It's go time.*

Tiptoeing out, I quietly closed the door behind me, then made a dash for it, breathing a sigh of relief when I reached the safety of my room. I was about to turn my door handle when a voice startled me from behind.

"My shower broke this morning."

I froze, practically turning into a human statue. He must have possessed stealthy, ninja-like abilities, because I didn't even hear him approach.

"Thought the spare bathroom was empty. Lights were off, shower wasn't running."

I slowly turned around, my breath hitching when I saw him, fully clothed, wearing those glasses. My damp towel was slung over his shoulder, his hands shoved in his pockets.

"Imagine my surprise. There you were, watching me getting turned on."

I was having difficulty breathing again.

Alec slowly sauntered toward me, his eyes never leaving mine. He stopped right in front of me, making me hyper-aware of my still-wet body, molded to his soaked white shirt. My brain sternly instructed my mouth to say something, *anything*, but I was incapable of forming a logical thought, let alone a sentence.

"I think you've got something of mine." His voice, low and husky, made goosebumps pop all over my skin. "And I think," he went on, his hands reaching out to undo those two flimsy buttons, "I'd like it back."

My skin felt like it was ablaze, every nerve ending on my body screaming and begging for him to touch me. I sucked in a breath when his fingers skimmed my shoulders, easing the shirt off, letting it drop to the floor. The shivers weren't from the cool air on my skin, but from his warm skin on mine. And because I was now standing stark naked in front of him while his gaze roamed all over me, feasting, the hunger in his eyes palpable.

"You're beautiful." His voice was gruff. "Perfect."

My brain was frantic, waving the Stay on Track Plan while yelling loudly through a bullhorn. *He's interested in someone else. STEP AWAY FROM THE MAN RIGHT NOW!*

"We can't."

There was confusion in his hooded eyes. "Why?"

"You. Like. Someone. Else," I whispered, my mouth struggling to get the words out.

Alec stared at me, his clouded eyes fighting an internal battle. "I don't," he finally said, as his hands took their time draping the towel around me, grazing my arms and shoulders, sending a raging inferno throughout my body, all the way to my toes.

I sucked in a breath. "What . . . do you mean?"

His fingers curled, tucking the ends of the towel. "There's no one else."

"But . . . all those late-night phone calls," I croaked out. "You said you're interested in someone else . . . you had your eyes on another girl. Your potential girlfriend. The one that you're taking things slow with. That cute brunette . . ."

"I don't know which brunette you're talking about." He skimmed one feather-light finger, a whisper of a touch at the top of my cleavage, and I suppressed a shiver. "There's no brunette. There's no one else. I was talking about you. It was always you, Ellie."

That's it. I was done for. Fire—or very likely, madness—flew through my veins. I caught his hand while untucking the towel with my other hand, letting it tumble to the floor.

Alec hissed a breath. "What are you doing?"

Instead of answering, I pulled him closer, pressing his body to mine.

His eyes burned hotter than molten lava. He looked like he was holding on to the final shred of his self-control, those eyes asking me, *Are you sure?*

"Yes," I whispered.

"Let me be very clear." His voice was low, throaty. "I'm about to kiss you. And once I start, I won't be able to stop. If you don't want that to happen, you better tell me right now."

My answer was to grasp his other hand and place it over my chest.

That last bit of control in his eyes snapped. With a loud groan, he crushed his mouth onto mine, pushing me against my bedroom door. I slipped my hands under his T-shirt, touching him everywhere, humming with pleasure when I felt him growing harder against my stomach. One of his hands stroked and worshipped my breast, while the other hand—*oh God, the other hand*—mercilessly teased me down there.

This was unreal. Beyond my wildest fantasies. I was naked against my bedroom door, and an eager participant in a frenzied make-out session with my fake boyfriend, like a couple of horny teenagers. All I had to do was reach behind me, turn the handle, and we could be on my bed within seconds.

So I did.

We tumbled onto the bed, his mouth on mine, our hands all over each other. My brain was fogged with lust, wanting—needing—more of him. I peeled off his T-shirt, desperate to feel his skin on mine. There was no finesse, just hunger, and I shuddered when the hard shape under his shorts nudged me. A hoarse groan escaped him as I arched my hips, shamelessly grinding against his solid length, begging him for more.

Then, of course, my phone had to choose that very moment to sing out.

"Ignore it," I mumbled against his mouth, my hands busy exploring his body.

"You feel so good." His clever lips pressed kisses on my jaw and my neck, tracing a path down to my breasts. He took one nipple into his mouth, licking and lapping attention at it. My eyes rolled to the back of my head, as the rest of my body perked up in gleeful anticipation.

But the phone didn't care that I was about to have the best sex of my life. It kept on ringing, as if us ignoring it made it even more determined to get noticed. It stopped for all of two seconds before starting its next round of melodies.

"Turn it off." His tongue did something mind-blowing on my breast.

"Mmmh." I shuddered. "Good idea."

It took every ounce of my willpower to pull away, because the sight of him worshipping every inch of my body would be enough to make a lesser woman succumb to temptation. Groping around the sheets, I finally found my phone on the bedside table, with the sole focus of turning it off, pronto.

Everything screeched to a halt when I saw my mother's face flashing on the screen.

This was the first time she'd called since I left home. *What does she want?*

Rejecting the call, I switched the phone off, then turned back to Alec to resume where we'd left off. But it was too late. Because he'd seen it, too. His face had turned pale, and he stopped whatever dirty, delicious things he was doing.

"Hey," I whispered, my hands gently caressing his face. "You okay?"

He jumped a little, then grabbed his discarded T-shirt from the floor. Straightening up, he slipped it back on, while wearing a flustered look in his eyes. "We shouldn't be doing this."

My mouth gaped open. Ten seconds ago, this man had his lips around one of my nipples. I was on the bed right now, lying naked before him, and that was what he chose to say?

Whatever the hell happened to his intense "*once I start, I won't be able to stop*"?

I was perplexed, stumped, and mortified. "What?" Pulling the blanket, I hastily wrapped it around myself. "A little too late for that, don't you think?"

"I'm sorry. That should never have happened." He covered his face with his hands. "What was I thinking?"

Anger and embarrassment rushed through me. Twice in my lifetime I'd given him my heart on a silver platter—this time, my body, too—and both times he'd rejected me.

That was two times too many.

"I don't understand," I said, my lips pursed tightly. "I thought we both wanted this."

"No." He shook his head. "Yes. I do. But I can't. We can't. I promised."

"*Promised who?*" A neuron snapped inside my brain. "Eric? Forget about it. I'm absolving you of that promise. You're no longer under any obligation. Is that all?"

"That should never have happened," he repeated. He backed

away, moving toward the door. "I should go. We have a long day tomorrow."

Without looking back, he rushed out of the room while I sat on the bed, covered with my blanket and shame. Then the humiliation faded into nothingness, replaced by indignation and rage. I was seething, furious at him, but more than anything, I was angry at myself.

Hadn't I known this was going to happen? That letting myself fall for him again would lead me to nothing but grief and heartbreak? Sure, he was being an asshole, but I had nobody to blame but myself. I'd known this was in the cards, but I still let my feelings for him dictate my thoughts, my words, *my actions*, like that naïve eighteen-year-old teenager that I had once been.

Getting up to get dressed, I made a vow: I'd grit my teeth and do everything in my power to get through this weekend, because I'd already promised to go. But the minute we got back from the GPG trip, I was moving out of his house as fast as humanly possible.

And then Alec Mackenzie could go to hell.

CHAPTER 21

We're Gonna Need a Bigger Bed

Despite my resolution, I was still a hot mess the next day, because I couldn't stop thinking about what had happened. My concentration was shot, and I found myself explaining the same things multiple times to Ruby, Jenna's friend whom I'd hired to work the front of store, because I wasn't making any sense. It took all my willpower to focus on the last two pending tasks on my To-Do List, but no matter how hard I tried, my traitorous brain kept repeating yesterday's humiliating episode over and over again, like one of my Engkong's old, scratched CDs that always got stuck on the same annoying track.

On the brighter side, my mother hadn't tried to call again, which was good, because I just didn't possess the mental capacity to deal with her *and* Alec right now.

After debating with myself the entire day, I finally decided to pretend that nothing had happened, and to treat him with cool indifference. Ignoring him would be the preferred solution, but we were heading into a weekend with Rob, Jacqui, and God knows how many GPG employees, so that option was obviously out.

When I arrived at the airport, it was close to 9:00 P.M. The resort was on a small island an hour away, and Alec and I were booked on the last flight of the day. Rob, Jacqui, and the others had flown out earlier. Carmel texted to say she'd already checked us in, reserving his seat and mine next to each other.

I'd taken an Uber to the airport, so I didn't see him until it was time to board the flight, which was practically empty. Pretending not to see Alec, I went to find a vacant seat as far away from him as possible. Sure, it wasn't very adult-like, but I had no intention of sitting next to him, while trying to suppress my murderous urge the whole trip, because it could end horribly—with me strangling him using my bare hands.

The island's tiny airport was deserted when we landed. There was only one available taxi when we exited the building, so I had no choice but to share it with Alec. He looked like he'd rather be anywhere but stuck in the same car with me, probably because I'd been shooting down all his attempts at making conversation. The air inside the Toyota minivan was colder than a tundra, thanks to my curt nods and one-word answers.

It was almost 11:00 P.M. when we finally arrived. The Pacific Palms was a five-star resort by the sea, ten minutes from the airport. Two majestic palm trees stood on either side of the main entrance, curving to form a welcoming arch. Bright lights illuminated the lobby, and I could hear gentle sounds of ocean waves lapping against the sand from a distance. A resort staff wearing a bright-blue shirt printed with colorful frangipanis ushered us into the foyer and took care of our luggage. I thanked him, then slumped into one of the comfortable sofas as Alec checked us in. My eyes started to drift closed, only for me to be softly shaken awake a few minutes later.

"There's a problem." Alec's eyes were unreadable, his tone flat. "No twin rooms available. We got a room with a queen bed."

A queen bed. Frustration clawed at my spine, but I took a deep breath and calmed myself down. "They don't have any other rooms?"

"They're fully booked."

My heart rate picked up speed. "Does it have a sofa bed?"

"Not according to the manager who checked me in."

He handed me a key card, and I grew quiet as we followed the concierge, who led us on a darkened garden path toward our room. My nerve endings were on high alert, because not only was I spending the next two nights sharing the same secluded room with him, but also the same definitely-won't-be-big-enough queen-size bed.

Surviving the weekend wasn't just impossible; it would be a miracle.

Our room was a boutique-style villa, one of the many individual huts dotting the property. After thanking and tipping the concierge, Alec slid his key card into the slot and pushed the door open. The luxuriously furnished room was bathed in warm, neutral colors. A spacious bathroom occupied the right side, and two comfortable armchairs flanked the transparent sliding door at the far end.

And in the middle of the room: one comfortable, heavenly-looking queen-size bed. With plush pillows, luxurious, satiny-looking bedsheets, and a pale beige comforter.

Not a sofa in sight.

My heart dropped to my shoes.

Alec's phone trilled. Sighing, he strolled toward the sliding door, stepping out to take the call. An automatic light switched on, and I could see an inviting patio with brown deck chairs, direct access to the sandy beach, and a spectacular view of the moonlit ocean. The amazing scenery did nothing to help the churning in my stomach as reality sank in. I was stuck in a beautiful, romantic resort for the next two days with him, sharing a room and a bed, while playing the role of his loving girlfriend.

I should really get an Oscar, an Emmy, and a Tony for my performance this weekend. At the very least, a nomination for Best Actress. Maybe I could even try to write a soundtrack about this trip and hope to be nominated for a Grammy.

Alec was still outside on his phone. If he wasn't taking phone calls from his potential girlfriend, then who'd be calling him this late at night? Maybe he'd lied about not being interested in anyone else? Maybe there really *was* another woman, and somehow things didn't work out, and now she was calling because she wanted a second chance? Perhaps that was why he ended things last night?

I shushed my neurotic thoughts as the patio door slid open.

Alec stepped in, frown lines pulling his forehead down. He saw me contemplating the bed, so he cleared his throat and gestured to the armchairs. "I can sleep there."

The two fat, fluffy armchairs would be heavenly to lounge in, but they weren't built for sleeping. He'd wake up in the morning with his body stiff and screaming curses.

Although . . . after last night? He totally deserved that, and so much worse. *He's lucky we're not kicking him out to sleep on the patio*, my brain argued.

But my mouth had a mind of its own.

"The bed is big enough to fit both of us." My eyes twitched, because even as I said those words, my brain was hastily sending instructions to *STOP TALKING RIGHT NOW!*

My common sense, along with my dignity, had clearly gone for a dip in the ocean and would not be returning for the rest of my life.

"I don't think that's a good idea." He wasn't meeting my eyes.

"Don't flatter yourself. I only offered because it wouldn't be comfortable to sleep in a chair." I hoped my raised chin conveyed disgust and indignation. Walking over to the bed, I reached for a pillow and plonked it in the middle. "That's your side. This is mine. We're both adults, so we can co-sleep on the same bed peacefully."

He eyed the bed with trepidation. "We can?"

"Absolutely." I ignored my wildly thumping heart and nodded a couple of times, more to convince myself. "But one snore out of you, and you're banished to the floor."

Alec considered me for a few seconds, before giving me a brisk nod. "Fine."

"Great."

"Awesome." He jabbed his thumb toward the bathroom. "You want to go first?"

My cheeks heated as memories of last night's shower episode came flooding back. Grabbing my pajamas and toiletry bag, I was done within ten minutes, then slipped under the blanket as Alec went into the bathroom. I closed my eyes and sent firm demands to my brain to relax and go to sleep. But no such thing happened; all the sensory neurons in my body were busily buzzing, still wide awake by the time he climbed onto the bed. The mattress dipped slightly under his weight, and even though I had my back to him, I wondered if he could hear my heart anxiously thrashing around in my chest.

"Ellie?"

I squeezed my eyes tighter, hoping that would somehow send me to sleep quicker.

"I don't snore."

My eyes creaked open.

"I sometimes hog the covers, though."

Forget pretending to be asleep. "Do that and I'll kick you off the bed."

There was a low chuckle from his side. "Just promise you'll be gentle about it."

I didn't answer, because obviously, I'd gone back to sleep.

"Thank you. For coming along this weekend. It really means a lot to me."

I let out a pretend snore. Loudly.

"Sleep tight, Ellie."

But of course I couldn't, because I was too aware of him. Of his clean-soap smell, his steady breathing, his warm, comforting body behind mine. A couple of hours later, as my eyelids finally succumbed to exhaustion, my last coherent thought was, *Two nights of this?*

God help me.

When my alarm quietly beeped in the morning, it took me a few seconds of staring at the foreign ceiling before realizing I wasn't in Alec's spare bedroom; instead I was at a beautiful, romantic resort, staging my last appearance as his fake girlfriend. The Grand Finale, the Swan Song, the Last Hurrah. The performance that was going to win me numerous awards.

I shifted my body to watch Alec's unmoving figure next to me. His eyes were closed, a gentle snore coming out of him, completely oblivious that he was the leading cause of the chaos and pandemonium inside my head—and my heart.

One night down. One more to go.

I only had to make it through to tomorrow, and it would all be over. In fact, I should update the Stay on Track Plan to include moving out of his house. Maybe I could finally put my sleeping bag to use and beg Kim and Jenna to let me sleep on their living room floor until I found a place of my own, no matter how uncomfortable it might be.

Anything was better than living under the same roof with him.

Quietly removing the covers, I tiptoed to the bathroom to brush my teeth and don my running gear. Ten minutes later, I silently closed the door, then made my way to the lush garden. Putting my earbuds in, I started around the jogging track as the sun made its way up. It was still early, but there was already a buzz of activities happening. When I passed the pool, shrieks and noisy chatters of little kids drifted my way, their parents watching as they lounged on the deck chairs. Some guests were on their way to the beach, carrying tote bags and beach towels, with some surfers already out enjoying the waves.

When I returned to the room, Alec was on the patio on another one of his mysterious calls. I slipped into the bathroom for a shower, and by the time I finished, he was back inside, frowning and typing furiously on his phone.

He glanced at me before pocketing his phone, looking like he was choosing his next sentence carefully. "Morning. How was your run?"

"Good." Even though I'd offered him the bed last night, it didn't mean I'd forgotten and forgiven him for what had happened two nights ago.

"Did you have a good sleep?"

"Yep."

He hesitated, before trying again. "Should we go for breakfast now? I'm starving."

"No."

Alec sighed. "Ellie, we can't do one-word answers. I know you're mad, but we need to present a united front for Jacqui. Two days, and you're off the hook."

I ignored the hollow feeling inside. "Not mad."

"You sound like it. You sure *look* like it."

"You're wrong."

"Am I? Because that murderous glare on your face tells me I'm right."

I folded my arms, exhibiting top-level mastery in denial and ignorance of my own feelings. "Let's move on. What does Jacqui have planned for the day?"

Another sigh, but he didn't press the issue further. "Carmel emailed me the schedule." He whipped his phone back out, and five seconds later, my phone pinged with an email notification.

My eyes grew larger as I scanned the contents, detailing all the things Jacqui expected us to do today: company lunch, then a series of team-building games (sandcastle competition, beach relay races, and beach dodgeball), followed by a casual company dinner. Tomorrow was a free day, but we were invited to participate in (optional) dolphin-watching, snorkeling, and hiking, before checking out and heading back to the airport.

Whoa. Even reading the schedule exhausted me. Whatever happened to sunbathing and piña coladas by the beach?

"We have a couple of free hours after breakfast. Any ideas what we could do?"

"*We?*" Raising my eyebrows, I snagged my backpack and marched toward the door. "There's no 'we.' *I'm* having breakfast, then a relaxing swim before lunch."

"Great idea." He followed closely behind, making me hyper-aware of his presence. "We should stick together. Jacqui will be suspicious if we do separate things."

"Whatever." I shrugged. We got to the breakfast room, and Rob waved at us from a table by the window. I schooled my features to portray the adoring girlfriend I was supposed to be and made my way toward Rob's table.

Then I felt Alec linking his warm hands through mine. He pulled me closer and planted a quick kiss on my temple. "Put on a smile, Ellie. Get ready for a weekend of fun."

CHAPTER 22

The Heroic Seagulls Saved the Day

R ob went to check out the waves after breakfast, so I—followed by Alec—wandered over to the pool and found two vacant chairs near the deep end. Draping my towel on one, I slipped out of my T-shirt, trying not to feel self-conscious in my bright-red bikini, aware that his eyes were tracking my every movement.

"I'm going for a swim," I announced. "See you later."

"I'll join you." Alec peeled off his own T-shirt and shorts, tossing them on the lounge chair next to mine. His navy swimming trunks hugged his lower body, sending my treacherous eyes to his mouthwatering abs, and the tantalizing V pointing toward body parts that I ~~probably~~ *definitely* should NOT be thinking about.

Nope, not going to ~~ogle admire~~ look at him. Eyes straight ahead.

Steeled with determination, I removed my pump, then strolled to the edge of the pool and went in, pretending not to notice that he slipped in next to me. He was blissfully unaware that several pairs of eyes were watching him with keen interest. On the other hand, I was *very* aware of how close he was, and how there was nothing separating us but water gently lapping between our bodies.

I mentally roundhouse-kicked myself and concentrated on doing a few laps across the pool. After ten laps, I took a break, resting my head on the edge. The water was nice, and the sun shone bright, warming my face.

Alec came up next to me a few minutes later, mirroring my position. Ignoring him, I closed my eyes, enjoying the cool water, and the chatter and laughter of people around us.

"Ellie?"

Too bad I couldn't pretend to be asleep. "What."

There was a long pause before he replied, "I'm sorry."

I didn't reply.

"For the other night," he continued. I could sense him drifting closer. "I was being inappropriate, and I promise it will never happen again."

I'd be lying if I said a huge part of me wasn't disappointed in hearing that.

"Come on, Ellie. Tell me how I can make it up to you. Please?"

"There's nothing you can do," I said, turning to face him. He stared at me, his eyes gentle and pleading. I had to escape him *right now*, because if he kept looking at me like that, I'd lose that last ounce of my pathetic, nonexistent willpower. "I've moved on, and we're never going to talk about what happened that night. Ever. Is that clear?"

Without waiting for him to answer, I hauled myself out of the pool. Stalking toward our chairs, I was determined not to look back and see if he was following me. But when I finally got to the chair and reached for my towel, I made the dreadful mistake of glancing back.

Alec was having a James Bond moment, emerging glistening and wet from the pool, his navy trunks dripping with water and hotness. In fact, he looked so damn sexy, Bond had *nothing* on

Mackenzie. I swore I could even hear a sharp intake of breath from the open-mouthed lady sitting way across the other end of the pool.

That's it. I *had* to get away.

Without waiting for him, I wrapped my towel around my waist and stalked off.

Unfortunately, I couldn't escape him for too long. We sat at the same table for lunch, and I spent the entire time making small talk with Jacqui while trying not to be distracted by the occasional hand rub and quick kisses on the cheek from Alec. He'd smoothly slipped back into his doting boyfriend role, trying to show affection for Jacqui's benefit. But it was sending confusing signals to my brain, causing the cells to go haywire, and thoroughly befuddling my heart.

Tomorrow night couldn't come fast enough.

When lunch was over, we all made our way down to the beach, where Carmel stood with a clipboard, flanked by two other women wearing ocean-blue shirts emblazoned with the GPG logo. She blew a whistle to get everyone's attention, then rattled off the rules of the competition. Three games, with a grand prize of five thousand dollars for the winning team, and the supposedly highly coveted Goodwin Games trophy.

That was a lot of money that could help my cash flow at the bakery.

First up—making sandcastles. My last encounter with sand-castles was when my age was still in the single digits. My mother hated sand, because it got everywhere, and she always complained that she didn't have time to take us to the beach *and* clean up the mess afterward.

We were split into teams of four, with ten teams in total. Jac-qui, Carmel, and the other two women stood on the sidelines as judges. Rob, Alec, and I were in the same group with a redhead named Marisa, who'd introduced herself as GPG's marketing manager.

The minute Carmel finished distributing the buckets, shovels, and trowels, mayhem ensued. We only had one hour, so everyone jostled to find the best possible site for their group's masterpiece, eager to construct the finest sand structure ever known to mankind. Alec and Rob had already claimed our spot, busy laying the foundation, while Marisa and I raced to the water to fill up our buckets.

When the hour was up, Carmel blew her whistle again, signaling us to put down our tools. One team had made a replica of the Sydney Opera House, with lumps of what were supposed to be koalas in front. Another group had built a literal sandcastle, with moats and turrets and flags, big enough to comfortably sit four people inside it. My favorite was a team that had constructed a collection of sea creatures—whales, turtles, dolphins, plus one lone mermaid.

Jacqui stopped to inspect our group last, and a smile tugged at the corners of her lips. We'd created a structure resembling a small city, with tall skyscrapers, houses, and a construction site at one corner. Alec had come up with the idea, and he was grinning from ear to ear, looking pleased with himself.

"I love this." She beamed at the four of us. "Sticking to the spirit of the company. I'm awarding you the first place. Fantastic effort, everyone."

Our team cheered as Carmel announced that we were leading with a score of fifty points.

Next, the relay races. Alec and Rob stood at one end, while Marisa and I were at the other end. The second Carmel blew her whistle, Marisa took off, only skidding to a halt inches away from Rob. He grabbed the blue-colored baton from her, sprinted, and practically threw it at me. I did my almighty best to pass it to

Alec, but it wasn't easy to run barefoot in soft sand. Alec made the final dash, but his superhuman effort still couldn't win us the game—we came second, after a team of tall, lithe twenty-somethings who were already cheering and hugging each other by the time Alec crossed the finish line.

That put us in a tie for first place, with a score of ninety points. After a quick fifteen-minute break, it was time for the last game.

"There are things you absolutely can't do in dodgeball," Carmel announced through her bullhorn. "You can't smack, spike, kick, or catch a ball. You should aim for below the shoulders. The first team to lose all their players will be eliminated."

Cheers erupted as the first two teams shuffled to the makeshift court. The game began, fast and hard. Everyone focused all their energy into destroying their opponents, and the balls flew sharper and harder as team after team went down. The game had recorded at least five minor casualties so far—sprained ankles, shoulder injuries, and one bloody nose.

We started easy, defeating a few teams without difficulty, and got into the final round. Our team was up against four muscly guys who looked like they ate two dozen eggs every morning for breakfast and wrestled professionally for a living.

Rob tossed the ball back and forth in his hands. "Listen up, y'all. If we win this round, that five grand is ours. We can do it, people. Who's with me?"

"I'm not too sure about this." Marisa grimaced as she glanced at the opposing team. "Have you seen who we're up against? Their arms are bigger than my whole body. They're the most competitive guys in the entire company. We're doomed."

"We're not," Rob said, looking dead serious. "They might be bigger than us, but we can be faster. So, same strategy as before. We'll go after the biggest guy first, that one in the white T-shirt. Just aim your ball at him, find a time when he's distracted. Remember, throw with one hand and aim below the neck so you don't hit their heads. Don't do straight shots and try to throw cross-court. Fake your throws."

I gave him a blank look. "Do you do this for a living? I thought you were a builder."

Rob grinned. "I've practically been playing this since I started walking. I have five older siblings, Ellie. I dodged things to survive."

Carmel and her whistle pierced the air again, and we took our positions. I fired up the first serve, pretending to aim for a tall guy standing in front of his teammates. Then, as I tossed, I curved the ball to the big guy in the white T-shirt. He dodged it at the last second, and the guy behind him picked it up, firing it back at Marisa, who jumped out of the way.

Alec scooped the ball and lobbed it at Tall Guy. It hit him, and he walked off the court with a loud groan. Marisa was the next to go, then another guy from the opposing team.

Two down, two to go.

Big Guy in White took possession of the ball, watching us from across the court as he bounced the ball in his hand, probably assessing which one of us would be the easiest to eliminate first. The next thing I knew, he pitched the ball toward me, and it whizzed at lightning speed in my direction. My brain froze, stripping me of the ability to react and protect myself, and for a few beats I thought—no, I knew, *for sure*—that the ball was going to hit me.

Because it was heading, in super slo-mo, straight toward my face.

I realized I needed to move, that if I remained where I was still standing, the ball was going to clobber me in the face, and I'd be eliminated. Which wasn't ideal, because the aim was to win, wasn't it? The aim wasn't to get intimately acquainted with a bright-red rubber ball, or worse, developing a bruise on my face because of high-impact contact with said ball.

But it took longer than a few seconds for my brain to thaw and the gears to properly turn, because I was still rooted at the same spot, even though the ball was less than three feet away from my face. I had probably two, maybe three seconds to jump into action, to move my feet and avoid becoming the next eliminated player. To avoid sustaining serious injuries to my nose, my jaw, and my eyes.

That was when a blur of black suddenly flew in front of me, shielding me from the incoming onslaught of the ball. The next second, a loud *thwack* reverberated in the air, and four things happened at once:

1. A raucous cheer from the opposing team,
2. A loud roar from Rob, followed by his angry, *"What the fuck?!"*,
3. A long whistle to signal the temporary pause of the game, and
4. Alec going down like a sack of potatoes.

I gaped at him, his body slumping at my feet, his face firmly planted in the sand, as my brain raced to catch up with the latest events.

Alec jumped in front of me and got clobbered in the face with the ball.

Because he was trying to save me.

Sure, it wasn't a life-or-death situation, but this man had made a split-second decision to intentionally place himself in harm's way to stop me from getting hurt. He was willing to be hit in the face, which could potentially break his nose, or his jaw, or split his lip, *for me.*

Rob and Marisa rushed over, snapping me out of my daze, and I quickly crouched down to check on him.

"Alec?" He hadn't moved, and a sliver of panic gripped me. "Are you okay?"

A few seconds passed, and my panic was about to skyrocket when he finally groaned. Relief washed over me when he rolled over. There was an angry red spot on his left cheek where the ball must have made impact, but other than that, he seemed fine. No blood, his nose wasn't broken, and his eyes weren't swollen. I made a move to sit him up, but Rob stopped me.

"Don't move him yet," Rob said. "Just in case he has a concussion or a neck injury."

The panic came back, more urgent than before. A concussion? What if Alec sustained a life-threatening concussion because he *was trying to save me*?

"I'm okay," Alec said. "It's just my cheek. My head's fine."

Another shrill whistle pierced the air, and Carmel announced that Big Guy in White was out of the game for hitting an opponent in the face. She ignored his protests, as Rob and I helped Alec to stand up.

I peered into his eyes, worry gnawing at my insides. "You sure you're okay?"

"I'm fine, really." He gave me a smile. "He didn't hit you, and that's all that matters."

And that was when it struck me. A realization so overwhelming, as if I were about to drown in the ocean behind me, the splashing waves refusing to let go until I gave in and acknowledged it.

That I was in love with this man.

One of the women in the blue shirts came and handed Alec a bag of ice and ushered him to the side of the makeshift court. She was talking to him in a low voice, checking that he was okay, asking whether he wanted to see a doctor.

"He's okay," Rob said, as Carmel blew her whistle again, resuming the game. "All the more reason we need to win this. For him."

I nodded and got into a ready position, adrenaline rushing

through my body. Rob pitched the ball across the court to our last opponent, missing him by an inch. He picked it up and hurled it back at us, too fast and too hard, hitting Rob in the foot.

He gave me a fist bump. "Do us proud, E. No pressure, but remember, five thousand dollars. Do it for Alec."

And then it was just me against a tall, fit, towering monster of a man on the opposite court. I glanced at Alec, who was sitting courtside next to Rob and Marisa, the ice pack still on his cheek. He flashed me a thumbs-up and mouthed, *"Go get him."*

The ball suddenly came flying at me, and I ducked just in time. I grabbed it and made a deliberate gesture of aiming it at my opponent, but missed him by mere inches.

The ball was now in his court.

He was taking his time, being dramatic about aiming it at me. I did a little jog on the spot, priming myself for a quick dodge. My opponent suddenly raised his hand and pitched the ball across the court. It whizzed straight toward my legs, and I dodged it within an inch of my life. Grabbing the ball, I walked to the middle and narrowed my eyes at him. He grinned at me, making taunting "come on" gestures with his hands.

That was when a colony of seagulls saved the day.

The birds cawed loudly as they flew above us. The next thing I knew, generous amounts of white droppings rained down on my opponent, perfectly landing on his face. Chuckles and disgusted groans echoed from the spectators as he swore and looked up at the offending birds.

Seizing the moment, I flung the ball across as hard as I could, hitting him squarely in the chest. Disappointed cries erupted from his supporters, while earsplitting cheers exploded from ours. Alec was the first one to rush to the court and hug me, lifting and twirling me with glee.

"You were amazing." He grinned and bent down to brush

my mouth with a quick kiss, lingering for a little longer than he needed to.

Before I could process what just happened, Rob and Marisa engulfed me with hugs, and all my thoughts were swallowed by the whoops and cheers from the crowd.

CHAPTER 23

You Weren't Ready for the Truth

E veryone was still in high spirits when dinner rolled around. The restaurant was full of chatter and laughter, and people I didn't know came up and congratulated me on our win. Alec had been grinning from ear to ear the whole evening, playing the perfect boyfriend role, hamming it up for everyone to see.

Completely, blissfully unaware that I was still reeling from my earlier revelation.

Halfway through dinner, Jacqui stood up and clinked a fork on her glass, sending a quiet hush throughout the room.

"Thank you all for being here tonight," she began, looking every inch the successful, awe-inspiring businesswoman that she was. "This has been such a wonderful day, and I trust we've all enjoyed this chance to get to know our colleagues a little better."

A smattering of applause went around the room.

"I'd also like to welcome our newest business partners, Alec Mackenzie and Rob Carmichael, from Mackenzie Construc-tions." She motioned for the two to stand up, then raised her glass in a toast. "Gentlemen, we're honored to have you with us. We have lots of exciting things on the horizon, and I look forward to a long and fruitful partnership. Welcome aboard."

Murmurs of "welcome aboard" echoed around us. As Jacqui continued her speech, my phone vibrated in my pocket. I pulled it out, my eyes narrowing when I saw my mother's number flashing on the screen. I hadn't bothered to call her back after that night, because I wasn't exactly keen to find out what she wanted. Knowing her, whatever it was, it couldn't be good.

I rejected the call, but another soon followed. It would take more than one rejection to deter Veronica Pang, and another call vibrated immediately after. I declined that one, too, and the next one after that, before finally turning the phone off.

Alec glanced at me. "Don't you need to get that?"

"It's not important."

He raised his eyebrows at my clipped tone. "Is everything okay?"

I clenched my jaw. "That was my mother."

His eyes widened, and he looked like he was about to say something but thought better of it. Without another word, he returned his attention to Jacqui, who was now announcing the employee recognition awards. I followed his lead and pushed the calls out of my mind, respectfully clapping whenever Jacqui called out a name and handed out the awards. All the while, my conscience nagged at me, whispering worries and doubts, making guilt rise a thousandfold inside my heart. My parents might be manipulative and overbearing, but they were still my family. What if she or my dad was sick, or in trouble? Eric would have told me if they were, wouldn't he? Or what if she was calling about Eric?

My upbringing and years of being under her shadow sneakily crept their way back into my brain. My guilty conscience rapped me in the head, nagging and berating me for being such an ungrateful, inconsiderate daughter and sister.

And it emerged victorious.

Sighing, I leaned over to whisper to Alec, "I'm going to call her back."

He turned to me, his eyes searching mine. "You want me to come with you?"

"Thanks, but I'll be fine."

Getting up, I walked out of the restaurant and found a quiet spot near the deserted pool. I turned my phone back on, then took a deep breath to compose myself before pressing her number. Two seconds later, the call connected.

"Why didn't you answer my calls?"

I let out a long breath and braced myself. *Here we go.*

"I had never, not even once, received any calls from you since you left home. And now, when I'm being the bigger person, picking up the phone to call you *first*, you rejected them? Is that how I raised you?"

The temptation to toss my phone into the pool was so, so great.

"Obviously you've forgotten about your poor, old, aging parents. Very disappointed in you, Ellie. *Very* disappointed."

Anger bubbled up behind my rib cage. *That's it.* The old Ellie would probably have swallowed the barrage of insults and guilt trips without thinking twice. But the newly updated, vastly improved, Ellie 2.0 wouldn't take this lying down.

"In case you've forgotten, you were the one—"

But she cut me off. "Are you in Port Benedict? With that man who nearly killed you?"

I could feel blood rushing to leave my face. *How did she know?*

"I don't know what you mean."

"You are, aren't you?" She spat out the question, her voice full of contempt. "Eric wouldn't say anything. I found out on my own, no thanks to you."

My mind raced, trying to connect the dots, figuring out where or how she could possibly have heard about it. Alec had been careful to post pictures only on Facebook, where Jacqui had her only account, and our family members were excluded every single time. Eric and Naomi were the only people who knew where I was, and I knew they would not say anything.

Who else could have tipped her off?

"Who told you? And what do you want, Mom?"

"Do you know how damaging it would be to have our family name associated with someone like him? Someone from a dishonorable family, whose father is a criminal?"

"His dad may have abandoned them, but he's not a criminal," I said. "His mother had to work hard to provide for the children on her own. Alec even had to move here for a job to support his mom and sisters financially. They're a hardworking, honest family."

Her reply was a sneering laugh. "Is that what he told you? That he moved away for a job? Oh, darling, he's not being honest. He's a liar, just like his dad."

What did she mean by that? My mind went into a tailspin. *What am I missing?*

"Nothing good could come from socializing with him and his family. If people—our business partners, the media—found out that a member of our family is fraternizing with someone like him, it's going to be a catastrophe."

"Stop exaggerating."

"I'm not. This is serious." She sounded offended. "Eric and George's new brewery just launched, and they can't afford any negative press associated with it."

I scoffed. "Of course. The business comes first, second, third, and last. The rest of us are only an afterthought."

"It has to come first. How do you think we could give you and Eric the best education money can buy? Afford all your medication? Your dad and I started from nothing, and we had to work our tails off when we founded the business. Everything that you and Eric had growing up, the private schools, the overseas trips, it was because we worked so hard and sacrificed so much. To give you two a good life. To guarantee a lasting legacy for our family."

"I don't want a legacy. I just wanted a normal family."

But my mother was unstoppable, on a roll.

"I won't let you ruin everything that we've worked so hard for, over him. So if you have even an ounce of empathy in your body, you're going to leave that man and fly back home first thing tomorrow morning. You hear me?"

My backbone was screaming bloody murder, wanting to get a word in, to remind her I was an adult. I didn't have to put up with her controlling and manipulative ways anymore. She needed to stop, and it was way past overdue.

"No. Who I see, or what I do, is none of your business. It's time you stopped running my life. If *you* have an ounce of empathy for your daughter, back off and leave me alone."

I hung up, my body shaking with anger. My phone vibrated again, but I switched it off with a snarl and shoved it back into my pocket.

The night was crystal-clear, with stars dotting the brilliant evening sky. I started walking, aimlessly, and found myself in the lush, darkened garden. The full moon cast shadows over the trees as I wandered along the jogging path, trying to calm myself down.

But the more I thought about her call, her words playing on repeat, the angrier I became. My brain raced, trying to figure out what had just happened. How did she find out where I was? Did Alec make a mistake, not omitting our families from his posts?

But more importantly, what did she mean about Alec being a liar?

Switching my phone back on, I sent rapid-fire text messages to Eric and Naomi, asking if they knew how she'd found out.

I needed some answers. *Now.*

Turning around, I rushed back toward the main building. I slipped into the restaurant, where the dinner was already winding down. Rob was chatting with a few people at the bar, but Alec was nowhere to be seen. I found him in the lobby, frowning at his phone. Gritting my teeth, I quickened my stride, marching toward him with purpose.

"Hey."

He looked up. "There you are. I've been trying to call you. How did it go?" Noticing my sour face, his frown deepened. "Not good?"

"Somehow my mother worked out where I am."

He blanched. "What? We were careful with our posts, and Eric wouldn't say anything."

"That's what I'm trying to figure out. She said it's not Eric."

"Who else knew? Would Naomi have said something?"

"I trust her. Maybe *you* did something wrong with your posts." My tone was accusing.

"I didn't." Alec scrolled through his phone and held up one of his posts for my inspection, showing that it was set to *Friends except* . . . "See?"

My phone pinged, and it was my brother, surprised to hear about the phone call. I racked my brain, trying to walk back the past few weeks.

Then it hit me. Something Jacqui had said about a press release.

I scrolled frantically through my phone, then waved it in his face when I found what I was looking for. "The GPG press release, announcing the acquisition. They used the photo from the dinner to accompany the article."

Alec took the phone, his eyes scanning the post, his face turning grim. He had his arms around me in the picture, both of us beaming at the camera. It was proudly displayed on all Goodwin Property Group's social media accounts for the entire universe to see. There was a short write-up about Alec and his company, calling him a "prominent, award-winning residential developer on the rise."

And the proverbial nail in the coffin was the caption.

Alec Mackenzie, CEO of Mackenzie Constructions, and his partner, Ellie Pang.

My heart—and my stomach—crashed to the ground.

"That's got to be it." Alec handed me my phone back. "She could have set a Google alert on your name and got notified when the article was posted."

"She said something else." My mind jumped back to the conversation with my mother. "About your father being a criminal. Said you're lying about why you moved here."

Blood drained from his face, and I was taken aback by his horrified look.

"What was she talking about, Alec? What aren't you telling me?"

His jaw clenched. "That's a private family matter. It's not her story to tell."

I gaped at him. "So she was right?"

"It's none of your business. Or hers." He turned around, walking away from me. "It's late. I'm going to bed."

"Don't you walk away from me. We're not done here, and you've got some explaining to do. Did you really leave home because of a job offer? Why did she call you a liar?"

Alec didn't reply and kept walking.

"Why did you really leave?" My head felt light, and I could feel the beginning dizziness of a hypo, but I brushed it aside and marched after him, because I was too fired up. "What happened with your dad?"

He only quickened his pace as we speed-walked on the quiet, dimly lit garden path.

"Alec. Stop ignoring me." My legs were a bit shaky, but I pushed on, moving faster to keep up with him.

He came to an abrupt halt in front of our room, turning around to face me. "You want to know the truth? Yes, my father is a criminal. He had an affair, had a second family with another set of children, nicely tucked away in some small town in God knows where. Whenever we thought he was on a business trip, he actually went to see his second family."

"You told me that. That makes him the worst father in the world, but not a criminal."

"Well, he's both. Because to support that second wife and set of sons, he stole money from his employer." Alec turned around to slide the key card, then pushed the door open. "He embezzled close to three million dollars over six years and went to prison because of it. The company he worked for paid off a lot of people to keep it hush-hush, so it didn't make the news. Nine years, Ellie. He was in prison for *nine fucking years*."

A soft gasp escaped me. My heart was beating faster, although not from his words. My pump vibrated, likely sending me a gentle warning that I was about to go low and that I should be eating some carbs to avoid that from happening.

Alec stalked across the room to the other end, stopping in front of the sliding patio door. "They let him off early a few years ago for good behavior. So yes, your mother was right."

"Why didn't you tell me?"

He glanced at me, looking exhausted. "Because I was ashamed. And I didn't need your pity, or anyone else's. That look on your face right now? I never wanted to see that. Even Eric didn't know. All I told him was that my dad had left us and started a new family."

I ignored the light-headedness that was knocking louder, making itself known. "But how did my mother know about the embezzlement?"

"Your mother knows a lot of powerful people."

"Have you seen your dad since he was released?"

"No." He shoved his hands into his pockets, his eyes watching the darkness outside. "He's probably living with his second family, or maybe even an entirely new family. We did just fine without him, and we don't need him coming back into our lives."

I was sweating, and my pump vibrated again, giving me another warning that I was about to crash. "And why did you move away?"

He was still staring out into the darkness. After what felt like forever, he sighed and finally said, "Because of you."

My legs wobbled, like they were about to crumble and send me toppling to the ground. The dizziness was now unbearable, and I shook my head, trying to center myself back into the present. But nothing helped.

I knew what was happening. My blood glucose level was dropping rapidly.

Taking a few tentative steps toward the armchair, I slumped down and closed my eyes. Alec was still talking, but I wasn't listening. My hypo kit was in my bag by the door, but if I tried to get up and walk over to get it, I'd probably collapse after a few steps.

The alarm on my pump beeped loudly this time, followed by my CGM app, both sending me urgent pleas to look after myself.

"Ellie?" Alec must have heard the beeping, because he turned to look at me, alertness snapping into his face. He marched over and knelt in front of me. "Are you having a hypo?"

My head was spinning, so I could only nod and point at my bag. "I need sugar."

Alec went to grab it, zipping it open as he walked back to me. Shivering, I took the bag from him, but my hands were shaking. Taking over, he pulled out a juice box and a bottle of glucose tablets. I pointed at the bottle, so he opened it and handed me several of the raspberry chewable tablets. He searched my bag, found my blood glucose meter, and pricked my finger.

"You don't need to do that," I said, closing my eyes. "I know I'm low."

"Just to be sure, right?" Alec gently tapped the test strip on the tiny drop of blood. "Better safe than sorry."

"How did you know?" I was still munching on the tablets as we waited for the result to appear. "How to use a blood glucose meter?"

"I've seen you do it when we were younger. And I might have looked up a video or two."

My eyes flew open, and Ellie the Human Goldfish returned, sashaying back into the room with wide eyes and heart thumping louder than the ocean waves crashing outside. I couldn't utter a single word, so I just stared at him in astonishment.

Although, really, after everything he'd done for me, should I really be surprised?

His attention went to the flashing red number and downward arrow on the meter. His brows drew together with concern. "Forty-five. That's very low, isn't it? Is there anything else we should do? Do you have a glucagon kit?"

Of course he knew about glucagon kits. "You really *have* been reading up, huh?" I let out a weak chuckle. "No, not yet. Now we wait." I shuddered, and Alec hopped up, grabbed the comforter from the bed, and wrapped it around me.

"Fifteen minutes? Until your levels are back up?" At my raised eyebrows, he shrugged. "Eric used to set fifteen-minute timers for you all the time, remember? Then another fifteen if you were still low."

This was grossly unfair. My heart didn't have a snowball's chance in hell of surviving this. How was I supposed to stay mad at him if he kept this up?

"How often do you have hypos? I haven't seen you have one since you moved here."

My pump and CGM app beeped again, reminding me that I

was still low. Alec was watching me, obviously expecting some kind of verbal answer.

"I have mild ones maybe once, twice a week. But I'm always quick to treat it. This is probably from the swimming and all the games," I finally said. "I should reduce my insulin intake whenever I do a lot of physical activities. But I was too hyped up with everything that happened today, and I miscalculated. It's a silly mistake. I should've known better."

He glanced at the timer on his phone. "Eight more minutes. How are you feeling?"

"Better." My brain fog was starting to lift. "The glucose tablets are working their magic."

We spent the next seven-and-a-half minutes sitting in companionable silence. He had dragged the other armchair and positioned it next to mine, alternating between checking the CGM app on my phone every few minutes, as we both watched the number slowly creep up, and watching the darkness outside, looking contemplative. When his timer went off, we did another finger prick, making sure I was back to normal.

"Eighty. Much better." Alec showed me the glucose meter, then checked the number on the CGM app to confirm they corresponded. He let out a long, relieved breath, his shoulders visibly relaxing. "That was scary, Ellie. I thought we were going to have a repeat of ten years ago."

"No, we weren't. It was my fault, because I ignored the signs." I reached for my bag again, where I always kept a small stash of low-GI snacks for after a hypo episode. Pulling out a mini packet of rice crackers, I waved it at him with a smile, trying to lighten the mood. "Would you like something to nibble on? Maybe it'll take your mind off things."

"Snacks are the last thing on my mind right now."

"You sure? These are honey soy chicken flavored. They're the best."

He sighed. "I'm being serious. You just shaved ten years off my life."

"Don't worry. I'm used to it."

"You don't understand." Alec got up and paced around the room. "You might be used to it, but I'm not. And it was a harsh wake-up call. I can't live through another episode, like the one you had all those years ago. I can't watch you being carried on a gurney into another ambulance again, because I *cannot* lose you, Ellie." He stopped pacing and stared at me. "Do you understand me? I can't lose you for the second time."

I was supposed to finish my packet of crackers, but right now, nothing else seemed to matter. Right now, I should be bursting with happiness, jumping with glee, and shouting my joy from the mountaintops. Because Alec Mackenzie, my fake boyfriend, my longtime childhood crush, the guy I used to hate *but was now in love with*, was all but confessing his feelings for me.

The question was, *What was I going to do about it?*

CHAPTER 24

Filthy Things to Make You Scream

Nothing. I wouldn't do anything, because once bitten, twice shy, and there absolutely wouldn't be a third time, not even if all the planets, the suns, and the moons in the entire universe had gotten out of alignment.

But why not? my rational brain argued. *You're in love with him, and he obviously cares a lot for you. What's stopping you?*

Because once I went there, there was no turning back. And despite all that he'd done to prove that he was a different person from ten years ago, it was still scary, and there was no guarantee that he wouldn't hurt me again, and I didn't know how I'd recover if he did . . .

Maybe I could pretend he didn't say anything. Or act as if I didn't hear him.

"Well, thanks for helping. And for staying with me. You should probably get back to dinner. Rob and Jacqui might be looking for you. I think I'll go to bed."

He was still staring at me, the look on his face inscrutable. Hoping my casual tone conveyed how cool and unruffled I was (*not*), I shoved the last two pieces of crackers into my mouth to hide my nervousness. I packed up my glucose meter and disposed of the used test strips while turning my back to him, so he couldn't see how flustered I was. Then I got up and started toward the bathroom, making sure to carefully maneuver my way around him.

But he had other ideas.

Alec stepped in front of me, blocking my path. "They won't even notice I'm gone."

I cleared my throat, not meeting his eyes, because I might lose all my already shaky willpower if I did. It was safer to avoid any forms of eye contact, or physical touch, or anything to do with this man; and I should really back the hell away from him, *right now.*

"Can you move out of the way?"

He didn't budge. "Ellie, look at me."

I didn't look at him. "Fine, then I'll move." I took a couple of steps to the right, attempting to go around him.

But he mirrored my movements, blocking me again, and this time, his hand lifted my chin, and I had no choice but to gaze into his eyes. Alec took another step closer, and I was practically nose to nose with him. He was chewing on his lips, drawing my gaze to his mouth.

"Life is short, Ellie. I think I'm done trying to fight this."

I was incapable of forming a coherent thought, let alone a reply, because he leaned down, his lips lingering only inches away. He paused, asking me for permission, giving me a chance to back off. My brain waved a tearful goodbye to my weak self-control, because all I had to do was tilt my mouth, and I'd be tasting those lips. Flames erupted inside my stomach, and I wondered if the room thermostat had malfunctioned because it felt twenty degrees hotter than normal.

What if this was a mistake?

But he was right. Life *was* too short, and I didn't want to have any regrets.

I wanted him.

Even if it was just for tonight.

I moved the tiniest bit, my lips grazing his. Alec hissed out a sharp breath, and courage shot into my blood. "The last time we did this, you jumped off me like I was on fire and said something about promising someone."

Both of his hands moved to cup my face, and he was slowly, gently, walking me back toward the bed. "Fuck the promise."

The back of my legs hit the bed. "I think I'd rather you fuck me."

The next thing I knew, his mouth crushed mine. He tasted like mint and champagne, and he was kissing me like his life depended on it, like the sky would fall and the world would come to an end if he dared to stop.

I fell back on the bed, pulling him with me. His hands slipped under my shirt, and in one swift movement, he undid my bra. His hands roamed free, touching, claiming, and caressing. His thumbs gently teased my nipples, sending exquisite shudders throughout my body. He took one of my breasts into his mouth and lavished attention on my nipple, licking and sucking it, before turning to the other. I let out a soft moan as his rigid outline pressed hard against my thighs.

Pulling off my jeans, he started to move down my body, planting kisses on my inner thighs. I shivered, my hands trembling as I disconnected and removed my pump, while he tugged on my panties, kissing his way to where I wanted him the most.

"Do you know how many times I've thought about this?"

Before I could answer, he pulled the flimsy fabric aside, and with one quick motion, sent my already soaked panties crumpling on the floor, then slid a finger inside. "Hundreds of times. Thousands, maybe. My imagination doesn't do this justice."

He began to stroke, and we both inhaled sharply as he gently added another finger and groaned, "Oh, fuck. You're so wet."

I didn't have a response to that, because my brain had turned into mush, and all the air had been sucked out of my lungs. If I were to hazard a wild guess, this must be what it would feel like to die and go to heaven. But his torture didn't end there. He bent down, adding his tongue along with his fingers, licking, feasting, and teasing, almost tipping me over the edge.

I sucked in a breath and hissed, "*Alec*. I'm close."

Instead of answering, his tongue stroked deeper, his fingers moved in a frenzy, and I rolled my hips against them, riding him unashamedly. Before I knew it, I went over the edge, letting out a loud, shameless moan as the orgasm crashed through my body and I convulsed against him. His mouth traveled up my body and found my lips, while his fingers continued to tenderly work their magic.

My eyes were closed, and I was still trying to catch my breath when he tugged my top off. Two seconds later, it landed with a soft thud on the floor, on top of my jeans, my panties, and my bra. Then he went quiet.

"Alec?"

I opened my eyes and found him staring at my stomach, where I had little dots of scars from old pump sites. His eyes found mine again, and the look in them was almost enough to give me another orgasm. Without saying a word, he bent down to drop kisses on them, as his hands gently stroked my breasts.

I swallowed the lump in my throat, his tenderness threatening to break open the tear ducts in my eyes. *Goddamn it, Ellie. Who the hell cries in the middle of sex?*

His mouth crawled back up my body and closed around a nipple, and I sucked in a breath, as thoughts of tears and tenderness were immediately forgotten.

"This isn't fair. Why the hell are you still fully clothed?" My hands shot out, trying to unbuckle his belt. I fumbled with the buttons on his jeans, my hands trembling as I struggled to peel them off.

"Remind me to wear a pair with zippers next time." Alec pulled away and took over, his impatient fingers shucking them off in just a few seconds.

I grinned at his words. "There's going to be a next time?"

"Hell, yeah." He kicked his jeans to the side, then leaned down to kiss me again, smiling against my lips. "More than once. Or twice. Or thrice. What's four times?"

"You need to stop talking." I reached inside his boxers, my fingers circling around his long, hard length, loving the feel of his hot skin in my hand. He groaned when I began to stroke him.

"And you need to slow down," he breathed out, his voice hoarse. "I'm only human, Ellie. Not going to last too long if you keep that up."

"I don't understand the instructions." I stroked him a little faster and rubbed his tip, drawing out the moisture. He let out a hiss, his head falling back and his breath quickening.

"Holy shit. Wait. Stop."

Pulling away, he tugged his shirt off and pulled his boxers down. My eyes widened at the sight of him, sending shivers of anticipation throughout my body.

"Hey. My eyes are up here."

I looked up at him, his face split in a sexy grin.

"Sorry." I returned the grin. "The view was just too glorious. But again, why are we still talking?"

He chuckled and bent down to pull out his wallet from his jeans, retrieving the thin plastic foil from inside. The five seconds it took him to cover himself felt like five minutes. When he made a move to remove his glasses, my hand reached out, stopping him.

"Keep them on," I whispered. The sight of him in nothing but his glasses made my heart ricochet behind my rib cage. Or maybe it was the amazing feel of him against me, skin on skin, his dick pulsing hot and urgent against my thigh.

Alec groaned as I curled my fingers around him, guiding him to my entrance. He slid in, just an agonizing inch, letting his tip graze me, giving me a preview of what was to come.

"Is this going to take all night?" I gasped as he pushed in a little deeper, but still not all the way in. "Because I would really prefer to keep things moving along."

"Why, do you have somewhere else more important to be?"

His grin was teasing, but his pupils dilated as I raised my hips to meet him, greedily commanding him to sink deeper.

"No, but you do." I moaned, as he did another circling motion at my entrance, teasing me, driving me wild. "*Alec*. You need to be inside me. Right now. *Please*."

The teasing grin disappeared, and in one swift motion, he plunged into me.

"God, Ellie," he breathed out. "*You feel amazing*."

He was hot and hard and slick, and felt *so good*. The cords on his neck stood out as he growled, straining to stay still, but I wriggled my hips to take him farther in. Alec let out another groan and began to move, sliding in and out slowly at first, the delicious friction between our bodies nearly sending me into oblivion, then faster, harder, as our sighs and his moans and my pleas of "more" filled the room. Our mouths found each other again, fusing and devouring, as he began to lose control, and before long, I was rocking and shivering against him, as his body shuddered together with mine.

And this time, I had truly died and gone to heaven.

CHAPTER 25

Don't Believe Everything You See on Social Media

Two weeks ago, if anyone had tried to convince me that hot, mind-blowing romance-novel-slash-movie-scenes sex *did* exist in real life, I'd have laughed in their face and told them they were out of their mind.

Well, it turned out I'd been missing out on that specific niche. A delicious, mind-boggling, bone-melting, earth-shattering niche. I'd been missing out on *a lot*.

The first thing I saw when I opened my eyes the next morning was his sleeping face next to me, looking positively adorable. I spent the next few minutes watching him, wearing a goofy grin, as I tried to carve his features into my memories.

Last night had definitely changed everything, although I still wasn't sure where we'd go from here. I knew how challenging it would be with my family, but I was hopeful there'd be a future for—

"Stop staring at me. It's creepy."

I blinked. His eyes were still closed, but the tiniest hint of a smile lifted the corners of his mouth. His eyes creaked open, and I loved how his smile lit up his entire face.

Not that I was keeping track, but that was three times now that I had used that word in conjunction with Alec Mackenzie.

"I'm not staring. I just woke up, and I happened to be facing in your direction, which is why it seems like I was watching you, but I swear to God I wasn't, because I mean, really, who does that? And you're right, it would be creepy. Stalkerish, even."

He cut my ramblings short as his mouth found mine, shutting me up. Groaning, I shifted my body and pressed it against his, sending an ache straight to that place between my legs. An encore of last night's multiple performances seemed very likely, and the mere thought of it sent tingles and lust jolting throughout my body.

But before we could get very far, his phone vibrated on the bedside table. He ignored it, but whoever was on the other end was as persistent as my mother.

"Maybe you need to get that."

"I'll turn it off." He reluctantly pulled away and reached for the phone, but when he saw the caller ID, a frown twisted his face. "Actually, I do have to take this. Stay where you are, because we're going to finish what we started." He gave me another kiss and hopped off the bed, heading toward the patio.

Heaving a contented sigh, I grabbed my own phone and scrolled through my text messages. My mother had left several, as expected, and so had Eric. And to my surprise, there were two missed calls, and nine messages from Naomi. Her first one read:

We need to talk. Call me.

I wondered if this had anything to do with the last WhatsApp conversation we were having. She'd sent me a long, rambling message about how my mother had been pestering Eric to have three big weddings: one here, one in Indonesia, and one in Korea, although Naomi much preferred a small, intimate ceremony with family and close friends.

But my gut told me it had something to do with why my mother had called last night.

My thumb hovered over the second message before giving it a tap, and my stomach sank when I read what it said:

Your mother is on the warpath. Call me ASAP.

Yep, I was right. And it was way too early in the morning to deal with this.

Deciding that it could wait a couple of hours, I tossed my phone back on the nightstand. I settled back and scooted over to Alec's side of the bed, sniffing at his familiar scent. Then, because I had no shame nor self-control, I took his fluffy pillow and covered my face with it, closing my eyes and taking in his scent. I wondered if the resort would notice if I ~~stole~~ borrowed this pillow and took it home with me.

Right then, the patio door slid open. I hurriedly tossed the pillow back, rearranging my position to imitate a tempting, seductive woman, wearing what I hoped to be a sexy smile on my face. Or at the very least, a semi-decent impression of one.

Alec strolled back in, staring at his phone, a worried frown creasing his eyebrows.

"What's wrong?" I sat up, wiping the sexy smile off my face. "Is everything okay?"

"No, actually. It's Gemma."

Something clicked in my brain.

"Your sister, Gemma? So . . . she's the one that's been calling you?"

That caught his attention, and he looked up, tilting his head. "What?"

"You know, all those late-night phone calls you've been getting.

I always thought it was the girl you said you were interested in . . . You mean it's always been your sister?"

"Yeah." Understanding dawned on his face, and a slow grin lifted his mouth. "Were you jealous, Ellie?"

A whoosh of relief flew through me, and it felt as if two heavy bags of rocks had just been lifted from my shoulders. I had an overwhelming urge to grab him and kiss him into oblivion. "Psssh. Don't be silly. Of course not."

His grin widened. "Yes, you were."

"I don't know what you're talking about."

"Yes, you do. You were jealous, because *you like me*," he sing-songed.

Love. I love you.

"Is everything okay with your sister?"

"No, but we can talk about that later." For a nanosecond, I thought I saw a brief look of sadness passing over his face. Tossing his phone on the bedside table, he crawled back to bed, his eyes fixed on mine, and a sexy grin on his face. "Right now, I've got something much more important to do."

We spent the morning tangled up in each other, before wrapping things up with a steamy shower session. We'd missed the optional dolphin-watching and snorkeling sessions, so it was almost lunchtime when we finally emerged from our room to meet the others.

Rob was nowhere to be seen. When I saw a free table for two by the window overlooking the beach, I made a beeline for it. Alec followed, but he was busy texting, the worried look returning to his face. We sat down, and I reached across the table to cover his hands with mine.

"Is Gemma okay? Anything I can do to help?"

Alec tore his attention away from the phone and gave me a small smile. "Thanks. We'll be fine." With an apologetic nod, he went back to the device, his face subdued.

I wanted to say more, but he looked so focused, barely noticing anything apart from the messages on his phone. Deciding to give him some time alone, I got up and went over to the buffet table to find some food.

I was halfway through my breakfast when Jacqui strolled over to our table.

"Morning. Slept well last night?"

"Didn't get much sleep," Alec replied, putting his phone aside. "Must be the leftover adrenaline rush from the competition."

He gave me a meaningful glance, sending heat rushing to my cheeks.

Jacqui's smile didn't quite reach her eyes. "We need to talk. Privately. Got a minute?"

Alec nodded. "Of course."

We followed her out of the restaurant, heading toward the lobby. Jacqui stopped to chat with a few resort employees along the way, but she was disconcertingly silent with us—no smile, no effort to make polite talk. We found a set of vacant chairs near the lobby entrance, and by the time we sat down, whatever small smile had been on her face had completely disappeared.

"I'll get right to the point," she said. "I received an email from Phil last night. You see, Phil and I go way, way back. We both started in the industry around the same time, practically from nothing, and we worked hard to get to where we are right now. And he and I, even though we've had our share of disagreements in the past, we've always had each other's backs. I'd trust him with my life."

Both Alec and I nodded, the confusion in his face mirroring what I felt.

"And Phil's gut instincts told him there was something not

quite right about your relationship." Her tone was calm, but her eyes were icy. "Something about the timing of Ellie showing up in Port Benedict being questionable. How it coincides too much with GPG looking into acquiring Mackenzie Constructions. I didn't want to believe him at first, because I liked and admired you both. So he took it upon himself to dig a little deeper into your backgrounds."

Blood drained from my face, and I could feel sweat beginning to pool on my forehead. *Shit, shit, shit.* I snuck a quick glance at Alec. He looked completely unfazed, but he was probably doing his best not to freak out.

"Phil seemed to think that you two hadn't been in touch for a long time. He couldn't prove it, because both your personal social media accounts are private, and neither of you are tagged together in any public posts anywhere. I tried to defend you, reminding him that you two were in a long-distance relationship for two years. Told him I've seen your photos on Facebook. That a lack of social media presence isn't uncommon, because not everyone is hooked on posting every single facet of their lives online."

"That's very true," I stammered. "I don't post a lot on social media. Once every few months, maybe. Once a year, even. Alec is the same."

"And our relationship is exactly what we've told you," Alec replied, in a surprisingly cool, unflappable tone. "You know you can't put too much stock in social media posts. Things aren't always what they seem."

I didn't know how he could be so calm, but I was glad at least one of us was.

She was watching us, her eyes cold. "That's true."

"Yes. And just like we've told you, I've been in love with Ellie since—"

Jacqui cut him off. "I want you to listen to this." She thumbed her phone, and I froze as Naomi's confused voice echoed between us.

"They're not a couple. They've known each other for ages, that's true, but they're not together. I would know if they were. Is this a prank call?" Her voice turned suspicious. "Wait, did you say you're from the *Port Benedict Gazette*? And you're writing an article about Alec and his company? What was your name, again?"

Naomi's messages. She'd been trying to tell me about this call.

Jacqui switched off the recording, her icy eyes now blazing with fury.

"Phil did some digging, Ellie, and found that your family owns Pang Food Industries. He then contacted your brother and Naomi Park to ask some questions. Naomi said she had no knowledge that you two had been a couple for the past two years. She even confirmed it with Ellie's brother. I had Carmel call Naomi herself to verify the stories last night."

I closed my eyes, silently groaning.

"This morning, I went to take a closer look at your Facebook account, Alec. You know what I realized?" She laughed, her frosty tone sending chills down my spine. "Phil's gut instinct was spot-on. You never posted any photos with her until several weeks ago. To be precise, a few days before my fundraising event."

"I can explain," Alec said.

"Are you going to spin me that lie about your long-distance relationship again?"

"The reason we never posted any photos online, or told Ellie's brother and her best friend about our relationship, is because her parents think that I'm an unacceptable match for their daughter. Nobody knows we're together. And I was never one to put up photos of my partners on social media anyway, until things got serious."

"He's right. My mother doesn't approve of our relationship, so we've been keeping it a secret from my family." At least this part wasn't a total lie.

"But after two years, we finally decided we couldn't hide it any longer. Which is why Ellie moved out here to be with me."

For a brief minute, Jacqui was quiet, her sharp eyes considering us. Then she shook her head, as if she'd reached a verdict. "No. I think the two of you never had any relationship, because it was all a lie."

She went back to her phone, then turned it around, showing us the screen.

It was George's viral proposal video, currently notching up close to twelve million views.

My breath hitched, while Alec swore softly under his breath, and the color had all but drained from his face.

"Phil managed to find this little gem. I had to watch the video three times to make sure that it was you, Ellie. At first, I thought the video was a few years old, because how can someone else propose to you if you were supposedly dating Alec? But then I realized the video was taken"—she turned the screen toward herself—"on New Year's Eve, less than two months ago. Which doesn't really fit with the timeline of your relationship, does it?"

I winced, as the guests in the video shrieked when the flame burst to life, before the video came to an end.

"So, Alec. Last chance." She pocketed her phone, her eyes piercingly cold, but also, now I realized, with a trace of disappointment. "Care to explain how one of the country's most eligible bachelors proposed to your supposed girlfriend only a couple of months ago?"

This time, Alec let out a defeated sigh. "Look, Jacqui," he began, his voice shaking a little, "I admit, it may have started with a lie, but Ellie and I—"

"Don't insult me. Did you do this because I was interested in you?"

He froze. "No, of course not."

"It was my idea," I blurted out. "I was the one who convinced him to do it." .

Jacqui lifted her palm, shushing us both. "It truly amazes me how you think it's acceptable to start our partnership with a lie. In all my years in the business, I have *never* come across anything like this."

Alec closed his eyes. "Jacqui. I can explain. Please."

She ignored him. "I clearly have misjudged you. I wouldn't have cared about the relationship at all, but it's the elaborate lie that concerned me the most. You've shown me that you have no honesty and integrity. I can't do business or be partners with someone so untrustworthy."

Alec went pale and looked like he was about to throw up.

Jacqui stood up. "I think it's fair to say that the partnership won't be going ahead. Our lawyers will be in touch." Turning to me, she continued, "And obviously, consider the order Carmel placed for the party canceled."

Without a second look, she walked away, leaving us in stunned silence.

CHAPTER 26

Tell Me Your Deepest, Darkest Secrets

After the confrontation with Jacqui, we packed up our stuff, checked out of the resort, and caught an earlier flight back to Port Benedict. All my attempts at talking to Alec or cheering him up were met with a quiet nod or a shake of his head. Rob had been frantically trying to call him, because word had gotten around that the Goodwin-Mackenzie partnership had ended just days after it had started.

When we arrived home, Alec only mumbled a quiet "see you later" and disappeared into his room, closing the door with a firm-sounding click. I stared at his door for a long time, torn between wanting to barge in and give him a comforting hug and assure him that everything would be just fine and giving him the space he was clearly asking for. Deflated, I went to my own room, my heart heavy and breaking, but not knowing how to help.

Later that night, as I unpacked my weekend bag, I realized I hadn't taken my phone off airplane mode. That was when I saw the flood of messages from my mother, even two from my dad, all newly sent in the past few hours. There were also several others from Eric and Naomi, rounding up the total new messages to twenty-two.

I took one cursory glance at the list, with my thumb hovering over the first message, wondering whether I should open them. But after everything that had happened earlier, dealing with my family was the last thing I wanted to do right now. Deciding I'd deal with them tomorrow, I left all twenty-two messages unopened and tossed my phone onto the nightstand. And as I slowly drifted off to sleep, my thoughts went back to Alec, wondering how he was doing, and wishing, more than anything, that I was there to support him.

Alec had left by the time I woke up the next morning. There was no note, but I assumed he'd gone to work, trying to salvage the deal with Jacqui. I was debating whether I should send him a message, but decided to give him some space.

Kim was standing outside her shop with a big grin when I arrived at the bakery. "Welcome back. How was your mini getaway with Loverboy Building Expert?" She peered at me, her curious eyes assessing. "You don't look like someone who'd just returned from a weekend of rest, relaxation, and incredibly hot sex."

"And you would be right."

She followed me inside the bakery. "Is everything okay?"

Her eyebrows dipped farther and farther down as I gave her the condensed version of what had happened. "That's strange. Why would this Phil guy do something like that? Has he got something against Alec?"

"Not that I know of. They've only just met each other at that dinner party."

Kim glanced at her watch. "I gotta go, but let's talk more about it. I'll text Jenna, and maybe we can figure out the missing piece in the puzzle over lunch."

I nodded, grateful for the support.

Our scheduled opening was less than two weeks away, so things were borderline chaotic right now. Rob's crew had finished their work, and I had started training Ruby on her main duties—running the POS system, keeping track of our inventory, and making sure our displays looked nice and pretty. And because Jacqui had canceled her order, which I'd been counting on, I had to make up for it somehow. I pushed the bakery launch harder on social media, offering a generous 20 percent discount during opening week. My To-Do List had grown by several more pages, and as it grew, so did the headache pounding in my brain. But even as I ran around all day, my mind kept wandering back to Alec. All my messages to him were read but unanswered, and when I tried to call in the afternoon, it went straight to his voicemail.

Right now, the shop was quiet, as it was close to 6:00 P.M., and Ruby had already left. I had just finished going over my list, ready to lock up for the day, when my phone beeped with a short message from Naomi. I decided to call her, and she answered on the second ring, sounding frantic.

"Ellie! Where have you been? Why haven't you returned my calls?"

"I'm sorry. Things have been super hectic."

"Are you okay? Eric has also been trying to get in touch with Alec, but he hasn't been returning Eric's calls. Some guy claiming to be a journalist from the *Port Benedict Gazette* contacted me a few days ago, asking a lot of questions about Alec, his company, and his relationship with you."

"I know."

"But I got suspicious, so I hung up after a few minutes. Eric called the *Gazette* to check, and they've never heard of that guy. Then someone else named Carmel, who said she worked for Goodwin Property Group, called a couple of nights ago to ask *more* questions." Naomi paused to take a breath. "Carmel said she wanted to verify some stories for her boss, but I was so suspicious, I hung up on her twice, before one of Eric's contacts in the property industry confirmed her identity. What's going on, Ellie? Why are people asking about your relationship with Alec?"

I finally told her everything: about our arrangement, the pretend relationship for Jacqui, and how it all went pear-shaped yesterday. Naomi was silent, listening, not even interrupting once, until I finished my story.

"You're in love with him, aren't you?"

There was no point in pretending with her. She knew me too well. "Yes."

Naomi chuckled softly. "About time. You two are meant for each other."

A wave of sadness tore through me, because right now, I didn't know how things stood between us. "But with everything that has happened . . . I don't know what to do. I want to help, but I don't know how. He's been avoiding me and ignoring my messages."

"Give him some time," Naomi replied. "Just be there to support him. And whatever happens, be firm and stand your ground, no matter what your mother says. It's your life, your relationship, and you've done so well to start a new life out there on your own. It won't be easy saying no to her face-to-face, but you're strong, and you can do this."

I went quiet. "What do you mean, face-to-face?"

There was a long pause before Naomi spoke again, her tone careful and measured.

"You haven't read my messages, have you?"

"Um." I put her on speaker, then tapped open her unopened messages. As I scrolled through them, my heart started to race, and panic began to overtake my consciousness.

Your mother has been asking questions about you. And Alec.
Eric isn't saying anything, but she's VERY suspicious.

Her next message, an hour after the first one:

She knows where you are. We don't know how she found out,
but she did.

And her very last message from last night.

Heads up. She's flying out to PB tomorrow.

I froze, as Naomi's voice echoed in the empty store. "Her flight
arrived at four."

Shit. I thanked her and hung up, then shoved my laptop into
my bag. I didn't even know where she would be headed, but in my
mind, the most sensible thing to do was leave now, get home, and
warn Alec. As I typed a frantic message to him, the front door
swung open. A familiar voice rang throughout the store, sending
chills down my spine.

"So. This is what you gave up the family business for, huh?"

Dread filled me, as the hairs on my neck prickled and my back
stiffened. I slowly looked up and locked gazes with the woman
I'd moved to the other side of the country to avoid.

She strolled into the shop, casting a critical gaze around. "Not
bad. Although I'd probably invest a bit more in the kitchen if
I were you." She nodded toward the *perfectly fine* commercial
kitchen at the back of the shop.

"What are you doing here?"

Her eyes were still assessing the place. "How much did it cost
you to set up this business? What's your projected monthly turnover for the first year? How long until you break even?"

I heaved a resigned sigh. "Seriously? You've been here for five seconds, and you're already dissecting and criticizing *my* business?"

My mother scoffed. "That's because I can't imagine how this is a profitable business model. There's a reason your father and I never went into retail, especially brick-and-mortar stores. The net profit margins aren't worth the time, the effort, and the investment."

I ignored her unsolicited business analysis. "Let me ask again. Why are you here?"

She finally turned to look at me. "I'm here to take you home."

"Yeah, that's not happening."

"It sure is." Her tone was condescending. "Because I said so."

"How did you know where I was?"

"It wasn't easy, trying to find you. Eric and Naomi wouldn't tell me where you were. You locked your Facebook profile, went private on all your social media accounts. It was a smart move, I'll give you that. Mimi suggested we hire a PI to track you down, but I didn't want to risk the possibility of this . . . *scandal* getting out. Can you imagine what our business partners might say? If they heard that the daughter of Henry and Veronica Pang ran away from home, and we needed *a private investigator* to track her down? How embarrassing would that be for us?"

I kept quiet.

"But I overheard Eric on the phone one afternoon, talking to Alec Mackenzie." At this, her face turned menacing. "So I began to wonder if maybe you were with him. His family wouldn't say anything. Turns out my hunch was correct. I'm sure I would have found you eventually, but it was fast-tracked when a journalist from the *Port Benedict Gazette* called."

So not just Naomi and Eric. Phil also called her. "What did he want?"

"He was writing an article about Mackenzie Constructions

and its founder and discovered his connection to the Pangs through you, *his girlfriend*." My mother sneered. "I made it very clear to him that you are not his girlfriend, and our family is in no way connected to Alec Mackenzie or his family. But thanks to him, we found out where you are."

"Well, congratulations, Mom. You found me. But I'm sorry you made the trip all the way here for nothing, because I'm still not going back home with you."

"I heard about your latest hypo. And how you ignored the signs."

My jaw unhinged. "How did you know?"

"You're lucky it didn't escalate into much worse. Have you forgotten that horrible episode ten years ago? Do you realize there's one single person connecting you to both incidents?" She advanced on me, her eyes narrowing. "Every single time, it's him. It's not a coincidence."

"It's just another hypo," I said impatiently. "You know it happens. It's not a big deal."

"Maybe that last one wasn't. But the next one could be. And if that happened, who's going to be there to look after you? Only your family. No one else can. Especially not someone like him."

"You're wrong. You're just saying that because you've never liked Alec and his family. He's been putting a lot of effort into learning about everything." I gritted my teeth. "And I can look after myself perfectly well."

"We're reinstating you in the will. Provided that you come home with me and cut off all ties with that man. Right now."

"Are you serious? Do you not see what I've built here?" I gestured around the bakery. "Do you really expect me to just walk away and leave everything? Should I just lock up and tell my employee that she doesn't have a job anymore?"

"Only one?" She waved a dismissive hand. "That's easy. Just pay her wages for the next three months."

"*How?* I need to *open* the business to have the money to pay her."

I could have sworn she looked bored with this conversation already.

"Fine. Pang Food Industries will foot the bill. We'll make sure she's paid and looked after." She gave an impatient shake of her head. "Stop wasting time. Is that all?"

"I. Have. A. Business." I enunciated each word, as if I were talking to a disrespectful toddler who was refusing to listen. "Something of my own that I started from scratch. Something that I'm *proud* of."

"Put it up for sale. You're going to work for the family," my mother said, with a finality in her tone. "Eric and George still need a capable CFO at their brewery. We were so lucky the Fitzgeralds were willing to move on from that humiliating proposal. You'll need to learn the ropes because one day, when your father and I retire, Eric will inherit the business, and he's going to need someone he trusts to help him manage things."

"Eric will inherit the business," I repeated, my ears ringing with anger. "And I'll be the one helping him manage things."

"Exactly." My mother looked pleased that I finally understood her grand plan.

"Maybe you could refresh my memory. Not that I wanted it, but explain to me again why I'm not inheriting the business alongside Eric?"

She raised her eyebrows. "That's pretty self-explanatory, isn't it? He's the firstborn son. You don't have the capability to shoulder such an enormous responsibility, and you don't need the extra pressure that comes with running Pang Food Industries. We can't have someone with a health issue holding the reins. *You have a disability, Ellie.* If something were to happen to you, it would leave the leadership of the group in a void. Thousands of people depend on us. We need someone healthy, strong, and of sound mind to lead the business, and Eric is the perfect person for the job. Not you."

I couldn't believe my ears. "Did you say disability? And of sound mind?" That was news to me.

"Well, you rejected a perfectly fine marriage proposal, then left your family without even saying goodbye. Your father and I think that shows immaturity and recklessness. What if we put you in charge of the business, and you suddenly decided to do that again? Bolt from all your responsibilities? That would be disastrous. Billions of dollars could be at risk."

Immaturity and recklessness? *Seriously?*

"Plus, Eric has his degrees, his MBA, and he's been involved with the business since he graduated. Whereas you chose to waste time working for other people and doing meaningless cooking courses and whatever the hell else you've been doing." Giving me a satisfied nod, she concluded her spiel, "That's why we're leaving the business to Eric, with you assisting."

My head spun. I needed her to get out of here. Out of my life.

"We've already been through this so many times. You're different. You have limitations, and you need to accept that your life will never be normal." She made a circling gesture in the air, indicating the bakery. "Trying to pretend otherwise, to prove it by running a business of your own, will never work. It changes nothing."

I wanted to scream. I wanted to grab the delicately embellished porcelain cupcake holder behind me and throw it against the wall.

Instead, I took a couple of steps away from her. "I'm not going back."

My mother's eyes narrowed. "Is this because of him? If you knew what he did, trust me, you'd run for the hills as fast as you can."

"Is this about his dad?" I raised my voice. "I know what he did.

But Alec is a good man. He's honest and dependable. He's not his dad, and definitely not who you think he is."

"How did you think I found out about that latest hypo?"

I gaped at her. "What?"

"He freaked out and told Eric. Told him to come and get you."

I went completely still. That couldn't be true. He was the epitome of cool, calm, and collected that night. Pricked my finger, patiently waited with me until I was fine. The total opposite of freaking out.

But . . . he *was* the only one who knew about it.

She nodded at my stunned expression. "Didn't know that, did you? That honest, dependable Alec isn't as trustworthy as you think?"

My stomach churned, and I felt like I was about to throw up. "He wouldn't do that."

"He did. Look, while we're revealing secrets, I have something else to tell you. I think it's time you found out."

Bile rose in my throat. *What now?* I'd had my quota of horrible news for two lifetimes, and I didn't think I could bear any more.

"Did he tell you why he left ten years ago?" At my confused look, she reached into her handbag and pulled out some folded papers. "Of course he didn't. Here. Read this."

I eyed the papers as if a three-headed monster was going to magically emerge and bite my head off at any second. My first instinct was to push the papers away, but curiosity got the better of me. I slowly unfolded them, afraid of what was to come. As I scanned the official-looking document, a sharp pain sliced through my chest.

It was a confidential agreement, dated ten years ago, between Alec and my parents. To be exact, one week after *that incident*, specifying that my parents would pay the Mackenzies a sum of three million dollars if he agreed to sever all contact with me for the foreseeable future. *Forever.* It was a legally binding contract, in boring, wordy legalese, with lawfully enforceable consequences. My parents had signed it. A lawyer had signed it.

He had signed it.

I blinked twice. Maybe I'd read it wrong. But no, even after flicking through the pages repeatedly, rereading it until I could probably recite all the words by heart, they still spelled out the exact same thing. His name was on it, and so was his signature.

My parents had bribed Alec with three million dollars *to stay away from me.*

And he had *taken the Goddamn money.*

Thoughts and questions swirled around in my head, and lumps of anger clogged my throat. This couldn't be right. Alec wouldn't do that, would he?

Would he?

"He obviously broke the agreement," my mother said, as my eyes drifted back to her in disbelief. "The terms specifically said he's not allowed to be in your immediate vicinity, or he could be liable for breach of contract. We'll be taking him to court, and the judge will rule him guilty faster than you can say 'three million.'"

I glanced at the papers in my hand, then back at her, refusing to believe her words.

"No. You made this up. He said he left to chase job opportunities here. He's the most decent, hardworking man I've ever met."

My mother sighed and shook her head. "You don't believe me? Fine. Go ahead and ask him. I'll be staying at the Plaza Hotel if you need to find me."

CHAPTER 27

I Don't Know How to Quit You

The Mackenzie Constructions office was fifteen minutes away from the bakery, in a converted warehouse on the outskirts of the city. My CR-V screeched to a halt in front of the building, and without bothering to properly park in a vacant spot, I killed the ignition, slammed the door, and marched inside. A young woman at reception was slinging her bag over her shoulder, getting ready to leave the office. She beamed at me when I told her my name.

"Ellie? So glad to finally meet you." She pointed to a corridor leading to a series of doors on her left. "His office is the first door at the very end. Just go right ahead."

Nodding my thanks, I took off in that direction. I could hear muffled voices as I approached, recognizing the second voice as Rob's when I got closer.

". . . so mopey the whole day, man. Want to talk about it?"

I stopped in front of the door, trying to be as silent as I could. There was a long pause before Alec finally replied.

"I screwed up." His voice was so quiet, I had to press an ear to the door to catch what he was saying. "I lost us the Goodwin deal. Ellie's parents are going to sue me, so chances are I'm going to lose her, along with this business, too. I'm sorry, Rob. I let you down."

There was the sound of a chair scraping against the floor, and Rob's voice came back. "We've got an hour before the meeting with the lawyer. Let's unpack everything. First things first. Why are her parents suing you? What did you do?"

"I called Eric. Told him what happened over the weekend."

So Mom had been telling the truth.

"But why?" Rob sounded puzzled. "He's going to tell their parents—"

"He already did. They have the right to know. She's not safe here with me, because I can't look after her. And my priority right now is salvaging the Goodwin deal. This is the best for everyone."

Rob said something I couldn't catch, followed by, "She won't like it. You're going to lose her, man. I thought you said you lo—"

I pushed the door open, storming in as the two men jumped.

"Ellie." Alec's eyes widened, looking like a deer caught in the headlights. "What are you doing here?"

I stopped in front of his desk and glared at him. "Guess who just dropped by?" At his blank look, I tossed him the crumpled agreement. "Explain that."

His face hardened at seeing the papers. He glanced at Rob. "Give us a few minutes?"

Without being asked twice, Rob sprang up, gave me a nervous smile as he passed, and skittered out of the room. The second he closed the door behind him, the anger I'd been trying to suppress bubbled to the surface, and I went on the attack.

"What the hell, Alec? Why didn't you tell me about the money?"

"I didn't have a choice." His tone was flat.

"That's a load of crap. We always have a choice. You chose to take the money."

His hollow laugh echoed in the room. "You don't understand. I really didn't have a choice. Things were terrible when my dad got caught embezzling the money. His employer had powerful, well-connected lawyers, so the court ruled that my family needed to repay the money he'd stolen, plus interest and compensation, and the costs of the lawsuits. There was no way in hell we could pay them back. My mother had to mortgage the house up to the hilt, worked three jobs, seven days a week, and even then, it still wasn't enough." He took a deep breath and looked away. "We never told anyone. Somehow, your parents found out.

"Your mother called a few days after you had the severe hypo. Blamed me for what happened and told me I was a danger to you. How she didn't want someone like me, whose father was a criminal, hanging around you and Eric anymore. Said it'd look bad for your family's reputation. She knew about the law-suits, about our financial difficulties, and bluntly offered me the money. No interests, no repayments needed, it was ours, for free. If I stayed away from you."

My heartbeat was pounding in my ears.

"I couldn't say no. The hard truth was, that money from your parents saved my family. We paid off the debt, and it gave us our lives back. Your parents were happy because you were safe, far away from me. It was a win-win for everyone." He finally looked back at me. "Me leaving home was a tiny price to pay."

Rage charged through me, and I had to grip the edges of his table to steady myself. To give my hands something to hold on to, because I was tempted to snatch one of the thick folders on his desk and whack him on the head with it.

"What about *me*?" I shouted. "It wasn't a win for me. Everyone thought they knew what was best for me, but no one, not one person, has ever asked me what *I* want. Not you, not my family."

He was quiet.

"Does Eric know about this?" I hissed. "Naomi?"

"No. They knew your parents blamed me for the incident. And that I'd left home to find work, to support my family financially. They didn't know about the agreement and the money."

He covered his face with his hands and stayed quiet for a minute.

"The contract was very specific. The reason you weren't invited to Sienna's wedding? It's because of this agreement. I couldn't be within fifty miles of where you were. That was why I had to leave, because it was the easiest. I kept in touch with Eric, so he'd tell me how you were doing. Sent me pictures of you, him, and Naomi every now and then. I saved every single one of them, because they kept me connected to you.

"When Eric called that day, asking for my help, I knew I shouldn't have said yes, that I should have stayed away. But Eric can be very persuasive, and he knows I couldn't say no when it comes to you. And I thought, we're on the other side of the country from your parents. They won't find out." Alec blew out a long breath. "These past few weeks have probably been one of the best times of my life. I knew it wouldn't last, that once the repairs at your store were done, I'd need to get out of your life. But I can't, Ellie. I don't know how to quit you. And then when you had that hypo on the weekend . . . I couldn't handle it."

"But you did! You did everything right and helped me through it!"

"I thought I could, but then I realized that you, being here with me, was a huge mistake. You didn't immediately treat your hypo because we were arguing. What if it happens again, and the next time it's too late, and you don't make it? You need to be with your family, because they're the ones who *do* know how to look after you."

"I don't know how many times I have to tell people this," I said, my voice rising again, "but I can look after myself. What happened this past weekend and ten years ago were entirely my fault, not yours. And I survived both."

"But you might not. I'm not willing to take the risk. You're better off without me."

"So that's it? You're just going to walk away?"

He went quiet, then slowly nodded. "If something did happen and I couldn't help you, I could never forgive myself."

I fisted my hand and leaned on his desk. "And you thought the best thing to do was to call my family?"

Alec's laugh was bitter. "You know all those phone calls I had with Gemma? It's because your mother had been harassing my family. She called my mom and my sisters, sent people over to our house, to their work, asking if they knew whether you were here with me. Even threatened to call the police on them."

I closed my eyes. My mother had really gone too far.

"My mom and sisters pretended not to know anything. And they would have continued, for as long as it took. But after this weekend, seeing you that way, it triggered all those dreadful memories from that night. I *had* to tell Eric. If something had happened to you . . ."

"I was *fine*. How many times do I have to tell you, it was just another—"

"It might've been just another hypo to you, but not to me," he interrupted. "You didn't see yourself being wheeled away into an ambulance ten years ago. Did you know how frightened I was? To watch you, unconscious and being taken away, not knowing whether you'd be okay, whether I'd ever see you again? I know hypos can be fatal in severe cases. I'm not taking a chance, not when it's your life." His voice shook a little, but his face was determined. "Your place isn't here. You should go home. Be with your family."

"I have a life, a business here. And what about us?" I asked, gesturing to the space between us, desperately trying—hoping—to convince him we were worth saving. "You're not even going to fight for us? Look, we're in this together. We'll hire our own lawyers, and we can dispute my mother's lawsuit. I'm sure once the judges hear that—"

"I can't."

My heart lodged in my throat, refusing to budge.

"My priority right now is to save the company." He glanced away. "I've got people depending on me. My family. My employees. I can't let them down. I need to focus on making this right, because one wrong step, and my life could go pear-shaped as early as tomorrow. You deserve someone better. Someone that's not me."

I stood in front of him, feeling like the entire universe was about to come crashing down, burying me alive under its rubble. He'd made himself clear—that he needed to prioritize his business over me, because I wasn't important enough for him. *Just like I wasn't important enough for my parents.* And history was repeating itself: he was breaking my heart, shattering it into a billion tiny pieces.

Again.

But this would be the last time.

Because I was *so done* with this man.

I took a deep breath, calming myself down, then launched into my speech.

"First of all, I'm an adult. A human being. Not a fucking baton you can simply pass back to my family once the going gets tough. Second, I am perfectly capable of looking after myself. Get that through your thick skull. I didn't need you, my family, or anyone else in the world to watch over me, or wait on me hand and foot." I paused. "And finally, I don't need someone who gives up on me after one hypo episode. Yes, they can be fatal. But it won't be if you learn how to manage them. It's not an excuse to freak out and pull the plug on a relationship. Do you know how many I've had since I was diagnosed? Hundreds. Maybe even thousands. And there's probably another few thousand in my future. It's part and parcel of having diabetes." I took a deep breath. "Obviously you're not the man I thought you were, because if you can't handle that, then we can't be together. I need someone who can be there for me, who's resilient enough to go through the ups and downs with me, because trust me, there will be plenty of them."

His eyes clouded, but he said nothing. Didn't even try to defend himself.

"I'll get my stuff out of the house before you come home."

Without another look, I turned around and stalked away from his office, painfully aware of the radio silence behind me. I didn't stop until I was outside, and the minute I found my car, I leaned on it and covered my face. And tears started pouring.

Because this time, it was finally over.

Alec Mackenzie was no longer a part of my life.

I wiped my eyes, knowing I still had one more piece of unfinished business. Pulling myself together, I got into my car and drove to the Plaza Hotel. My mother had texted me, letting me know she was at a café at the Plaza's rooftop area. When I got there, she was sipping at what I knew would probably be her fifth or sixth cup of coffee for the day. The woman lived and breathed the concoction, just like Eric. Maybe it was the real reason I couldn't stand coffee.

Because it subconsciously reminded me of her.

I pulled out the chair across from her. "You were right about him."

She looked satisfied. "I'm always right."

"But I'm still not going back home. Even if you reinstate me back in the will and shower me with all the money in the world. Until you realize you need to stop controlling my life, you can't be a part of it, and I can't be a part of yours."

She placed her cup back on the table, her gaze furious. "That's not the correct response. I'll give you five minutes to reconsider your answer."

"That was the right answer, and my final one. I'm staying, and no amount of emotional or physical blackmail can change my mind."

She let out a loud, impatient sigh. "Stop being dramatic. You're always acting as if I'm doing something horrible, but you know I'm only looking out for your best interests."

"No, you're not. All you care about is the family business, the status and privileges that come with it. You don't care about my best interests or my happiness."

Her tone turned frosty. "Listen carefully, Ellie. I'm saving you from making a terrible mistake. If you're doing this for him, it's not a smart decision, and you'll regret it. You don't belong here, and people like us don't belong with people like Alec Mackenzie."

"I'm doing this for myself." My tone rose. "You may not care, but I have a life here. I'm running my own business. I truly appreciate everything you've done for me and our family, but it's clear that you value the family business more than your own child. I've had enough of living my life being controlled and suffocated by you. It's time for *you* to move on."

She flinched, and a flash of something—fear? surprise?—flitted across her face, only to disappear the next second. People at neighboring tables were starting to stare, but my mother's attention was laser-focused on me.

"You know that's not how things are done in our family. If you go ahead with this, consider yourself cut off from whatever you stand to inherit in the future. You're giving up all the privileges you grew up with. Choose wisely, because you're not getting a second chance."

I gave her a sad smile. "I don't want your second chance."

Her face paled, and her eyes, so much like mine, held nothing but anger. "You're being disrespectful, and you're making a huge mistake."

For a brief minute, I waited for the familiar guilt that would normally engulf me in a world of shame and regret.

But it never came.

Instead, a tidal wave of sadness washed over me. I knew I was about to lose my parents for good, but if keeping them meant giving up my future and my freedom, then I knew which choice to make. An enormous, empowering urge to walk away surged inside of me. I had never been more confident in my life, and I knew that it was the right thing to do.

"It's not your life to run, and please don't get started on your grand, self-sacrificing speech. Go ahead, cut me out of the family, out of the will, whatever you want."

"You're going to regret this," my mother hissed. "In six months, you'll come back, begging us for a handout, because you're going to fail."

"That's what you thought when I left home, right? But you're wrong. I had a lot of challenges when I first came here, but I handled everything without your help. Or your money. I turned a horribly damaged store into a beautiful bakery, and we're opening in less than a month. I started a new life all on my own, and I'm doing just fine. So no, I won't fail." I paused to take a breath. "And one more thing. My condition isn't an impediment. I'm not defined by it, and it doesn't limit me. It doesn't make me less, or different, and even if I fail, I'll just get back up and try again. So please don't come back into my life, unless you understand it isn't yours to run." I whipped out my phone and tapped on the Uber app. "I've requested a car to take you back to the airport. Goodbye, Mom."

Without waiting for a response, I walked away from the café. From her.

And for the first time in a long while, I felt peace.

CHAPTER 28

Hashtagging the Shit Out of Everything

After packing up my stuff, I called Kim and asked if I could stay with her and Jenna until I found a place on my own, and she immediately came over to help me move my things to their apartment.

We had a movie and bubble tea session that night, where we ignored the movie and drank every last drop of our tea. They listened to my story, then very supportively trashed Alec and called him all sorts of names for accepting the bribe money and breaking my heart. It didn't make things easier, but having the two of them to chat with helped take my mind off ~~him~~ things.

The first few days after the confrontation with Alec were the worst, because almost everything I did and saw reminded me of him. My green plaid pajamas. The takeouts I'd bring back to Kim and Jenna's place from Java Spice. The matcha and dark chocolate chip cookies that became one of the bakery's staple items. Even removing and changing the site for my pump. The hardest of all was being in the bakery, which was supposed to be my safe haven, because he'd played a huge part in the place coming together.

As for my parents, well, I'd sent my father a long email to explain and apologize, which went unanswered. As expected, my mother called and left voicemails, sent emails and text messages, her tone starting at rage and quickly escalating into frightening hostility. Knowing that her threat of cutting me out of the will wasn't working, she'd resorted to the oldest tactic in her book: guilt trip and manipulation. Her latest were increasingly aggressive messages of how she didn't deserve to be treated this way by her daughter.

The more I read her messages, the more I doubted my decision. What if she was right, that I was throwing away a relationship with my own parents? Maybe I should have given them—her—another chance to work things out. After all, familial bonds were supposed to be the most important ones in our lives, right? Wasn't that what the old Indonesian saying was all about? Always honor your elders?

But then my phone would light up with her latest angry text, and it would bring me crashing back to the realization that she would never change. Trying to resolve my issues with her would be futile, and no matter how hard I tried, or how much I wished for it, she would never be the mother that I needed. I was overcome with grief when reality finally set in: that I should stop hoping for the day when we might have an actual relationship. I had to accept that I needed to find ways to make peace with the past on my own.

So the next thing I did was to delete her messages, change my phone number, and remove theirs from my contact list, despite Eric and Naomi pleading with me not to. It felt strangely liberating, although I'd be lying if I said I wasn't completely heartbroken about it.

But I knew that this was for the best.

And after what had happened, I knew I could handle whatever came my way.

It had been eleven long days since I'd confronted Alec and sent my mother away. Today was the bakery's grand opening day, and I'd been a nervous wreck since I'd woken up. I'd arrived at three to start baking, a flurry of things-to-do on the checklist racing through my mind. Were the glass displays clean and shiny enough? Did I order enough napkins and pastry boxes? Where did I keep the display labels and pricing? Had I made enough cupcakes and donuts and brookies for the first day?

But as I slowly folded and kneaded the dough for some cinnamon rolls, feeling it grow smooth and springy under my palms, I began to calm down. I was prepared, and I'd completed everything on my list, so I shouldn't have anything to worry about. I'd also been promoting our opening special on social media—free cupcake giveaways for the first hundred customers, banking on the hope that it would help usher in some much-needed cash for the business.

Thankfully, it looked like my instincts were right. Ever since we opened the door this morning, business had been a constant stream. Most customers only walked in to have a look because they were curious. But we'd prepared trays full of samples, and a lot of people were surprised that our desserts were low in carbs and sugar-free, because they still had the same delicious flavors and textures. Once they had a taste, the majority converted into a sale. It was a great morning that turned even better by lunchtime.

"Hey, Ellie." Kim walked through the door, followed by a grinning Jenna. "Guess who we found at the airport."

My jaw dropped open as Naomi and Eric burst in, beaming.

"Surprise!" Naomi wrapped me in a tight hug. "Congratulations, Ellie! The place looks *awesome*. We're so proud of you."

"Good job, sis." Eric gave me a hug as well. "You've done very well."

I still hadn't recovered from the shock of seeing them here. "When . . . how did . . . ?"

"I got in touch with Kim," Naomi explained with a grin. "Told her we were coming today and not to let you know. She insisted on picking us up at the airport and bringing us here."

I turned an astonished look at Eric. "And *you* took time off? To be here? Are you even allowed to do that?"

He chuckled. "If you're asking about the parents, they don't know we're here. I'm traveling for work, and no questions were asked. Don't worry. I can handle them, okay?"

Happiness—and gratefulness—swept over me. I didn't know what was going to happen with the bakery; it could go well, or things could be so bad I'd have to give up everything in a matter of weeks. But no matter how challenging things might be, knowing they had my back was more than enough.

"Thanks so much for coming all the way here. It means a lot. And Kim, thank you for picking them up. You guys are the best."

"I'll take a dozen of those dark chocolate chip cookies as payment. I gotta go, but let's catch up for dinner later." Kim gave me a hug. "Congratulations. You did it."

Jenna did the same. "I'm so happy for you. Go kick some ass."

"Okay." Naomi rubbed her hands and looked around. "How can we help?"

I assigned her to the front of the bakery to hand out samples to passersby. She gave me a salute, put on our mint-green apron, and grabbed a tray of low-carb maple pecan mini tarts.

"You." I turned to consider Eric. "What are your café-related skills?"

"I'm an excellent barista. I make a very good cortado."

"I don't even know what that is, but you're hired." I pointed at Ruby, who had been on her feet since we opened this morning. "You can take over so she can have her break. And this is only our first day, so please don't screw up any coffee orders."

"I'll do my best. And hey, Ellie?"

I looked up at him.

"I know I don't say this often, but I'm very, very proud of you. You've worked so hard for this, and you deserve all the success coming your way. And even though the parents aren't happy you've abandoned the family business, I'm always here for you, okay?" He gave me a sad smile. "I'm sorry. I hope they'll come around one day."

He gave me a hug, then slipped behind the service area and strolled toward the coffee machine. My heart expanded a thousandfold, reassuring me that I was doing the right thing here, and everything would turn out just fine.

By the end of the first day, we'd sold half our stocks, which wasn't bad. It wasn't ideal, though, because it wouldn't be enough to pay for the raw materials and Ruby's wages. But it was still a pretty good start, and I would gladly take that any day over a quiet, deserted bakery.

But then it only got worse.

Eric and Naomi had left the next day for Eric's work conference, but we made promises to visit more often. It was a good thing they hadn't stuck around, because after their declarations of being proud of me the day before, I didn't think I could bear them being here to witness the slow and embarrassing death of my brand-new business.

The following week was quieter than a library in the middle of the night, and the initial flurry of interest seemed to have dwindled to nonexistent, despite the push I'd done on social media. Jenna had stopped by on her lunch break on Friday and ordered a dozen of the matcha cronuts to bring back to her office, and Kim had bought some maple pecan mini tarts for a knitting class in her store. There were a few more walk-in customers during the day, but apart from that, the bakery was practically dead.

The weekend was coming, though, so I had high hopes—the

Plaza was always busy on the weekends, and I had ramped up our promotions, because if we could get just a fraction of their visitors spilling over to the bakery, then I'd be happy with that.

But of course, no such thing happened. Not even the 20 percent discount advertised on social media had made a difference.

I was screwed six ways to Sunday.

By the time Sunday afternoon rolled around, I had almost lost all hope.

We only had two walk-in customers during the day, and I was so dejected, a million different doom-and-gloom scenarios played on repeat in my mind: I'd have to declare bankruptcy and lose the business, the CR-V, and every single possession I had. Probably even my trusty sleeping bag. Then, because I had no money left over, I wouldn't be able to afford my next meal, let alone my diabetes supplies. And since I couldn't live in the same city as Alec, I'd have to move to another state. But because I didn't have a car, or money for a plane or train ticket, I'd have to hitchhike my way across the country—and run the risk of spoiling whatever small amount of insulin supplies I had—while praying and crossing my fingers I wouldn't run into a serial killer who'd kill me and chop up my body before dumping it in a remote area for the coyotes and vultures to feast on. Although I probably would, and when Alec and my family heard about my tragic demise on the news, they'd be filled with grief and remorse, wishing they had treated me with more respect when I was still around.

Pushing the blockbuster horror movie out of my mind, I went to the kitchen to try out a recipe for low-carb strawberry lemon cupcakes, hoping it would help me relax. But fifteen minutes and two messed-up batters later, it was clearly not working.

Great, now I didn't even have baking as my safe space anymore, because of course the moment I had made it my live-
lihood, it had all spectacularly come crashing down on me. I
knew and had factored this into my business plan, that most
new businesses take time to make money and be profitable. But
now that I was running one myself, it was much harder than
I'd expected.

And after everything that had happened, I couldn't help but
think that this had been nothing but an expensive, colossal mistake.

Groaning, I decided to tell Ruby to go home early while I
figured out my next move. Just as I was about to flip the CLOSED
sign around, a young woman strolled in, followed by two other
women. All of them were staring intently at their phones. I recognized the first one, who had been here on Thursday. She had
been enthusiastically taking pictures and videos of the food,
telling me that she was making a reel for her social media
accounts.

Yes. I did a mental fist pump, grateful for the repeat customer.

I gave them my friendliest, most enthusiastic smile. "Welcome
to Twisted Sweets. How can I help you?"

The first woman beamed back. "Hi. We'll take half a dozen of
your low-carb strawberry and cream donuts, three of the peanut
butter cupcakes, and three of the matcha cronuts."

She turned to her two friends as I started boxing her order.
"Trust me, they're so good, *and* guilt-free. You're going to love
them."

One of her friends finally looked up from her phone, catching
my eye. She stared at me for a few beats, then her face brightened.
"Hey. I know who you are."

My stomach sank, as she looked down at her phone, her fingers
frantically scrolling.

I knew what was coming.

"I was right." She looked back up at me, a satisfied grin on her face. "You're the girl from that viral video over New Year's. The one who rejected George Fitzgerald's proposal."

That caught the attention of her two friends, who immediately snapped their heads toward me, their eyes wide with astonishment.

"No way! Seriously?" The third woman shook her head, her mouth hanging open. "Who in their right mind would reject *him*? You actually said *no* to this country's most famous, hottest, and richest bachelor?"

"She did." The second woman shoved her phone at the friend, undoubtedly showing her the clip. "See? Same eyes, different hairdo. But that's her."

"Girl, you must be out of your mind."

I gave a weary sigh. "Probably."

"Probably? No, definitely. Without a doubt. I'm going to tell my cousin about this. She's obsessed with George Fitzgerald. She's never going to believe it."

I knew for a fact that her cousin wasn't alone in her undying devotion, because I'd had strangers gushing to me about how lucky I was to have dated *the* George Fitzgerald, no matter how brief it had been.

An idea suddenly bloomed in my head. *What if I could use that to my benefit?*

"My cousin wanted to know what he smells like. Do you remember?"

I didn't, but I said the first thing that came to my mind. "Musk, sandalwood, and leather." Ignoring their giggles, I finished their order, then rang up their total. "That'll be fifty-one dollars, thanks. Cash or card?"

"Card." The first woman whipped out her purse. "Thanks, um," she peered at my name tag, "Ellie? Thanks, Ellie."

"Thank you. Enjoy the goodies." I processed her card and

printed her receipt. And the minute they walked out the door, I went to work on my newest idea.

I'd created a TikTok account for Twisted Sweets weeks ago, but the two videos I'd already posted were probably best described as pitiful and uninspiring.

Or, as Kim had bluntly called it, "fucking pathetic."

One was a brief look at the front of the bakery, with my voice-over welcoming people to Twisted Sweets. The other one was a ten-second shot of our display case at the bakery, proudly showing off the many different cookies, donuts, cupcakes, and brownies. Combined, the two videos had garnered an extremely laughable fifty views.

Clearly, I still had a lot to learn.

So that night, I spent more time watching and studying Tik-Tok and YouTube videos than I cared to admit. But it was for a worthy cause, because after too many weeks of cringing and covering my face whenever random people on the street recognized me from George's viral proposal, I was going to finally capitalize on my unwanted fame.

Enlisting Kim and Jenna's help, the next day we took several videos of me working in the kitchen; of me giving a tour of the bakery; of me serving customers (Jenna and Ruby each pretending to be one) and boxing up their orders; and finally of me behind the coffee machine, (also pretending) to make a latte. Kim brought her DSLR camera and took professional snaps of the baked goods, and the results were so much better than what I could have taken with my phone.

"I think we've got enough." Kim lowered her camera and scrolled through the pictures. "I'll send these and the videos to you."

"Thanks. Let's hope this works."

I uploaded everything during lunch—Kim's gorgeous shots on all our social media accounts, and fun and catchy edits on both TikTok and YouTube, including a short snippet of George's proposal video. I'd also scheduled several posts in advance, hoping the consistency would help me collect more views and followers, and hashtagged the shit out of everything.

My grand idea was to show the face behind the bakery, humorously exploiting the fact that I was *that* girl who had rejected the famous George Fitzgerald. I was banking on the hope that the now twelve million people who had watched the viral video and the ones who were obsessed with George would see what I'd uploaded, and hopefully spread word about the bakery. I texted George the previous night asking for his permission to include his failed proposal, because I knew it might bring back humiliating memories for him. He was surprisingly cool about it, even wishing me nothing but the best for the bakery.

I didn't glance at my phone again until it was time to close, because I was too scared that my bright idea would turn out to be another disappointing flop.

Thankfully, it didn't.

Later that night, I had so many notifications on my phone alerting me about new followers and messages on the bakery's social media accounts. In a few short hours, my posts had gained over thirty thousand likes, and almost fifty thousand views. Sure, there were plenty of nasty comments on the videos, mostly from people who laughed at me because, apparently, I'd fallen so far from being George Fitzgerald's almost-wife, to working my ass off frosting cupcakes at a small bakery.

But for every one mean remark, there were four thoughtful comments to make up for it. People from all over the country offered their best wishes to me, warming my heart with their encouraging words. Some people congratulated me on the "next chapter of my life," and strangers I didn't even know cheered me on for being brave enough to follow my heart and turn down a very public and elaborate proposal. And thanks to the posts, the bakery had racked up forty thousand new followers in less than a day.

Forty. Fucking. Thousand.

And the good thing about the power of social media?

It was that the effect didn't just stop online.

When I arrived at the bakery bright and early the next morning, the sight that greeted me made my jaw drop.

It was still dark, but there was already a queue a mile long outside, snaking past Kim's yarn store, around the corner, and beyond, even though we weren't open yet. In fact, we weren't supposed to open for another three hours. When I cautiously squeezed through the crowd to get to the front door, some people at the front of the queue called out and greeted me with my first name, as if we were next-door neighbors and had been BFFs since we were in our mothers' wombs. I could even hear someone exclaiming, "It really is her!"

We were slammed from the minute I flipped over the OPEN sign, and Ruby and I were on our feet the entire day. One of the videos I had posted yesterday—the one with the snippet of George's proposal—had gone viral overnight, although still not as impressive as the original proposal video. It was quoted and reposted on all the major social media platforms, even on some I hadn't even heard of before. Word had well and truly spread that the woman who hadn't been smart enough to accept George Fitzgerald's proposal was now holed up in Port Benedict, slaving over hot ovens to eke out a living.

My plan *had actually worked.*

Some people who came in to the store weren't even there to buy anything, but because they wanted to see me, as if I were a well-known celebrity chef with multiple Michelin stars. Some asked for a selfie, and almost every single customer had a similar set of questions: (1) Was it really me? (2) Why did I reject the proposal? (3) Was I out of my ever-loving mind? And finally, the overwhelmingly most popular questions coming from young women, (4) Is George still single, and (5) If yes, can I introduce them to him?

The queues and the steady stream of customers kept coming and going throughout the day. The last customer walked out at eight, two hours after our normal closing time. I held my breath as I tallied the day's taking, before letting out a loud whoop and breaking into a crazed happy dance, because we had achieved our budgeted revenue for the entire month.

In just one day.

Hopefully, this was a sign that things were finally looking up.

CHAPTER 29

He Made Things Right

The next couple of weeks were a dream come true. The bakery was busy round the clock, both from walk-in customers and online orders. On days when we announced a special, limited-edition menu item—matcha cinnamon rolls for today—customers would flock and form long queues outside, hours before we were open, and we'd sell out within the first two hours. We'd gotten so busy that I'd had to hire two part-time employees: one to assist Ruby at the front, and one to work in the kitchen.

Someone from the *Port Benedict Gazette*—an actual journalist from the actual newspaper this time—got in touch, wanting to feature us in their weekend edition. Thanks to the article, which raved and spoke glowingly about our "*delightful choices of guilt-free, decadent baked goods, guaranteed to satisfy your sweet tooth*," a few businesses in the city had reached out, wanting us to cater for their next corporate events.

So far, so good. Life was finally turning around. Business was picking up, and our profit and loss for the first month—I was putting my finance training to good use—was looking solid. I was finally free of my parents. I made plans to move out of Kim and Jenna's sofa, scouring real estate listings for one-bedroom units to rent, preferably close to the bakery. Everything was perfect, and absolutely *nothing* (and no one) was missing from my life.

When I announced that to Kim and Jenna, they'd snickered and said I was full of shit.

I was most definitely not. In fact, I liked to think of myself as careful and cautious, because I now planned all my trips in advance and made it a point to avoid all the places *he* would usually go to. Instead of getting my Indonesian food fix at Java Spice like I used to, I drove twenty minutes farther to find another restaurant, thereby eliminating the possibility of running into him. I had even rescheduled my weekly grocery shopping trips to fortnightly, because I now had to drive twice as far to find a supermarket in another area, so I wouldn't accidentally bump into him in the fresh foods aisle.

But the city wasn't big enough for the two of us, so I knew the odds were probably not in my favor. One day, be it in the near or distant future, I would run into him. It was inevitable, just like getting old and dying. And I hadn't prepared myself for what to do when that day came. (The day that I ran into Alec, not the day I died.)

A knock on the thick glass windows of our open-plan kitchen broke my reverie.

"Ellie? A customer is here to pick up their order and asked to see you."

"Thanks, Ruby. I'll be right out."

I'd gotten used to requests like this. Ever since our videos became viral, two out of five customers that came into the store had asked to speak to me—especially on busy Fridays like today—either to just say hi, or have a selfie taken, or ask questions about our recipes. Some of them genuinely wanted to have a chat, while others only wanted a picture with me so they could post it online, hoping to boost their followers. I was fine with that, because it was still advertising the bakery in some way.

I quickly finished what I was doing—slicing the matcha cinnamon rolls with dental floss to get nice, clean cuts on them—then placing them in a pan and leaving them to rest for a while before they went into the oven. Taking off my apron, I washed my hands, then turned around and fixed a friendly, customer-service-appropriate smile on my face.

Then froze in my tracks when I saw who it was.

I'd been so preoccupied in the kitchen, I hadn't noticed that Alec had come into the store. He wasn't in his usual suit-and-shirt attire, which was highly uncommon for a weekday. Instead, he wore a navy T-shirt with dark jeans and sported a few days' worth of stubble. His hair was also slightly longer than when I saw him last.

What is he doing here?

My heart thumped loudly, breaking out the taiko drums once again. He was watching the customers queuing outside, with one hand shoved in his jeans pocket, and the other holding one of our Twisted Sweets boxes. For a brief second, I wondered if I should go back to the kitchen and hide there until he went away.

No. Ellie 2.0 was made of stronger stuff. I steeled myself, viciously stomping on the tiny seed of hope that was beginning to sprout in my heart. My reasonable, levelheaded brain wisely advised that I should approach him with the caution I would reserve for great white sharks, taipan snakes, and saltwater crocodiles.

As if sensing my gaze, he tore his attention away from the ever-growing line outside and looked at me. I blinked once, working hard to organize my facial muscles to show zero emotions. As if to say, *Screw you, Alec Mackenzie. I don't need you in my life.*

Without saying a word, I slid behind the counter to serve the next customer in the queue. Flashing the petite woman a friendly smile, I began boxing up her order, then dutifully answered all her questions about the plant-based sweetener used in our cupcakes. For the next twenty minutes, I continued to ignore him, attending to customers and chatting with them about the weather, the news, and the latest episode of the reality TV show they were currently watching.

As my latest customer turned to leave, I glanced at him. He was watching me, his expression unreadable, with one hand still in his pocket. I was tempted to make him wait for another twenty minutes, or for the rest of his life, but that wise, levelheaded voice in my brain came back, reminding me it was a clear violation of Basic Manners 101 to keep people waiting.

Curse you, levelheaded brain.

I strolled over to him, pretending it was just another ordinary day, and I was clearly unaffected by his presence.

"Alec." I nodded at him, cooler than a frozen cucumber. "Can I help you?"

"I was here to pick up an order."

I folded my arms, not saying anything.

"How have you been?"

"Fantastic." I waved my hand around the shop, indicating the customers milling about, and the long lines of people queueing outside. "Business is going well. No complaints."

"Glad to hear that." He shifted his weight from one foot to the other. "Where are you staying now?"

"Let's skip the small talk. Why are you here? Something wrong with your order?"

"I just want a chance to explain things," he began, but I cut him off.

"There's nothing to explain. You signed a black-and-white agreement. It's legally binding, it can't be undone, and you took the money. Can't be any clearer than that. Anything else? Otherwise, I've got a bakery to run."

I was about to walk away when his next sentence stopped me in my tracks.

"I went to see my dad."

That . . . wasn't what I was expecting.

"I felt like I owed it to myself, seeing how he was pretty much the cause of all my family's troubles. Closure and all that, you know?"

I watched him and said nothing.

"I spoke to my aunt, his younger sister, then tracked him down. Thought he'd be living with the family he'd left us for, but he said they didn't want to have anything to do with him anymore." Alec gave a rueful smile. "Prison wasn't kind to him. He looks different, a shell of the man I remembered. It was difficult to find work after he got out, so now he's doing odd handyman jobs here and there, for anyone willing to hire him."

"Does your mother know? That you went to find him?"

"Yeah. She's okay with it. My dad said he regretted everything he'd done, but he was too ashamed to come and find us." Alec blew out a long breath. "I wanted to yell at him, Ellie. For causing our family hardship for so many years. For breaking my mother's heart and making her life hell. But I didn't. Yelling at him isn't going to change anything. It won't bring our family back together. Or reverse all the terrible things that had happened to us in the past."

Some customers who were waiting for their coffee orders were starting to watch us.

"I still haven't forgiven him, but I felt sorry for him. He's done time, paid for his sins, and now he's got the rest of his life to live with the consequences, alone and miserable. Everyone that used to matter in his life left him, because he turned his back on them, on the people he was supposed to love. And I thought to myself, *what a sad, sad life.*"

The crowd watching us slowly grew, and God forbid I had another viral social media moment—this time with the man who broke my heart. I gave them all a polite smile, then dragged Alec away to the office and closed the door.

"Why are you telling me all this?"

"Because seeing him has made me realize that I didn't want that kind of life. I didn't want to spend the rest of my life being sad, miserable, and away from the people I care for, from the people I love. From you. I've wasted the past decade living thousands of miles away from you, Ellie. And I don't want to waste even one more day if I don't have to."

My heart stilled for a couple of beats. *Do I need my ears thoroughly checked and cleaned, or did he just imply that he . . . loves me?*

I held my breath and ignored the uninvited cheers and fanfare that erupted from the depths of my brain. *So much for being cautious, brain.*

"I thought about what you said to me. That one hypo episode isn't a reason to freak out and pull the plug on a relationship. And you're right. I might have turned my back on you once, ten years ago, and I still don't know if I'm good enough for you, but I want to be there for you, Ellie. To go through the ups and downs together with you, no matter how hard. I promise to do better, if you'll give me another chance."

As I stood there gaping at him, still trying to process everything, he pulled out a thick white envelope from his back pocket and handed it to me. I didn't take it, and my brain took that as a cue to hum ominous doomsday soundtracks, and vivid mental images of sharks, snakes, and crocodiles began to play in Technicolor. He placed the Twisted Sweets box on my desk and the thick envelope on top of it.

"Eric also told me how your mother is still raging at you, and me, because you refused to return home to be with your family. Kept ranting about how your family name couldn't be associated with someone like me, how you belong with someone who comes from a family of your financial status. And I finally understood that she will never change. She never cared about you, or your health, or anything else, and probably never will. All she cares about is your family's reputation, the business, the money, and all the privileges that came with it."

"Yeah." It was a bitter pill to swallow, but he was right.

"I also went to see Jacqui. Last week."

"You've been busy," I said.

He gave a small chuckle. "I apologized to her. Told her everything, and explained that yes, it was a ruse at first, but it's gotten real for me, and how I've had real feelings for you from a long time ago. That it wasn't your fault, because it was all my idea from the beginning." He shoved both his hands into his pockets, his eyes searching mine. "And I asked if she would consider giving you another chance."

I gaped at him. "You did . . . what?"

"She agreed. Carmel will be in touch with you to place a new order for the party."

"But . . . what about your business agreement with her?"

"We worked something out. She was still offended by our elaborate stunt, but she's also a shrewd businesswoman. The numbers didn't lie. It was still a wise business decision to invest in my company."

"That's wonderful, Alec." Relief went through me. "Did she say why Phil did it?"

"He was trying to get her to invest in his business, to save him from financial trouble. Jacqui wasn't interested, so Phil thought he could persuade her that his company was a better investment than mine. That's why he started looking for dirt he could use to discredit me. Last I heard, he's dissolving his business and filing for bankruptcy."

For a moment, I felt a twinge of pity for Phil. No matter what he'd done, he was just doing what he thought was best for his company.

"I know you might not want to see me again after this, given everything that I did. So I'm going to give you some space to think about it." Alec pointed at the white envelope. "Everything you need to know is in there. I'll leave it with you, so you can read it in your own time."

He walked backward toward the door. His eyes were still on me, his hands paused on the doorknob. "It's good to see you, Ellie. I've missed you so much."

With one last look, he walked out and disappeared from view, and I stood there, trying to compose myself. My eyes drifted to his envelope, and that's when I realized he'd left his Twisted Sweets box underneath it.

I grabbed the box, with every intention of rushing out and going after him, but something caught my attention. My name was scribbled at the top, written in his handwriting.

He ordered these . . . for me?

Placing it back on the desk, I untied the white ribbon and lifted the lid open, immediately recognizing some of our customized sugar cookies. He'd ordered cookies shaped like oven mitts, mixing bowls, aprons, and colorful swirly cupcakes, all neatly arranged in rows inside the box. Behind the row of apron-shaped cookies, there were some alphabet-shaped, pink-and-light-green dotted ones.

I didn't know how long I stood there, just staring at those pink-and-green cookies.

Because the letters read,

I.

Love.

You.

CHAPTER 30

It All Ended with a Grand Romantic Gesture

For the next few days, I ignored the envelope, giving it a permanent home inside my desk drawer instead. I avoided it as if it might trigger an unseen bomb, detonating and obliterating the bakery, the neighboring shops, and even the nearby Port Benedict Plaza.

Carmel got in touch to place a new order for Jacqui's party. It was the same varieties and quantities as their first one, with a few hundred extra mini cupcakes to be boxed up as party favors. With only a week to finish the order, my new routine was leaving home at crack-of-dawn o'clock and coming back past midnight.

By some miracle, we managed to finish everything in time. It was an hour before I was supposed to deliver them to Jacqui's mansion, and I had been rushing to load the boxes of baked goods in the CR-V when the door to Kim's shop opened and she strolled out.

"Hey. You need any help?"

"Thanks, but I'm nearly done." I stacked the last two boxes and closed the car door.

Kim raised her eyebrows at me. "Is that what you're wearing?"

I glanced down at my pair of faded black jeans and old blue-and-white stripy top. "Yes. Something wrong with it?"

"Not if you're going for a walk on the beach. But massively inappropriate if you're a guest at a property tycoon's party."

"I'm not invited. Well, I was, but after all that's happened, I'm sure she doesn't really want me there. I'll just deliver the cakes, find her to say hi, and then go."

Kim wrinkled her nose. "Still. That's not how you dress to go to a party of the rich and famous, even if you're just delivering an order. You should know that, of all people. What if you run into Alec there?"

Hearing his name sliced my heart into tiny little pieces.

Kim must have noticed the look on my face, because she sighed. "Seriously? You still haven't opened his envelope?"

"No."

She gave me a shrewd look. "Because you don't want to? Or because you're afraid?"

"Afraid? What should I be afraid of?"

Kim folded her arms. "Oh, I don't know. Maybe because you're madly in love with him, and you're afraid that whatever's in that envelope will prove he isn't the bad guy you're making him out to be. Then you'll have no choice but to find him, to kiss and make up. But of course, you're terrified that he's going to hurt you again."

"Nope. Couldn't be further from the truth."

She gave me a smug smile. "Liar, liar, pants on fire." Then her expression turned serious. "Ellie, I wouldn't be saying this if you weren't my friend. But for the love of all that is holy, open the envelope and give the man a call, will you? You've been so mopey and cranky, and I'm pretty sure it has nothing to do with your blood glucose levels."

"How do you know? It might." My tone was defensive.

She gave me a look that said, *I wasn't born yesterday*.

"Fine. I'll think about it. But no promises."

"That's what you said two days ago, and two days before that. I'm going to ask you again in another two days, and if you *still* haven't done anything by then, I swear to God I'm going to rip the envelope open myself, then lock you in a room with it until you tell me you've read and memorized every single word."

"Yes, ma'am." I grinned and started back toward the bakery. "I have to run. See you when I get back."

Kim only shouted at me, "Open the damn envelope!"

Glancing at my watch, I realized I only had forty-five minutes left before the agreed delivery time. I hurried inside, grabbing the paperwork I needed, and quickly rifled through it to make sure I had everything. Tugging my desk drawer open, I rummaged inside to find a pen and saw Alec's white envelope.

Kim's words echoed in my brain, egging me on.

I made a swift decision right then and there to read it, even if just to tell her I'd done what she'd asked me to do. Then his letter was going straight into the trash bin. I tore the envelope open and pulled out the folded pages.

My eyes bulged, nearly popping out of their sockets, as I read the contents. It was a copy of a recent sale and purchase agreement between Alec and Goodwin Property Group, stating that he'd sold the majority of his shares in Mackenzie Constructions to Jacqui.

I blinked. *No*. He would never do that. He'd worked so hard for that business, and it was his pride and joy, his whole life, so there was *no way* this was right.

But it was. I went over the pages several times, and they still read the same, even after the fifth time: that Goodwin Property Group was now the major shareholder of Mackenzie Constructions, holding 80 percent of the ownership. Rob still owned his 10 percent, and now, so did Alec.

And there was more. The last page was a copy of an electronic funds transfer receipt from Alec's bank account to another account with a familiar name.

My *mother's* name.

For the sum of three million dollars.

My breath caught in my throat.

Alec sold and gave up his business to return the bribe money to my mother.

For me.

There was only one thing left to do.

I only had thirty more minutes before I was due at Jacqui's party. As I raced back outside and got into my car, I speed-dialed Alec, but it went straight to his voicemail. I probably broke every road rule and speed limit driving to Jacqui's house, making it there in fifteen minutes.

Unloading the boxes of goodies from the car, I rushed to set everything up on the dessert table, assisted by Carmel, who was there with her trusty clipboard to make sure everything was perfectly in place. Once I was finished, I went back outside, whipping out my phone as I speed-walked back to my car.

Alec still hadn't replied to any of my messages.

My heart sank. I didn't know if he was still attending the party or not, given how things were between him and Jacqui. Maybe I should go over to his house. Or the Mackenzie Constructions office. Or call Rob. Rob would know where to find him.

As I stood on the side of the road, debating my next move, a familiar black SUV swung into an empty spot, a few cars behind mine. Alec got out, and my stomach lurched at the sight of him. He was dressed in a casual, light-blue Henley and dark jeans.

I took a deep breath, then shoved my phone into my back pocket as I approached him, hoping to look and sound casual.

"Hey. I've been looking for you. Um, I left you several messages just now."

"My phone's dead." He took off his sunglasses, revealing the dark circles under his eyes, as if he hadn't slept for a few nights. "Forgot to plug it into the charger last night."

"Right. Uh, lucky I found you here, then."

He frowned at me. "What's wrong? You look flustered. Are you okay?"

That question broke me down. I was done trying to play it cool.

"I finally opened your envelope. Did you . . . Did you really do that? You gave up your business to pay my parents back?"

Something—maybe hope?—flickered in his eyes. "I did. Well, not everything, though. I still own ten percent."

"But why? You're giving up something you've worked so hard for. What about the people who work for you? Your family?"

He gave me a small smile. "It's all good. Jacqui agreed to keep all the employees. Rob still owns his share. I'll still be involved in the company, although in a much smaller role. And both my sisters are working, so they're helping me support my mother. We'll be fine."

"Oh." I swallowed. "Thank you. For giving up everything for—"

I trailed off. He'd never said that he sold his business and re-paid my parents *for me*.

As if he knew what I was going to say, Alec replied, "I did it because I don't want your parents to lord that money over my head for the rest of my life. I don't want to owe them anything. Not even a single cent. But more importantly, I don't want to keep any more secrets from you."

I nodded. "No more secrets."

He took a deep breath, composing himself, before continuing, "And I wanted to prove that you're all that matters to me. That you are *the* most important thing in the world to me, more than anything. And I want to be there for you. Nothing else, no one else, but you. I was a fool for letting you go once. I won't make that same mistake twice. If I had the business, and Jacqui's investment, and all the money in the world, but not you, well, then I don't really want that."

I could only nod again, as my brain cheered and applauded his speech, while my heart swooned and melted into a puddle of goo.

He took a couple of steps forward, closing the gap between us. "So . . . if you've opened the envelope, and you're here, does this mean you've forgiven me?"

I folded my arms and pretended to consider him. "Not yet. I'll have to think about it."

His mouth slowly curved into a smile. "Yeah?"

"Maybe I *will* forgive you. Just as long as *you* don't lord this . . . sacrifice over my head for the rest of our lives."

"I believe the correct term is a 'grand romantic gesture.' Like what the guy does at the end of a rom-com movie to win the girl back." A twinkle lit up his eyes. "So? How did I do?"

"Well, let's see. Grand romantic gesture, check. Big speech, check." I gave him an approving nod. "I think as far as grand gestures go, this was pretty epic. Nine out of ten."

He took my hands in his. "Only *nine*? I was expecting a full ten. I don't get any points for the customized cookies?"

"Maybe, if you'd baked them yourself. But you bought them."

"Trust me, if I'd baked them myself, you wouldn't want to eat them."

"And might I add, *from my bakery*. I should take points off for that."

His smile grew bigger. "It's the thought that counts, Ellie. And the idea was all mine."

I finally broke into a grin. "Fine, I'll give you nine and a half. Happy now?"

"Not yet." He pulled me closer. "Just in case the message wasn't clear enough from those extremely thoughtful cookies, Ellie Pang, I'm in love with you."

My heart felt like it was about to break free from behind my rib cage and bust into a happy dance. "Really? I must have missed that message."

"Probably since the very first day we met." He brushed a light kiss on my lips. "And as corny as this might sound, I won't be happy until you tell me that you love me, too."

"I'll tell you, if you promise never to leave again."

"Done. I'm not going anywhere," he said, the smile in his eyes warming my entire universe. "I love you, Hello Kitty. You're stuck with me. Forever, whether you like it or not."

"I think I'll take the risk," I said, my grin splitting my face. "I love you too, Sir Grouchiness. You're not so bad. I think I'll keep you."

As his lips found mine, I knew that this life I'd chosen, here in Port Benedict, running my dream business and being with him, had all been the right decision.

And I certainly didn't need any pros and cons lists to tell me that.

Epilogue

Funny how different life could be in just under a year.

Less than twelve months ago, I'd been trying to get my bakery off the ground, flailing and failing in confidence, life, and love. And now, here I was, a month away from opening the doors of my second bakery and still together with Sir Alec McGrumpyface.

I'd moved back into his house, and we were getting ready to usher in the new year with a small, low-key gathering at home. His family had come over for a visit, so his mother was there, and his sisters and their partners, plus an auntie, an uncle, and two cousins. After too many years of enduring my parents' over-the-top new year's celebration, the intimate get-together had been a lovely change. Instead of gowns and stilettos, I was in jeans and flats, and I had spent the night getting to know his family better, instead of making polite small talk with my parents' business partners.

At ten to midnight, I'd settled on a comfortable Adirondack in the quiet, dimly lit backyard next to him, waiting for the fireworks to begin. One by one, everyone disappeared into the house, and a string of fairy lights suddenly lit up the garden.

Then Alec turned to me with a nervous grin.

"Ellie," he began, "how long have we known each other?"

I narrowed my eyes at him. "I feel like this is a trick question, because I know you know that we've known each other for almost twenty years."

"That's correct." He flashed me a more relaxed smile. "Do you know, though, which of those twenty years is my favorite so far?"

"Okay, this is definitely a trick question, because it's got to be this year, right?" I waved toward the strings of fairy lights. "And when did you put those up? They're so pretty."

"This afternoon, when you were out with my mom." He took both my hands in his. "This year is a close second, but it's actually twenty years ago. The year we first met. You remembered what I told Jacqui, the first time you met her at her party?"

"You're going to have to jog my memory."

"I'd said that I knew I was going to marry you one day. Even when I was twelve. And it was true. That hadn't been a lie to sell our fake relationship to Jacqui."

I only stared at him. Where was he going with this?

"I know I've said this to you before, but I want you to hear it again. You're the strongest person I know, Ellie. Your strength and resilience never cease to amaze me. You've gone through a lot, but you've done and achieved so much in the last twelve months, more than anyone else I know. You make me want to be a better person. Because that's who you deserve. Someone who doesn't freak out during your hypos. Someone to help you count carbs and prick your fingers and change your pump site. Someone who can be there for you through all your ups and downs. I want to be that person, if you'll let me. For the rest of our lives."

I was holding my breath. *Is he . . . doing what I think he's doing?*

Alec pulled a black box out of his pocket and popped it open, revealing a simple yet stunning ring, and I let out a soft gasp. "I won't be able to top that first proposal that started this all. Nobody's recording this, so it won't go viral and make you famous again. Although I'm sure my family is watching with bated breath from inside the house." He gave me a grin. "I know I'm not down on one knee or anything, but I meant every word I said, Ellie. Please say y—"

I pulled him in and gave him a kiss before he even had a chance to finish. Loud whoops and cheers floated our way from the direction of his house, just as the fireworks started in the distance.

It was, hands down, the best New Year's Eve ever.

At the annual Lunar New Year parade and festival, I stood at the side of the road, waiting for the dragon dance troupe to start their performance. Kim, Jenna, and I agreed to make this our new yearly tradition, and it was extra special this year because my fiancé—I still got goosebumps at that magical word—was with me. Even after several weeks of having the stunning rock on my finger, the memory of that night still brought a blissful sigh and a contented smile to my face.

"Oh. My. God. Ellie! You're wearing that annoying dreamy look again on your face." Kim rolled her eyes and took a long sip of her taro pearl milk tea. "Mackenzie, this is all your fault. Ew, you two," she said with disgust, as Alec leaned down to give me a quick kiss. "My eyeballs hurt. Some of us are single, so please spare us the PDA."

I pulled away from Alec. "You can't be bitter forever just because what's-his-name broke up with you. Trust me, you deserve someone better."

"I know I do," Kim replied. "I'm just furious because *I* should've dumped him first. I wasted six months of my life on him! That's one hundred and eighty precious days I'm never getting back. Meanwhile, my time is running out, because I have a deadline, and the pool of single, decent, available men is shrinking and getting smaller as we speak."

Jenna grinned and gave her shoulder a consoling pat. "Well, if you're willing to relocate to Qatar or UAE, you might have a better chance of finding someone there. When I went to Abu Dhabi last year, I was told they have twice as many men as women."

Kim considered this for a moment, then shook her head. "It's too hot there. You got any single friends back home in Melbourne?"

"Speaking of single friends," Alec said to her, "Rob is single now."

She scoffed. "Carmichael? Yeah, I'll pass. So not my type. Jenna can have him."

I raised my eyebrows at her. The drums and cymbals from the dragon dance started to play, prompting me to raise my voice so she could hear me over the noise. "Really? Handsome, funny, and kind isn't your type?"

She placed one hand on her hip, looking indignant. "I have standards, you know."

My eyebrows hiked higher. "You do? How high is this so-called standard of yours?"

"Higher than yours, apparently." Kim glanced at Alec. "No offense, Mackenzie."

The dragon dancers were strutting and prancing toward where we stood, and the noise was almost unbearable. I was now yelling so Kim could hear me. "Because Rob checks even all my boxes, and if it weren't for Sir Fiancé here, I'd probably go after him myself."

The drums paused right as I shouted the last few words, earning me frowns and judgmental stares from people around us. An elderly woman shook her head and muttered in rapid-fire Cantonese while throwing dirty looks at me. I couldn't understand a single word, but no doubt she was condemning me for showing extreme disrespect for this much-revered cultural performance. I gave her an apologetic smile and mouthed, "I'm so sorry."

Alec placed a palm over his heart. "Wow. I really am the luckiest man alive. My new fiancée loves me so much, she's already planning to go after other guys even though I'm still around. At least wait until my body is cold, honey."

I stuck out my tongue at him, just as the drums and the dancers started again.

Kim waved a dismissive hand. "I know men like Rob Carmichael. Good-looking guys who think they can get a woman to do whatever they want just by flashing a cute lopsided grin. Just like Leo. Well, I'm steering clear of the Leos and the Robs of this world. Can we just focus on this majestic, magnificent dragon, please?"

My phone vibrated in my back pocket, prompting me to pull it out. Alec did the same thing at the same time. It was an email sent from a bank, and as I read the contents, my jaw promptly dropped.

The message notified us of a funds transfer made into our joint account—mine and Alec's—late yesterday afternoon, for the sum of three million dollars. My breath caught as I scanned over the sender details.

It was *V Pang*.

"Is that who I think it is?" Alec looked up from his phone, his eyes wide.

I looked up from mine, the bewilderment in my eyes matching his. "I think so."

"Why is your mother returning the money I paid her? What does she want this time? And why now, after almost a year?"

I shook my head, equally confused. "Maybe she's paying you to leave me again. Or paying *me* to leave you this time?"

Just then, his phone trilled, and my mother's name and number flashed on his screen.

Alec frowned, making no attempt to answer it. "Why is she calling me?"

"Because she doesn't have my new number." I gestured at the phone. "Pick it up. And by the way, I'm not here."

He answered the call, muttering a cautious "hello." The dragon dancers had now moved farther down the street, followed by the crowd, the drumbeats slowly fading away. Both Kim and Jenna had drifted toward the stalls on the sides of the road, so there were fewer people around us.

I watched as Alec spoke on the phone. A rainbow of emotions played across his face as he answered in clipped one-and two-word answers. The call didn't take long, ending after five minutes.

"Well?"

He didn't answer for a while. When he finally looked at me, his eyes were dazed. "That was your mother."

I nodded, impatient. "Yes, I know. What did she say? What does she want?"

"That was *really* her."

"Come on, babe. Tell me something I don't know."

Alec stared at the phone in his hand, still looking shell-shocked. "She's giving us back the three million dollars I paid her."

My eyes widened. "*What*? No, no, no. Call her back, tell her we don't want the money, because I'm *not* doing whatever it is she wants us to do."

"She's not asking us to do anything. She said we could keep the money. It's ours."

"Yeah, right. And I moonlight as a superhero during my lunch breaks. No, seriously, what does she want?"

Alec shook his head. "Nothing. Said she'd heard about our engagement from Eric. It's her wedding gift, and her angpao for the Lunar New Year. No expectations, no demands, nothing. Hard to believe, but that's what she said."

"*That's it?* No, that doesn't sound like her. Are you sure you spoke to *my mother*?"

"Believe me, that was her." He handed me his phone. "Call her back, if you don't believe me. Ask her yourself."

I shook my head. "No, not now. Are you sure? And she wanted nothing in return?"

"No. Absolutely nothing."

We were both silent for a few minutes, trying to process the news.

"She did say, though, that I wasn't who she had in mind for you, and how she'll never, ever think I'm good enough to marry a Pang."

"Okay, now *that* I can believe," I said. "That definitely sounds like my mother."

Alec sighed and pulled me into a hug. "But she knows we've loved each other since we were young. And that you've made your choice. As long as I look after you, and you're happy, she's not going to stand in our way. But she said she'll never accept our relationship or acknowledge me as a son-in-law."

A big dollop of sadness flooded through me, at her stubbornness, at losing my parents. But there was also the tiniest flicker of hope, and relief, because maybe not all hope was lost.

Because knowing my mother, this gesture was extraordinarily significant.

"Do you want to call her?" He tightened the hug. "I don't know what's gotten into your mother, but maybe she's not as coldhearted as we thought she was."

I was quiet as I considered it. Perhaps one day I'd be able to make peace with her, and she could finally accept Alec.

Accept us.

But that day wasn't here yet. We still had a long way to go.

"I will. But not right now." I looked up at him, then stood on my tiptoes and gave him a kiss. "Because right now, all I want to do is just enjoy us."

Author's Note

This story contains something personal to me and my family. In September 2020, during the height of Covid lockdown in Melbourne, my youngest son—then six, three weeks away from his seventh birthday—was diagnosed with type 1 diabetes. It was a huge shock to us all, as we didn't have any family history of T1D. The weeks that followed were a roller coaster of highs and lows (literally), sleepless nights, and lots of curious questions from well-meaning friends and strangers. And that gave me the idea for this book, in the hope that I could help raise some sort of awareness about T1D.

The symptoms that Ellie had in the story were exactly what my son had gone through, although thanks to our quick-thinking family GP, he avoided going into diabetic ketoacidosis. T1D usually develops in children, teens, or young adults, but anyone can be diagnosed with it at any age. There are four early warning signs of T1D: excessive thirst, frequent urination, unexplained weight loss, and feeling more tired than usual. If you or any of your loved ones are exhibiting these symptoms, please reach out to your healthcare professional. Knowing these signs could save someone's life.

Please note that I wrote the story based on our family's experiences, and I tried to make it as authentic as possible, but everybody's experience with TID will be different. Any errors in the book are all mine.

I'd like to thank the team of doctors, nurses, endocrinologists, and diabetes educators at the Royal Children's Hospital Melbourne for providing excellent care for children in Victoria. Thank you to our GP, Dr. Yassa, and the staff at SJPS for making sure school is a safe place for my son. And to all the TID warriors out there, I am in awe of how courageous, resilient, and tough you all are. You're all heroes in my eyes.

To learn more about type 1 diabetes, please visit Breakthrough TID (formerly JDRF) and Beyond Type 1; or if you're in Australia, please visit JDRF Australia and Diabetes Australia.

Acknowledgments

To be here writing my first ever author acknowledgments (!!) is beyond my wildest dreams. I'll try to make this as quick and as painless as possible, and if I missed anyone, please know that it wasn't intentional. My apologies, and bubble teas are on me.

This book wouldn't be in your hands without the support of so many people. Thank you to my brilliant agent, Ann Rose, for believing in me, and for being the most supportive, the most awesome, and the best agent in the entire world. I don't know what constellations were aligning the day you read my manuscript and decided to offer me representation, but I'm so lucky to have you in my corner.

My immense gratitude to Monique Patterson at Bramble for taking a chance on a debut author and for giving this story a home. You've made my dreams come true, and for that I will be forever grateful. A massive thank-you to my incredible editor, Erika Tsang, for your invaluable feedback, your guidance, your wealth of knowledge, and your patience with all my questions. I'm truly privileged to be able to work with you. My heartfelt thanks to the team at Bramble/Tor Publishing Group who've had a hand in bringing this story to the world: Mal Frazier, Tessa Villanueva, Hannah Smoot, Nicole Hall, Esther S. Kim, Rafal Gibek, Ryan T. Jenkins, Tyrinne Lewis, Ariana Carpentieri, and Cassidy Sattler. The biggest thank-you to the talented Jacqueline Li for her stunning cover illustration and for bringing Ellie and Alec to life.

Many thanks to my Australian publisher, Alex Lloyd, for your enthusiasm for the story and for warmly welcoming me into the Pan Macmillan family.

To the Rosebuds, the best agent sibs anyone could ever have. Thank you for helping me brainstorm the title! I'm so honored to be a part of such a talented group of authors. Thank you also to the team at the Tobias Literary Agency for all your support.

My endless appreciation to the best writer's group a girl could ever ask for: Alexandra Almond, Amanda Robinson, Kylie Mulligan, Paul O'Doherty, and Jennifer Tomlin. Thanks for always giving me such thoughtful, kind, and encouraging feedback. You are all incredibly talented and I'm enormously blessed to have your support and friendship.

I owe a huge debt of gratitude to Anahita Karthik, my SmoochPit mentor. Thank you for choosing this book out of the SmoochPit slush pile and for loving it as much as I do. You are an amazing writer and friend, and I am extremely fortunate to have you in my life.

My Indo author buddies: Melody Thio, Melly Sutjitro, Anselma Widha Prihandita, and Quinn Huang. I am so lucky to call you all my friends and to have the privilege to read your words. Here's to more Indo reps on the shelves!

Idawati Zhang, my childhood bestie. Thank you for always cheering me on, and for always being willing to read my crappy first drafts from many moons ago, when publishing a book was just a pipe dream. Shout-out to Grace Pan, Melinda Bott, Amy Wen, and Cindy Husein, thanks for all your support. Thank you to Bobbi Diemer for reading a very early version of this book. Thanks to Christine Cowan and the SmoochPit team; to writers Victoria and Amy Adams; to Curtis Brown Creative UK, Jenny Colgan and Anna Bell; Hannah Langdon and Clare Rhoden.

To my family: Mama, who never said no to all those Enid Blyton and Sweet Valley High books and Archie Comics, even though you're not a reader yourself. Thank you for everything you've done for us. I hope you're proud of me. Papa, I wish you were here to see this. I know you would've gotten a huge kick out of this. Tatah and Oom David—thank you for always being the voice of reason, for always being so encouraging and positive, and for always being there for me. To Chris and Lala, you're the best bro and SIL anyone could ever ask for. Thank you for all your support and for being so excited for me when I told you both I was writing a book.

And of course, Ludi, Maxwell, and Jasper. Thank you for always being proud of me and for believing in me, even when I didn't believe in myself. I couldn't have done this without your support. Special shout-out to my boys, for asking me every day how many chapters I've worked on that day. You two bring me so much joy and love and I couldn't be prouder to be your mum.

And finally, to the readers, thank you, *thank you* for picking up this book. It's a dream come true and the greatest gift ever to be able to share my words with you.

About the Author

Cynthia Timoti writes fun, sexy multicultural rom-coms with plenty of heart and snark, where happy endings are always guaranteed. She was born and raised in Jakarta, Indonesia, and moved to Australia when she was seventeen. She spent too many years working in finance, even though numbers aren't her strongest suit.

When Timoti's not writing, she's probably trying to make a dent in her TBR pile, hunting for the perfect cup of bubble tea, and collecting pretty notebooks that she'll never use. Timoti currently resides in Melbourne, Australia, with her husband and two sons.